continued . . .

Heart Change

Robin D. Owens

BERKLEY SENSATION, NEW YORK

THE BERKLEY PUBLISHING GROUP
Published by the Penguin Group
Penguin Group (USA) Inc.
375 Hudson Street, New York, New York 10014, USA
Penguin Group (Canada), 90 Eglinton Avenue East, Suite 700, Toronto, Ontario M4P 2Y3, Canada
(a division of Pearson Penguin Canada Inc.)
Penguin Books Ltd., 80 Strand, London WC2R 0RL, England
Penguin Group Ireland, 25 St. Stephen's Green, Dublin 2, Ireland (a division of Penguin Books Ltd.)
Penguin Group (Australia), 250 Camberwell Road, Camberwell, Victoria 3124, Australia
(a division of Pearson Australia Group Pty. Ltd.)
Penguin Books India Pvt. Ltd., 11 Community Centre, Panchsheel Park, New Delhi—110 017, India
Penguin Group (NZ), 67 Apollo Drive, Rosedale, North Shore 0632, New Zealand
(a division of Pearson New Zealand Ltd.)
Penguin Books (South Africa) (Pty.) Ltd., 24 Sturdee Avenue, Rosebank, Johannesburg 2196,
South Africa

Penguin Books Ltd., Registered Offices: 80 Strand, London WC2R 0RL, England

This book is an original publication of The Berkley Publishing Group.

Copyright © 2009 by Robin D. Owens.
Interior text design by Kristin del Rosario.

PRINTING HISTORY
Berkley Sensation trade paperback edition / November 2009

Library of Congress Cataloging-in-Publication Data

Owens, Robin D.
    Heart change / Robin D. Owens.—Berkley Sensation trade paperback ed.
        p. cm.
    ISBN 978-0-425-22997-2
    1. Life on other planets—Fiction.   I. Title.
    PS3615.W478H38 2009
    813'.6—dc22

                                                    2009029840

PRINTED IN THE UNITED STATES OF AMERICA

10 9 8 7 6 5 4 3 2

To all who love cats, and to Tommy and Dingo,
my Du and Beadle.

Characters

Calendula SIGNET D'Marigold: The last of the GrandHouse of the Marigolds, Signet has great but unknown Flair. Her Fam animal companion is cat Du.

The Hawthorns:

Cratag Maytree: Distant kin of the Hawthorns, Cratag was born on the southern continent as the son of a shopkeeper, sold his sword as a caravan guard, and joined the Hawthorn household just as they were beginning a feud several years ago. He is now the chief of the Hawthorn guards. His Fam animal companion is cat Beadle.

GreatLord Huathe T'Hawthorn: Head of the Hawthorns, Cratag's sworn lord. His Fam animal companion is cat Black Pierre.

Huathe LAEV Hawthorn: T'Hawthorn's Son'sSon (grandson), a young man of seventeen who is like a younger brother to Cratag. Laev is experiencing his Second Passage to free his psi power, his Flair.

Nivea Sunflower: A girl of seventeen, Laev's first love.

The Vines:

GreatLord Muin T'Vine (VINNI): The thirteen-year-old prophet of Celta, his eyes have a disconcerting way of changing when he is experiencing his Flair. Vinni already knows his HeartMate is young Avellana Hazel. His Fam animal companion is housefluff (bunny) Flora.

Hanes Vine: Chief of the Vine guards and bodyguard to Vinni.

Arcto Vine: Vinni's tutor.

The Hazels:

GreatLady Coll D'Hazel: The head of the Hazels.

GreatLord T'Hazel: The GreatLady's HeartMate and consort.

Coll Hazel: A girl of fourteen, the Heir to the Hazels.

Avellana Hazel: A girl of seven who had a fall at three resulting in brain damage. She is experiencing her First Passage, a dreamquest/fugue to free her psi power. Vinni T'Vine's HeartMate. Her Fam animal companion is cat Rhyz.

Others:

GreatLord Rand T'Ash: Jeweler/blacksmith, T'Ash has the premier testing stones to discover a person's Flair (*HeartMate*). His Fam animal companion is cat Zanth.

GreatLady Danith Mallow D'Ash: HeartMate of T'Ash, Danith is an animal Healer and the person who usually matches intelligent animal companions (Fams) with people. Her Fam animal companion is cat Princess.

GreatLord Heather: The premier Healer of Celta.

SupremeJudge Ailim Elder: SupremeJudge of Celta, she is telempathic (telepathic and empathic).

Note: Other unnamed characters show up who regular readers might recognize.

241 RANGE

GREAT WASHINGTON
BOGHOLE

ÔRUIÔA

HARÔ ROCK MTNS

GAEL CITY

GREAT
PLATTE
OCEAN

ÔEEP
BLUE SEA

BRITTANY

CELTA

One

DRUIDA CITY, CELTA
407 Years After Colonization
Early Spring

Signet D'Marigold stood on the crumbling edge of the cliff and dared fate to take her. The sky was more winter than spring, flat and gray. The ground, frozen and dead. The wind, bitter and mean. Her life was as gray as the light, as dead as the land. She had no doubt that fate was as mean as the wind.

Far below, the ocean smacked spray at the sawtooth rocks, as they did every moment of every day, cold enough to suck the life out of her if she survived the fall.

She really didn't care.

Today was her thirtieth Nameday and she had no one to celebrate it with, not even one acquaintance close enough to meet for a cup of caff.

It had happened again. A couple of weeks ago she'd attended the celebration of Imbolc in the GreatTemple, had participated in the circle and felt vitality humming through her, enough to add pink to her pale cheeks and a slight golden color to her washed-out blond hair. She'd made a new acquaintance, Whinna Furze. They'd begun to take the steps to deepen the friendship, then Whinna's life had changed dramatically and she'd left the City yesterday— leaving Signet with only an excited, offhand good-bye in her message cache.

Signet was alone again. Thirty and no one to celebrate with: no friend, no man, no child. Soul deep loneliness ached inside her.

Alone except for the D'Marigold Residence. She turned her head so she could see it—all pale peach walls and tall, arched windows framed in white, an airy fantasy of a house, looking as if laughter itself had shaped it. But it was empty. Like many of the Families of Celta, the Marigolds had dwindled, and now there was only herself.

She could have opened one of the windows to the winter, leaned out . . . but the loss of the last Marigold in such a manner would have damaged the Residence, the sentient house, and she loved it. Instead, she'd walked to the cliffs and looked down on the endless movement of the sea. It whispered her real name, "Calendula." She didn't like that name, so she ignored it.

There had been two messages in her scry cache when she'd returned from her cliff walk yesterday, something that hadn't happened in years. One was Whinna's. The other was from T'Ash.

Signet was a challenge to T'Ash and his Testing Stones. His deep, rough voice had said his stones were better, stronger, more finely tuned this year—enough not only to measure the great strength of her Flair, her psi power, but to determine what her particular talent was.

He said that every year.

She wondered if she could dredge up the will to trudge to T'Ash Residence and be tested again for the gift that should have shaped her life, filled it with direction and purpose. This time, she didn't think so. It was painful seeing how T'Ash's life had changed, how his Residence, once as lonely and empty as her own, was now full of love from a menagerie of animals, a precocious child, and his Heart-Mate, Danith, glowing with the pregnancy of twins, *twins*.

Signet was sure that if she didn't make an appointment, T'Ash would forget her until her next Nameday rolled around.

She glanced at her home, couldn't bear going back to the loneliness there. She looked down to the sea, the same gray ebb and flow against black rock. The wind whipped her cloak around her, seemed to whistle through her. It called to her, too, mocking, "Calendula." She couldn't stay here, not today. She'd be tempted to do something irrevocable.

She'd go to CityCenter and let the false cheer and warmth of people surge around her. She'd fill the hours and when she woke tomorrow, she'd feel better. That she knew.

There was a new play with Raz Cherry, a tragedy. It would probably make her life appear good in comparison. Tomorrow would be better.

A gust of wind caught her. "Calendula!"

That wasn't waves or wind. She pivoted. Dirt crumbled under her heels. She jumped forward, heart pounding at the skittering fall of rock behind her. A young teenaged boy shot toward her, arms waving. "Calendula."

Blinking at the sight of a visitor on her land, it took her a moment to understand he was coming too fast. "Stop!" she shrieked, but the wind snatched her words away. She set herself in his path, held out her arms, braced.

The collision knocked her back, knocked *them* straight into air. The teen's green brown eyes went wide with horror.

But Signet knew every inch of her land, the strength of her Flair. His Flair, greater than hers, added power. She visualized them in the sacred Marigold grove and teleported them there.

They slipped on the frosty ground, fell hard under the huge-boled, leafless trees, both expelling breath, then fighting for it. She recognized him, the thirteen-year-old prophet, GreatLord Muin T'Vine. She looked into his changeable eyes, now green.

"C-c-calendula," he gasped. "I know what your Flair is, and I have a mission for you!"

His words buzzed in her brain then solidified into meaning. He knew her Flair! Had divined a purpose for her life.

Knew her future.

She nearly moaned with needy anticipation. She yearned to ask a dozen, a hundred, questions but the boy shivered with cold.

She didn't really want to touch him again, trigger any change in his variable eyes that meant he was seeing her future.

On the other hand, a warmth bloomed inside her that she *had* a future—a good one. Ignoring her fears, she moved behind him and curved her hands onto his shoulders, holding tight. "I'm teleporting us to my sitting room on three. One, Marigold, two Muin T'Vine, *three.*"

They were there, in the circular tower room with huge arched windows showing only the sky from this viewpoint. She settled T'Vine on a twoseat, drew a llamawool throw over him, and ordered him cocoa with a thick topping of white mousse from the beverage no-time storage.

She said a spell for the room to heat. For herself, she took a mug of hot, strong, and sweet caff, wrapped her hands around the crockery to still the trembling in her fingers and warm them.

Waiting for Vinni to take one sip, two, ready himself for talk was exquisite torture. Finally, after he had a brown and white moustache on his lip, and she'd finished her caff, she cleared her throat. "You were saying?"

He drank again, and she refused to prod. Despite the fact that he was a boy, he was of far greater rank than she, one of the thirteen GreatHouses, the twenty-five FirstFamilies. He had power and status and wealth beyond her own.

She was also more afraid of his words than plummeting into the ocean. She had hope now, and hope was a fearsome thing. If it crashed, she could shatter.

Vinni wiped his mouth with a softleaf, burped discreetly. "That was close." His eyes were wide and had returned to green brown.

"I didn't see that coming." He shook his head, trembled under the cover. The corners of his mouth twitched up in a painful smile as his changeable eyes met hers. "I can't always see the future when it concerns myself."

"A blessing of the Lady and Lord. Otherwise I'd suppose you'd go mad."

His face lightened, and he sighed. "You're right."

Finally he pushed down the blanket. Color had returned to his face, and his freckles were lost against his skin and not light brown against stark white. Signet kept watch on his eyes, deciding she'd be a perfect coward and run if they started to change color with prophecy.

Looking at her over his mug, Vinni slurped the last of his drink. She said nothing, and he grinned, his brown and white moustache dashing. "You're a nice lady. Good news for you. I know your talent, GrandLady Calendula D'Marigold."

"Call me by my middle name, Signet."

He nodded. "I will since we'll be seeing a lot of each other. You can call me Vinni."

She didn't mind his rudeness, did mind his game-playing. Of course he couldn't understand how desperate she was to *know*, could he? "Yes?"

"I've set up an appointment for you with T'Ash and his Testing Stones," Vinni glanced at the timer on his wrist, frowned. "In three-quarters of a septhour. This is taking longer than I anticipated." He looked back up at her, hazel eyes keen. "You're a catalyst, Signet. Being around you changes other people's lives, and always for the better."

She sat, frozen. Catalyst. Images of her entire life flickered before her. Since her Second Passage at seventeen, she'd been losing friends. Because their lives would change and they'd move on. Did she only draw people to her because their lives needed to be changed and once that occurred they didn't want her near anymore? Had no one ever liked her for her very own self?

"*Signet, listen to me!*" Vinni demanded.

She focused on him, much better than thinking hurtful and dreary thoughts. This had already been a horrible day. "A catalyst," she said.

He nodded again. "And we'll prove it with T'Ash's Testing Stones."

"Managing my life, like the GreatLord you are?" she asked.

He winced. "Sorry, I'll make it up to you. We'll get you a Fam from D'Ash while we're there."

"I'm on the list for Fams. Low on the list." She'd thought an animal companion wouldn't leave. Would it? How much would she change that one's life?

Vinni shifted uneasily in his seat under her stare. "I've arranged more than the appointment with T'Ash." He paused, fixed his gaze on hers. "I desperately need a catalyst."

Cratag Maytree's liege lord, GreatLord T'Hawthorn, called him into the ResidenceDen. Cratag knew by looking at the man's face that he wouldn't like what his distant relative and the head of his Family was going to say.

So Cratag sat stoically and waited as T'Hawthorn went behind his antique desk, sat, intertwined his fingers. T'Hawthorn's comfortchair put his head lower than Cratag's since the lord was smaller than himself. Most people were smaller than Cratag. That didn't undermine T'Hawthorn's power or authority in the least.

"I have had a request for your services," T'Hawthorn said.

Cratag's mind went blank. "My services?" He was a personal guard for the T'Hawthorn Family, the head of their force. He cherished the fact that he was an important part of the Family. At least he'd thought so.

Cratag gazed at his quiet lord, the man's violet eyes, black hair, and impassive expression. Anxiety twisted Cratag's gut. Was the man he'd sworn a loyalty oath to going to make him a merchant guard? He'd been a mercenary before, but he'd longed for Family, so had come north to offer his sword and blazer to T'Hawthorn.

He'd made a place in the Family, especially with T'Hawthorn's Son'sSon and Heir. Cratag wanted to stay with them. He didn't want to go anywhere, do anything else. Had never thought he'd be asked to leave. He'd worked hard for T'Hawthorn, had fought, killed, been willing to die for the man.

Now he was being shuffled aside. He kept his face a mask as T'Hawthorn went on.

"I was approached by GreatLady D'Hazel. As you may or may not know, the Hazels keep no Family guards. The female side of that line is the strongest in Flair, and the title has passed to females. They haven't settled their problems with dueling or feuds for generations." His lips curved in a wintry smile. T'Hawthorn had needed Cratag's fighting expertise because the lord had made a disastrous mistake in feuding.

"I don't understand," Cratag said.

T'Hawthorn rubbed his temples with thumb and forefinger. "I'm not putting this well. D'Hazel is in need of a guardsman."

Cratag's stomach sank, he already knew where this was leading.

"She went to the Green Knight Fencing and Fighting Salon and requested the name of the best fighter from Tab Holly."

Cratag tried to visualize a gentle FirstFamily GreatLady at the Green Knight and couldn't.

"GreatSir Tab Holly gave her your name."

Cratag tensed. The Hollys were former enemies. "It's the best salon—"

T'Hawthorn waved a hand, cutting him off. The lord's smile went a little crooked. "Our feud with the Hollys has been over for years, but I thought you held a personal animosity to them."

"No." He hadn't liked the idea of the feud, hadn't liked fighting, but he'd known his duty and had been grateful to T'Hawthorn.

"It's past." The lord's nostrils widened with his deep breath, lines showed in his forehead. He'd lost his son. "You are a good guard, and you keep your skills honed. I would imagine that you would prefer to work with the best, and those fighters are found at the Green Knight."

Cratag kept his reply to a brief nod.

"I understand." T'Hawthorn sighed, leaned back in his chair. "D'Hazel has been neutral over the years, making very few, very shrewd alliances. If I supplied her need for a guard. . . ."

Alliances. That was what FirstFamily politics and maneuvering was all about. Cratag knew enough about the noble class to understand that. Though he'd lived among the nobles of Celta for four years, he still didn't know their ways. He figured that only those who grew up in those ways fully understood them.

He didn't want to go, wanted his rooms here at the Residence and his daily life with the Family, his mentoring of Laev, T'Hawthorn's Son'sSon.

T'Hawthorn said, "Of course, I would not force you to accept this temporary position in any way."

"Temporary? How long?" Not that this feeling of betrayal would go away even if the job lasted a week. All too evident that his life was not his own to command. "What's the job?"

T'Hawthorn hesitated. "Apparently D'Hazel's information comes from GreatLord Vinni T'Vine, the boy prophet."

Worse and worse, a whole mess of FirstFamily nobles with "Great" in front of their names. No way out. Cratag sat and suffered.

"The prophet convinced D'Hazel that her younger daughter should be fostered with GrandLady Calendula D'Marigold. D'Marigold's household doesn't run to guards either."

Cave of the Dark Goddess. D'Marigold. He'd met her once, participated in a ritual with her, had been attracted to her. That recollection almost distracted him from the feeling of being a tradable commodity.

"Avellana Hazel is . . . fragile. There was a past threat of a kidnapping of the girl, and T'Vine believes her First Passage fugue may come very soon."

Cratag said, "Your Son'sSon, your Heir, Laev, is facing Passage, too. His second." Cratag couldn't keep quiet about this. He'd wanted to be here to help the young man of seventeen, a boy he thought of as a younger brother. Laev's father had been killed in the feud. Passages could be dangerous.

"I am aware of that," T'Hawthorn said coolly. "But Laev has Grove and Hawthorn blood and is not much at risk."

So much for interrupting his lord. It had gotten Cratag nowhere. Nobles rarely listened to commoners.

"Avellana suffered brain damage as a toddler. Her Family is worried for her. The Hazels are convinced that her survival of Passage depends on being with D'Marigold." T'Hawthorn rubbed the line between his brows. "I don't think it will be an arduous task, but you should know that the Household is a very small and quiet one, not like here."

"How small?"

"Including D'Marigold, Avellana Hazel, and you, it numbers three."

Cratag just stared. "I'll be alone with D'Marigold and the little girl." He didn't know what to think, but his pulse quickened at the recollection of the ethereal D'Marigold. She'd seemed like a legendary princess, unapproachable. Now he'd be her guard. The situation, all so mythic, appealed to him.

"Yes, only three of you. The Residence is quite large, a beautiful estate bordering both the river and ocean. You will, of course, draw your salary from me, and I'd imagine that D'Hazel will pay gilt for your services, also."

That was nearly an insult, and grounded him from foolish flights of fancy. "Gilt is not why I came to Druida or why I offered you my sword."

"No. I know. But I'd like you to take this job." T'Hawthorn raised a finger. "And not only for any alliance. We have a Family in distress." Another ironic smile. "Through my own experiences, I've come to a modicum of compassion. Your presence at D'Marigold's will ease minds. Celta is still harsh enough that Families perish. If you wish for a divination reading—" T'Hawthorn reached for his runes.

"No." Cratag's jaw flexed. "So I am to be a guard at D'Marigold's, check out her security and increase it, watch the child, keep them both safe from any danger. Including trying to mitigate Passage for the little girl." How he was supposed to do that he didn't know. He'd never had enough Flair to experience more than a woozy few minutes of Passage.

T'Hawthorn smiled briefly. "Succinct as always." His brows lowered. "Keep them safe. D'Marigold has never impressed me as a practical woman, aware of FirstFamily politics or threats. She keeps very much to herself. Your decision, Cratag?"

Always nice to be put on the spot, to make important choices with little consideration. "I'll take the job. Tell me where and when to start."

T'Hawthorn consulted a sheet of papyrus on his desk. "D'Hazel, the boy prophet, T'Vine, and D'Marigold are all meeting at T'Ash's shortly. I'll have a glider take you there." Since Cratag couldn't teleport worth a damn.

"Thank you."

"No, Cratag, thank *you*. You have been—are—a valued member of this Family and this household. If I haven't expressed my thanks very often, please know that I have blessed the day that you came to us."

Warmth unfurled in Cratag's chest, almost enough that he could swallow the lump of betrayal.

He stood and bowed.

T'Hawthorn did the same, another sign of respect.

Cratag turned on his heel and strode to the door, left the room, and walked through the castle to the courtyard, where a manned glider waited.

He was leaving a place he'd tried so hard to fit in to. He shrugged. By the time he returned, this feeling of hurt would be gone, worn away by the mission itself.

The mission. He set aside the past to focus on the future. Anticipation surged within him. He'd see D'Marigold again. He'd never forgotten the feel of her fingers clasping his, the fizz of her energy as it passed through him around the circle.

He found a smile on his face that faded when he realized D'Marigold, the princess, would have to live with his scars.

Two

Signet was seated in *T'Ash's octagonal ResidenceDen, sweating.* The place was warmer than her house by the sea with the heat given off by people and animals . . . people who needed warmth to do their jobs. Family who cared that each other would be warm enough.

The heavy gold curtains were pulled aside from the tall, narrow windows to show the gray day looking out over dormant lawn and bare flowering bushes. In the distance she could see the building housing T'Ash's forge.

She sat in an intricately carved wooden chair, with back and seat a plush gold, facing T'Ash's big desk. The desk itself had a few cat-made nicks and scratches that had been stained to "disappear." A large cat platform was near the desk.

Each year since the first time she'd consulted with T'Ash, the room had a bit more furniture. Then it had been distressingly spare. Before he'd met his HeartMate.

His fees had risen, too, but she'd only paid the first time. She was a challenge to T'Ash since his stones hadn't been able to determine the form of her Flair.

T'Ash himself was standing in the corner of the room frowning down at a fast-talking Muin—Vinni—T'Vine.

More noise came from another room. People had teleported in. With senses heightened from nerves, she understood that they all had great Flair. A young girl's piping voice sounded. Avellana Hazel, the life she was supposed to change, and change greatly, so the girl would live through her First Passage.

The youngest, pampered incredibly Flaired child of a FirstFamily GreatHouse was in Signet's hands, and she had no idea what to do to save her. If she failed, the consequences could be disastrous. No one would ever trust her. Sweat coated her palms. She wiped them on a softleaf. Soon she'd have to hold all of T'Ash's egg-shaped stones. All of his many stones indicating type of Flair that grew in number year by year, none of them reacting to her.

She heard Danith D'Ash welcoming the Hazels, and Signet relaxed a little in her chair. She wouldn't have to meet them until her Flair as a catalyst—and what exactly did that mean?—was confirmed by T'Ash's Testing Stones. Finally having a good Certification of Flair would be concrete validation.

T'Ash coughed, and Signet swung her gaze from the door to the large man who'd seated himself behind his scarred but glossily polished desk. "You know what to do, Signet." He smiled, and she thought he meant it to be reassuring, but it only reminded her that of all the people in the Residence, she was the least in nobility and power.

Vinni came away from the door where he'd been lingering and hitched himself up to a chair next to hers. "I promise, Signet, that you won't suffer for this."

"Of course she won't," T'Ash sounded offended. "None of my stones hurt anyone if used properly. In all the times she's tested, they haven't harmed her."

"I meant the whole situation, T'Ash," Vinni corrected.

T'Ash snorted. Then his piercing blue gaze pinned hers. "I witness that GreatLord Muin T'Vine offers reparation for any harm that comes to Calendula D'Marigold as a result of his request that she foster Avellana Hazel."

Vinni looked surprised, but T'Ash nodded. "Always wise to ensure a man's word is good." Signet remembered that T'Ash had lived on the streets as a boy and young man, worse off than she.

She wasn't afraid she'd lose gilt or status, which didn't mean very much to her. She might be shunned, lose more bits of her heart.

Already her own life had changed—could it only have changed when she'd fallen so low?

Now she knew how her Flair affected others, she'd figure out how to use it for good. If she thought about it, she should be able to make it into a business like others used their Flairs.

Would the effect she had on people's lives be less extreme if she were less emotionally connected to them? Still be for the better? So many things to think about.

But Vinni had straightened at being called a man.

"Now, Signet." T'Ash opened a heavily carved box that contained only two of his eggs that measured the strength of a person's Flair. He slid the box to the edge of his desk and, sighing, Signet picked up the clear crystal egg. As always, it felt neither cool nor warm. She closed her eyes and spiraled down into her center serenity. Her core seemed stronger, brighter . . . because she had hope. When she opened her eyes, beams of light shot out from the space between her fingers, as bright as a summer's day on this relapse to winter.

Turning her hand over, she opened her fingers and let the egg dazzle.

Vinni gasped. T'Ash made approving grumbles, then rubbed his hands, a gesture of excitement Signet had never seen. "I always knew your Flair was greater than you tested." He grinned. "And it's a new, better-calibrated stone." He narrowed his eyes, shot Vinni a look. "Catalyst psi power, you said."

"Yes," Vinni said.

Doubt crossed T'Ash's face. "I checked the Flair records. There is no listing for 'catalyst' or any people who have been 'catalysts.'"

Giving a casual shrug, Vinni said, "Might have been some we didn't know about. Records of everything but the FirstFamilies' talents are scarce." He made an encouraging gesture to Signet.

After exhaling a little sigh, she said, "It seems whenever I make a good friend, their life changes and they . . . leave. Move on. Usually literally. They move away from Druida."

T'Ash was making notes. "Big change in their lives." He looked at her from under lowered black brows. "So you make at least one large change, but what of someone who lives with you on a constant basis?"

Her face stiffened. "I don't know."

"Your parents are dead?"

"Yes."

T'Ash winced. "Sorry, insensitive."

Vinni lifted his chin. "She causes lives to change. She's a catalyst, and I want her Flair for my HeartMate, my Avellana." His expression turned mulish. "Signet is Avellana's best chance to survive First Passage." He looked away. "If there is no change in Avellana . . . as it is . . . what I've seen . . ." His small shoulders slumped.

Signet's mouth dried.

"What of your own Passages?" T'Ash asked her bluntly. "Have you had them all? Did the third come early or at twenty-seven? How rough were they?"

"I've had them all. Third Passage came when I was twenty-one." She didn't want to remember that time. "It was difficult." She could barely force out the next words in a harsh whisper. "My parents died during my Third Passage."

Both males stared at her.

She bit her lip. "They weren't here in Druida. My Passage came untimely, none of us knew it was coming until they'd left for a sailing holiday with several other couples. Their boat capsized. . . . I always wondered if I . . . if my Passage somehow affected . . ." She couldn't go on.

T'Ash sucked in an audible breath, his face was stark. "Perhaps their Flair was stifling you, or keeping your Passage at bay, or some such, and when they left, it surged."

Signet had never thought of that.

Vinni's eyes unfocused, turned a grayish blue. In a calm, bland voice he said, "Nothing you did, nothing you were, affected their deaths. It was their time."

A relief and a slight comfort.

T'Ash grunted and made more scratchings with his writestick. Then he put the instrument down and stood, opened another carved box, larger than it had been the year before, holding more Testing Stones. He set the top aside, glanced at the stone eggs and at Signet, waved for her to stand, so she did. This was a different step in their little process. Usually he brought a table to set in front of her and let her hold each stone. Some were odd and unpleasant, some slick, some dulling . . . but none had truly reacted to explain her Flair.

The chairs she and Vinni sat in were drawn close to the desk. T'Ash waved at the stones. "Just run your finger over them. I don't think anything there is what we want," he muttered. Then he paced toward a corner of two walls of the eight-sided room that were covered with books. "Catalyst," he grumbled. "Catalyst. What sort of stone might . . . a type that's not in the box." He left.

Signet shared a glance with Vinni. She straightened her shoulders and took a big breath, then touched a fingertip to the first stone, a creamy quartz crystal with streaks of darker silk. Warm. Not right. She continued quickly, bumping her finger down the row of stones, then the next and the next, through all six rows, getting little bursts of feeling from them and ending at obsidian, then a dull black. When she was finished, she felt a little nauseous. She'd had too much strange input from them.

So she sat back and rested her arms on the chair's curved ones. Vinni patted her hand. "I know I'm right."

He was a GreatLord with great Flair, so she believed him. The more she thought about her life, the more the particular theory that she was a catalyst fit. After her First Passage as a child her grovestudy group, which had been stable for years, disintegrated and reformed. After her Second Passage, the young gallants who'd been vying for her had all found their true HeartMates, or good and loving wives. She'd begun to lose friends then.

T'Ash strode through the door, letting it slam behind him. He cradled something wrapped in light green velvet. "This is a lambenthyst that I recently acquired. They are living stones, but not sentient—or can be alive sometimes." He frowned. "I've been trying to buy all the lambenthyst mines I find—"

"T'Ash, can we get on with it? The Hazels are waiting for us," Vinni said, as if he'd heard talk of lambenthysts before.

Grimacing, T'Ash said, "Fine. We'll see how you interact. If you're a catalyst for more than people."

A catalyst for rocks! Signet just stared. She couldn't believe it.

"Living creatures," Vinni said, looking interested.

Carefully, T'Ash set the cloth on Signet's lap. There was no weight to the stone, but her thighs warmed, began to tingle. He stepped back and watched as she unfolded the velvet, ready to pounce if she dropped the thing, she was sure.

When she saw the crystal, she gasped, and Vinni made a surprised noise. The stone was cut and faceted like a huge violet white diamond. She cupped it in her hands, it seemed all sharp cutting angles, and she cried out as it sliced, felt the slipperiness of her blood, then a throbbing warmth. A vision enveloped her, like she walked into a bright dream, showing pieces of her life from her Third Passage on. Once again the leavetakings of her life flashed before her in exquisite and painful detail. This time she saw that when she met people, there was a flash between herself and them. If they stayed near her for a while, the "flash" sank into them, changing the pattern and balance of their inner selves. Then "sparkles" appeared inside them, lovely designs. They were more cheerful, healthy.

Then the people left.

Wondrous and strange that her Flair had caused this, enough to dry the tears behind her eyes.

"Did you see that?" T'Ash asked Vinni in a hushed tone Signet never thought would come from the tough lord. She became aware that his large hand rested on her shoulder. Vinni's fingers were linked with hers. They'd shared her vision.

"Looks like you were right. A catalyst for sure, maybe a type of Healer. As she balances their inner Flair, their lives change. Amazing." T'Ash shook his head. "She also gathers something, some sort of Flair into their lives. The power of change? Then they, um . . ."

"They leave," Signet said flatly.

T'Ash looked uncomfortable.

"And the time it takes for her innate Flair to work is decreasing," Vinni said softly, releasing her hand. "A month at first, then becoming shorter, perhaps as short as two eightdays with—Whinna Furze?" He glanced at her.

Compressing her lips, Signet nodded. He was right. Her friendships had shortened over the years.

"Look at the rock," T'Ash said.

Signet became aware that it was heavy in her lap and stared. It was no longer the pretty piece of crystal, but a dull surface of glowing purple surrounded by other rock. All the same, it felt better and shot off little waves of sparkles.

Vinni sucked in a breath. "How did that happen?" Vinni asked. "*What* happened?"

T'Ash stared. "I'd guess that it has gathered back to itself the part that was cut away to make the 'jewel'." He frowned. "Happened fast. Rock is different than people, patterns less complex, more structured. There was blood. Bodily fluids can emphasize Flair." He waved a hand between them. "You've got three strongly Flaired people here."

The rock began to hum, deep and low, then there was another bright flash of purple, and it disappeared, leaving her cut hand Healed.

Both men appeared a little pale.

Signet's mouth dropped open, she snapped it shut. "Gone. The story of my life."

Vinni took her hand in his smaller one and lifted the back of it to his lips, kissed it reverently. "You may be left behind, and I'm sorry for that, but the lives you change are enriched. You help people, and I thank you for that, on behalf of them all."

"And you need me to help Avellana Hazel."

Vinni's green brown gaze met Signet's squarely. "Yes."

T'Ash had returned to his desk and the box of his stones, looking at them with frustration. "I don't have the right stones to indicate your power." Like her, he ran a finger over the stones, polishing them, giving some of his own Flair. "I'll look for some." Now he met her eyes. "I *will* find some."

"No matter that we don't know exactly what her Flair is or how it works," Vinni murmured.

"New types of Flair are evolving all the time," T'Ash said. "I like to keep up with them." He drew out a piece of thick, expensive papyrus, set his hand casually on the sheet, and a Certification of Flair appeared. It stated Signet's name, her rank, that she had GrandHouse power and a talent for "Catalyzation, with Other Effects to Be Determined."

Before she could say anything, T'Ash had ordered the sheet to the NobleCouncil Clerk. T'Ash stared at her and rubbed his chin again. "I've seen you at rituals at GreatCircle Temple." Her duty as well as a futile attempt to be a part of Druidan life. She inclined her head.

"Hmm," T'Ash said. "I'll research those. I'd bet the ones where you're present have better results than if you aren't." He gave her a slashing smile. "You might be in great demand soon."

"She must help Avellana, first," Vinni said.

"Speaking of that . . ." T'Ash's face softened, and he went to the door, opened it to his hugely pregnant wife, Danith. They were HeartMates, so he would have known she was outside the door. Another, different, pang went through Signet. What would it be like to have a HeartMate?

The GreatLady animal Healer beamed up at him. She was dressed in a dark tunic that showed a lot of cat hair and a few stains Signet didn't want to think about. D'Ash's boots were cracked and scuffed.

T'Ash leaned down and kissed her, put an arm around her waist.

D'Ash's gaze went to Signet, who was rising, and to Vinni, who'd hopped to his feet. Vinni bowed, and Signet curtsied.

"Greetyou, D'Marigold, Greetyou, Vinni. The Hazels are waiting in my Fam adoption room. Some Fams arrived last night and this morning. Would you like to come back?"

Time to meet GreatLady D'Hazel, who held Signet's future in her hands—and Avellana Hazel, whose future Signet had to save.

Three

*S*ignet flushed. *They were keeping GreatLady D'Ash from matching* Fams with people on her list—her very long waiting list, with Signet near the bottom. Danith's eyes were kind, and she smiled at Signet and leaned into her husband. "Now that we have more information about your Flair, I'll be able to place a Fam."

T'Ash said, "After a few minutes in her presence the lambenthyst coalesced into its original shape and returned home."

Danith blinked, stared at Signet, let out an audible breath. "Great and unusual Flair indeed." Her brow lined. "A catalyst? I have a thin tom who could use some change mixed with stability in his life." She moved slowly down the hallway, and they all followed her. "He's a very beautiful cat, a light beige and white with yellow eyes." Her laugh rippled. "He is elegant."

"Then he'd be at home in D'Marigold Residence," Signet said.

They went through Danith's office and back to a long room that was unlike anything Signet had ever seen. The floor and the walls were carpeted. There were perches and posts and cubes and walks and rails, like a crazy playroom for rambunctious children.

Several animals looked at her from various places. The impact of the stares made her self-conscious. These were telepathic animals hoping to bond with a human. Were they as lonely as she? How much would she change the life of the Fam she chose, or who chose her?

One stare became more penetrating, and she looked over to see a young girl of about seven scrutinizing her. Avellana Hazel. Signet could almost feel the intensity of the great Flair the child radiated. And what did Signet know about handling . . . living with . . . teaching . . . children? Nothing.

"Just be her companion," Vinni murmured.

But the girl had a look to her blue eyes—bluer than Signet's own, lake blue—that bespoke an old soul in a young body. The person behind those eyes might know more than Signet had ever learned.

"She's not as wise as she seems," Vinni said, proving *he* had excellent Flair for guessing what Signet was thinking. His body went tense. "You are her best hope, always remember that."

Signet made a noncommittal noise and walked forward, offering her hand to the girl. "Greetyou, GreatMistrys Avellana Hazel. I'm Signet D'Marigold." She sensed the child preferred formality. Perhaps it was because the girl was dressed in miniature adult clothes of long tunic and bloused trous.

Avellana frowned. "I thought your name was Calendula."

"I like Signet better," Signet said.

"A cygnet is a young swan, and a signet is a seal like on a ring. Is the swan your Family animal?" The girl petted a housefluff on a cube waist high to her with one hand as she offered her other hair-bedewed hand to Signet.

"Yes, and my name is spelled with an *S*." Signet took the girl's hand and shook it firmly. Avellana's hand was warm, as if life and Flair flowed too hot in her veins. Avellana wiggled her fingers. "You have a strange Flair."

Signet winced.

Avellana's mother, D'Hazel, sighed. "We have discussed making personal comments, Avellana."

"It's a fact," Avellana said.

"Your comment was rude."

Avellana swung her wide blue gaze from her mother to Signet. "I apologize for the rude but true comment."

Inclining her head, Signet said, "Apology accepted."

"Muin says that it's best if I stay with you during my First Passage," Avellana said, and Signet was confused until she remembered Muin was Vinni's real first name. For a moment she wondered if he'd chosen "Vinni" or if others had called him that. If they actually had something in common.

"That's right," Vinni and D'Hazel said at the same time, a little too heartily.

The girl picked up the housefluff. "But I get to return home if I feel I need to, and we will visit Mother and Father at least once an eightday."

"That sounds good," Signet said gravely, then groped for memories of her girlhood. "We'll make out a schedule."

Avellana relaxed. "Schedules are excellent tools." She smiled a winsome smile up at Signet. "You should choose this wonderful, soft and pretty and gentle housefluff as a Fam." She offered the hybrid between an Earth rabbit and a Celtan mocyn to Signet.

Signet took it, but didn't like its earthy smell or its big ears that tickled. Since it squirmed in her arms, she didn't think it liked her fragrance either. So she set it back down on the cube. It hopped to the floor, across the room and into a tunnel.

"A sympathetic connection is more important than outward beauty," Signet said, and received an approving glance from D'Hazel.

"Very true," Danith D'Ash said. "And I have a fellow who I think would fit well with you, D'Marigold."

"Please call me by my middle name, Signet," she said, sweeping the area with her glance, "All of you." She didn't know if the other nobles would do so, but she'd made the gesture.

"New tom cat, can you come, please?" Danith called.

A cat Signet hadn't noticed jumped from a high perch to land in front of her. He *was* beautiful, if too thin, and had a graceful, elegant aspect. As he stared up at her with gleaming yellow eyes, Signet heard, *Greetyou.*

"Greetyou, Sir," she replied.

"I think you two would be good for each other," D'Ash said.

The cat stretched. *I think so, too.*

"He will tell you of his past when he is ready, as all Fams do, but he is as healthy as I can make him," D'Ash said.

Just that easily Signet had a Fam. Dizziness swept through her, and she straightened her spine. No thinking about how fast things had changed—changed for *her*—right now in the midst of such important events. She had to keep her head, keep her serene manner. People—many, noble people—were counting on her, judging her.

"Thank you, Master Fam, I am pleased to welcome you to my household."

You have a name for me? the cat asked her, his ears tilting expectantly.

She hadn't given a name a thought. "Don't you have one?"

The cat sniffed. *No.*

She didn't think that was the whole story, but would find out when they learned of each other. If the cat didn't leave her.

I heard that, FamWoman, the cat said. *I will not leave.*

"Thank you. I would like to call you Du. It's part of my own given first name, Calendula."

"Duuuuu," the cat rolled his name out. Signet was surprised that it could actually speak the word.

"That's taken care of," D'Ash said with satisfaction.

D'Hazel gave a little cough. "If you don't mind, GrandLady—ah, Signet, could I impose upon you to show us your home where Avellana will be staying?"

Signet froze. "I do have guest rooms, of course, many." And they should be clean and aired, but she didn't know that for sure.

"Avellana can have her choice—" She stopped babbling at D'Hazel's frown.

"I think Avellana should be close to you."

"Ah, um, of course." Signet took a deep breath. "I didn't have time to prepare a room specifically for Avellana, but she is welcome to use the HeirSuite. It was mine as a girl and is furnished for a female."

"The *HeirSuite*! I get the HeirSuite, just like big sis Coll?" Avellana perked up. "My very own rooms? More than one room? Not on the ground level?"

"It's on the third—" Signet stopped in time, recalling that Avellana had tried to fly as a very young child. That had led to a terrible fall, resulting in brain damage. The reason everyone feared for her chances during her First Passage . . . the whole basis of this entire situation.

Signet drilled Avellana with a serious look that she knew she'd be using a lot in the future. "Can I trust you not to do anything to endanger yourself or others by opening or hanging out the windows or any time you go out on the balcony?"

"Excellent wording," Vinni muttered.

D'Hazel's expression was torn between the glance of approval she sent Signet and anxiety as she turned her gaze to her daughter.

"I get a *balcony*!" Avellana was so thrilled she was jumping up and down.

"If I get your word about the stated conditions," Signet said. "Whether you stay in the HeirSuite and are not moved to a ground floor oldie's room is completely dependent upon your good behavior."

"Oh, I *promise*. I promise not to do anything to endanger myself or others by opening or hanging out the windows or any time I go out on the balcony. And I won't teleport from the balcony to anywhere." She beamed a smile. "I teleport very well, but am not allowed to do it by myself."

Teleporting at seven? When most people came into the power

after their Second Passage at seventeen? "I accept your promise," Signet said.

Avellana slipped her small hand into Signet's and the trust in the gesture made Signet's heart squeeze. She had another new friend.

Oh, Avellana would only stay with Signet for a while, until the girl survived her First Passage, but at least Signet knew the time was limited to begin with. Maybe, when word got out that she was a catalyst, she would learn how to keep friends after she changed their lives. Avellana would certainly be staying in Druida and not leaving to follow other dreams.

Signet looked at Avellana's mother, D'Hazel, whose smile appeared to be cautiously optimistic.

Signet smiled back. "I would be honored to show you my home." She lifted her chin. "It is one of the loveliest Residences in all of Celta." She looked down at Avellana. "The HeirSuite has wonderful arched windows and looks out over the ocean." She gave Avellana *The Look*. "You are not allowed to go down the path to the beach and the ocean without me or with anyone other than me. If you do, you will get the old person's room on the ground floor. It *smells* like oldie." That was a fib. There was such a room, but it hadn't been used in generations, and Signet and the Residence kept the house meticulously. That particular room faced inland and looked out onto lovely gardens, but Signet was sure Avellana wouldn't appreciate that.

Avellana wrinkled her nose. "May we go see, Mother?"

"Yes, of course," D'Hazel said.

Vinni coughed, and D'Hazel glanced at him with a puzzled look. He shifted from foot to foot, shot a look at the door.

"Oh, someone is going to meet us," D'Hazel said. When she met Signet's eyes, there was a hint of GreatLady to lower noble. "I am very conscious of Avellana's safety."

"Of course," Signet said, feeling wary.

"So I have hired a guard for her during the time she is away from our Family and Residence."

"A guard?" Signet didn't quite understand.

"Yes. I assure you he has the best credentials from T'Hawthorn himself."

T'Hawthorn had once been the Captain of All Councils of Celta, the most powerful man in the world. The most important of the FirstFamilies GreatLords. Finally the meaning of what D'Hazel was saying filtered into her mind. "You want me to house a guard."

"I want Avellana to be safe," D'Hazel repeated.

"I don't need another person to watch me." Again Avellana looked up at Signet with wide eyes and a charming smile, squeezing Signet's hand.

"I think your mother knows what should be done better than you or I." Signet thought sharing the responsibility for Avellana's welfare sounded like a good idea, even if it meant another person in her home.

"Thank you," D'Hazel said. "In this instance I'm quite sure I'm right."

"He will be arriving shortly," Vinni said. "I asked that he meet us here."

Avellana dropped Signet's hand and went over to a corner that held a teleportation pad. "I already have a FamCat, and he will want to see our new rooms, too. Rhyz, will you come to me?"

"Another Fam," Signet murmured. "It will be good to have company." But so many, and so soon!

"Yesss," hissed Du. *I am ready to leave this place for my own home. T'Ash's Fam has everyone here under his paw.*

Signet chuckled and replied mentally, *And you want your own household under your paw.*

Yes.

Signet sensed the many auras of a busy household around her. When Du jumped into her arms, she cradled his thin body. *Our household is only you and me.*

I must start somewhere, Du said.

The dizziness returned. She was no longer alone. Her household was now herself and Du, but guests—including Fams—made it four more. People in a house that had been empty of everyone but her for so long. The sound of a child's laughter. Two children, if Vinni visited. Cherished Fams.

Avellana's orange tabby Fam appeared on the teleportation pad, and she hauled him up into her arms.

Signet looked around the room full of people—the Ashes, the Hazels, the animals. "D'Marigold Residence will be pleased to welcome you all."

She heard voices from the hall outside the room. All the unattached Fams who had been lying around casually arranged themselves. They wanted to bond with a person as much as people wanted a Fam, Signet realized, and held Du tighter to her chest. He revved up his purr.

*T*he ride to GreatHouse *T'Ash* Residence had been silent. Cratag had sat stiffly in the luxurious backseat of the Hawthorn Family glider. Though there had been no shield between him and the driver, another Family member, Cratag hadn't spoken. The driver's manner had held a pity that set Cratag's teeth on edge. It wasn't only himself who believed this outside job was more like a demotion.

T'Ash's greeniron gates had opened, and the Residence had come into view, a large pale yellow building of curves and jutting shapes. The newest fortress of the FirstFamilies, in an equally new style, was made of armourcrete and the shields were the best. The gliderway was smooth, without any dips or bumps, and the driver was as competent in his profession as Cratag was in his. Their lord didn't promote fools.

But that hadn't stopped their lord from assigning Cratag to another household. Cratag had to meet GreatLady D'Hazel and be gracious to her even while he resented her. At least the scars on his face helped keep his expression unreadable.

T'Hawthorn had indicated that D'Marigold would be here, and that was the only bright thing in this whole cloudy mess. He remembered her from the times they were at GreatRituals, and there was a single meeting a few years ago where they'd held hands during a Healing Circle. He had little hope that she'd recall him. Would she be frightened of him—his size and his aspect? Women often were, common and noble. Those who lived in Druida were accustomed to excellent Healing that left minimal scars, particularly on the face. The slash from his jaw to his nose—his obviously once broken nose—was white from a slicing claw of a now-dead slashtip. The smaller claw punctures were less noticeable.

Cratag followed T'Ash's butler down the carpeted hallway. He was much friendlier than T'Hawthorn's butler, and from the general looks of the Residence, it seemed like the house and the Family were more casual.

A cold chill slicked his gut. The only Family he'd known, the only Residence, was T'Hawthorn's. He'd have to adapt to a new place, something he'd never anticipated he'd have to do again. D'Marigold's household couldn't possibly run along the lines of T'Hawthorn's.

He was led to an office suite, then through it, the odor of animals in the air. Obviously the animal Healer's portion of the house. Danith D'Ash was also the person who matched rare Fams with nobles.

The butler opened the door and announced him.

Cratag sought D'Marigold immediately. She looked more ethereal than ever. Her hair was pale gold, her eyes a summer blue, her lips soft and pink.

Vinni cleared his throat.

Cratag figured he'd stared too long at her and moved his gaze to the Hazels, mother and daughter. The GreatLady was gazing at him. She seemed unsurprised at his size and scars, but he hadn't seen her reaction when he'd entered.

He had seen D'Marigold's, whose eyes had widened, but she hadn't flinched, a good sign.

The little girl said, "You are going to be our bodyguard, Mother told me." She smiled. "You look big and strong. How did you get those scars?"

D'Hazel closed her eyes. "Personal comment, Avellana."

"No, it wasn't. It was a question."

"It was a question about his personal appearance. We have discussed this before." More than anger was in the woman's tone, distress, too, as if she feared for her daughter's mind or memory.

Four

Cratag answered Avellana, "I'm from the southern continent of Brittany." He laced his tones with the lilt of his native land. "There aren't as many people there, nor as many Healers. I was hurt fighting a slashtip."

"Thank you for your forbearance," D'Hazel said. He thought she wanted to swoop down on her daughter and pluck her up and take her away, but Vinni T'Vine stood in her path and D'Marigold held Avellana's hand.

"It must have hurt a lot." Avellana was still looking at him.

"It did."

"But you killed the slashtip."

"Yes, because he was trying to kill me."

The little girl nodded decisively. "Then you are a good person to take care of Signet and me."

"I intend to be."

"You need a Fam, too."

Cratag nearly rocked back on his heels at that. No one would give him a prized Fam, not a common, minimally Flaired person like him. But the little girl and D'Marigold and the animal Healer, GreatLady D'Ash, were all nodding.

He looked at the animals, none of whom had been a threat, so he'd dismissed them without truly observing them. There was a beige cat sitting elegantly by D'Marigold's feet in a proud pose, with an interesting triangular face, white muzzle, and yellow eyes. Obviously D'Marigold's Fam.

The little girl had an arm around a big cat who was nearly limp in her arms. Two cats already.

Well, cats were more common than dogs. Maybe there would be a fox? He'd heard foxes were good Fams.

There *was* a fox, aloofly watching from a cube set in a strategically defendable area. Two housefluffs watched him and a black and white cat gazed at him from upside-down eyes, all paws in the air, with a goofy smile.

Cratag stepped toward the fox.

I am not for you, the fox snickered.

Cratag pivoted back . . . and nearly tripped on the goofy cat who'd thumped down from his perch and run to him. The cat fell over, between Cratag's feet, and he had to settle into his balance or windmill like a fool.

Lying on Cratag's shoes, plump side rounded, the cat gazed up at him with cheerful delight, a little drool escaping his mouth. *Greetyou, FamMan.*

He heard it clearly, as clearly as any Family mindspeaking, the only sort he'd been able to hear. Maybe he had a better connection with animals.

"He gets clumsy when he's excited, but he's perfect for you." Danith D'Ash beamed.

The cat grinned. *What will you call me? I will call you FamMan.*

"Or you could call me Cratag." He nodded to each person in the room. "Please call me Cratag."

FamMan. The cat jumped to his paws, raced back and forth across the room, his run mixed with an occasional bow-legged hop. Then he ran around Cratag, hit the rise of his sturdy boots, and fell over, grinning again. *What will you call me?*

Damn. He had a silly Fam. Cratag searched Family names, Maytree and Hawthorn, for an appropriate one. "Beadle," he said.

*C*ratag, the Hazels, Vinni T'Vine, and D'Marigold—who'd told him to call her Signet—walked through T'Ash's Residence to the front door where the glider Cratag had come in waited.

D'Marigold's fragrance of delicate spring blossoms drifted to Cratag, making him very aware of her. Soon they'd be at her Residence, and life would never be the same. He'd look back on this interlude as a time different than his previous life at T'Hawthorn's and his ultimate return there.

The glider driver had made himself comfortable in the kitchen that was well known for good food and hospitality, and now met them on the portico, along with another man.

Vinni heaved a sigh when he saw his bodyguard. The boy tended to slip away from his guards. If Families continued to produce children who could teleport at a young age, Cratag foresaw problems protecting them, though as far as he was aware, Vinni and Avellana were the only children who could teleport. Just his luck to be tangled up with them both.

Hanes Vine, Vinni's bodyguard, winked at Cratag, but made his expression serious as he fastened his gaze on his charge. "We got your note, T'Vine, but would like to reiterate that you should take at least one of us with you wherever you go."

D'Hazel gave Vinni a sharp look. "Vinni, I thought we also discussed being a good example for Avellana. She looks up to you. Something dreadful could have happened on your own."

"Something nearly did," Signet muttered.

Cratag glanced at her but said nothing, since D'Hazel had continued to talk in that patient voice most youngsters hated. Which reminded Cratag of Laev, T'Hawthorn's Son'sSon, and how much he wanted to see the young man.

Had T'Hawthorn bothered to tell Laev personally that Cratag would be here at D'Marigold's when Laev himself was experiencing his Second Passage at seventeen?

Hanes slid his glance toward Cratag, both of them commiserating for Vinni and the gentle scold he was receiving before his social inferiors and men whom he respected.

D'Hazel may have been a canny noblewoman with her peers, but she knew little about adolescent boys.

Hanes and Cratag held similar positions in their households—extended Family that worked for a GreatLord. Cratag as the chief of T'Hawthorn's guards, Hanes as chief of Vinni's bodyguards. They'd met when they'd taken Laev and Vinni to their training sessions at the Green Knight Fencing and Fighting Salon. The main difference between the two men was that Hanes had more than average Flair and had grown up in the Vine household under old D'Vine.

When D'Hazel stopped for a breath, Cratag said, "Perhaps Avellana can have a warm drink when we reach D'Marigold's."

As expected, D'Hazel switched her focus back to her daughter. "Yes. The wind is cold."

Neither he nor Hanes had been much affected, but they were both big men. D'Marigold and Vinni appeared cold despite the weathershields surrounding them. They'd teleported to T'Ash's and hadn't worn heavy outer garments—another deficiency that D'Hazel had pointed out to Vinni. At her exclamation, the driver swept the door open.

Hanes stepped forward and lifted Avellana—warmly dressed in a thick winter coat and with a weathershield, too—into the glider. "Here you go, GreatMistrys Avellana, enjoy the ride. Greetyou, Rhyz," he said to her Fam. Then Hanes winked at her, and she smiled back. He eyed the glider, turned to the driver. "I'll sit up front with you."

"You're welcome to," the driver said.

D'Hazel stepped into the glider, Vinni slid next to Avellana on the large leather back bench facing forward, and Signet followed gracefully. Cratag was last, and though there was still room on the bench, he sat on the one facing the rear. The driver initiated the privacy shield between the front and back of the glider, retracted the stands, and smoothly took off.

All three FamCats scrutinized each other and vocalized lowly in their throats, working out status.

D'Marigold's Du sat upright, staring the other cats down. Though he had just been adopted, he obviously considered that the Residence would be his own, and he would be top cat. Since Avellana's Fam dropped his eyes, and to Cratag's disgust, his own plump puss rolled to expose a white furry belly, forcing Cratag to catch him before he fell off his lap, the littlest cat won.

The people, of course, knew their status, highest to lowest: D'Hazel, T'Vine, D'Marigold, Avellana Hazel, and Cratag. Vinni was only second because of his age, Cratag was a commoner and lower than everyone else.

Once past the walls and through the greeniron gate of the D'Marigold estate, Cratag saw the beautiful Residence. It was of smooth construction in a peachy color. He was sure the shell wasn't armourcrete.

It was not a secure fortress modeled after Earthan castles like the FirstFamilies had built. Not even a smaller armored house that other nobles had constructed. This home was designed to be pleasing to the eye with tall arched windows, smooth curves, flowing balconies, and a gracious presence. Beautiful and essentially indefensible from any sort of threat—given any thief or army, the Residence would fall.

The glider stopped before the house, and paneled wooden doors inset with fancy colored glass opened . . . inward. Cratag sighed. D'Hazel was looking approvingly at the pretty Residence, Avellana was squirming with excitement under the weight of her Fam, Vinni was watching Avellana, and Signet was radiating pride.

The drive was raked, the few steps up to a porch were spotless.

Hanes Vine was the first out of the glider, and circled around to open Avellana's door. Once again he lifted the girl from the glider with a flashing smile. He set her on her feet with a wink that had the girl giggling and thanking him by name. Obviously she was no stranger to the Vine household. Hanes offered his hand to D'Hazel, who accepted it. He didn't patronize Vinni, merely stood by as Vinni jumped the three-quarter meter to the ground.

Cratag took the opportunity to slip from the glider and turn to hold his hand out to D'Marigold—Signet.

Lovely color tinted her cheeks as she put her bare hand in his. Again, like when they'd met years ago, he felt the small zing through his nerves that he'd half-thought was faulty memory. He liked it and the feel of her long, cool fingers in his hand.

She was taller than D'Hazel and stepped easily from the glider, completely balanced every second, like someone who knew her body well.

Best not to think of her lovely body. Though as soon as she dropped his hand and walked with long strides toward her home, his gaze fastened on her nice ass—muscular for such a slender woman.

As soon as they entered, stepping onto an antique but still vividly colored carpet set on a beige marble floor, the Residence spoke, "Greetyou ladies and lords. I've been informed of the wonderful news that we will be having long-term guests." The voice of the house was as mellow and smooth as the surroundings.

Avellana placed her cat on his feet, then ran to the richly polished wooden staircase at the right of the entry hall. As beautiful as everything else about the house, it was gracefully curved and had a bannister as wide as a child's butt. "Where's my room? I have the HeirSuite on the third floor. Where?"

A creak came as if the Residence laughed. D'Hazel sighed and followed after her daughter, steps looking quicker than the pace she preferred. Cratag figured she must have been running after Avellana since the child found her feet.

Keeping a keen eye out for any missteps by Avellana as she

hurried up the stairs, Cratag strode past D'Hazel, a running Vinni, and Signet, bringing up the rear carrying Du.

Signet answered, "Up two flights of stairs and to the right. The MasterSuite is slightly down the corridor to the left, the Mistrys-Suite, my rooms, a little to the right. The HeirSuite is just beyond mine. Then we have a teleportation room and the corner turret with my meditation room, angling to the east wing."

Cratag was appalled. A straight shot from the entryway up stairs to the Master- and MistrysSuites! Probably the most beautiful and richly appointed rooms in the Residence, and so accessible to threat. No one else seemed to be thinking of that, though, and he still didn't know what real threats might be. Difference in status or not, he had to speak with D'Hazel.

Avellana slipped, and he steadied her with a hand.

"No running on the stairs. That's a rule," Signet said.

"Now, Avellana," D'Hazel said, "We know you like to be in control of your surroundings, but you are *not* an adult. Nor will you be the one giving the orders here. Your father and I expect you to follow D'Marigold's rules."

Avellana stuck out her lower lip.

"Indeed," added the Residence. "As generations of Marigolds have said, a true lady never runs anywhere, and stairs are to be ascended with grace and descended with the knowledge that one is making an entrance."

Avellana tilted her head. "Really?" She glanced at Signet. "You never got to run up and down these stairs at all?"

"Ladies don't—" D'Hazel started, but Signet answered.

"Oh, just like you, I slipped once, and a riser took a chunk out of my leg. Running is fine, and you can run in the gardens, but *not* near the cliffs or any stairs. That rule can apply to gentlemen, too." She sent a look to Vinni, who flushed. He stroked the smooth glide of the bannister with his hand.

Signet said to the girl, "It would pain me if you were hurt."

"Oh." Avellana considered that. "And if I don't follow the rules,

I don't get the HeirSuite, but will be moved to the smelly oldie room."

"I beg your pardon!" the Residence said. "We have no smelly rooms."

"How do you know? Do you smell?"

"Avellana, that is quite enough. I think instead of seeing your rooms, we should go back home and have a long talk about manners and personal comments," D'Hazel said.

"Oh, no! It is so much lighter here. D'Hazel Residence has dark rooms and halls! I apologize, I apologize, I apologize, D'Marigold Residence."

"A-vel-la-na!"

"Uh-oh." The little girl sank down onto the step and put her face in her hands. "I'm sorry, Mother, I shouldn't have said that about our Residence. But this place is so pretty!"

"Thank you. I accept your apology," D'Marigold Residence said. "It has been a while since I have had a child in my halls, but I do recall how curious they are. To answer your question, I can . . . sense . . . odors, I believe. They sink into my walls."

Cratag picked up Avellana and swung her up the few steps to the landing. "Let's check out your rooms."

She giggled. "You're so bi—." She stopped. "I admire how strong you are, Cratag Maytree."

"Thank you," he said, and the procession got under way.

Then Signet was beside him. Another flight of stairs later, she waved to the opposite wall and right. "Those are my rooms, the HeirSuite is just beyond."

As they neared Avellana's rooms, the door swung open, again inward, revealing a large sitting room of a light orange yellow.

Signet sighed a little. "Ah, everything is fine."

Everything was better than fine. It was obviously a room made for a cherished and refined noble girl. All was clean, and the furnishings were comfortable with a look that was essentially female: light-colored fabrics with flowers and such, as feminine as Signet.

Now that he thought about it, T'Hawthorn's Residence was dark with tall walls and narrow windows. A protective Residence. A proper warrior's Residence.

Cratag wouldn't admit that he liked this better.

Light shafted in from the high windows that took up most of the wall facing the sea. In the summer the room would fill with afternoon sun. Today clouds dominated the scene until he moved close to the door-like windows and looked out to see a balcony. It was enclosed with slats of wood higher than Avellana was tall. There were occasional fancy cutouts about the size of his cat's head from low to high. Safe for a child, as long as she or he didn't climb up on the top rail.

Avellana threw open the door and let in the cold spring air, then shot out onto the balcony.

Signet followed fast. "Shield on!" The air shimmered in a bubble around the balcony. "Residence, please activate the security field whenever the door from the bedroom to the balcony opens."

"Yes, D'Marigold," the Residence said.

"Good," D'Hazel said. She was studying the field and looking thoughtful. Avellana and all three cats were poking their faces through various cutouts. Du stretched tall to his full height, paws on the side of the balcony to see, and Beadle was craning his neck. Avellana's cat was going from hole to hole to check on the view. Vinni T'Vine went to the rail and looked out. It was chest-high on him.

"Ooooh. Look at the ocean and the clouds and the rocks and the ocean!" Avellana said. She stooped down and lifted her Fam to look out the next-to-highest hole. He accepted the rough handling with a purr.

Cratag's Fam ran to him. *Up! You are the tallest, so I will see the best.* Pride infused his mental tones, warming Cratag. Only a few minutes with a Fam, and he was already beginning to love it. He reached down and cradled Beadle's butt in his hand, held him up. Beadle's whiskers twitched. *Too high. No ground. Down!*

He put Beadle carefully on all four paws, and the cat staggered.

Eyeing the shield, Cratag thought it was only good enough to keep children from falling. He'd have to talk to Signet about that.

"Me, hold me up!" Avellana was hopping in delight again.

Setting his hands around her waist, he lifted her. "Oooh. So beautiful. Does my bedroom have a balcony?"

"No," Signet said, "but it has windows so you can see the ocean better. From the bed."

"Ooooh!"

Cratag put Avellana down, and she danced a little as she said, "Thank you, GentleSir Maytree."

"Call me Cratag."

"Thank you, Cratag." Avellana zoomed back into the sitting room and unerringly went to the bedroom door, flung it open.

"It is *orange*," Avellana whispered.

Signet winced. "I'd forgotten that. We can tint—"

"I have wanted an orange room forever!"

"She has," D'Hazel agreed wryly.

"I believe it's a phase," Signet said. "At one time every girl I knew wanted an orange room."

"Nothing like green!" Avellana said. "There is very much green on Celta. My room has always been green."

"And we're blessed that we have such abundant plant life here on Celta," Signet said.

Cratag grunted, and all eyes turned toward him. "I come from the tropics." He didn't need to touch his face. "There can be too much green."

"I knew I would like you," Avellana stated. She smiled at Vinni. "Vinni told me so."

Cratag made a half bow.

"This is really a top-of-the-pyramid suite," Avellana pronounced, testing the bedsponge by flopping onto it, then scrambling up. "Let's go see yours, Cratag. Will he have the MasterSuite?"

"Yes," Signet said.

"I'd rather he stay close to Avellana," D'Hazel said.

"I'll take the room across the hall." Close to both Avellana and

Signet. There was a slight flatness to D'Hazel's gaze. Did she sense his attraction to Signet? He let his face set into impassivity. Attracted or not, he understood he was here as a caretaker cum bodyguard. Besides, D'Marigold was far above his touch, the Residence had shown him that.

Five

$\mathcal{V}$ery well, Cratag." Signet frowned. "*Those rooms are for a second child. My father's younger brother who died when I was four kept that suite, so it should be furnished for a man.*"

Avellana swiveled her head to stare at her mother. "Second child has a *suite* here? This Residence isn't as large as ours."

D'Hazel rubbed her temples. "If you behave well here and after your First Passage, we will speak of changing your room to the second child's suite."

"Where is it?" Avellana demanded.

"In the northeast corridor of the second floor, around the corner from the HeirSuite," D'Hazel said.

Avellana opened her mouth, but Cratag decided he had had enough of female pique and opened the door to his suite. The sitting room was full of light from the east, showing as watery sun patches on beige marble floor—that the Residence would always keep warm in the winter.

The view through the tall windows was of the front gardens and gliderway. The walls were a pale gray and the furniture was dark maroon leather. He was disappointed, realizing that he liked warmer colors, liked the peach of Signet's old rooms—and what colors did she live with now?—and his own cream-tinted walls at T'Hawthorn's estate. But he agreed with little Avellana, a suite was much preferable to a room. Though he had a private bath at T'Hawthorn's, he lacked a sitting room, and this was pure luxury. Two walls were filled with shelves of books, holospheres, music flexistrips, and even Family memoryspheres.

"Oh." Avellana dismissed his suite with a glance, turned back to her mother. "You promise I can have the second child's suite at home if I'm good here? I *am* the second child."

"I said so." D'Hazel's expression turned stern. "While you are gone, I'll examine the rooms and consider how they can be improved for you."

"Thank you, Mother."

D'Hazel nodded. She glanced along the hallway. One end had the large tower and many-paned glass doors to a sitting room, the other long windows at the end of the hall. Cratag's and Avellana's doors were still open, and squares of light from the rooms showed on the floor. A wistfulness came to D'Hazel's eyes. Her Residence was probably some Earthan-looking castle, much grimmer than this airy place.

"Vinni, why don't you and Avellana teleport home to D'Hazel Residence and select her things to pack," D'Hazel said.

Cratag thought he heard/felt a little pulse from the GreatLady, and a few seconds later he heard steps on the stairs, and Vinni's bodyguard, Hanes, rounded the corner.

His gaze went to the group of people and cats first, checking on their health, then swept the bright corridor and luxurious rooms. His eyes sparkled, and there was a quick lift of his brows at Cratag before he arranged his face in serious lines and bowed to D'Hazel. "You called, GreatLady?"

So he'd been summoned telepathically. Cratag was surprised he'd even felt a tingle.

"Can you accompany T'Vine and my daughter to D'Hazel Residence?"

"We're only 'porting," Vinni grumbled.

"Nevertheless, I want you escorted," D'Hazel said.

"Of course," Hanes said with another inclination of his torso. He held out his hand to Avellana, and she walked over and put hers in his, looked up at Hanes, and said, "I need my wall holo paintings."

Signet made a surprised noise. "You craft holos?"

Avellana smiled widely. "It is my creative Flair."

Child was precocious. Cratag would be earning every piece of gilt he was paid on this job.

"The nearest teleportation room is at the end of the hall, between Avellana's suite and the turret."

That had Avellana pulling away from Hanes and running down the corridor again. "There's a turret near my room. I am not allowed in any of the D'Hazel towers."

Signet raised her brows at D'Hazel, but answered the girl. "I use the room on this floor as a meditation room, so it is off-limits to you."

"Oh." Avellana stopped, but her cat continued to trot on to the designated door. Again, the Residence opened the door.

"Welcome, Fams," the Residence said. "We have not had Fams in the house in my memory."

Signet picked up her Fam. "Residence, this is Du. He's our new Fam."

"Greetyou, Du," the Residence said, with an undertone of pure joy that made Cratag uncomfortable. If he listened closely, he thought he could hear the empty silence of all the other rooms in the Residence. A quietness he hadn't experienced since he'd joined the T'Hawthorn Family, hadn't experienced much at all except when he made the journey to Druida by himself.

Continuing, Signet said, "We will modify my suite for Du."

"Of course," said the Residence.

"This teleportation chamber is another lovely room," Avellana said, in an almost adult voice. Hanes and Vinni had each taken one of her hands.

Cratag had followed them and glanced into the room with the teleportation pad that he would never use. The place was no bigger than a large closet and was paneled in a honey wood. It had a stained glass window. People who could teleport were always concerned with light.

Avellana's Fam accepted Hanes's offer to be carried with his free arm. Vinni counted down slowly, and all four teleported away. Cratag blinked, still a little surprised that children so young were proficient at 'porting.

"Now, shall we settle some details?" D'Hazel said smoothly from behind him.

"Of course," Signet said. "Please come into my main sitting room, at the opposite end of the hall."

"Ah, that lovely curve of house that can be seen and envied along much of the coast," D'Hazel said.

"Yes, the main turret facing the sea, the largest one, though I think of 'turret' as stone, and these circular tiers are mostly glass set in arches." Signet's face softened with love.

"A most beautiful architectural feature. Which tier is this floor?" D'Hazel asked.

"Thank you, the third."

"I don't want Avellana to go up into the last and smallest. It's more of an observation room, nothing but windows?"

"That's right," Signet said, "but it would be a shame for her to never visit that room, so let's put it off-limits like the beach path, unless she is with someone else. Another human adult," she corrected.

D'Hazel smiled briefly. "You learn fast."

"I hope so."

Cratag soon realized that Signet being firm about Avellana's rights was different than how she treated her own. Though the next few minutes were very polite, Cratag was surprised at the strange reverse bargaining. D'Hazel opened the negotiations with an offer to pay for updated security spellshields for the Residence. Signet was being politely insulted and willing to give away her services as Avellana's companion for much less. He was hard put not to shift in his very comfortable chair.

Finally, he stood and went over to Signet, took her arm, and drew her up and out of her chair. He sent a cool smile to D'Hazel. "Please excuse us for a few moments."

The GreatLady's lips tightened, and she nodded then rose herself and moved to the windows and the fabulous view of the ocean framed by the tall, arched windows.

His hand firmly under Signet's elbow, Cratag opened the door and took her out into the corridor with him, moved them down to the far end of the hallway.

Signet's brow furrowed as she looked up at him. "What's wrong?"

"What are you doing?" he asked at the same time.

"What do you mean?" she asked.

"Your bargaining skills—" He stopped before he made a rude personal comment.

Her brows arched. "I haven't had to bargain for anything since grovestudy."

He groaned.

"I suppose it's obvious." Then she actually smiled. "But it's not important."

"*Not important!*" For a moment his mind boggled. "You have a GreatLady, one of the highest nobles of them all, wanting to engage your services as a companion for her daughter, ready to pay you . . . anything. Her very first offer is to upgrade the security of this Residence, so you need to ask for more."

Signet shrugged, still smiling. "I have enough gilt for my own and the household's needs. Gilt isn't important. I'm glad to have people here with me . . . us."

Cratag didn't open his mouth again until he knew he wouldn't sputter. "First, take the GreatLady up on her offer to immediately update your Residential shields."

"That's an enormous expense, and I don't need—"

Lifting a hand, Cratag stopped her. "It's security that D'Hazel needs to be calm in her mind—and me, too. You, too, if you think about it. We're going to be protecting Avellana. And after that— what of all the pretty objects in this pretty house? Wouldn't you miss a few . . . or a few dozen? Don't know why this place hasn't been burglarized before."

"Most of our objets d'art are quite unique, people would recognize them," Signet said stiffly, then added, "and no one comes here. We're the last noble estate before the river, and the land is cliffs down to the river and to the ocean. I have walls, and the greeniron gate and shields. The Residence would warn me of intruders, but no one pays any attention to me."

He grunted. "Isolation is great for thieves and you'll be fresh gossip by this evening, I guarantee that."

"Me?"

"T'Hawthorn sending me, his chief of guards, here. Avellana coming here. Adopting three Fams . . . lots of good juicy gossip."

She frowned. "My Testing at T'Ash's was filed with the Noble-Council Clerk, publicly available." She lifted her chin. "Very well, point taken. I'll accept the security spellshields being updated." She turned away, but Cratag caught her arm. His jaw hurt, and he realized he'd been clamping it tight.

"You owe it to your Family to make the most of this opportunity."

"I am the last of my Family, and I doubt we'll continue," she said simply, then repeated. "The gilt is not important. Having people in the Residence is important." A lovely flush stained her cheeks. "Being valued is important, and D'Hazel and T'Vine have already given me that."

"For now. What happens if Avellana doesn't survive her First Passage?"

Signet's blush faded and took even more color from her. She stood straight. "I will do my best to ensure that doesn't happen." Her face set. "Just being with me will . . . I hope."

He didn't understand everything that was going on, didn't have to. "I've sat in on hundreds of negotiations with T'Hawthorn." As an intimidation factor that sometimes worked. He knew this part of noble life, if nothing else. "Don't sell your services short. Don't sell yourself short, either. You're a beautiful, greatly Flaired noblewoman. You'll marry, have children. Take advantage of this opportunity."

She huffed a breath. "I hear you." Spine straight, she turned and walked back to the room. He followed.

D'Hazel had returned to her chair, and Signet and Cratag took their own.

Signet smiled at the GreatLady, and Cratag was glad to see the curve of her lips had taken on an edge and her eyes a keenness. He'd overstepped his bounds in speaking with her, hoped he hadn't disgusted her. Much harder to adore a woman from afar when she disliked you.

Signet cleared her throat and said, "I accept the immediate upgrade of the Residential spellshields by Lahsin Holly."

D'Hazel nodded. "Good. I've made the appointment, and Great-Mistrys Holly will be here in a couple of septhours."

Sitting even straighter, Signet said coolly, "That will be the payment for boarding Avellana. My personally helping her through her First Passage, doing my extreme best to ease her . . . with my Flair, will cost one golden favor token to be redeemed upon demand by my Family of yours anytime in the future."

A stunned look came into D'Hazel's eyes. Cratag swallowed his pleased and surprised exclamation. Golden favor tokens were the stuff of legend—promising aid up to the life of the head of the household. But then, the life of the child of a household was in the balance now. He'd had no idea Signet could be so tough.

"Since the price is so high," Signet continued in a voice that held a hint of breathiness, "I will only claim the golden token after Avellana returns to her home after her First Passage. I will take a silver token now for being her companion, which I will exchange for the gold later."

"There is no price I wouldn't pay for my child's life," D'Hazel said.

"Of course not," Signet said, appearing to soften.

"Don't," Cratag muttered, hoping she heard him.

Listen to the big man, Du advised. The cat hopped up onto Signet's lap. She waited a few seconds. "Agreed?" she asked.

"Agreed." Then D'Hazel looked at Cratag. "T'Hawthorn has taught you well."

"I just advised the lady to bargain, not on the terms." Cratag smiled. "Now, I want to know exactly what you're expecting of me and Signet."

D'Hazel lifted her hands and dropped them. "I want Avellana to be safe, to suffer no accidents while she is here. She is a very curious—"

"Precocious," Signet said.

"—girl. She always has been."

"What about enemies?" Cratag asked pleasantly.

"I don't have any."

He raised his eyebrows and stared at her.

She flushed. "None who would be so cruel as to harm a child." She narrowed her eyes at him. "I have few, but strong, alliances. Male heads of households who would duel or go to war beside me. And no one wants to make a precedent of harming a FirstFamilies child."

That sounded straight. "What of this kidnapping threat?"

Signet gasped and protectively gathered Du close. She was bonding quickly with her Fam, too.

Beadle rumbled from where he'd sprawled on Cratag's feet.

D'Hazel's eyes flashed. "Avellana was briefly a target of those mad Black Magic Cultists. The last died some time ago on that island they were banished to," she ended with satisfaction.

"How terrible," Signet said.

"Not likely to occur again," Cratag said.

"No, craziness like that comes along rarely, thank the Lady and Lord," D'Hazel said.

"But one of the murderers escaped," Cratag said. "It's a good idea to strengthen the spellshields here."

"Ours have already been replaced," D'Hazel said. Her fingers tapped the cloth arm of her chair. "I haven't thought of that man for a long time. I doubt he would return to Druida."

Cratag shrugged. "It's my job to keep villains like him in mind. It would be well if he was not forgotten."

"I'll ensure the Clerk of All Councils schedules a yearly reminder for all councils, perhaps on the anniversary of——" she stopped.

"Yes," Cratag said, "the anniversary of which of the six deaths?"

D'Hazel's mouth tightened before she said, "The anniversary of the conviction of the murderers."

Nodding, Cratag said, "Good enough. So, we are to keep Avellana safe from her own adventurous nature and mischance. No specific threats?"

"No."

"And what else?" he pressed.

Pain came into D'Hazel's eyes. She stared at Signet. "Vinni has convinced me that Avellana will weather First Passage if she is here with you. Your specific Flair will help her somehow." Again she raised helpless hands as if it were a common gesture when it came to Avellana. "No one knows how her damaged brain will handle Passage. Please, both of you, be there for her. Help her through Passage." It was a plea.

Cratag snorted, bringing the lady's gaze back to him. "Precious little I know about Passage. I've never had an intense one. But I will guard them both during that time." He considered the matter. "And how does Vinni T'Vine figure in with Avellana?"

The women gave him the look that said that they'd expected him to know something they did, have some knowledge—noble knowledge—that he didn't.

"Avellana is Vinni's HeartMate," Signet said.

The words rolled around in his mind for a minute before he truly understood them. "Who said?"

"Vinni," the women replied in unison.

"And he knows? How?"

Signet looked uneasy, D'Hazel glanced away. "However Vinni knows anything, I believe," D'Hazel said. "He saw it in a vision, or multiple visions." Then she smiled sweetly at him. "You could ask him."

Grunting, Cratag said, "Most of you folks are uneasy around the young GreatLord, because he's a prophet, afraid of what he will tell you." The women pokered up, but he'd seen the reaction around Vinni T'Vine often enough. T'Hawthorn's Son'sSon, Laev, trained in fighting with Vinni, and Cratag always took Laev to the class and back.

He went on. "But I don't have much Flair, just enough to work our machines. He probably doesn't see much of my future." Cratag stood, and Beadle flopped over from his feet to the floor and protested with a mew. Cratag already knew his Fam was not one who vocalized much; one good thing about the guy. He picked him up, bowed to D'Hazel and Signet—an equal bow. D'Hazel was of greater rank, but Signet was his hostess for the next while. "I need to settle my affairs at home—at T'Hawthorn's. I will return this afternoon. GreatLady D'Hazel, I will do my extreme best to ensure Avellana takes no harm in any way and survives her Passage. She's an interesting little girl. Signet, until later. D'Marigold Residence, please inform T'Hawthorn's driver I'm ready to leave." He wanted to see Laev, talk to him.

"It is done," the Residence said.

"Good, and thank you. Please be aware of security." He aimed the words at the Residence but a look at Signet.

"Of course," said the Residence.

Signet nodded.

One last bow, thank the Lord and Lady. "Ladies." He strode to the door, holding his plump Fam. The door opened.

"One moment, GentleSir Maytree. Your price?" D'Hazel asked.

He met her gaze coolly, his gut tightening again. "I thought you'd negotiated it with my lord, T'Hawthorn."

D'Hazel inclined her head. "Very well. But as an aside, I wouldn't discount Vinni's Flair when it comes to you."

If his gut squeezed any more, he'd get a bellyache. "Noted," he said, and left.

I can 'port, said Beadle. *But I can't 'port both of us. You are too big.*

"Don't think we'll be moving around much," Cratag said. "We're stuck here."

Six

*C*ratag brooded on the way back to *T'Hawthorn's Residence, mostly* about Signet D'Marigold.

The more he was in the lady's presence, the more he felt as if there were faint waves pulsing from her. He knew it was a foolish idea, but he couldn't shake it. Perhaps all nobles gave off emanations of Flair, and he was just too dull to feel them. Maybe he was more attuned to D'Marigold because . . . because he was attracted to her. So, he acknowledged it. That didn't mean anything, wouldn't change anything.

Being careful of his speech and his accent and his manners around so many nobles wore on him. He was beginning to know D'Hazel and was sure that Vinni and Hanes would accompany Avellana back to D'Marigold's, probably by glider this time. There was a limit to how often even powerful people could 'port.

Everyone should be safe enough in the bright light of the sunny afternoon. The clouds had blown away with the strong wind, and the day turned from shades of gray to blue and yellow.

Beadle was stretched out on Cratag's bed, snoozing with all four paws up and white furred belly exposed, while Cratag stood staring at his closet and the many clothes for different purposes he'd somehow accumulated in the past four years. When had he acquired *four* sets of tunic and trous ritual robes? A couple even had fancy braid.

Well, yeah, he recalled the damn white on white brocade that was a bitch to clean, spells or no, that he'd worried about getting blood or food on. T'Hawthorn, as Captain of All Councils, had led a Winter Solstice ritual at GreatCircle Temple, and Cratag had been his bodyguard.

He'd seen D'Marigold at that ritual, too, hadn't he? He snorted. He might hide his feelings from everyone else, but it wasn't wise to hide them from himself. Of course he had noticed her. He'd looked for her every time since he'd held her hand and linked with her during D'Holly's Healing circle.

Staring at the white ritual robe, he recalled that he'd had a fizz of excitement when dressing in it—because he was sure he'd glimpse D'Marigold. She always participated in the important quarterly rituals at GreatCircle Temple. He snorted at the memory. He'd still had a summer tan and had thought the white would look good on him, maybe attract a female—D'Marigold's—eye. Instead when he put it on, he saw the white was the same color as the scars on his face. It was the last time he'd cared about the ritual robes that T'Hawthorn gave him.

She'd seen him that night, he recalled. She, too, had been dressed in white, and it had accented her pale coloring—her light blond hair, her summer blue eyes, her pale skin, with the hint of rose in her cheeks. She'd looked like a winter goddess.

Disgusted with himself, Cratag packed some old sets of work clothes, a couple of newer tunics and trous, several sparring robes, a set of generic purple with gold trim ritual robes— T'Hawthorn's colors—which looked like hell on him, and a set of more fashionable clothes he wore for dressy. Underwear. That should be enough.

Another bag for his weapons—sleeve and ankle knives, some throwing discs, his tri-blazer case, and some long daggers—and he was ready. He exchanged his regular sword with his best, buckled the belt, and settled the sheath at his hip.

There was a rapping on his door, Laev's knock. Did the young man know that Cratag was leaving? What did he think?

Cratag opened the door, and Laev flung his arms around him in a hug, surprising both of them. Hawthorns didn't often display affection. Cratag hugged Laev hard, feeling how he was filling out from boy to man. Laev seemed to be sending off waves of emotion. Strange. Definitely a strange day.

Though they'd often talked in Cratag's room, now it seemed dark and cramped as he recalled the bright and spacious suite he had at D'Marigold's. A view of gardens tipped with light green spring growth instead of a paved and walled courtyard.

Laev stepped back, and Cratag let him go. He searched the face of this young man he'd raised as much as the Hawthorns had. Cratag had spent time with the boy since they'd first met, when Laev's father and T'Hawthorn had been busy with the business of planning, then fighting a feud.

Cratag had comforted Laev in those dark days when all thought D'Holly would die—and her HeartMate, too, the great warrior T'Holly—from a wound the boy had given her. Laev had lost his head during a street melee, forgetting what little Cratag had taught him, and injured the woman with a poisoned blade he'd found.

Cratag had been the one to convince Laev to do what was honorable and go to D'Holly's Healing. Though with the loss of Laev's father, T'Hawthorn and the boy had developed a closer relationship, Cratag believed he was the one to whom Laev told his hopes and fears and dreams. He loved Laev like a son—or a younger brother.

At thirty-four, Cratag would have had to be very promiscuous in his southern village to have a son of seventeen.

"I hear you're leaving us for a little while," Laev said, his words rushed.

Cratag frowned, gestured to his bags that took up most of his bedsponge, then said, "We'll speak of it in your rooms."

Laev nodded jerkily. Cratag narrowed his eyes, lately the boy had been clumsier than usual for a young man coming into his growth. "Or maybe we should see whether you've learned those fighting moves Tab Holly has been trying to teach you." Fighting was the best lesson around for coordination.

Grinning, Laev rubbed his hands. "Now you're talking." He glanced at Beadle. "You got a cat!" Laev went over and rubbed the feline belly. Beadle didn't even open his eyes, but purred.

Warmth suffused Cratag, he found himself puffing out his chest. "A *Fam*."

"A *Fam*!" Laev's eyebrows rose. The only Fam in Residence was T'Hawthorn's haughty Black Pierre who didn't deign to notice anyone else. Laev cocked an eye at Beadle. "Good thing you're not staying, Black Pierre would eat him for lunch."

Cratag grunted. "Thought we were going to spar."

"Right," Laev swung around and was a mite off balance.

They strode to the nearest workout room in the castle, only a few doors down. As far as he was concerned, two sparring rooms were too few, though one was a converted ballroom and good and large. He frowned. D'Marigold Residence *must* have a fighting room—probably called a salon—wouldn't it?

Soon they were in the minuscule locker room, changing into gear. Laev wrinkled his nose. "Smells in here."

"Not enough ventilation," Cratag said, as always.

"Did I tell you? After my Second Passage, as a gift, FatherSire will let me remodel the HeirSuite! We're going to put in a sparring room. New." Laev rubbed his hands again, not a usual gesture for him.

This was the first Cratag had heard of a remodel or a new sparring room. His expression must have given him away, because the young man's excitement dimmed. "It's the same design you and I talked about a while back."

Cratag nodded. "Good, and I'm glad you'll have it."

"*We'll* have it," Laev said.

"Yes." Cratag stowed his clothes tidily in his locker and set his hand on Laev's shoulder as they walked into the room. Laev's shoulder twitched with nerves, and Cratag squeezed it comfortingly . . . standard gestures between them that settled them both.

They stepped onto the mat and bowed to each other. "Fifth fighting pattern," Cratag said. Laev's class was working on that one at the Green Knight Fencing and Fighting Salon. None of them had mastered it.

An intensity came to Laev's eyes, and Cratag readied for the attack, the kick and leg spin. But Laev shot a short jabbing blow instead. Cratag countered, and they fought. As always, Cratag modulated his strength. He took some kicks, a fall or two, and gave back as good as he got, teaching with technique Laev could observe.

They circled each other, sweating, adding heavy scent to the already odor-burdened room.

"So tell me about this deal with D'Marigold," Laev said.

Cratag's mind flashed to an image of the woman sitting in her beautiful Residence that so suited her.

Laev took him down, properly pinned him to end the bout, crowed with panting laughter, and rolled off Cratag. "I won!"

"Sure you did," Cratag said.

"I did."

"I said so, didn't I?"

Chuckling, Laev said. "It's that D'Marigold diverts you."

Cratag stilled. How did the boy know that?

"I've watched you at GreatCircle Temple rituals." Laev glanced aside. "I watched you the first time you met. At D'Holly's Healing circle." His voice was a little rough. "I'll never forget that."

"You did very well, then and now." Cratag shoved to his feet, offered Laev a hand up. "And I don't recall that move in fighting pattern five."

Laev shrugged. "Some variation Tab Holly taught us."

Something nobles knew and commoners didn't. Cratag had

spottily learned the fighting patterns in his youth, learned more after he'd come to Druida and trained at a gym.

Picking up a towel, Laev rubbed it across his neck. "Think the Hollys, maybe Tab himself, developed it."

Definitely a move Cratag didn't know—or hadn't. Now he did. But the boy's excess energy had drained. His movements were smoother, like a fighter's should be. No more clumsiness for a while, Cratag congratulated himself.

Laev slanted him a glance. "Odd how fate circled around with this—you and D'Marigold met first at a ritual presided over by the Hazels."

Ah, the boy was considering his own personal philosophy and what his culture had taught him. Cratag didn't care what the young man believed as long as it included a strong sense of ethics. If it didn't—well, Cratag'd failed.

Cratag grunted. "It was the Hazels' month, and as for meeting..." He stopped in midstep as he recalled more details just *before* they'd met. He'd been focused on Laev's well-being, walking into a Healing circle for an enemy, but Laev had wounded the woman. It was the right thing to do.

Vinni T'Vine had helped arrange the circle. Insisted that D'Marigold be beside Cratag. "Vinni T'Vine. Again."

Laev stopped right before he got to the locker room door, flashed a smile. "Mixing in, is he? Everyone seems to quiver when Vinni acts on one of his prophecies." Then Laev's expression went serious. "But we've learned to know him in training. He's a good kid. Too isolated at that castle of his, with those old female relatives. A good kid," he repeated. So said the seventeen-year-old about the thirteen-year-old.

"I'll drop a word to Hanes," Cratag said.

Laev's voice echoed back, "Yes. Convince him and the other bodyguards that Vinni can have us over at T'Vine Residence more. Even FatherSire lets me bring friends home, and host a grovestudy class and young-gatherings and overnights."

Cratag had worked hard to make that happen. But T'Hawthorn was also aware of the contacts Laev was making with other noble Families that would be valuable for the rest of his life. Cratag followed Laev to the waterfall room, considering those in Laev's training class at the Green Knight Fencing and Fighting Salon—a class Vinni T'Vine had put together. All sons of the FirstFamilies except the Clover boys, who were from a commoner Family rising fast. Cratag would have to keep an eye on Vinni T'Vine, much as the boy's uncanny eyes made him wary . . . probably not a hard thing to do if Avellana Hazel was Vinni's HeartMate. Vinni would be hanging around. Imagine knowing you had a HeartMate at such a young age, and who she was.

Imagine having a HeartMate at all.

That thought made more than Cratag's muscles ache, and he increased the temperature of the water to hot and the spray to pounding. Why wasn't D'Marigold mated?

*S*ignet was courteous to *D'Hazel,* signed a contract, and accepted a silver "favor to be rendered" token and a note that it would be exchanged for a gold token when Avellana returned to the Hazels after her First Passage. Signet's emotions were mixed. Delight that she'd negotiated such a boon, trepidation and pity that it was to help a small girl survive her First Passage. But she thought she kept her face bland as she dropped the small piece of papyrus into the long sleeve of her tunic.

Events piled upon events this day, nearly spinning out of control. Too much company in a house she'd thought would be empty for the rest of her life. Too much change too quickly. Is that what people felt after they'd been with her, a catalyst? She hoped not, but she'd have to consider that later.

She might panic if she let herself. Panicking in the presence of a GreatLady was not acceptable or wise behavior, even though she liked D'Hazel.

There was a small stretch of peace when D'Hazel left to oversee Avellana's packing. For a few minutes Signet collapsed in a large, soft chair in her sitting room. "Residence, I'm a catalyst."

"I did overhear that." The male tones of the house were as rich and mellow as always, but the almost subliminal soothing was gone. It had understood how lonely she'd been, how desperate thoughts had crept into her mind.

"I love you, Residence." It had always sounded silly when she'd said it, but just because she felt silly didn't mean she shouldn't say the words or they weren't true.

You love Me, too. Back from another of his brief forays around the Residence, Du jumped on her lap, circled around.

"I suppose I will love you," she said, petting him.

Do.

"Do, Du." She chuckled.

One window of the sitting room opened a crack, and the scent of the ocean came. The day had turned beautiful.

"I am contacting the PublicLibrary, all the noble Residence libraries regarding this matter of being a catalyst," the Residence said. "I spoke to the starship *Nuada's Sword*, and it, too, is searching for information. However, it said that most of the Earthan information about psi powers was carried by the ship that made a hard landing and was later lost, *Lugh's Spear*."

"I can't think that old Earth would have more knowledge about us than we would or the libraries and the Residences." Another chuckle escaped her, more chuckling than she'd done for a long time. She anticipated laughing tomorrow with Du and the other cats—especially that funny Beadle—and with Avellana.

Signet thought that she and Avellana needed more laughter in their lives. Cratag, too.

There came a slight clink, and she recalled the silver token. She lifted her sleeve and found the marker in the bottom corner of her pocket, pulled it out, and stared at the silver coin. D'Hazel had made it in front of her, embossed with the date and her sigil on the back and the picture of a hazel leaf on the front.

A favor token. Her first. Some heads of households never got one, and that she, lady of a GrandHouse of one, had managed was an extraordinary feat.

Of course she hadn't done it alone. She had been too busy concentrating on impressing D'Hazel, assuring her that Avellana was in good hands, underselling herself. Cratag Maytree, the pragmatic man, had had to remind her to bargain. She thought she'd seen surprise and approval in his eyes when she'd named the price—the spellshields as he'd recommended and a silver token to be turned into gold. A very fine price.

But D'Hazel saying she'd already set up an appointment to update the spellshields had irritated Signet. She'd been manipulated enough today, so she'd named the outrageous price. And had gotten it.

She was no longer useless D'Marigold who lived off Family investments and didn't get a yearly NobleGilt from the Councils because she had no marketable skill. She was *prized* D'Marigold, a noble with something to offer.

An agent of change. That sounded good. Need a drastic upturn in your life? Call on D'Marigold. She smiled. Feeling bubbly, she held Du close and went to a secret stair. "Going to the House-Heart," she told Du and the Residence.

Du straightened in her arms. *I am a GrandLady's Fam. I deserve a HouseHeart.*

"And you have one."

A few minutes later she arrived there, a narrow hall deep in the cliff under and angled inland from the Residence. This was the place that held the sentient stones of the Residence, all the knowledge and character of the Residence and Family, the most important treasures.

She set Du on his feet.

You're not carrying Me in?

Another ripple of amusement escaped Signet, more than chuckle, not quite a full bodied laugh.

She looked down at Du, ran her hand along the rock shoulder

high and to the right of the HouseHeart's gleaming brass door. A secret cache about a half-meter square was revealed as a slab of rock slid aside.

A FAM door? Du actually hopped.

No. Rumor has it that some Families chant, or sing, or recite poetry spells to open the HouseHeart door. The Marigolds don't. She paused expectantly.

Du didn't disappoint. *What do We do?*

Seven

We dance. She took out some special shoes from the cubbyhole, pressed a stone to close the door.

Today the fact that there was only one pair of shoes didn't give her a pang of grief. Today she *wanted* to dance.

The shoes were a bright yellow with an orange design of flowers—marigolds—but most important were the soles. They had bits of metal on the heels and toes. Inside the HouseHeart were hundreds of metal taps shaped for all sizes of feet. Marigolds made their own shoes.

Tucked inside the shoes were a pair of traditional short white liners of the softest silk, with a frilly edge.

Marigold took off her fashionable ankle boots and liners and put on the ones from the cache, balancing on each foot, not leaning a hand or shoulder against the wall. Tradition again.

Du looked at her, then away. *I have heard that some people go without clothes into the HouseHeart.* He licked a patch of hair on his shoulder, then nosed her liners and boots, sniffing deeply, purring. *Mmmm, FamWoman shoe smell. Wonderful.*

This time she truly laughed. *We don't dance naked outside the HouseHeart. You'll see why. I'll remove my clothes inside.* She shook out her limbs, wiggled her feet, grinned down at her Fam. *Ready?*

He stopped rolling on her boots to sit.

It's the staccato rhythm that's important, she said, as hundreds of Marigolds had told mates and children through the ages. Maybe even a Fam or two.

Then she began to "tap" vigorously, feet moving rapidly in the right pattern, hands held *so*, a slide, a shuffle, tap!

It echoes! Du ran a few feet along the corridor.

Yes. She tapped the pattern, whirled, feet moving so fast they'd be a blur to even a Fam eye. When she finished the third turn, the HouseHeart door was open. She followed Du into the golden light and onto the thick moss and closed the door before the last of the sound had faded.

The HouseHeart was a round and domed chamber, cut of brown rock, but with the ceiling smoothed. A continuous mosaic of small alabaster and obsidian and amber tiles rimmed the room in a pretty abstract pattern.

She wanted to sink down into the thick moss, maybe even roll around, but followed tradition again and stripped. Her shoes and liners were cleansed with a spell and put back in the cache from this side of the wall. Then she let the moss cool her feet, twirled in the golden light.

"I'm glad to see you so happy, Signet." The HouseHeart had a female voice, and though it wasn't *quite* her mother's tones, she burst into tears, sank to her knees, and wept.

She hadn't been responsible for her parents' deaths. That idea had lodged in her during the wild swings of emotions, the heat and chills and spiking of her freed Flair during her Third Passage. But the idea had been *wrong*.

Vinni T'Vine had said so, and Vinni was usually right. His eyes had changed color, and that meant he was "seeing." But Vinni was a prophet, supposed to see the future, not the past.

"Dear one," the HouseHeart said, "your parents would have been distressed to know you blamed yourself. Our beliefs are that we pass on to circle the wheel of stars when it is our time."

"I didn't want them to die!" It was something she'd never said aloud, and it came out in a wail. "I didn't want to become D'Marigold at twenty-one and lose my Family and have all my friends go away and no one come back to say they loved me." Oh, this was too much. She sounded like a whiney little girl, so she shut her mouth and cried out the self-pity until her tears were exhausted and she felt better.

Du lay beside her and purred, rubbing his body along her side. When she was done, he brought her a softleaf for her to wipe her eyes with and blow her nose. *This is a very interesting place*, he said. *The moss does not smell like permamoss. It smells nicer.*

"That's because it's Earthan moss." Tended long and well to grow so lushly. Dark grooves caught her eye, and she sat up, looked over toward the wall where there were deep scratches in the moss. Looked down at her Fam's paws. Guilty.

Du gave her an ingratiating smile. *Smells different and better.*

It will grow back, the HouseHeart said. *Welcome, Fam.*

Signet stretched and rose, glanced around to make sure nothing else was too disturbed. The round room was small. A circular marble piece was set into the floor in case one wanted to dance, especially with the special shoes, otherwise the place only held the four elements and an altar. A small trough around the marble held ever-burbling water, and rainbow banners fringed the ceiling and fluttered in the sweet, fresh air that brought the tang of the sea, flowing through tiny rock vents. A large brass brazier on the altar with an airy top showed smoke rising along with a lick of flame.

The essence of the Marigolds.

"HouseHeart, am I the first catalyst in the Family?"

Indeed, the HouseHeart said. *As you were taught, the Family has no one strong psi talent. Most of us were botanists, or geologists, or,*

*like your father, architects. We have had entertainers, a few Healers,
an engineer or two.*

"Just checking." She went to the wall safe, chanted a few couplets, and the door swung open and the interior lit. There were ancient papyrus journals, recent memoryspheres, personal to her predecessors. At one side was a brass box. She took it, went back to sit near her discarded clothes, and opened it.

Inside the larger compartment were more than a dozen "favor" tokens, small brass ones, larger silver ones, even three "great" ones. She stared. She'd known they were there, of course, had seen them once as a child and Heir. Had been told not to use them unless she was in dire straits.

She could have called them in at any time since she was twenty-one. But why? She sighed. Not one of them could have mitigated her loneliness. She picked up a brass one, Horehound. Should she have gone to the Horehounds and asked for one of the men in that household to accompany her to a dinner and play? Stupid.

She looked at the three gold ones. Yew. Very powerful First-Family GrandHouse, and the current D'Yew was a mean and mad woman. Sage and Aloe. Signet smiled. Good Families from which to claim a favor if one needed one. She plucked D'Hazel's token from her pocket and added it, once again pleased with herself.

It would have been better if D'Hazel had offered an alliance with the Family, but that was too much to expect. Signet opened the smaller compartment and saw bits of sturdy foil fashioned like the tokens. Five. Five favors she owed if someone from that Family called on her. Only two were in gold foil—Cherry and Cilantro.

If either of those were given to her, she'd have to use her utmost skill to help that Family, just short of death. She shivered. The reason she'd gotten the golden Hazel favor was to help prevent Avellana's death.

At that moment, the HouseHeart said, "D'Hazel's glider has entered the gates. The spellshields noted four people, adult male and female, and two female children."

All the Hazels, no Cratag Maytree yet.

Signet's heart picked up beat. She liked the aura of the big man. Solid, unpretentious, keen-witted in every sense. A Hawthorn guard, he'd notice things other people wouldn't—or at least she wouldn't. He was very male, though; how would he feel being in D'Marigold Residence?

She didn't have more than a couple of minutes to get dressed and meet them. So she put the box away, hurried into her clothes and out of the HouseHeart, shielded it again with the most powerful spell she knew, then sped to the entryway. She welcomed the Hazels and translocated the luggage.

As T'Hazel walked through the house, D'Hazel and Signet and Avellana and Avellana's sister, Coll, arranged her rooms just so. Then Vinni T'Vine and his bodyguard arrived by glider. They were followed within minutes by Lahsin Holly to survey the estate and begin work on the spellshields surrounding it.

Cratag Maytree was last and put two large duffles in his room. Then the men accompanied GrandMistrys Holly as she studied the outdated security of the estate. Lahsin Holly appeared as if she was accustomed to having men with her every step of the way to comment on a project.

By mid-afternoon, it was obvious that all of the visitors would be staying for evening meal, and Signet told the Residence to use the best crystal, china, and table linens and take food of the highest quality from the no-time storage. Good luck that she'd restocked from the catering company just the week before.

Two additional people teleported in, Lahsin's HeartMate and Avellana's ex-governess, who had just given notice since she was getting married. Another reason for Avellana's move.

The meal went off well, as did after-dinner drinks, then the ex-governess and the Hollys said farewell. Lahsin would be back in the morning to continue her spellshielding. She looked tired from practicing her skill and using a great amount of Flair.

Had Signet ever felt so tired and fulfilled, or was her Flair essentially passive? She thought back. Sometimes when she'd participated in a great ritual, she'd felt like that.

Then Avellana yawned, and the Hazels got back to business. Preliminary schedules were drawn up. Visits to the Hazels, and from the Hazels and Vinni, lessons with Avellana and the ResidenceDen. Time for Avellana's wall holo crafting. Educational outings that Signet racked her mind for—a couple to the starship, *Nuada's Sword*, a few to various theaters, to the PublicLibrary, where Avellana had never been. . . . .

Finally Signet and D'Hazel took Avellana up to bed. Signet showed her how to activate the full wall and ceiling holos. She had preferred a night sky with bright twinkling stars and scudding clouds. Avellana wanted the ocean and surf, so she was surrounded by the ocean—illusion on the walls and the real one from the windows— with a double echo of surf that Signet thought strange, but pleased the girl. Music flexistrips were threaded into the wall slot, enough to play all night but timed to play for half a septhour after the last voice in the room was heard.

D'Hazel had brought some *real* illustrated papyrus and leather books to read from and teach Avellana that ancient art. D'Hazel and Signet took turns reading the girl an epic story, Signet struggling a little, because it had been a long time since she'd actually read instead of watching holos.

D'Hazel held her daughter's hand until she fell asleep, then appeared torn.

"It's the very best thing for her," Vinni said from the doorway. Behind him stood T'Hazel, holding the hand of Coll, the older Hazel girl, who appeared more concerned now that her younger sister wasn't playing lady of the manor.

She is not afraid of being here or of her Passage. It is an adventure special to her, said Avellana's Fam, Rhyz. *And I will be here. We can teleport to you at any time.*

T'Hazel and the older girl came in and kissed Avellana, then he held out his free arm, and D'Hazel went and fit herself to his side. They stepped back into the hallway but stopped as if unable to go farther. The small Family looked at their youngest.

"It's the best thing for Avellana, to remain here in Signet's home and presence," Vinni repeated. "Signet's catalyst Flair will work subtly on her, as it does for all those who make friends with her. You *do* care for Avellana already, don't you, Signet?" The last was a command that Signet answered instinctively.

"Yes, she's a wonderful and interesting girl."

The three other Hazels relaxed a little, and Cratag slipped into the room. He checked the windows, went into the other rooms, then returned. "Lahsin Holly does good work," he said. "These rooms are well protected from any assault." He looked down at Avellana, who had flung off her cover while they were talking, and bent down and pulled it back up over her.

The gesture seemed to reassure the others.

Coll glanced around the suite, stared at the windows, and tilted her head at the sound of two counterpoint rolling surfs—one real and one illusion. "I'll come over sometimes and stay the night."

Signet nodded. "That will be fine."

Coll's father squeezed her. "That isn't on Avellana's precious schedule. You know how she likes her schedules."

"It will be a surprise," Coll said loftily.

Her parents laughed and stepped into the hallway, leaving the sleeping girl and purring Fam. Signet was loath to join them, but she *was* in the suite next door.

Residence, guard her well. Our Family may very well perish if she does.

I hear you, and so it will be, D'Marigold.

She could only trust her Residence as she had always done and went into the hall. Cratag followed her, shut the door quietly, and tested the latch. He grunted. "The lock is bespelled to let Signet and me and all the Hazels in and out. No one else." He moved to the sitting room door. "Here, also." Then he came back to stand behind Signet as she faced the Hazels, his body radiating an astonishing amount of warmth. "She is as physically safe as she can be this night. The new Residential spellshields will be finished in the next couple of days. You have me, Signet, our Fams, and the Residence to watch over her. Be at ease."

D'Hazel smiled wanly. Her husband tightened his arm around her, gave his HeartMate his own sweet smile. "I feel . . . hopeful . . . about Avellana." His breath came out in a quiet sigh. "The most hopeful since her accident."

"She'll be fine," Coll said a little loudly. She sniffled. "She always gets what she wants."

"That's not true," D'Hazel said in a tone that showed she repeated these words often, and began moving down the corridor to the stairs and the glider that awaited them. "No more than her complaint that *you* always get what you want because you are Heir."

Signet and Cratag accompanied the Hazels to the entryway, and as soon as the greeniron gates closed behind their glider, Signet sagged against the wall. She hadn't known how much tension had kept her going until then. "By the Lady, what a day," she murmured.

Cratag slanted her a wry look. "Surprising to you, too?"

"Very." She pushed herself upright, rolled her stiff shoulders. "Those FirstFamily lords and ladies move people around like markers on a gameboard." She recalled he was close to T'Hawthorn. "Beg pardon."

His smile turned grim. "Consider me another marker."

Then he'd had no real choice about this either. "I'm sorry that you were forced into this." A sigh wended up and out of her, and she told the truth on a breath, meeting his eyes. "But I'm very glad you're here." He was strong. Gorgeous.

I am glad to be here, said Beadle, trotting down the stairs. The cats had explored the Residence all evening, sometimes with T'Hazel and Coll.

Signet stifled a yawn, but Cratag's sharp gaze hadn't missed it. "Sorry," she said.

He went to the front door and tested the lock and spell. "Long day," he said.

It wasn't as late as she usually retired, but she was exhausted at the events crammed into this day. Thinking back to her morning sadness was an effort. That seemed years past, and she was a different person. A person with purpose. The recollection that this was her Nameday pushed through her hazy thoughts, and she chuckled.

"What?" Cratag asked.

But the Residence, as usual, had picked up on her thoughts and emotions. "It is Signet's Nameday."

Eight

Cratag paused, his face inscrutable. "I have no gift."

Signet laughed quietly again, shaking her head.

"She has already received her gifts," the Residence said in a smug male tone. "But small iced teacakes, Signet's favorites, await in the kitchen."

Music unrolled through the rooms, a Nameday waltz.

To Signet's surprise, Cratag turned to her and bowed with elegance. Well, she *had* noticed how well he moved, but that was a guardsman's, a fighter's grace. "You dance?" she asked a little foggily. Then wanted to sink with embarrassment. She didn't mean to insult him.

But he didn't look offended. Maybe she'd just sounded as dazed as she was. Barely able to lift her feet. Good thing this was a waltz and not a tap routine.

Cratag smiled slowly. "Oh, yes, I dance." He took her into his arms, and she knew she'd received another gift. His body was big and strong and flexible. His hands on her were warm and comforting with an easy, commanding lead. He was light on his feet as he twirled her down the long atrium, making her breathless with more than the exercise. She liked how he affected her, with tingles. And the way he looked at her and held her—as if she were precious and beautiful.

Sensuality spun between them. He held her close, so their bodies brushed, and she felt his rising passion—and her own. She looked up and was snared by his violet eyes, beautiful, unusual eyes, darkening as she watched.

They twirled, their steps matched, their bodies moving together, and her breath came unevenly as she wondered how they'd move together in bed.

He felt it, too, this attraction.

A gift indeed.

Then they reached the kitchen door, and he stopped, held her in his arms.

The Residence opened the door and broke the moment. Signet cleared her throat, forced her mouth to curve in a smile when she wanted her lips to form a kiss. "Do you like teacakes?"

His large chest expanded with deep breaths. "My favorite."

This was the best Nameday of her life.

The sugar in the icing and the teacakes, and the tea itself, revitalized Signet enough that she followed her usual nightly ritual of bathing and changing into a nightrobe. This time, though, she didn't go to her meditation room to sink into a trance, but turned the opposite way to go to the main sitting room and review the events of the day, smiling.

The sound of the ocean was loud here, the constant ebb and flow soothing.

So.

She had a gorgeous man she was attracted to and who felt something for her staying in her house for a time. He wouldn't leave.

She had a Fam and a new friend in a child.

And Signet knew her Flair. She was a catalyst.

Though no one, including her, knew exactly what that meant. Furthermore, so far her Flair was a passive trait. Somehow she'd have to discover how to make it active. Signet sensed that helping Avellana through her First Passage would tax all her innate skill.

What she must do was think back on the times during GreatRituals and how she'd tried to help, one way to discover how to actively use her Flair. She frowned, surely she'd made some memoryspheres about those times . . . particularly after her parents had died and she'd been the sole Marigold in the noble ritual circles. Hadn't she journaled then? Feeling a shift and blossoming of her Flair, even though she didn't know what it was?

Groping for memories, she realized the time she'd felt most in control of her Flair was during the Healing ritual for D'Holly. The time Vinni had insisted she be placed beside Cratag Maytree.

Now that she sent her mind back, it was after her First Passage that the Marigolds had been invited by the FirstFamilies to participate in their august circles. She had a shadowy memory of a very old woman with a deep voice and a phrasing that sounded like . . . Vinni's? Old D'Vine, the previous prophet of Celta? Her parents had been excited by the old woman's visit, though Signet had been settled in the craft room to work on new shoes.

She'd *known* they'd talked about her, but the Residence hadn't told her what or why when she'd asked.

How had she forgotten that?

Perhaps because at first the memory had made her think she was special, but along the years it had seemed to be proven wrong, and that was an inner hurt.

She'd have to view her parents' memoryspheres. She had some that she'd never listened to after their death, first because she'd been wrapped in grief, then because she'd been so lonely. She'd get those tomorrow.

Cratag had remained downstairs, shooing her from the kitchen after their little sugar feast, telling her he would clean up. She'd been aware that, guardlike, he was checking the windows and doors and the security spellshields—something she'd stopped doing years before. No sound from him alerted her, but when she looked up, he was a large dark shape standing in the doorway.

She studied him, this huge, quiet man who was both vital and calm, had participated in this day—unusual for him, too—with reason and utter dependability. She wasn't quite used to men like him—not used to men at all, of course—but the several affairs she'd had had been with men of subtle intelligence and quicksilver charm. Since her father had been a man like that, she knew what to expect of such gentlemen.

This was an altogether different man, a very intriguing man. She didn't think he was the type to create on-the-spot love poetry for her. But she wouldn't be surprised if he read her love poetry—and from one of those old-fashioned books.

Yes, she could imagine an antique album in his strong hands as easily as the sword and blazer he wore on each hip. She could still see in her mind's eye how his large hand had steadied Avellana on the stairs, how he'd lifted the girl easily and with complete assurance of his strength.

She could still feel his muscular arms around her in a dance, the ease of his footwork.

If you only looked at his scars and his once broken nose, his face was fearsome. But his beautiful violet eyes were steady and held depths and interesting shadows. His chin was strong. His hair was cropped so close to his skull that it was difficult to see what color it was except it was darkish, perhaps the color of his brows, a dark uncompromising brown. Such a hairstyle was favored among some household and city guards, but she thought he wore his hair so short for some reason she didn't know.

Her gaze went from his face, imperturbable but not offended, though she knew she was rudely staring. His shoulders were wide, the muscles of his arms and legs thick—naturally, she thought, as well as being developed by his profession. He was a strong, solid man.

He looked a little odd standing in the white framed doorway of the room that suddenly seemed too feminine, though her father had designed it for the Family. The cream-colored walls were too light, and the gilded furniture upholstered with cream-colored cloth with pastel embroidery looked frivolous next to this man.

But the Marigolds had always loved their frivolous home.

And he could dance.

He didn't move, merely stood there casually, and Signet reluctantly dropped her eyes, flushed. "I'm sorry for staring."

He shrugged massive shoulders. "You have a right to look at the man who was foisted on you, who will be guarding you."

Impulsively she stood and held out her hand. "You don't need to guard me."

He nodded briefly, touched her fingers. She didn't see acceptance of her words in his gaze. He was a man who would do what he planned to do unless you gave him more than weak words to change his mind.

For a moment he awed her with his size and his solid presence, and she stood wordless. Could only hear the beat of the sea and her heart and feel an intense awareness of him.

Then he spoke. "It will be a pleasure to guard you."

Cratag thought his words were utter foolishness. The woman didn't need him to guard her, need him in her life. There she stood like a beautiful princess in a beautiful home that loved her and would protect her. With new excellent security spellshields soon to be in place. A woman surrounded by more magic than any other he'd ever known.

Yet he felt a pull to her, a very earthly sexual attraction, a visceral longing to see hot color in her cheeks, her hair mussed and tangled, her eyes wild . . . as he lay over her, in her. That image was new and had insinuated itself into his thoughts in the hours in her company, during that dance that had made him ache.

He hadn't expected that she would still be up, had thought that she'd be in bed or in the meditation room. The light and the open door of the sitting room and her floral scent had drawn him. He'd ignored it as he checked every lock on this floor.

In the end he'd been drawn to the room and the woman inside. He couldn't refuse her gesture to come near, and trod as softly as he could on the expensive rug, feeling like some thick and clumsy animal in this room of ultra civilization.

"I have some questions." He winced inwardly at his blunt sentence. He'd planned on having a nice conversation, working up to nagging concerns. Not just blurting something out so she frowned, then withdrew behind a polite manner and sat again.

But he pulled up a chair—not as heavy as those in T'Hawthorn Residence—close enough to her that he could see the rim of gold around her pupils. Lovely eyes, fringed with light blond lashes that were longer than they seemed.

"I have some questions," he repeated in a gentler tone.

When her eyes softened, he had to look away. Then he glanced at the dark glass of the windows, and the room reflected the watery outlines of himself and Signet. Now *he* felt enveloped by magic, aware of little frissons that had touched him all day. He was imagining things.

"Yes?" she prompted.

He shifted, and the soft chair cushion settled around him as if welcoming his weight. More imaginings. But he met her gaze again and said, "I was told by T'Hawthorn that Avellana's life was at risk in her upcoming First Passage, and everyone else confirmed that. But, ah, I wasn't informed why . . . ah. . . ."

She nodded encouragingly, but he was all too aware of *rudeness*. The word had been used a lot. Including when she'd stared at him . . . but since she'd had admiration in her eyes, he hadn't felt it was rude. He couldn't recall the last time a woman looked at him with such innocent appreciation. Occasionally he got heated sexual appraisal . . .

"Cratag?"

"Sorry, thoughts wandering." Down a road they shouldn't go. He cleared his throat. "Why will Avellana be staying here?"

Signet stared at him. "This is my home. No one said a thing about having me move in with the Hazels." She hesitated a few seconds.

"I don't know that I would. Even FirstFamilies wouldn't expect me to leave my home and live with them." She sat up straighter. "Even if I am a GrandLady, and my household only consists of me, I *am* the head of my household and have duties here. I couldn't leave the Residence empty!"

Now he was agitating her when he hadn't meant to. Worse and worse. He ran his palm over his head, realized he'd given in to an old nervous gesture and put his hand back on the chair arm. "I meant why did they choose you as Avellana's companion?" There, it was out.

She went very still, and he thought she paled, though she was very fair skinned. Her tongue swept her lips. "No one told you." Was there a hitch in her quiet voice? She glanced aside. Her mouth pressed tightly and her chin rose as their gazes matched once more. "You should have been told."

His senses went on alert. "Some danger?"

Her hands half rose, then fell back to the padded chair arms. "Yes. No. I don't believe so." She drew in a large breath, and he kept his gaze from falling to her breasts rounding her nightrobe.

Looking him straight in the eyes, she said, "One of the problems in my life was that though it was known I had great Flair, the type of Flair had never been uncovered. Apparently Vinni discerned that I am a catalyst."

That made no sense. "A what?"

"Someone whose Flair changes the lives around her."

He considered that for a moment. "I don't think I've ever heard of such a thing."

Signet grimaced. "No one knows much about it, including me. People come into my life and if they stay long enough . . . their lives change." Her mouth twitched up in a smile that didn't hide the hurt in her eyes. "So far, for the better."

There was a moment of quiet. Then her face set into impassive lines, and she looked at the dark windows. "So you see, if you spend time with me, your life will no doubt change." This time her mouth curved down. "A passive Flair."

"I don't believe that."

"What?"

"I've seen you at GreatRituals, experienced your energy cycling. Your Flair is strong and active." He realized in that moment it was true. He'd always been aware of her energy. He'd always been placed in some particular spot to balance energies or something. Usually he felt little, maybe a nudge, when others felt great sweeping waves. When D'Marigold was there, he'd always felt her energy, but never so much as the first time.

Her smile bloomed. "That's a lovely thing to say."

"It's the truth."

She nodded, but he didn't think she believed him. "But if you stay with me, my Flair will act on you to change your life."

"My life has already been changed today."

Again her expression froze, and this time he couldn't resist reaching over and putting a finger under her chin, requesting she look at him full on again. Her blue eyes were large. "My life won't be the same when I return to T'Hawthorn Residence." His turn to frown. "But your Flair wasn't responsible, it was Vinni T'Vine and D'Hazel and T'Hawthorn." Her skin was so smooth under his fingers. Did she feel his hard calluses from blazer and sword? He shouldn't be touching her, but he didn't want to stop, and this was a time of truths. "Your life changed, too. It won't ever be the same after today, will it?"

She shook her head slowly.

He continued. "We're like two dice shaken in a cup."

Her pale arched brows went up. "I'll take the roll."

A sigh came from deep within his chest. "Me, too."

He leaned to her, slowly, slowly, letting her pull away. But though her eyes widened even more as she understood he was going to kiss her, he thought they went as dazed as his own must be. He angled his head to brush her lips with his own, press. Sweet softness. Or soft sweetness. To his surprise, there wasn't only sweetness as he expected, but a hint of tart, like lime. Then his mind went dizzy just from the wave of feeling from his mouth.

Her lips opened, and the tip of her tongue touched his mouth, and not-so-sweet hunger clawed him.

No.

He would not roll onto the floor, put her under him, give in to all sorts of new urges, new needs, new images flooding his mind along with the heat flooding his sex. He was harder than he'd been in a long, long time.

When he pulled away and stood, he was panting.

She still appeared princess-like, then her cheeks reddened, and he followed her gaze to the front of his trous, erection evident. It looked rude to him. He made an involuntary noise, also rude.

Signet looked up at him and smiled with that hint of tartness. Then she rose, too, her body brushing his, and he grunted-groaned again. Yeah, that was sweet and a little mean. Woman, not princess. He thought he might like the contrast.

She put her elegant hands on his cheeks, and they were cool, so he knew the heat of his desire was pumping off him. Her smile faded, and that cleared his brain a little. Then her hands dropped away, and he focused on her serious face.

"Avellana is with me because everyone hopes that my Flair will change something in her—her aura or Flair or brainwaves, so that she will survive her First Passage." Signet's chin set. "If I can link with her somehow during her Passage, if I can learn to direct this Flair of mine, I'll make sure she survives. But you should know that my Flair will probably work on you, too. I will change your life."

He found his voice, raspy but under control. "Signet, we all change each other's lives when we come in contact with each other. Alter opinions or points of view. Share experiences." Maybe he shouldn't have said that, now his mind had gone to the kiss and the wanting. "Change each other when we rub up against—" He simply stopped.

Laughter rippled from her.

"Lives usually change when people interact." His jaw flexed. What a mess. But he was serious.

She looked him in the eyes, serious, too. "I agree."

His brain started to buzz.

"And thank you. I hadn't thought of it that way. I haven't thought much about this Flair of mine. I just learned about it today."

Before he could move, she rose to her toes and kissed him again. Nice pressure on his lips. Then she glided from the room, and he thought he saw more of a swing in her walk.

And left him with a tart-sweet taste that he wanted more of.

Nine

The next morning was so full that Signet didn't take her usual walk along the cliff. Breakfast was lively, with a high-spirited Avellana and three Fams jockeying for status. Du won.

Then Lahsin Holly came to finish the spellshields, and Cratag asked for a full tour of the Residence. That interested Avellana, and she came, too. They started at the top, in the small circular observation room that was the highest of the tiered layers of the main turret. Avellana ran to each of the windows and oohed at the view, especially of the ocean. Her Fam stopped on the threshold, but both Du and Beadle hopped-walked around the window seats and peered out.

Signet hadn't thought of Cratag's kiss more than fifty times. For being so short it had been remarkably sexy, sizzling through her in a fashion she'd almost forgotten. Making her recall sex. Making her consider sex with Cratag, and that sent more than tingles through her body. So big. In every way . . . a heart as big as his . . . .

Beadle sicked up food and hair on Cratag's shoes, and the Residence cleaned the room and Signet his feet as he stood stoically, a pained expression on his face.

Avellana laughed.

"I'm glad I could amuse you," he said to her.

The girl whirled, arms out. "This is the first day I've ever spent without my Family."

She wasn't acting like the formal miniature adult Signet had met the day before. Signet would have thought that Avellana would have been worried at being with strangers, but it seemed not. She must know, sense, that neither Cratag nor Signet nor the Fams would let anything happen to her. Signet herself could feel determination radiating from Cratag.

Five more beings to cater to Avellana? No.

"You aren't allowed up here without a human adult," Signet reminded. She hadn't told Avellana how to open the windows.

"I know." Avellana nodded.

A housekeeping spell whisked the room, leaving the spicy scent of marigold behind. Signet smiled approval and thanked the Residence.

"The third floor next," Cratag said. "I've already seen the sitting room, the teleportation room, and Avellana's and my suites, but I want to check all the others."

Signet slid a glance to him. It wouldn't be just a ploy to look at her suite. The man took his work seriously, but when her gaze caught his, he reddened a little. She smiled smugly. He was aware of her.

He'd wanted her last night.

Avellana descended the spiral stairs then ran through the long hall of the main wing, turned right out of sight into the short north wing, the cats streaming after her. Cratag lengthened his strides to catch up with her.

"There's a big turret on the end of this wing, too," she called. "I didn't know."

Signet hurried along. "For aesthetic integrity," she answered.

"The first T'Marigold was an architect. We have lessons on architecture in your schedule."

Avellana was waiting by the tower door hopping from foot to foot. Cratag opened it.

"It's a bedroom!" Avellana exclaimed.

"It's a full suite with its own staircase," Signet said. "This is the top floor, below is the sitting room, and on the bottom is a small dining area with no-times, though they are quite old." She looked at Cratag. "There isn't a hot-square."

He nodded. He was being very polite and quiet today.

And he was wearing fashionable loose trous.

The Residence said, "An incoming call from Laev Hawthorn for Cratag Maytree."

Cratag raised a brow. "Is there a scrybowl—"

"Here it is. Oooh, how pretty. Like everything else," Avellana cooed. The bowl was thick pottery of navy blue, the contrasting color of the suite with blue-gray walls.

"Is there water in it?" Signet asked. She didn't think she'd been in this room since Yule two and a half months before.

"Of course," the Residence said.

"Yes." Avellana looked into it. "Vinni's colors are mixed in with the Hawthorns'."

Smiling, Cratag said, "That settles it, I must answer."

"Yes," Signet said.

He crossed to the bowl set on a simple redwood table and ran his finger around the rim of the bowl, initiating the spell. Water droplets formed over the bowl, showing images: a handsome boy of about seventeen with brown hair along with the Hawthorn violet eyes. At his shoulder stood Vinni T'Vine.

"Greetyou, cuz," Laev said.

That sent a little jolt through Signet. Obviously Cratag was regarded *very* well in T'Hawthorn's household if he was "cuz" to the Heir. More than just distant Family and the chief of T'Hawthorn's guards. Close to his Family. An integral part of his Family. Envy twisted inside her. Wisps of notions of maybe more than an affair vanished with a painful throb of surprise that she'd even been imagining something so vague in the future.

"Do you need privacy?" she asked coolly.

Of course he'd caught her tone, he was the most observant man she'd ever met.

"No," Avellana answered for him.

"No," he said, smiled at Signet, and turned back to the scry.

"D'Marigold," said the Residence, "Lahsin Holly would like to speak with you in the main sitting room."

"I'll be right there." Signet smiled brightly at Cratag. "Excuse me."

He nodded. Since Avellana didn't budge, Signet deduced the girl was interested in talking to Vinni. The bond between them was touching. Signet strode out.

Cratag was slightly preoccupied by Signet's manner . . . something had changed—again—between them, but he had a feeling that during this whole time at D'Marigold Residence change would be the order of the day.

"Cratag?" Laev said. He was smiling and a little flushed, but there was a shadow behind his eyes, as had been there during the terrible time of the feud. What had happened to put that haunting there? What had T'Hawthorn said to him of this business? Less than a day away from home and Cratag was already out of touch.

"Yes, Laev?" He kept his tone brusque. Laev would be more concerned if Cratag gentled his voice.

"Our training session is done, and there is a youth holiday—no apprenticeships or journeyman septhours, no grovestudy. Vinni said he was going there, to D'Marigold Residence. May I come, too?"

"One moment, I'll ask D'Marigold." If he'd been anyone else, a nobleman, he'd be able to speak to her mentally when she was at the opposite end of the house. As it was, he thought he could vaguely sense she was talking with Lahsin Holly. Which was more than he could have done two days before . . . was his minuscule Flair growing? No time to consider that.

"Signet would say that since you are living here, you should invite whom you please," Avellana pronounced with a lift of her small nose, just as if she hadn't been making faces at Vinni a moment before.

"Residence?" Cratag asked.

"Avellana is correct," the Residence said.

"Sure, come over, Laev," Cratag said, satisfaction washing through him. The boy loved him. Cratag recalled the beautiful suite Signet had given him. The day was sunny, and his view of the greening gardens was nice. Laev would appreciate a view of gardens more than of ocean.

"Vinni, we are at the end of the other wing," Avellana said. "Left when you teleport, but I'll beat you to the teleportation room!"

With a muttered word from Laev the scry ended.

"Avellana," Cratag said as she raced from the room. "You are not to go into the teleportation chamber."

She didn't slow down.

"Avellana, stop!" He used his tone of command.

Huffing a breath, she stopped, stuck out her lower lip. "I won't win, now."

"No, but when I make a request of you, I'd like an acknowledgment that you heard me."

"You were shouting down the hall. I heard you!"

"I wasn't shouting. I was projecting my voice. Again, I'd like an acknowledgment when I request something of you."

"Yes, GentleSir Maytree," she muttered.

"Good."

Boys' hoots came from the teleportation room. Avellana grumbled under her breath, then marched at a slower, long-suffering type of pace to the end of the hall and around the corner.

Laev had been such a subdued boy for his years that Cratag had worried. Looked like he wouldn't have such a peaceful time with Avellana.

The boys appeared, and Vinni went immediately to Avellana and hugged her, grinned when he saw her in high spirits.

Laev looked around. "Very pretty place." He glanced down the opposite end of the hallway where the glass-paned double doors to the sitting room were open, bright at the end of the hall. If Cratag had left his own doors open, sunlight would be streaming into the corridor from them.

Narrowing his eyes, Laev stared at the sitting room. "Oh, this is that house with the big peach tiered turret that looks like a wedding cake."

Cratag hadn't considered it before, but now the image was stuck in his head, he knew Laev was right.

"I didn't know this place was D'Marigold Residence. Fab place," Laev said.

"Thank you," D'Marigold Residence said in its rolling voice.

"Welcome," Laev said.

"You've seen it?" Cratag asked.

"Yeah, the turret can be seen from along the river or the beach."

From other Noble Country estates. But Cratag hadn't been on the beach or the river very often. Since they were opposite Cratag's rooms now, he opened the door. When Laev made sincerely appreciative noises, Cratag's pride got a boost. He may not live like this in T'Hawthorn's Residence with a whole suite, and his lord might have traded him out, but here he was valued.

Then Signet came in and blushed at the sight of him, and his ego lifted more. Cratag introduced her to Laev—who winked at Cratag as he bowed over her hand—and they finished a quick tour of the Residence. The little girl looked at Signet with a scrunched face when they came to the nice "oldie" room tinted a pale gold and with doors opening onto the grounds.

Vinni was happy to be with Avellana, and Laev had been polite. He studied the style of the Residence as if considering options for his own rooms or—Cratag realized with a jolt—for T'Hawthorn Residence when he'd become the lord. Signet and the Residence answered his questions on the use of tinting and mirrors and murals to make a Residence seem lighter and airier than its actual space.

Then they went to lunch. Cratag's only embarrassment was when Beadle slurped his meal with gusto.

The early afternoon was spent examining the river and beach side of the estate for security purposes, and Signet showed them the limits of her property. The south edge of her estate bordered a river. The cut in the land for the zig-zagging stone steps down the hillside held a gate. There was a walk to a boathouse that had a wide deck over the opening for a couple of boats. The skinny strip of river bank was muddy, so they didn't go down all the way.

In the west were cliffs to the ocean. Another stone gate was at the top of the path to the beach. The steps down and switchbacked path itself were in excellent repair but very steep. The beach was wide and sandy near the stairs, then narrowed to rocks toward the south and the river outlet and to the north and the Residence. Once again Avellana and Vinni had to promise that they wouldn't attempt the ocean steps without a human adult.

To Cratag's surprise, Beadle had said that he'd been kept strictly indoors with his former elderly owner who'd passed on peacefully in his sleep. The Fam was very excited and a little wary at being outdoors. He kept close to Cratag, or ran around, then returned to him.

Du, Signet's Fam, sniffed and offered to show Beadle the three Fam doors in the Residence to "out."

At MidAfternoonBell, Hanes arrived to escort Vinni home. By that time they were all taking refreshments in the sitting room. Hanes bowed to Signet and Avellana and Vinni, inclined his torso to Laev—HawthornHeir—and nodded to Cratag, giving each person their proper due. He complimented each Fam.

Then he eyed the slight wavering haze around the open windows and smiled in satisfaction. "I see GreatMistrys Holly has been here and the Residential spellshields are up."

"Yes," Signet said, frowning. "They *are* evident, but Lahsin gave me spellwords to drop them if I want to appreciate the view more." She glanced at Avellana and Vinni. "A couplet I won't be telling you."

Hanes nodded. "Youngsters should not have such knowledge."

Since he included Laev in this, the young man's pride was ruffled. Hanes went on. "We have a First Quarter Twinmoons Ceremony tonight, T'Vine, that you will lead at moons rising." Hanes glanced at his wrist timer. "Preparation time for the GreatLord is two septhours. We are cutting it close."

The other nobles glanced at Vinni.

Avellana stuck out her chin and said in her most adult voice, "Most houses think that preparation time for a First Quarter Ceremony can be only a septhour."

"We don't," Hanes said politely. He glanced at Laev. "Shouldn't you be returning to T'Hawthorn Residence to prepare, Hawthorn-Heir?"

Cratag knew that T'Hawthorn didn't celebrate twinmoons quarters unless he had some specific goal that demanded such a ritual. Cratag opened his mouth, but Laev didn't move from his casual pose and answered, "Heirs don't need the same amount of sacred cleansing time, and T'Hawthorn has not requested my presence tonight." Implying that there was a ceremony at T'Hawthorn's. As far as Cratag knew, there wasn't, but he hadn't been in contact with T'Hawthorn all day, and from that circumstance, understood that his lord would not be consulting with him as usual—or checking up on him regarding this job.

"Ah, adults only," Hanes said to Laev, as a reluctant Vinni stood and crossed to the door.

Hanes wasn't usually this undiplomatic, but then Cratag usually met with him at places and situations much more casual—except when they were working as bodyguards for their lords at events. Then Hanes had been all business, but so had Cratag. Perhaps he didn't know the man as well as he thought, but Cratag *had* known the Vines kept a more formal household.

Hanes followed Vinni to the threshold and bowed again, met Signet's gaze. She was sitting with straight spine in one of the plush chairs. "You don't celebrate First Quarters?"

She smiled politely, inclined her head. "Despite the recent influx of residents, I am a Household of one, and I live next to the ocean—the mightiest cleanser of them all. I usually celebrate rituals at twinmoons apex, not rising. Apex is after midnight tonight."

Cratag thought his mouth dropped open. Signet was implying that she danced naked on the beach in the twinmoonslight. Hanes's eyes widened, and his lips quirked as he slid a look to Cratag. Laev was looking at him, too.

Ten

Oh!" Avellana clapped her hands. "Can I do that tonight with you, too?" she asked Signet.

Signet's cheeks were nearly red. "I think it's a little too cool for you tonight," she said.

Good thing, too. Cratag would have had to accompany them, and he wasn't sure even the cold ocean would have kept his sex down if he and Signet were skyclad.

"Oh," Avellana said with disappointment.

There was a little pause.

"Merry meet," Vinni said.

"And merry part," they all chorused in response.

"And merry meet again," Hanes finished the little ritual. He shut the double doors behind them as they left.

Avellana stared after them. "That was a rude personal question."

Signet burst into laughter. "Yes, it was."

"Hanes is a good man," Avellana pronounced. "But all Muin T'Vine's oldie female relatives and his tutor are too rigid."

Cratag couldn't decide whether she was repeating something she'd heard or stating a conclusion of her own.

Laev rose with a smile, bowed, and thanked Signet, but didn't actually look at her. The tips of his ears were red. Druidans and nobles weren't modest about nudity, but teenaged boys in the presence of the opposite sex . . . Laev said his good-byes and left.

Rhyz, Avellana's Fam, stood and stretched, looking at her. *Nap time for us.*

Avellana blinked in surprise, glanced at the large schedule hanging on a wall. She'd insisted on having schedules in all of the rooms she might occupy, and Signet had agreed. "Yes." Avellana rose, smiling sweetly. "I might nap." She curtsied to them. "I will see you before dinner."

Laev hadn't shut the doors, and Avellana hesitated at the threshold. "Are you really going down to the beach for a First Quarter ritual after midnight?" she asked Signet.

Signet chuckled. "I can praise the Lady and Lord during my regular meditation time. I think it's a little too cold for *me* on the beach, too."

Avellana nodded. "Good." She looked at Cratag. "Don't you think that's good?"

Once more, an image of Signet, as pale as the moonslight and dancing naked, came to Cratag's mind. He couldn't find words, so he just nodded.

Avellana nodded solemnly back, closed the doors, and walked down the corridor, talking to her Fam.

Signet turned to Cratag, frowning. "Do you think we should follow her and tuck her in?"

He had no idea. There'd been no time for naps when he'd worked in his father's store growing up. By the time Cratag had joined the T'Hawthorn household Laev had been thirteen, beyond naps. Finally Cratag said, "What about you, did your parents accompany you for naps?"

"No . . . not usually."

"And she needs to feel that we trust her," Cratag said.

"Do we trust her?" Signet whispered.

"I trust her to keep the promises we've hedged her in about," he said, then smiled. "Though I don't think that 'oldie' room is much of a threat anymore."

"No. I'll have to think of another consequence for poor behavior." Signet nibbled her lip and glanced toward the HeirSuite. "How much personal alone time should she have?"

That had been rare in his childhood as well. "I think we can trust Rhyz."

Signet blinked. "You do?"

"Yes. He's a mature Fam, aware of his status and that of his mistress. He will inform us if we stray too far from what the Hazels would approve. T'Hawthorn's FamCat is vocal about what he expects."

Letting out a quiet breath, Signet said, "I'm sure you're right. I do wish I'd had a little more time to prepare, though."

"It's been my experience that when a FirstFamily lord or lady wants something, they roll right over the opposition as quickly and efficiently as possible."

Signet cleared her throat, met his gaze, then looked aside. "At the cost of being impolite and asking a rude personal question, I don't know much about you." She met his eyes again, and they were darker. "You probably don't know much about me, though I've seen you at GreatTemple rituals and social events."

Warmth unfurled inside him, and he smiled. She wanted to know about him, and for more reason than just because he was here to help watch Avellana. Signet was interested in him personally. "I grew up in Tref, a small town on the southern continent of Brittany. I wasn't meant to be a shopkeeper like my father, so I left home at fifteen." He'd been concerned about his older sister, who'd run off with a man Cratag hadn't trusted. "I was big even then and had some arms training, signed on as a merchant guard, and got even more. Sold my sword for a while." He shifted his shoulders. He'd looked for his sister until he'd discovered her in a mass grave of victims who'd succumbed to a deadly virus, then he'd found and dealt with her lover. A long four years. "Was a merchant guard for quite a while." He rubbed his scar. "Got this when looking around the jungle alone. Bad idea. Took me a while to heal."

"I should say so!" She appeared distressed. When she picked up her cup, it trembled in her fingers, and another spurt of gratification went through him. She was beginning to care.

He continued his story. "Thought a lot when I was Healing. Took on a job that got me across the Plano Strait. Didn't like the Strait towns." Too wild and dangerous and corrupt. "Drifted northward." Seeking something inside and outside himself. "Finally decided I'd apply to T'Hawthorn for a job. The Maytrees split off from the Hawthorns a century or so back." Cratag had decided that what he missed was a real sense of Family. A couple of his childhood friends had had close families, so he knew those sorts of bonds could be loving and tight. He'd wanted closeness and Family, no longer wanted to be alone.

He shrugged again. "T'Hawthorn was glad to hire me on." He met Signet's eyes, knowing he didn't have to remind her of the Hawthorn-Holly feud. He'd been the only good fighter T'Hawthorn had had.

Silence spun between them with Signet looking out the windows. Cratag didn't think her eyes were focused on the ocean view. Eventually she met his gaze and smiled a little. "You've come a long way, found your place."

It didn't surprise him much that she understood that.

Her lips curved in a sad smile. "I haven't moved at all and should know my place." She brightened her smile, and he was glad to see her determination. "But I'm learning it." She hesitated then said, "It's obvious that Laev, HawthornHeir, respects you."

He liked hearing that. "Thank you."

A small frown formed between her brows. "But do you think it's wise having Laev here?"

Cratag didn't understand. "What?"

"Having a young man flushed with oncoming Passage around Avellana. One who is experiencing Passage can affect others, you know, bring on their Passage, too."

"I didn't know." Of course that's why Laev had been jumpy when he'd come, despite his workout. Maybe some sort of Passage thing had put that shadow in the teen's eyes.

Cratag's jaw tensed. "I have little Flair, don't know much about Passage." His voice was sharp with anger at himself, embarrassment. He tensed. Would she think he'd snapped at her?

But her eyes went soft. She put down her cup and walked over to him, looking at him in a way that made his heart thump faster. "Of course you didn't know." She held out her hand. He took it, and a *zip* of desire went through him. Of sexual tension or her Flair, it didn't matter. She affected him, and he liked that. Liked the feel of her fingers in his, her tall, slim body next to his.

She drew him to the tower windows and said, "Open," and glass vanished. The air still wavered in front of his vision with the new spellshields. Signet said the couplet and squeezed his hand so he knew she wanted him to remember the words. The spellshields vanished, and there was nothing between them and the drop to the rocks below, the rolling of the gray ocean. The breeze was warmer than he expected and carried the sound and scent of the ocean. She breathed deeply, unafraid of the height.

But she'd lived in this house all her life, learned her place in the circles of Druida society as she'd grown. An Heir to a title herself, then GrandLady.

"The height doesn't bother you," she said.

"No."

She sidestepped even closer, until their bodies touched—her shoulder to his biceps, the roundness of her hip against his thigh. "I'm sorry that this situation takes you away from Laev at this tender time in his life." Her words were nearly a whisper. She understood. "The first twinges of oncoming Second Passage is when a person is considered an adult."

He recalled that, now that she'd said it. Nobles with great Flair would think so. Commoners held that the seventeenth Nameday was the mark.

"So when you return to T'Hawthorn's, Laev will be of age."

Yes, that was the ache inside him.

She turned to him, gazed up with her light blue eyes. "I want you to know that if Avellana isn't experiencing Passage, you are free to go back to T'Hawthorn Residence."

To the room he had in the dark fortress. He grunted. The next bit would be rude, but it had to be said. "I don't think my contract with D'Hazel allows that."

Signet pressed her lips together. "No, it isn't my decision, is it?" Something like glee lit her eyes. "This has happened so fast. Have you even seen your contract with D'Hazel, Cratag?"

He reddened under her stare. "Uh, no."

Signet chuckled. "And you scold *me* for not watching out for my interests."

"I should have said the contract between T'Hawthorn and D'Hazel might not allow me any time off. My lord would have looked after my interests." Cratag was pretty sure.

Signet poked Cratag. "You get a copy of that contract."

"Right." He'd do that later, right now all he could think of was Signet and the heated blood throbbing through him. He didn't want to think of D'Hazel or T'Hawthorn or even Laev, let alone First-Family contracts.

She was a tall, willowy woman, but he still had to bend to kiss her. Her lips looked pinker, plumper today, and he figured that was because he knew how she tasted. Sweet with an edge of tartness. His mouth watered, and desire curled in his groin.

Her lips opened slightly in invitation, and he held hard on to his control, but knew he'd taste her even more deeply, probe the moist cavern of her mouth with his tongue. Even the thought made him shudder, but it didn't stop him from setting a palm around her nape, feeling her shiver, too. He traced her soft skin and lovely cheekbones with his thumb. Then he closed his eyes, angled his mouth, and put it on hers.

Her tongue darted between his lips, inside his mouth, jolting him with fiery passion. His cock, rarely soft the whole damn day, thickened and surged. His tongue tangled with hers, battled in a sensual duel, thrusting, curving around hers, sucking. Then he explored her mouth, and he was lost as the last, exquisite taste of her slid through him with total inevitability.

He groaned and sent a hand down her slender back, curved it over her nice ass, and pressed her to him. He yearned, he needed, like never before. Red mist of desire swirled in his brain, fogging his thoughts.

She wrapped her arms around his neck, stood on her toes, arched against him, so he could feel the roundness of her breasts against his chest, the pebbles of her nipples. She closed her teeth on his tongue, and he moaned.

She sighed into his mouth, warm, wet air, with the fragrance of her and the taste of her, and all thought vanished. One of her arms hooked around his neck, then her free hand trailed down his thigh, and he moved instinctively, rubbing his sex against her softness. He hadn't worn regular work trous today, and these were made of silkeen, and the sensation was perfect. His hands clamped on her ass, pulling her up. His tongue thrust inside her mouth like he would inside her.

Beadle yowled, zoomed into the room, hitting Cratag's calves. Du and Rhyz chased him, and a girlish shout echoed.

His brain sharpened with painful clarity. Cratag broke the kiss, flung himself and Signet to the side, where they lit on a soft twoseat. He ordered the spellshields up and the windows to thicken back into sturdy glass. He stood, took a mussed and dazed Signet and placed her properly sitting on the twoseat, managed to turn and pretend to look out the windows at an angle that wouldn't show the bulging of his trous to Avellana as she swept into the room, chasing the Fams. "Naptime's over!"

It hadn't been very long. Cratag glanced at the schedule and decided that her twenty minutes wasn't enough time, he needed— she needed—a septhour at least. "I guess it is," Cratag said, heard his own voice rough and gravelly.

Avellana went to her schedule, nodded. "Time for a walk in the gardens before dinner."

"I'll accompany you," Signet said, her voice warm and throaty, which didn't help his desire subside.

Had she been mussed? Now every hair was in place, though her cheeks and lips were noticeably darker. Some female spell.

What was his part of this timetable? He couldn't recall.

"I'm dressed for the walk and dinner," Avellana said, now a little adult again.

Ah, dressing for dinner.

Signet blinked, glanced down at her clothes, which were casually elegant, but not something any of them would consider appropriate for dinner in a noble GrandHouse.

"Yes, Cratag and I must change," she said. Did she linger on his name? Give it an extra lilt? He hoped so.

She moved to Avellana. "Not quite perfect," she said. Cratag noticed the girl's shoulder tabs were uneven and gaping. Signet smiled. "I think you were preoccupied with the Fams."

Avellana stuck out her lower lip. "Perhaps."

"Let's take care of this."

Sniffing, Avellana looked at him. "I think we should put your schedules up, too."

Before he could answer, Signet did. "I like to keep my schedule flexible."

Avellana's expression went from pouting to shock. "You don't schedule!"

"Not all my septhours." She smoothed the cloth of the girl's tunic on both shoulders. "There, you look perfect."

But Avellana was standing completely still, blinking, mouth open. She looked at Signet, then her own schedule board, then Cratag. Her gaze lasered on him. "You come from a FirstFamily household. You must have detailed schedules, too."

Signet flinched.

"That was rude, Avellana," he said. "Not every Family or household does things the same way, not even FirstFamilies. It was rude of you to imply that Signet's Family is wrong in doing things because hers isn't a FirstFamily."

Avellana frowned. Glanced at Signet. "The Marigold Family is an ancient and honorable GrandHouse, which has contributed to our society, well worthy of respect."

Cratag heard D'Hazel's admonition behind her daughter's tones. He nodded. "That's right." Holding up a hand, he said, "We all know that the twenty-five FirstFamilies have the greatest status on Celta, and you are a daughter of that line, but it is not honorable to imply that Families are lesser because they aren't FirstFamilies."

"Even if they are?" Avellana persisted.

"Are they? Each Family, each individual, is respected more if they contribute to our society, and each can contribute in an equal but different way."

Avellana frowned.

Cratag waved a hand around him. "When has your Family, for instance, created and built such a lovely home as this? When has any Family?"

"D'Marigold's home is unique," Avellana admitted, looking at the wide curved windows of the sitting room, framed in white arches.

"Would Druida be less without this house?"

"Yes." Avellana nodded.

"Then the Marigolds have given Druida and Celta something that no other Family has."

Signet stared at him, eyes wide.

Avellana curtsied. "I'm sorry, GrandLady D'Marigold."

"Forgiven," Signet said. "The FirstFamilies are the most ancient and the most powerful, but it isn't wise to think that their ways are the only ways, or their households are the best."

"I guess." Avellana was shifting from foot to foot.

"I don't have a schedule because I'm the only one in my Family, but I did have habits." Signet walked to the board. "I usually breakfasted later and walked along the cliffs after breakfast." She waved a hand, and Avellana's schedule column shrank to a third of the chart, but stayed in the middle. Signet opened the drawer in a table and picked up a writestick. With quick strokes, she carried over some lines to the left, blocking most of her time as with Avellana's. When she got down to after Avellana's bedtime, she marked in a septhour and a half as "Meditation Time." Signet glanced at Cratag, flushed a little, then looked at the trio of cats who all sat watching her. "I'll be depending on Cratag and you Fams and the Residence to be watch—ah—keeping Avellana safe at this time."

Then Signet walked to Cratag and handed him the writestick. Their fingers brushed as he took it. The coil of desire inside him tightened, her cheeks pinkened. "I think most mind Healers would say that you needed alone time, too, Cratag."

He'd certainly need some training time. On the tour of the house, he'd noticed a couple of dance studios, one of them might do. He'd have to talk to Signet and the Residence about that, sooner rather than later. Especially since he needed to syphon off excess energy. He studied the boards and, again, blocked most of his time as Signet and Avellana had. Even as a bodyguard to T'Hawthorn, he had never had such a structured life. He set training times, not naming them, for three-quarters of a septhour midmorning and midafternoon. He extended Avellana's naptime, and she scowled at him and folded her arms, but said nothing. Her FamCat, Rhyz, smirked.

During Avellana's naptime, he printed "Consult with Signet regarding household matters," and glanced at her.

"That will do very well," she said. "We had visitors and tea today, but that may not continue." She looked at Avellana. "This seems reasonable to me. Items may change on a daily basis such as when we go on excursions. Why don't we agree that this will be the main schedule, and if anyone needs to change it, they notify the Residence, and all the boards will be changed."

"Good." Avellana nodded. She looked at her Fam, the small half-circle of cats. "Perhaps Rhyz should have a schedule, too."

Rhyz thrashed his tail, lifted his nose. *Cats do as they please. We do not need schedules.* He sniffed. *I choose to be with you most of the day.*

Beadle yawned and curled up.

Du said, *I am still exploring My Residence. My time is My own.*

"Of course," Signet murmured, smiling.

"Time for a walk in the gardens," Avellana said.

"That's right," Signet said. "I'll go with you, but we will return to the Residence a few minutes earlier than the schedule so I can get ready for dinner." She looked at Cratag.

"I'll go get ready now," he said.

"Thank you," Signet said. She brushed a hand over Avellana's hair, brown and to her shoulders, and a weathershield formed around the child. "It's sunny out but still may be cool. Do you want your winter garments?"

"I can go outside *without* my heavy winter hooded coat and my scarf and my hat and my gloves and my mittens?"

"We'll just use a light weathershield, it will be a treat. You will get a surprise treat every day for good behavior."

"I *will*?"

"Yes."

Cratag found himself smiling. This would work. "See you shortly," he said, winking at Signet as he left the room. He shook his head at the schedules. Life could be constricting, or it could be freeing. All depended on how you looked at it.

He'd be spending a lot of time with Signet.

And those nights of hers, of his, were open space when all sorts of wonderful things could happen.

Eleven

$\mathcal{A}$ *few minutes later Signet was leading Avellana along the winding* paths of the spring garden. Thanks to the previous D'Marigold botanists, the soil had been enriched time and again. The Marigold gardens were by no means the most beautiful in Druida, but they were colorful and serene and complemented the house. The paths were of smooth gray flagstones with flakes of orange and green lichen on them, surrounded by thyme groundcover. Blossoming spring flowers of Earth stock—grape hyacinth and crocus—lined the paths, with drifts of violets and spears of daffodils and narcissus giving hope to the bare bushes and the trees with the hint of buds.

Avellana had reverted to her staid persona, mainly because she was wearing new, shiny shoes and didn't want to dirty them, Signet thought. She'd had to admire and comment on the shoes. They were pretty, but Signet knew she could make better—her parents had been very pleased when Signet had demonstrated that her creative Flair was shoemaking. Cobbling. Signet had hundreds of shoes in her closet . . . all handmade by herself. Currently she was wearing soft furrabeast leather half-boots of a butterscotch color with rusty red marigolds tinted on the toes. Avellana had admired those, too.

Neither time did Signet disclose that she was a cobbler. She would probably make Avellana some shoes . . . and that might be a real treat for both of them . . . but first she wanted to understand the little girl better.

She'd make Cratag a pair of thigh-high warrior boots in a heartbeat.

"Cratag Maytree is a very competent and special person, isn't he?" Avellana asked as if she'd been privy to Signet's thoughts.

Signet tensed. The words sounded more like a comment D'Hazel might have made than Avellana. More and more it was obvious that the girl's mother had had a long chat with her daughter regarding the people who would be her companions. And how much had Avellana seen when she'd walked into the sitting room? Had Signet been sprawled or sitting on the twoseat? How dazed had she looked? Had Avellana seen their embrace? For the first time, Signet wished that the sitting room doors were not simply glass panes. Maybe she'd put back up the door curtains that she'd taken down after her parents died. She hadn't known, then, why they would have such heavy drapes.

Signet hoped Avellana hadn't seen her kissing Cratag. Not that she was ashamed of her feelings for Cratag, or felt guilty about the kiss. She'd like to do more, soon. But Signet didn't feel right about being sexually flagrant in front of the child. Though Avellana hadn't been expected. She'd shaved a few minutes off her very short "naptime," especially since she'd also dressed for dinner.

"Signet?" Avellana prompted.

Oh, Signet was supposed to reply to Avellana's question. Keep small conversation going.

"I'm sorry, Avellana, I have been much alone most of my life and walking these gardens, so I get lost in my thoughts. What did you ask?"

Avellana frowned, and Signet hid a smile.

"It's good that I and Rhyz and Cratag have come to keep you company."

"I think so, too," Signet said, but as the day was wearing on and she was finally falling into the rhythm of this new change in her life, she was beginning to think about how she could *use* her Flair, make it active instead of passive.

"Signet, I am talking to you!" Avellana stopped, hands on her hips.

Signet raised her brows. "Well, I was *thinking* about you."

Avellana stared. "Really?"

"Yes."

"About me and my First Passage. Everyone worries."

"Yes. Are you worried?" Signet asked.

Grimacing, Avellana kicked a pebble in the path into a flower bed. "I don't know." She looked up at Signet with wide eyes. "Will it hurt?"

Signet recalled her own Passages, shivered a little. "Probably. But Rhyz and I, and probably Cratag, will be there."

"Mother has some teas for me. She always has teas. Perhaps that will make Passage easier?"

"Perhaps. Your mother gave me some recipes, so I can make teas fresh from the herb garden. Also your medical records. It's true that no one knows how Passage will affect you, but you're a strong person."

"But my Flair is strong, too." The girl walked on, not looking at Signet. "I don't feel strange. Like my brain is damaged. I just feel like me."

"And we all care for you just because you're you. And we all want to make sure your First Passage goes well."

"Cratag, too."

"I'm sure."

"That wasn't a question." Avellana's voice was smug. "I can *feel* his caring, and yours. Can't you?" Her smile was smug, too.

"I suppose," Signet said, knowing where this was going.

"And I can *feel* his aura frequency emanations when he's with you. He likes you."

"I like him, too."

"He is big and strong and competent and a special person."

"Yes, we are all special."

Avellana sent her a side glance. "Your Flair is unique."

Not quite a rude comment. "It feels unusual to you."

"Yes." Avellana slid her hand into Signet's, surprising her. Now she grinned. "Sparkly and tingly." She nodded decisively. "And Cratag doesn't have much Flair, but his is like a rock. Solid and immovable. Very complementary."

Signet's stomach tightened as she thought of the man, of spending time with the man, of kissing the man and maybe having sex with him or even more than sex, loving. They complemented each other. That would be good for working and playing together, but when the inevitable end came, it could be very bad.

Cratag stood under the waterfall longer than usual. The gray granite ledge was wider than the one in his Hawthorn rooms, and it was higher than he, a blessing. Furthermore, it had a nice rush of water. He hadn't brought toiletries with him, and the liquid soap that the Residence—or Signet—had provided had a good scent. Nothing too floral—a nice tang of herbs.

A few minutes later when he surveyed the only good clothes he'd brought that were appropriate for dinner, he realized he'd have to send for more—or return for more. He also figured out that he'd usually partaken dinner with the Hawthorn Family about once a week and had rotated four outfits. No one had ever said anything to him about that, especially when he wore the Hawthorn colors, but now he'd need at least six good trous and tunics. He frowned, trying to think if what he had would mix and match.

He was getting a feel for this job and, he guessed, what Laev would call the energy of the people around him. Avellana's was definitely picking up beat, so Cratag didn't think her Passage would be too far away. He frowned. Not that he knew enough about that. But he didn't think he'd be here, staring at a few clothes in a huge closet next month.

As for Signet . . . he didn't want to consider the emotions she stirred in him. He thought that being with her might be as dangerous as walking along one of the cliffs. Big drop ahead! He liked her, he liked this house, he liked how she treated him.

He saw respect in her eyes. When they kissed, he saw passion, felt her desire for him in the pliancy and heat of her body.

There was no denying that her Flair was working on him. All day long he'd been more sensitive to things he might have missed before. Energies he'd been feeling more strongly, an idea when Signet and the Residence were conversing telepathically, other mental conversations going on around him that he wouldn't have discerned before. Or maybe he just hadn't cared much about telepathic conversations before. Certainly the life of a young girl had never hung in the balance.

But the lives of the Hawthorn Family had. When he'd joined them during the feud, the atmosphere had seethed around him as if bees swarmed in the Residence. T'Hawthorn's energy, determination, and his now-dead son's. Cratag'd been too new to the Family, concentrating too much on the duels and the life-and-death situations, to care whether folk talked mentally around him. He'd known his place and done his job.

It had not been a good time. If things had turned out differently, if the current lord had died and the younger man, Laev's father, had lived, Cratag didn't believe he'd have stayed. And what was he doing thinking of such strange notions? The past was over and done with. The present was what a man concentrated on so that the future would be shaped the way he wanted.

But maybe it was good to reflect on the past a few minutes because it *was* the past. One thing he knew, with or without Signet's catalyst Flair working on him, his life had changed. He would not be the man he'd grown into at T'Hawthorn's.

The more he considered Laev, Cratag understood that he, too, would be different. No longer a boy, but a man. The teen's energy had been nearly as spiky as Avellana's.

A gong reverberated throughout the house. Before Cratag could react, the closet door deliberately creaked closed. He eyed it. He'd once overheard Laev and his noble friends talking about their Residences and nonverbal punctuation. If he recalled correctly, this was the Residence clearing its throat.

May as well try something new. *D'Marigold Residence?* He thought hard at it, knitting his brows.

Yes! The one word was infused with satisfaction. *You heard me and understood.*

Yes.

I wished to say how pleased I am that we have company. It has been a long and ... tiresome ... time for Signet.

Lonely? Cratag guessed. It wasn't hard. The more he thought about it, the more he remembered that when she was at the GreatRituals she wore a sense of being completely alone. Coming in and keeping to herself, or talking to one or two people who moved away. Leaving with no one.

Yes, the Residence said. *It is good that she will have a lover who will stay in Druida.*

Cratag froze. He was glad all this mental talking thing was pretty new. The Residence couldn't possibly hear his thoughts, could it? No. He was sure. Maybe. "I wouldn't have thought you the type of being who would monitor us."

You make my lady happy.

"Ah." He finished setting his belt into place. It was fancy and had a blazer holster that would look odd if it wasn't used. So Cratag went to the floor-to-ceiling vault hidden behind a panel, unlocked it, and took his weapon case from the top shelf. He slid his jeweled-hilt blazer into the holster, pressing studs in a pattern so he was the only one who could release and fire it.

Since the Residence didn't say anything else, and a happy little housekeeping spell was whisking around his room, tidying things,

Cratag figured he wouldn't be getting any warning away from Signet. The Residence also seemed canny enough not to press the matter. But Cratag's thoughts wandered down the path of sex with Signet anyway. He wanted her, and he didn't see himself leaving Druida anytime soon.

Despite the fact that his pride had been hurt when T'Hawthorn had sent him on this job with a perfunctory request, Cratag knew that being part of a Family—an older, established Family, hell, an honorable Family—was important to him. He wondered idly if there was a way he could become indispensable to T'Hawthorn. Cratag's position might solidify when Laev became T'Hawthorn, but the current lord was only late middle-aged, and that might be a very long time in the future.

The gong rang again, and Cratag glanced at the antique wall clock that was a funny-looking little carved house. If he waited thirty more seconds, a tiny bird would spring out with an equally silly noise, coo-coo.

As he'd settled into the suite, Cratag had discovered that Signet's uncle had been a man with generally polished taste that showed an occasional oddness.

Signet herself was feminine and polished. He hoped she'd be odd enough to like a different kind of lover.

*F*or Signet, dinner was only slightly less lively than breakfast. They sat in the elegant and candlelit small dining room, all well dressed. Like many other rooms in the Residence, Signet had not used the room in a long time because of all the memories she'd had of dining here with her parents. When they had taken dinner alone, it was in this small square room.

The Residence had gone all out to make the dinner special. The wall and ceiling murals were set for a clear night sky with full twinmoons, as if they dined on the roof of the observation room. A candelabra dripping with crystal sat on the polished wood table.

Silverware gleamed, and the china was the best, cream colored with tiny flowers around the rim.

Avellana ate her meal with perfect manners and amused Signet with her observations on the day, and the Residence, and Vinni "Muin," and Laev, and Signet, and, with sidelong glances, Cratag. Despite herself, Signet realized an atmosphere of intimacy and even family was spinning between them. More, she sensed her own Flair rising within, slipping through her blood.

After dinner they watched a good holo of a light comedy that had been a hit the year before, then Cratag and she took Avellana to bed, settled her with Rhyz, and read to her. Cratag had better reading skills than Signet, and his low rumbling voice was comforting. Signet could have listened to him a long time.

He walked her the few meters from Avellana's room to the meditation room. Though she'd shown the room to others on the tour, no one had entered it, to keep her own energy pure. She had appreciated the courtesy, since the Residence was humming with so much energy from others—but their Flair seemed to tweak hers, too.

When they reached the door, he said with a wry smile, "Beadle is exploring the gardens, tempted by night hunting. I will be just down the hall in your uncle's suite."

"*Your* suite."

He inclined his head. "My suite, but I'll do the usual Residence check later, before I retire. It's my habit, and I want to be very well acquainted with the Residence."

Signet chuckled. "The Residence might talk your ear off."

Cratag's eyes went keen. "He's had a few words to say." Then Cratag took her hand and bowed over it, actually kissing the back and sending a delightful sensation shooting through her. He hesitated, released her hand, and said, "Later."

She hoped so. She wasn't sure when it would happen, but she was sure, now, that they would share passion.

Entering the room, she closed the door and removed her shoes, opened the midnight blue curtains swagged around the circular room. To the north was the gleam and sparkling lights of the huge starship, *Nuada's Sword*, filling the horizon, bright enough to block out the stars in that direction. To the west was the ocean and the occasional spume of wave on dark sea, otherwise the water gleamed black except where the twinmoonslight tempted with a glittering path. To the east were the gardens, tree branches showing only when they moved in the wind.

The light blue room had little furniture . . . a cabinet, a small altar for rituals, a couple of large soft chairs, and a tall twoseat was set in a reclining position where she could sleep if she wanted. All were in tones of midnight blue.

Signet sank down onto the pastel silk rug, angling so she faced the east wing, and beyond it, her land.

Unlike most nights, her mind roiled with thoughts like a tempest-driven sea.

She had embarked on an enterprise that would change her life forever.

Twelve

Thank *the* Lady *and* Lord *that her loneliness and uselessness were* over. She had a new life path.

Now if she could only shape it.

She *would* learn to make her Flair active instead of passive. She *would* direct it. No matter that she'd tried to master her slippery Flair before. Now she knew what it was, she could, *would*, visualize it better.

But right now, her mind hopped from thinking about her Flair to thinking about the desire Cratag stoked in her, to her feelings about him. Too huge to understand, and how could that happen so quickly?

Unless it wasn't quickly at all. Unless she'd unconsciously noticed he watched her during the GreatRituals when he accompanied T'Hawthorn. Not as many lately as when T'Hawthorn had been Captain of All Councils.

She acknowledged that; knew, too, that she hadn't known what to make of Cratag's long stares. Not then. Now when he sent a look at her from those violet eyes, she knew what he wanted, what she wanted.

Could he be her HeartMate? She'd once thought she had a HeartMate, thought she'd touched him momentarily during her Second and Third Passages. Maybe his mental touch was like Cratag's aura . . . and maybe she was deceiving herself.

It was widely accepted in her circles that HeartMates were to be found and treasured. That HeartMates had more stable marriages, produced more and greater Flaired children. So a person who had a HeartMate usually went searching for them.

But Cratag hadn't been brought up in the noble circles of Druida like she had. He was a fascinating man from the southern continent, had lived an exciting life on the frontier that she could barely imagine. Big and tough, strong in more ways than the physical. Hadn't he accepted a guardsman's position with T'Hawthorn during a time when that lord was feuding and Cratag knew his life was on the line? That bespoke more than a physical toughness, a mental and emotional strength that Signet found incredibly attractive. He was a survivor.

And she'd had leanings toward . . . not surviving. Shame suffused her. Maybe it had been underlying guilt that had kept her from doing something stupid. Yesterday had been a very low day in her life. Her thoughts were fizzing off in all directions. She wasn't even grounded. She wouldn't be meditating much tonight, first quarter twinmoons or not. The new blessings of her life demanded a ritual of thanks, but that wouldn't happen, either. Next full twinmoons would mark the beginning of the month of Ash, perhaps she'd celebrate that outside in a sacred grove. She grinned. Now that the FirstFamilies knew her Flair was for change, she'd be in demand. Most of the noble rituals were about shaping their planet and society, about change.

Circling back to her wonderful future.

But all was based on the past. She rose and went to a cabinet where she'd placed her parents' memoryspheres that she'd retrieved from the HouseHeart that morning before breakfast. Even then she'd sensed that she wouldn't want to meditate in the HouseHeart tonight.

Signet had never experienced the spheres. She'd always thought they'd be wrenching. She hesitated to access them, but it was necessary. Yesterday they would have broken her. Today she was stronger.

They were dated a couple of weeks after her First Passage at seven. She took one in each hand. They weren't large . . . enough for a septhour or two, or an important visit by Vinni T'Vine's predecessor, the old D'Vine, who'd been the prophetess of Celta for over a century.

Signet's mother's and father's energy pulsed through the spheres, and tears welled in her eyes and trickled down her cheeks. Even nine years later she still missed them.

She couldn't decide whose memories she wanted to experience, felt she could only bear one. Without thought her hand replaced her father's sphere. She wanted to *see* him the most and she wouldn't if she saw through his eyes.

She walked to the center of the room. Cradling the small citrine sphere in both her hands, she shut her eyes and nudged the memorysphere with her Flair.

Time rolled back to a hot, bright summer's day.

Cara D'Marigold, she who had been a Sorrel, glanced up at her tall, dapper husband with the golden hair and lines beginning to etch into his face. *He is so handsome, and I love him more after all these years than I did when I wed him.*

Signet choked, clenched her hands around the sphere.

Thank the Lady and Lord he is with me, that we will do this together as always. He squeezes my hand in reassurance. His thoughts are excited and not as wary as mine, but his eyes gentle as they meet mine, and he says, "We don't have to do this if you don't wish."

He knows very well that I won't back away from this visit, no matter how nervous it makes me, and he squeezes my hand again.

"One does not deny a request to visit by a FirstFamily Great-Lady, especially if she is the powerful oracle, D'Vine," I say as I lean against his shoulder. I smile because I sound like the Residence, that arbitrator of all that is correct.

Cal brushes a kiss on my temple, soothing us both. "It must be about Signet."

"Yes." Our only child recently had her First Passage, and though she was Tested and showed great Flair, it wasn't determined what kind of Flair she had. The latest small problem that niggles at us, making our lives less than boring perfection.

"We should have had D'Vine as an oracle at her birth," Cal frets.

"She probably wouldn't have come. T'Bay was good enough." Though he couldn't tell us Signet's Flair, either.

Cal follows my thoughts. "Maybe we'll find out now." Sucking in his breath, he opens the door as the Residence tells us GreatLady D'Vine has arrived.

She stands before us, aged and straight and looking at us with uncanny blue green eyes. She shivers, an oldie who likes the heat, and Cal is disarmed. He leaves my side to slip a hand under her elbow and says, "You grace us with your presence, GreatLady. Please come up into the main sitting room and have some tea and cakes."

Signet lost the train of conversation as it passed through courtesies, as they all went to the sitting room. The room was done in a mint green that Signet barely recalled, with many potted plants. She was swept along with her mother's emotions . . . interest and pride and love for her child and husband. Signet didn't focus on the talk until D'Vine put her teacup down, folded her hands, and said, "As you know, the FirstFamilies invite certain GrandHouses to participate in the GreatRituals throughout the year. I am pleased to say that they have usually listened to my recommendations, and also pleased to inform you that your Family has been chosen."

Awe washes through me like high tide, followed by wariness.

Usually when a FirstFamily wants something from the rest of us there is a price to pay.

Cal is tapping his fingers on his knee like he does when he is thinking about all angles of a problem. His toes tap the carpet softly in one of our dance patterns. "And you would want us to bring our young daughter, Signet, with us to those highest of noble rituals."

I swallow back a bubble of nervous laughter. Cal doesn't do "haughty" very well. Him calling the rituals "noble rituals," which would include us, of course, as opposed to FirstFamilies and Favorites rituals, which is what most of us call those GreatRituals, might offend D'Vine. But he is not diplomatic, because he's concerned for our Signet.

D'Vine inclines her head. "Yes, please bring Calendula."

Tap. Tap. I can't hear Cal's fingertips, but I feel his emotions. Pride, above all, in our child, but protectiveness, too.

"She will have the benefit of being accepted by the First-Families," D'Vine says persuasively. "Make the acquaintance of the powerful."

I wonder about that. Signet isn't as outgoing as Cal or me, more like her uncle who hid in his rooms.

D'Vine gives me a sharp look, so I go with impulse and say, "What have you seen about Signet? Do you know her Flair?"

Temerity, and D'Vine's expression goes impassive, but her eyes are bright and piercing.

She rises. "Please consider coming to the next Full Twinmoons Ceremony in GreatCircle Temple. You and your daughter will always be welcome." She sighs, reminding us that despite her vitality, she is an old woman. Cal and I stand. "It is a shame you did not ask me to be an oracle at your child's birth, it would have saved much time." She shakes her head. "Ah, what will happen will happen when and how it needs to." Then she *fixes* me with a look. "Signet is important to our generation and her own and those to come. Do not forget that."

Cal escorts her to the door and when he returns he rubs his cheek against my hair and I relax. We do fit so well. "We'll go to the rituals, and someday will find out what D'Vine knows."

I tuck doubt into the back of my mind and savor the love of my husband. Finally our emotions settle into our strong and true bond, and I find he feels the same relief as I. Our wonderful Signet, our ugly duckling, will someday bloom into a swan.

*S*ignet was weeping by the time her mother's memory faded. She'd tried to be quiet, but sobs ripped from her, and she was helpless to speak when a tapping came at the door. Cratag looked in, then pushed the door open and walked silently over polished wood and silk rug until he crouched down before her.

"What's wrong?" he asked.

She couldn't tell him, just shook her head. Such love she'd had and lost! The precious sight of her father, and her mother's feelings about him, which he'd returned.

Cratag picked her up, and the memorysphere fell from her fingers. Even holding her, he caught the small orb, sucked in a breath. "Memorysphere."

Nodding against his chest, Signet managed to snag a clean softleaf from her sleeve pocket and wipe her eyes. In a thick voice, she said, "About when D'Vine came and asked my parents to start attending the FirstFamily rituals."

"Your Family wasn't always part of those GreatRituals?"

"No, we only s-started after my F-first Passage." She blew her nose as her own memories swam to the surface—the excitement of being in GreatCircle Temple with all those powerful lords and ladies and having new robes of orange trimmed in gold and the *Flair* of everyone in the circle. "We aren't a sufficiently important Family to have been part of the rituals until then."

"I didn't know."

Signet shrugged. Cratag placed her gently on the twoseat and started to draw away, and she kept hold of him, her arms around his neck. "Please stay."

His nostrils flared as he inhaled, then he followed her down, keeping an arm around her, setting the memorysphere on the table in a way that it didn't roll. He was a man conscious of his strength, with muscular grace in his every action. Not at all like her father.

More tears came to her eyes. Unique men, both of them.

Cratag settled next to her, flicked his fingers. "Female energy. Your mother's memories?"

"Y-yes."

For a couple of moments, they held each other in silence. "She loved you."

"They both did."

"You were lucky," he said, his body tensing, then releasing . . . at the thought of his own mother?

"I know." Signet moved until her head was on his shoulder, and she could feel the length of his side against hers. "I'd forgotten that lately, but I have been lucky." The long time of people she cared for leaving her had been all the more painful for the love she'd remembered. She sniffed. "Like I said, D'Vine came here after my First Passage and asked us to be part of the GreatRituals. Yesterday T'Ash said that he thought my Flair might have helped those rituals."

"T'Ash is generally right."

"Yes. But I don't think my parents ever found out what D'Vine knew about me."

"That would have been Vinni's MotherDam?"

Signet waved a hand. "A few generations more between them than that."

Cratag grunted.

"But after my parents died and I continued to go to the rituals by myself, she never said anything to me. After she died, no one seemed to care whether I was at the rituals or not. So I went whenever I felt like it." Most of the time, but not all, and not to some of the most important rituals, where her Flair might have made a difference if anyone had known of it. "I suppose I could ask Vinni to check old D'Vine's records." But young teen or not, he was still a GreatLord and with Flair greater than his ancestress's and secrets of his own.

She shook her head. "So I didn't learn much from the memory-sphere." She'd thought it would answer all of her questions.

"That's too bad." Cratag began to sit up.

"Stay awhile, rest a bit. It's been an eventful couple of days for you, too. We can trust the Fams and the Residence to watch over Avellana, and she's only a couple of rooms away."

As if conjured by Signet's thought, Du and Beadle trotted in. Du hopped up and settled at Signet's hip, purring.

Beadle thumped onto the twoseat and draped himself over Cratag's ankles. *Mousies outside very interesting. Skirls ran away from me! But night is cool and FamMan is warm.*

He felt very warm to Signet, the man gave out heat as well as energy. Du said nothing.

"Glad you're in," Cratag said, the pauses between his words telling Signet that she'd been right. He was as tired as she. Unlike her, he'd slept in a strange place last night, been in a different environment all day.

"Rest," she murmured, and it wasn't until his breathing had slowed into sleep that she focused on something else—the twinmoons shooting light through the windows, both waxing and at the apex of their First Quarter.

It seemed appropriate to whisper a small prayer of thanks and for blessings in her life to grow like the twinmoons, though she knew that had already started.

She was looking forward to the next day. The man beside her, and Avellana, and the Fams, would ensure it was an interesting one.

*C*ratag *woke to a woman in his arms and a raging case of lust.* Beadle bounded up his body in three hops and licked his cheek. *New day. After dawn. Critters stirring. I am going *out,* but back for breakfast.* He jumped from the twoseat with a thunk and trotted out the door.

Du uncurled from a neat circle, stretched, and yawned. He

slipped down from the twoseat and slid from the room with a muttered *Residence showed Me a no-time just for Me. I will have a nibble before breakfast.* Since the cat was too thin, Cratag thought that was a good idea. Almost as good as him getting the hell out of this sleepchair before he rolled over and took Signet.

But she was opening blurry blue eyes and smiled at him, and his breath stopped. Her gaze was gentle, affectionate even. She didn't seem to notice his scars, and that was good, damn near a miracle. He couldn't recall the last time a woman he'd met only a few hours before had looked past his scars to *him.* Though they hadn't just met. They'd been acquainted for years, long enough for her to get used to his face.

Her own face was flushed more than usual, giving her a rosy color, tinting her lips darker, plumping them, tempting him beyond resistance. He leaned down and brushed her mouth with his own. Soft.

Her body would be soft under his, too.

Thirteen

*H*e *leaned closer and closer, his blood throbbing in his body all the* way down to his groin. Her eyes got wider and bluer, the air around her seemed to lighten and turn golden. She reached up and slid her palms behind his neck, and her touch there dragged a groan from him.

No, his control was gone. He pulled her close and rolled so she was atop him, her breasts against his chest, the softness of her stomach against his raging erection. He set his lips on hers, swept his tongue across her mouth, ready to plunge in.

The doors banged shut with a crack, and he rolled again, jumping from the twoseat to put his body between her and the entrance.

Breakfast is served, the Residence said, then, *Avellana has been down to the dining room and the kitchen and is now returning to this floor. I have reminded her not to run up the stairs.*

"Fligger!" Signet snapped, and Cratag stared at her.

She scowled and ran her hands through her hair curling around her shoulders. "I can curse if I want to."

Cratag lifted and dropped a shoulder. "'Course you can. Just didn't expect it of you."

She sniffed and rose from the twoseat. For an instant her tunic pressed against her breasts, showing the small hardness of her nipples. Cratag's body clenched. He wanted this woman under him, mingling her panting moans with his, rising in passion so she'd cry out in ecstasy.

She swished by him and opened the doors, frowning at the glass panes. "Curtains are going back on these doors."

"Signet!" Avellana cried. "It is time for breakfast. You didn't answer your door so I let you sleep, but the Residence wouldn't let me choose my own breakfast, and I came back and—"

"Avellana, it is *not* time for breakfast. We have a half-septhour yet." Signet was walking toward the child, keeping her from seeing Cratag in the sitting room. He was irritated with himself. If he was a noble, or had better Flair, he could have teleported away.

"It *is* time! It is half-septhour after RisingBell." Avellana stamped her foot, and he shouldn't have been able to hear it on the hallway rug, but he did. Were his senses expanding?

"We do not eat at half-septhour after RisingBell, Avellana." Signet was patient. He sensed them walking away and drifted to look out the doors. Signet had her hand on Avellana's shoulder. "We eat later. Let's look at your schedule."

"I'm hungry now."

"Hmm. We should adjust the schedule." Signet glanced over her shoulder. Eyes full of affection met Cratag's. That warm look punched harder than pure lust, and emotion filled him. He watched as they went down the hallway, turned into Avellana's sitting room. To relieve some tension, he sprinted down the hall and into his own suite, stripped, and flung his clothes into the cleanser then stepped into a cold waterfall.

"Signet has informed me that breakfast will be in half a septhour," the Residence said. "Pre-breakfast treats of fruit and yogurt, honey and grain mix will be available to Avellana in the mornings."

"Fine," Cratag said. "You kept an eye—ah, monitored Avellana—this morning when Signet and I were in the sitting room and the Fams were out?"

"I did. She was in no danger. All outside shields were up. She looked at her balcony but did not attempt to go out on it."

"Good." He set his head against the granite of the wall and let the water roll over him. For a while he didn't think, just let the water cool his blood. He shivered under the cold fall and suspected he'd be doing this a lot in the coming days . . . unless he had Signet under him and was inside her. His shaft rose again, and he cursed. The plain truth was no woman had excited him like this one since his teens.

A *flash* came to him, and he stilled. What was that? A dark image? A spear of jangled negative emotions?

He tried to grasp it, but it was gone. And he wasn't erect anymore.

It was almost as if his survival had been threatened. Almost but . . . not . . . quite. Or the survival of his House, of his Family.

Roiling, jagged fear punctuated with despair shattered inside him like shards of broken glass. He fought for breath. What was this? Then he knew.

Passage.

Not Avellana's—Laev's.

He stumbled from the waterfall room, uncaring of the thick rugs soaking up his wet footprints, to the bedroom scrybowl. With clumsy, trembling fingers he touched the rim. Voice raw, he said, "Scry T'Hawthorn Residence."

"T'Hawthorn Residence here, Chief Guardsman Cratag."

"Laev? T'Hawthorn?"

"Yes, Cratag, T'Hawthorn is with his Son'sSon, Laev, who is undergoing the first fugue of his Second Passage. It is bearable and progresses well. From my experience I believe this time will be short, only a quarter septhour, and not as intense as many Hawthorns' Passages. I doubt he will have more than the now-standard three episodes for Second Passage. It was well done for the late HawthornHeir to marry into the Grove Family."

Cratag grunted as he reeled into a chair.

"Are you sensing the Passage, Chief Guardsman?"

"Yes."

There was a pause, then the Residence continued in its cool, level, masculine voice that Cratag had always accepted but seemed lacking compared to the mellow, varying tones of D'Marigold Residence. "If you are sensing Laev's Passage, then you are bonded to him emotionally."

Cratag grunted again. Any Hawthorn with a lick of sense knew that.

"I have been told that D'Marigold is a catalyst, an instigator of change in others' lives." There was the hint of disapproval as if change was inimical. Just how old was T'Hawthorn Residence, anyway? Was it stratifying? Cratag didn't think that was a good thing for man, woman, Fam, or house.

Beadle had come back to the suite, and now the cat was batting a cloth mousekin around the room and pouncing on it. No chance Beadle would stratify into dignified behavior soon.

"Chief Guardsman?" T'Hawthorn Residence prodded.

"Yeah?"

"It may be that D'Marigold's Flair is affecting you, amplifying your bond with Laev, or even your own Flair. Perhaps even changing your Flair."

"Wouldn't be too bad a thing to get a little more Flair," Cratag said, knowing everyone would agree with him, even T'Hawthorn Residence. He wanted to speak to Laev, more, to go over and hold him, comfort him, keep him safe from the Passage fugue. Which Cratag had never experienced himself and had only rarely seen traces of among the Hawthorn Family. But he couldn't do that. Laev might have wanted him there, but Cratag had to remain here. He'd read his contract. He had free time when Avellana was with her Family and could return to T'Hawthorn Residence if the lord summoned him.

"Not too bad a Passage, then—Laev's?" he croaked.

"No, I doubt it will last longer than two eightdays."

"Good." He cleared his throat. "Laev's message cache, please."

"Certainly."

"Laev Hawthorn here, give me some words." Laev's voice came young and enthusiastic, immediately recalling to Cratag the boy's— young man's—joyful smile.

"Understand you're in Passage and doin' well," Cratag said. "Know m'thoughts are with you." He cleared his throat again, spoke clearly. "I'm very proud of you. You are a fine . . . man." Cratag hadn't forgotten that people here in Druida would consider Laev a man, though as far as Cratag was concerned, there was a lot for Laev to learn. "End message."

Of course Cratag had declared himself a man at fifteen when he'd left Tref. He'd had a lot to learn and had learned it hard, was still learning. But he'd been more mature than Laev in some ways.

Cratag dressed, feeling sure enough of his control to don less blousey work trous. He was behind schedule. Even as he thought that, a small silver calendarsphere appeared in front of his nose, flashing red. "You are late for breakfast," the thing said in Avellana's most officious tones.

"I find this reminder obnoxious. It is not *my* calendarsphere reminding *me*. That is very rude." He didn't have enough Flair to have a calendarsphere draw on his psi power and manifest.

The object vanished.

He thought he could hear a question from Signet, could feel suppressed irritation from Avellana. The girl he and Signet would have to help through *her* Passage fugues. Dreamtimes that would not be as "easy" as Laev's. Cratag shivered again as he recalled the darkness that had shrouded him in the waterfall.

Everyone except he had known on an emotional level what a bad Passage might entail for the girl. Death, worse, madness.

Before he could dwell on this, Beadle trotted to the door. *Breakfast time, FamMan.* The cat grinned his goofy grin, and Cratag couldn't help but smile back. "Yes, you think they have porcine strips?"

"How many do you want?" asked D'Marigold Residence.

*W*hile *Avellana was at lessons in architecture in the* downstairs library, Laev scried Cratag. So he slipped away to his suite and took Laev's call. The Hawthorn colors of purple and gold, along with a slight tinge of green light, pulsed through the room. Laev's colors. He strode to the bowl. "Cratag here."

The water drops above the bowl showed Laev's smiling face, but there was a hint of trials undergone and survived behind his eyes. Cratag blew out a relieved breath. "You look good."

Laev stood straighter, his smile brightened, as if Cratag couldn't have said anything more complimentary. Cratag thought he felt—no, did *feel*—a wave of satisfaction from the seventeen-year-old. "My first fugue went well." His voice was slightly deeper, more resonant, from emotional storms. "I have more Flair than ever, and I think the Hawthorn talent for business will be confirmed." He frowned a little, and a distant look came to his eyes. "I think . . . I think I understand more of the web of the alliances that FatherSire has made." Then a flashing smile with more warmth than Cratag had ever seen from T'Hawthorn. "I did a few fighting forms, and I believe I'm more flexible, have more strength."

A seventeen-year-old was plenty flexible. Cratag eyed Laev. There seemed to be colorless waves around the young man. Cratag thought it was his own meager Flair in action. "Could be," he said. "Congratulations on reaching your manhood, Laev HawthornHeir."

Laev beamed. "There will be a huge celebration later. When you're home again. It wouldn't be the same without you."

Cratag's heart squeezed. "Thank you."

Rolling his shoulders, Laev said, "I miss our workouts already. May I have your consent to come there and train with you? Father-Sire has given his permission."

Even more emotion choked Cratag. This was a man who would not forget him, who would value him as a part of the Family. "Of course. Will MidAfternoonBell work? That's when my next session is scheduled. We run on set schedules here."

Laev raised his brows. "I wouldn't have thought D'Marigold—ah, it's the little one, Avellana Hazel."

"Yes." Then Cratag recalled what Signet had said about Laev perhaps triggering Avellana's Passage. He'd consult with Signet, but he wanted to see—to hug—the man who had been like his younger brother.

While he was considering this, a masculine gleam came to Laev's eye. "And Cratag, I think, I really think that I connected with my HeartMate!"

That admission tangled Cratag's emotions. Pride that the youngster was growing up and at his achievements, his potential. But also a sharp envy for such a love. He forced a smile. "Come this afternoon."

"I will." Laev tilted his head, grinned. "T'Hawthorn Residence has told me that I only have a few more minutes in my morning break, and that I should eat. Since I'm hungry . . ."

"See you later," Cratag said gruffly and ended the scry. He rubbed his head, feeling more helpless than he had in a long time. He didn't know, exactly, what he was doing here, no solid mission. He didn't understand—in his gut—great Flair or Passage or HeartMates.

Fourteen

Signet showed Avellana the small room that they'd skipped during the tour. The chamber held her bench and dyed leathers, wooden patterns, and hard soles. Avellana seemed as fascinated with Signet's creative Flair as Signet had been with the child's.

Since the time was right to offer a new reward for good behavior, Signet measured Avellana's feet for a pair of shoes and a pair of slippers—to be awarded at the end of a full week.

Then they went to the gardens and took a small break from each other, with Avellana playing with Rhyz and Beadle as Signet and Du sat on a sunny bench. She could still barely believe that her life had changed so much for the better, so quickly.

And she thought she was noticing small changes in her housemates. She stroked Du, believing that he was putting on weight already, he certainly was eating enough—of course the Residence was tempting him with the choicest tidbits from the no-time storage units.

Even as she thought of the Residence, it spoke to her. *Cratag Maytree wishes the primary dance studio on the second floor for a sparring area.*

Signet blinked. *Yes, show him how to remove the barres and where our mats are stored.* She frowned. *Make sure whatever equipment he needs is acceptable. If it is too old or substandard, you have authority to refurbish the studio, dressing and waterfall rooms, and office as they were in the past.* She wrinkled her forehead. Surely at one time it had been a fighting salon. Hadn't that been mentioned in the Residence's history?

We should have already anticipated his needs, the Residence fretted, voicing her own guilty thoughts.

Yes, she agreed. *A chief guardsman would want to train daily. I will continue to use the smaller dance studio.* After her parents' deaths, she had closed off the main practice room, where she'd studied and played with them. She'd moved to a small studio that had belonged to one of the previous Marigold daughters who'd become a prima ballerina and had insisted on her own space. Though as she thought about *that* room, she realized it, too, should be refurbished. She had ignored the prods of the Residence about refinishing the floors and panels for the last few years. *Go ahead and update my dance studio, too.*

Thank you!

Signet smiled, and Avellana came over. "What did your Residence say to make you happy?"

Hugging the girl, Signet said, "I told the Residence that some rooms need to be more fashionable. It is always happy when it gets more handsome rooms, and because I love it, I am happy when it is happy."

Avellana looked up at Signet with clear eyes. "You have been too much alone if you only have a Residence."

"Yes, I have." She looked down at the child who was becoming dearer by the minute. "But now I have you as a friend, right?"

With a short nod, Avellana said, "Yes. We are friends." She stared into the distance, then said, "I haven't gone to regular grovestudy, but have taken lessons from a nurse and a nanny and a governess." Her lips pushed in and out. "I have no grovestudy friends. I only have my Family and Muin and Rhyz."

"But all of them love you very much," Signet said.

Avellana let out a sigh. "Yes, they all love me too much."

"I don't know that it's possible to be loved too much."

Sticking out her lower lip, Avellana said, "They watch me all the time. Everyone watches me all the time."

"We are all concerned for you—"

"I know!"

"—but perhaps we will watch you less after your First Passage."

The girl grabbed Signet's hands and gripped them fiercely. "Do you really think so?"

Signet met the child's intense gaze. "Yes."

Of course, said Du, walking over Signet's lap to rub his head against Avellana. His amber stare was steady. *You will climb through Passage well.* He purred.

Avellana transferred her gaze to him. "You think so?"

"Yesss," Du vocalized.

"Yesss." Rhyz hopped up on the bench and nudged Du aside, purring louder. *I know human Passage. You must not fear.* He nosed Avellana's hand. *Now it is lunchtime.*

The whole gang of them, cats and girl, pivoted on the path and marched back to the Residence, and Signet could only hope that the Fams knew more on an instinctual level than the humans. Because even Vinni T'Vine, the prophet, feared for Avellana.

After lunch, Cratag and the Residence displayed the changes they'd made to transform the main dance studio into a sparring room. He had forbidden Avellana to cross over the threshold and made it a "no new shoes" violation, up there with being on the balcony or the sea path without an adult human.

It was during Avellana's nap time when Signet realized he'd

withdrawn a little from her and wondered at it. She'd adored waking up next to him, had yearned to feel the slide of his bare skin against hers, inside her.

But he had barely touched her all day, and when he spoke with her, his voice was gruff. She had dared to hope that they might have sex when Avellana took her nap, but he seemed more preoccupied with Laev Hawthorn, who had teleported directly to a newly specified area within the training room. Signet and Avellana had lingered outside the closed door and shared a glance or two at the thumps and mutters. Then there had come a ripe swear, and Signet had reluctantly realized they had to retire somewhere else and had taken Avellana back to the craft room and started on her slippers.

Just before nap time, Cratag had shown up, newly cleansed, had glanced at her work and grunted in approval, then escorted Avellana to her suite for her nap. They saw her safely abed with Rhyz and Beadle then went to the sitting room. He left the doors open and went to a large chair and sank into it. Signet suppressed a sigh. Frowning, he rubbed his head and the scent of soap and man came to her, and she shifted in her own chair. She wanted him. Had she been too passive? Perhaps she should be bolder.

"You know that Laev had a Passage fugue early this morning," Cratag said.

She thought he meant his voice to be expressionless, but she heard tones in it, and more, she *felt* emanations from him. Resignation that he hadn't been there to help this young man he loved, a trace of anger and, worse, helplessness. "I don't know much about Passages. Never had a deep one. Not even one fugue. Twinges, I guess."

"You said things went well?"

He shrugged. "So they told me, and he wasn't as tense as he'd been lately, but I still don't know what to expect." His violet gaze met hers. "What are they like?"

The day had been warm, and sun still spilled through the windows, making the room comfortable and cheerful, but Signet shivered. It had only been a couple of days since she'd understood that her Third Passage had nothing to do with her parents' deaths.

"Powerful," she said. "They wring emotion from you, as if Flair demands that all of you—mind, body, spirit—be integrated so it can manifest." She shook her head. "I don't know that I'm saying this well."

"You're the only one who talks to me about it," he said in a low voice laced with anger.

She glanced up sharply. "What have you been told?"

"That Laev's first fugue wasn't bad, but he looked older—different—more *there* afterward. He moved better, too. More integrated, you say?"

"Yes, Flair is a part of us all." She bent an admonishing look on him. "You, too. You can speak telepathically to your Family, and this Residence as well." *Can't you?* she sent the last mind-to-mind toward him.

His mind was dense, his entire presence was dense, solid. But he nodded. *Yes, I can mindspeak some.* He formed the words slowly and precisely.

I knew it. Do not think you are a lesser man because you have different skills.

He grunted again at that. *I cannot teleport.* His words were wistful.

I cannot handle a long and heavy sword, a broadsword.

Do you want to? His reply was immediate, and his thoughts lit as if he was considering how to ensure she could do so.

Perhaps, but it would take me years before I could do so, and I'd never be as good as you.

But you could master the craft. You have—

Do I? She held out her arms, waved them, flexed her minuscule muscles. *My broadsword could not match yours, my skill could never match yours. I am sorry that you cannot teleport, but that is a skill some people have and some don't, like all the rest.*

Cratag's fingers flexed as if he wanted to be moving instead of pretending to be relaxed in a chair. "They think he will have only three major fugues and they won't last too long. What is too long?" His jaw flexed.

"Three seems to be normal, now." Signet added a bit of soothing Flair she'd learned from her parents into her voice. "Too long would be more than a night . . . or a day." She bit her lip, thinking of all the rumors she'd heard, and phrased her next question carefully. "The gathering of Flair and determining its aspects and freeing it tends to—ah—plumb the depths of a person, test one. If there are any guilts or concerns . . . they may be magnified and play a great part in Passage." She thought of Avellana. Surely the girl would have only tiny negativities within her.

Cratag stared at Signet and narrowed his eyes. "If you're asking if it's true that Laev wounded D'Holly with a poisoned blade years ago, that's right." Cratag's voice was harsh. "But the entire Family worked through those consequences and the feud with the Hollys." He smiled, and it was crooked. "T'Hawthorn brought in D'Sea, the mind Healer, to help us. Especially Laev. So, yeah, that may come up during Passage, but he's a strong and reasonable young man. I don't think it will bite him any more than any tough and stupid life-turning mistake does." Cratag frowned. "But I suppose I should expect to see more shadows in his eyes next time."

"I suppose so, but he has others to help him, like we will be helping Avellana."

"*You* will be helping Avellana. I do not have the Flair."

Signet tilted her head. "I believe you have more than you think, and what you have is presence. And strength. You will be a rock I can count on."

They lapsed into silence, him still working ideas out in his mind, thinking things all the way through to conclusions. Signet was more accustomed to immediate decisions based on her emotions, a Family trait.

"What of HeartMates?" Cratag asked in words she could barely hear but that definitely resonated. She felt herself flush and glanced at him, but he was looking outside to the waves rolling in against the headlands marching toward the north.

She told him the bare truth. "HeartMates are usually connected with in Third Passage. I have heard that occasionally people can mentally touch each other in Second Passage if the bond is strong, perhaps if they are reincarnated souls. Vinni knows that Avellana is his HeartMate already—and don't ask me how that happened—but Vinni T'Vine is a law unto himself."

"And you?" He still didn't look at her.

"I thought I touched my HeartMate during my Third Passage." She tried a smile, but it felt brittle on her lips. "I believe I imagined that since he hasn't shown up in my life."

Then Cratag turned his gaze on her, and it was powerful enough to stop her breath. Banked desire ignited between them. "You don't think you have a HeartMate?" he asked.

Was that another reason why he'd stepped back from her? "No."

"You aren't waiting for him?"

Had she been? She thought about it. "I did, for a long time." She shrugged. "I let that dream die." Along with so many others. "I don't expect a HeartMate to come to me." Another shrug, this time of one painfully casual shoulder. "Unlike mythic tales and new legends, no man has hunted for me. I am not the type of woman to inspire such dedication."

He stood now, moved toward her. "You are the most beautiful woman I've ever known."

Then he was towering over her, and she felt the air around her heat with passion from them both. She didn't know what kind of relationship he wanted, didn't care as long as she could stoke and share and release her own desire with him. Yearned to feel his large and calloused hands on her body.

Yes, she is a beautiful FamWoman. Du trotted into the room. With one leap, he cleared the arm of her chair and landed on her lap. He wasn't heavy enough for her to flinch, but he certainly broke the moment.

Holding on to the shreds of it as long as she could, matching Cratag's smoldering gaze, Signet felt her lips heat, her core liquefy. "Tonight," she whispered.

He dipped his head just enough, and grazed her lips with his own.

Beadle swaggered into her view, sat on Cratag's feet, and burped. *Night is fun outside.*

The Residence chimed a tune notifying Signet of a scry, and she tore her gaze away from Cratag to look at the crystal bowl on a side table against the wall. "D'Hazel scries."

Cratag scooped the plump black and white Beadle up with one hand and retreated to his chair. Beadle settled into his lap with a purr.

Signet wrenched her thoughts back to her duty and, holding Du, went to answer to the GreatLady who held her fate in her hands.

D'Hazel had requested a report on the day, particularly any interaction between Laev HawthornHeir, who was known to have experienced a Passage fugue, and Avellana. Signet was glad she could truthfully say the two young people had not met or even seen each other. She spoke of the revised schedule and sent a copy to D'Hazel's mail cache.

As soon as she'd finished with D'Hazel, Vinni T'Vine called to heavily hint that he be invited to dinner. Signet complied, and though she was pleased the Residence was humming with happiness, she was feeling as if there were too many people and Fams around for her to do what she really wanted—to roll around in complete abandon on a bedsponge with Cratag. She had the suspicion that "complete abandon" with Cratag would not happen for many a day, but that she could anticipate some hot bouts of passion.

Vinni—Muin, as Avellana continued to call him—arrived with his bodyguard Hanes in tow, who was persuaded to eat with them. Vinni had also brought his Fam, a female housefluff—a hybrid between an Earthan rabbit and a Celtan mocyn that proved that both Celta and Earth had the same space-faring ancestors. The fat fluff stayed close to Vinni, eating beside his chair, hair raised so she appeared like a big brown and white ball with large feet and ears. All the cats stared at her, and found her sadly lacking. Du and Rhyz stalked away from the creature with sniffs, and Beadle looked her up and down, licked her pink nose, bumped her with his body, and bounded from the room.

After dinner the humans and the housefluff had tea sent from D'Hazel's Residence and watched the spring sun go down on the ocean through the sitting room windows.

Signet was amused at the lounging of two very large and male individuals in her own feminine room and their occasional scanning glances for trouble.

Avellana brought the housefluff over to meet Signet. "This is Flora. She is Muin's Fam and is very soft and pretty."

"And brave," Vinni said, stroking the long ears of his Fam.

"Not as brave as my Rhyz," Avellana said loyally, "but brave."

Taking the white fluff with brown splotches, Signet settled her in her lap and looked into big brown eyes. She stroked the housefluff and sighed at the Fam's emanations of pure sweetness. Signet didn't think she'd met a gentler, more loving soul, though she sensed a darkness in the housefluff that she finally identified as a lingering scar from emotional abuse. For an instant she was shocked, then realized that the darkness was before Vinni adopted her.

The children stood near Hanes. Vinni was having a man-to-man discussion about spending the night since the weekend started the next day. Avellana leaned against the man's knee and looked up at him with soulful eyes.

Still petting Flora, Signet glanced at Cratag and saw *his* eyes blazing. With another trained guard in the Residence, Cratag could relax his vigilance.

Desire . . . anticipation . . . wonder . . . swirled through her as she held his gaze.

Then the housefluff made a soft sound and seemed to sink bonelessly into Signet's lap as if she finally trusted her. Cheeks warm, and not wanting to betray herself, Signet focused on the gentle Fam. She was not nearly as complicated a creature as a cat or a girl . . . or a man. Could Signet actually summon her own Flair and try to affect the dark smudge within the housefluff?

Settling into her balance, Signet floated into a light trance and examined the smudge. Nothing she'd ever seen or experienced, even during the FirstFamily GreatRituals. She drifted to it and saw it was old terror and horror and torture. Flora flinched. Signet withdrew. She'd touched others' trace energies who had tried to Heal the injury.

She let a sigh at her inadequacy filter through her, though it didn't make it to her lips. She rose from the trance to see that more time had passed than she'd felt. Cratag stood hand-in-hand with Avellana near the open, unshielded windows. Vinni was looking intently at Hanes as if speaking telepathically. Hanes stiffened, then gave the briefest of nods.

"The ocean is so beautiful from here!" Avellana said. "These windows are perfect, all tall and with arches to look out of. Muin, do *any* of your Residence's towers have such windows?"

"D'Marigold Residence is unique," Vinni said as he and Hanes sauntered toward the windows. Holding Flora, Signet rose and crossed to join the others. Not wanting to scare the Fam, Signet stopped a meter away.

Flora said, *Closer*.

Signet tightened her grip on the soft fur that suddenly seemed a little slippery against her palms. Accidentally killing a GreatLord's Fam would be bad.

Vinni grinned at Signet, then took the fat housefluff from her. "Flora isn't afraid of heights, and she likes the wind flowing around and through her ears."

Asking a question that had occurred to her more than once, Signet said, "Do you prefer to be called Vinni or Muin?"

"Vinni is fine."

"I will call you Muin," Avellana said firmly.

"And I'll call you T'Vine," Hanes said. He turned to Signet. "Do you mind if T'Vine and I spend the night? I believe there's a suite next to Cratag's—"

"Yes," said D'Marigold Residence. "There is a wall bed in the sitting room, and GreatLord T'Vine can have the bedroom."

"Sounds good," Cratag said, his voice only a little husky. He didn't look at Signet.

We will use my bedroom, she said to him mentally.

His jaw flexed. He nodded.

"That is done, then," the Residence said with satisfaction ringing in its tones.

Signet wasn't so sure. Vinni wouldn't look at her or Cratag, and she didn't think it was because he was shy about sex. More like he'd had a vision, and that's why he wanted to stay.

Fifteen

Cratag's trous got too tight as the evening progressed. Finally he and Vinni and Signet read to Avellana after she was tucked into bed. The little girl fought valiantly to stay awake but slipped into sleep.

After that, he, Hanes, and Vinni walked through the Residence. Hanes seemed impatient with this, happy with the report by D'Marigold Residence on each of the rooms. Vinni had stopped halfway through at the craft room to look at Avellana's holos in progress. Hanes stayed with the young teen, and Cratag continued with his physical check. He *knew* when the duo went up to their suite, Hanes checked it, then Vinni and his bodyguard fell asleep.

Cratag was alone again, everything in the Residence silent. Now that he was without muted conversation, he burned.

Even the fact that he knew Signet was meditating . . . could *feel* her meditating . . . didn't help. He wanted her, but he was wary. She had a life here—a very different life than what he was used to, and today had taught him that being with Laev was important to him. Of course, Laev had visited today, and they'd trained in an excellent professionally fitted salon . . . except for the hardglass mirrors along one wall. Then he'd taken a fall against that wall, and by the time he'd rolled to his feet even the smudge of his robe against the glass had been gone. D'Marigold Residence in action.

He liked the Residence, so cheerful and respectful and humming to itself in satisfaction when it had fulfilled even a small request.

Beadle loved it here. He had never known T'Hawthorn Residence.

And why was Cratag's imagination even forming hazy dreams of living here?

Pure fantasy. Signet was a GrandLady with connections to the FirstFamilies. She moved in those circles with elegance and polish and sophistication.

He'd never taken such a lady to bed.

He groaned as he rounded back to the thought of Signet in bed with him.

Once again he sent his mind reaching for hers. Once again he touched her with surprising ease. Colors he couldn't truly see pulsed around her, energies he couldn't comprehend. Great Flair.

They were definitely from two different worlds that wouldn't intersect for long.

Du curled on Signet's crossed legs as she sat in the middle of her meditation room.

Time to stop playing around—though playing with Avellana in the craft room and Du and the other Fams in the garden had been good. And the idea of playing with Cratag curved her lips in a smug smile. Soon they'd play together, and she figured it would be the best playtime of her life. Her smile spread into a grin, and she wriggled her butt, just because it felt good.

She began to breathe deeply. She must work on her Flair, so she could understand how her Flair worked—on her and on others, particularly others. Trying to casually send her Flair to help Flora hadn't been effective. An ominous weight in the back of Signet's mind told her that Avellana would need her own *and* Signet's Flair during her Passage fugues.

The thought of Avellana dying during Passage was horrible. Signet cared for the little girl more every minute and would feel deep and abiding guilt if Avellana died under her care.

Not to mention the dreadful consequences of failing a First-Family. Despite what anyone said, Signet D'Marigold might as well move to a continent across the ocean as expect to have a normal life in Druida if she couldn't protect Avellana. No one would trust her with anything else. The tentative inquiries regarding her Flair and prospective commissions would vanish in an instant.

And she would have failed to save two lives, Avellana's and her own. Signet swallowed hard. Her throat was beginning to close with fear and grief. Lifting and holding Du, she stretched to reach a cup of cool mint tea and sipped, put the beverage back. Du rubbed his head under her chin and purred, then dropped back to her crossed legs and kneaded them, purring.

We will be fine. I will not have to leave My Residence.

This time she swallowed a chuckle. "I'm glad you have faith in me."

Of course. You have lots of nice Flair. He stretched his skinny body across her legs and curled up once more. *We will play with it now.*

Taking heart, she redirected her thoughts to the positive, an exercise she'd become familiar with in the last couple of years.

She must become an active user of Flair instead of a passive . . . emanator. So she breathed deeply and grounded herself and sent her mind, her instincts spiraling down, down, down into the deepest part of her self, the spark that was Signet. Until she was in a dark blue space surrounded by sparkling flashes of light . . . light of all colors of the rainbow that appeared like glittering and flashing dandelion seed balls. Spindly but delightful, pretty.

Flair.

Her Flair, in various colors and sizes. Just floating around having a good time. Partying.

She needed the balls of Flair to work, so she tried to push them into a bunch, or a stream.

That was futile. She tried to herd all the pinks together. Another failure, they refused to clump. Signet felt hot, flushed, thought she might be sweating and panting. Again she *pushed* mentally at the nearest, a pink. It floated gently against another pink, bounced slowly, slowly off, wheeled, sparkling merrily, until it hit a yellow, and they clung together. Their energy and light more than doubled.

With an inner shout of joy, she strained to push them at a blue or a white or a green or an orange or a purple or some of the darker colors she was beginning to sense, dark pulses against the midnight background.

All this pushing was tiring. She became aware of her hot, damp skin and dragged in a large breath—and sucked the flashing puff-balls to her. They *zoomed* to her.

Gathering, not pushing.

That realization was the breakthrough. She gathered them and arranged them in chains and patterns and loosed them to stream away. When she was tired of that, filled with success, she rested . . . and sensed the Flair outside her: the massive and ancient Flair of the Residence, powered and added to by generations of Marigolds, stretching back into the past and forward into the future after she passed on to the wheel of stars and her next life. For an instant she considered that. She loved the Residence, would like being a Marigold again in a future life.

Would even like being a catalyst again, if she could master this talent and be more aware and confident of it.

Of course, her next life wasn't completely her choice. There was destiny to be played out, with nudging by the Lady and Lord. Vaguely she thought she recalled a pattern in the sparkles of her Flair before she'd gathered them together. She released all hold on them, and they floated freely, but already seemed more trained, more organized, not in the apparently random brilliance that her mortal and human mind could not comprehend. Not the arrangement of the omnipotent universe or the goddess and god.

A warmth shifted on her legs, and she glanced down to see sparkles too pale to be named any color, ill-arranged, some emotional hurt that had made him thin. Du. She stroked and tickled him until his Flair—flashing strongly—settled into a brighter flow through his body, a lucent green. He purred, and the vibration went through her, and she felt the sensitive palms of her hands as his hair slid over them when she petted him.

She let her senses expand to test the rest of the new guests of her household. Sent her mind to Flora, Vinni's housefluff, first. Gentle waves of life lapped through the animal. She wasn't very intelligent and didn't have great Flair, but a first-generation animal Fam would lack those qualities. Humans and the other Fam animals had been breeding for psi power for centuries. But Signet could visualize Flora's slight aura of pinkish Flair, with some of her lifeforce and magic clustered protectively around the dark smudge.

Pink Flair, which meant that some of the pastel yellow florets would bond with it and work the best. Perhaps.

Signet gathered her Flair and connected with the animal through telepathy, sending her mind to caress the housefluff's. Then Signet loosed the restraints on her Flair. Some of her dandelion flowers separated and flowed toward Flora's negative emotional memories. Signet's catalyst energies clumped together and hovered near, then the outer portion was absorbed. For a while Signet observed, but nothing else happened. Change didn't often happen overnight.

Unless Vinni T'Vine entered your life.

So Signet let her mind drift toward him, sprawled on the bedsponge in the guest suite. Even asleep, huge and potent energies pulsed in the thirteen-year-old. His Flair was well integrated, under control. He rolled, and his energies overlapped his Fam's. Flora was on a pillow near his head. Both drew together, and Signet thought that a portion of the boy's Flair was drawn to Signet's, reinforcing her "change" in Flora.

Pleased, Signet turned her attention to the other person in the suite, Hanes. His Flair aura was of medium intensity, well ordered, as straightforward as the man. He slept lightly and seemed to sense that Signet observed him, so she withdrew her consciousness from the suite.

Did she dare check on Avellana? Perhaps it would be better to "see" Avellana with her newly found Flair. Even as her mind drifted toward Avellana's suite, she experienced flashing strobes of colorful energy. Avellana's usual lifeforce? Or her innate Flair coalescing into Passage?

Signet hesitated, then reached for the bond she already had with the little girl. The moment she brushed Avellana's mind, the girl woke aware and energetic.

Signet began to rise to the top of her trance, and Du pricked her with his claws. *Others will care for Avellana. This is Our meditation time.* His purr was louder than it had been before. *You have appreciated Me, helped Me. I chose well.*

She smiled and petted him and let all worries go, settled into herself to experience her own Flair again. She *had* helped Du, the being she was most connected to. She'd eased Flora's tangle of memories until the Fam accepted the old horrors as only a part of herself, and not something to be dwelt upon or allowed to influence the future with fear.

Signet's energy flowers had changed when she withdrew to herself to see them. It appeared like one or even two were *multicolored*! Florets of yellow and blue and pink on one flower. Was that progress in handling her own Flair?

Then she smiled as she distantly heard Avellana's piping voice. Here and now she was filled with hope that she'd be able to help the child.

"But I want to see Signet," Avellana insisted. "Meditating this long means napping or having sex. You're with me, Cratag, so Signet's just fallen asleep in her meditation room. She would feel better sleeping on her own bedsponge," Avellana said virtuously. "So we should check on her."

Signet saw a bright irregular smear of surprise and orange embarrassment . . . Cratag's feelings.

"That may be true in D'Hazel's household—" Cratag started.

"I felt her earlier, when I was in bed. Serene. She doesn't feel like this now."

"Perhaps she wants some alone time."

"Why?" But Avellana didn't wait for an answer; she flung open the tower door.

Signet reluctantly opened her eyes and only saw a dark background and throbbing swatches of color. The smaller red-and-green-and-blue-paisley one with dark streaks gasped and shrank close to the very big bright shades-of-purple one with a brilliant lightning-white aura.

"She's glowing," a small voice said.

Signet felt her legs under her, shifted. Du hopped off her. She rose and turned her head; the smears of color became encased in harsher colors of skin and clothing.

"Her *eyes* are *glowing*. Even Muin's eyes don't *glow*."

Blinking, Signet saw Avellana's fingers twine with Cratag's.

"Avellana," Signet said, her voice tasting low and rusty. If she narrowed her eyes, she could distinguish Avellana's dandelion seed balls of Flair. Most were nearly too bright to see, but many were mis-shapened, with dark areas. "Your Flair is very strong." Signet glanced at Cratag, and the streak of color was gone, replaced by tiny purple-colored sparkling puffs of Flair marching in regulated order within him. "Cratag, you don't have much Flair."

"I know."

Signet wobbled to them, reached for him, missed his shoulder. Her hands slid down his thick biceps to his wrist, her fingers found his bare, free hand, and she clamped hers around it. Skin to skin was best. It always worked skin to skin, she realized, finally recognizing a portion of this feeling from the past. "But what Flair you have I can . . . enhance . . . until it is the strongest possible."

He grunted but said a polite "Thank you."

The little girl had dropped his hand and was hopping up and down. "My Flair, tell me about my Flair."

Du sniffed. That sounded in her mind more than in her ears. *Rude child.*

"Oh, oh, I'm sorry. But tell me, Signet. You *see* Flair?"

"Yes."

"Fun!" Avellana threw herself in Signet's arms, and their skin touched, and Signet jolted as if lightning had struck her, gasped, coughed, and spun away. Avellana cried out.

"Got you," said Cratag's steady, calm voice.

Since Signet was still spinning, her mind whirling faster than her body, he couldn't mean her. Then she felt his large hand on her back, propelling her to one side, his grip around her upper arm, pulling, then releasing, and she sprawled onto the soft, silk embroidered twoseat. All the extra Flair in her, around her, zipped into the silk, down the wooden curved legs of the sofa and to the silk rug, the narrow planked and polished floor, and into the Residence itself.

Everything came into focus.

Signet giggled. She heard light, racing footsteps, and Vinni rocketed through the door, didn't stop in time, and hit Cratag, who had Avellana tucked under his arm as if he held a pig.

Cratag didn't budge. He fended Vinni off until he spun, too, into a winged chair.

Avellana was gasping with laughter. "Whee. Spin me around, too, Cratag!"

With movements too fast for Signet to see, he flipped her until his hands were at her waist, then over until she dangled head down, then up again.

Du jumped out of the way and onto Signet's sofa arm. Lifted a paw to clean it. *Child will puke.*

In between giggles, Avellana said, "No, I won't. My stomach is fine."

I am hungry, Du said. *I need a nighttime snack.*

Signet straightened into a more dignified sitting position and scratched his ears. He would eat more, now. His hurt hadn't been physical, or Danith D'Ash would have Healed him.

I was not long enough at D'Ash's to settle. And that Residence is too busy with other animals. I needed My own space and My own FamWoman. I needed you, he said to her privately. *My other Fam-Woman was old and died and was found, and I watched but did not come out, then I got lost in the city when they tore down the building she was living in.*

From his projections, she thought the woman had not been emotionally balanced, either, and had been one of the last shadows living in the old Downwind slums. *She called me "Tinky." I do not like "Tinky." I like Du.*

"I love you, Du."

Her Fam licked her face. *I love you, too, My FamWoman, but I am hungry now.* He jumped gracefully from the sofa to glide from the room.

Signet turned to look around, saw Vinni, and stilled. She could see his Flair! More brilliant, nearly incandescent, now that he was awake. Tightly packed florets in prismatic colors . . . with an incredible variety of shades. All spiraling through the teen in a double helix.

She blinked and blinked again. Stared.

"D'Marigold," he said coolly.

Avellana giggled. "Signet is being rude."

Signet dragged her gaze away from the GreatLord, sat up straight in a proper posture, then narrowed her gaze to change the focus of her vision from Flaired to mundane—though colors were still vivid, texture more detailed. "My apologies," she said, but didn't mean it much. This new aspect of her psi talent was fascinating, and she wondered what Vinni's Flair looked like when he was having a vision. Small of her, she knew, but she'd never had the lovely fun of knowing and experimenting with her Flair after Second Passage.

"I think we should all get back to bed," Cratag said.

"It's not even grown-up RetireBell," Avellana said.

Vinni moved to her. "Do you want some more bedtime tea, Avellana?"

"No. And I don't want stories, either." She shot a look at Signet. "And if she wanted me to sleep, she shouldn't have come poking at me mentally."

"I'm sorry," Signet said. She nodded to Vinni also. "Like those who are just developing their Flair, I was experimenting with it."

The boy's expression cleared, turned interested. He smiled. "We should talk, T'Ash—"

"Bedtime for Avellana and T'Vine." Hanes clumped in, perfectly groomed, his face set in benevolent lines that didn't match the irritation radiating from him.

"I won't be able to sleep," Avellana said.

"Sure you will," Hanes said. He plucked her away from Cratag. "Rhyz and Flora and Du and . . ." he looked around.

"Beadle," Cratag said, "is out enjoying adventures."

"Well." Hanes jiggled the little girl as if jollying her from her pout. "All the other Fams will come and tell you Fam stories." He looked at the cats and the housefluff. "Won't you?"

Of course, Flora said, hopping along after them.

Of course, Rhyz said, purring. *My favorite thing, telling you all My great adventures.*

Signet thought she heard a reluctant giggle from Avellana.

Du trotted in, licking his chops. He'd obviously had a quick snack from the no-time in Signet's suite. He sniffed, then rubbed back and forth across Signet's ankles before catching up with the others. *She has not heard any of My stories yet, and they are exceptional.*

Without looking back, Hanes waved a hand at them.

Signet sighed. "Even though he has some strict ideas, Hanes is good with those two children."

"Yes," Cratag said, pacing. "I've already done my house check," he grumbled. "If I was at T'Hawthorn Residence, I'd get a couple of men from the night guard and spar."

He needed physical action.

All her senses gave one last whirl then settled into pure sexual yearning.

Be bold.

She caught his hand with hers. It was hot and made her hotter. "Dance with me."

Sixteen

*S*uddenly the night hummed with possibilities, and Cratag's need for action changed into something a lot more basic—lust.

"I'd love to dance with you," he said, responding to the slightest pressure of her fingers, and followed her downstairs. She trailed her fingers on the wide bannister, very ladylike, but his gaze was focused on her ass, which was all tempting female. As soon as they reached the base of the staircase, she pivoted into a close dance hold. He kept step and swept her into an intimate dance. The Residence piped lush, romantic music into the grand hall.

She was finally in his arms. He could hold her and move with her and anyone watching would believe them to be respectably dancing.

Hardly.

His gaze was focused on her face, looking at the rim of gold around the irises of her eyes. He thought his expression was as granite as his shaft since he was trying desperately to be a gentleman and not back her up against the closest wall.

She smiled, and it seemed tender, and he knew he was losing his wits. The beat of the music thrummed through his blood until he was moving fast, spinning them down the wide north corridor to the warm and private dark.

*I*t took all Signet's skill to keep up with Cratag. She didn't think he knew he was using Flair to quickstep down the hall. He seemed impassive, but she could feel the heat emanating from him, smell the scent of the man—physical and even the elusive *other* fragrance of his Flair. With him, her senses expanded.

His body beneath his loose shirt and work clothes was all tense muscle. His dancing lacked his usual fluidity and was raw determination. As they whirled down the hallway, she murmured in his mind, *The ResidenceDen has a large, soft sofa that I'm very fond of.* She suppressed a giggle. Now she knew why her parents had had couches or lounges or reclining twoseats in nearly every room.

She felt him shudder. Her thoughts began to fade beneath the onslaught of rising desire. She was breathing rapidly, and not just from the dance. She needed him, felt empty places inside her that he could fill. Not only her body, but the caring of another—a man—for a woman who was his lover. Cratag would give her that. A connection with a man after so very long. Not just simple and casual sex, but an affair based on respect. And he wouldn't leave her afterward.

Now she understood that idea had been keeping her from intimate relationships for long years. The moment she met an attractive man she'd consider whether there was any way for him to disappear from her life. All too often the answer was "yes." Another past mistake to be ashamed of, if she let herself.

But desire and Cratag and the liquefying of her body . . . and Cratag's thick sex against her . . . and the yearning for the climb to ecstasy and his thudding heart against hers made thought disappear.

The door opened to the ResidenceDen, and Cratag spun them in, dipped her until she slid onto the leather couch. He followed her down, heavy, wonderful. His mouth was at her neck, nibbling, and she'd never realized how sensitive she was there. She slid her hand down the front tab of his tunic, opening it, gliding her hands around his already damp sides to his back, smooth of hair but rough with the occasional scar. Her insides clenched. She cared for this man, cared that he'd been hurt and suffered pain.

His teeth closed gently on her earlobe, tugged, and a bolt of sheer passion flamed into her core. All that mattered was touching him, arching against him to press her needy flesh against his. Whimpering moans escaped her, and her hands explored the steel of his biceps. She moved against him, trying to settle his arousal where she wanted it. There was a ripping sound and coolness as her robe fell away. Her arms were still caught in the sleeves, and she ached for all her skin against his. Her arms, her legs, all.

His fingers curved into the waistband of her pantlettes, and his hand was hot against her hip. He yanked, and the cloth ripped, and she thrilled. Then his clothes were open, and he pressed into her, and she screamed in delight at the sensation of slick desire, the sense of utter fulfillment. Of closeness.

She set her fingers in his hard butt and grabbed on, felt the flex of him as his hips pumped, caressing her.

Bliss came fast and fierce and wild, and she exploded and spun away. Before she could draw more than a couple of breaths a riptide took her fragments, melded her, then shattered her again in a pleasure so intense she thought she might be another star exploding in the night sky.

A few minutes later her ears stopped ringing and she heard his ragged breathing. She opened her eyes to a moonslit room of gray and silver shadows and night. Cratag's eyes were closed, his smile that of a man savoring an experience. Her arms clamped around him tight. She wanted to keep this experience in her memory always. He didn't seem to notice the extra pressure, but that was fine. Her arms encompassed all she needed tonight.

"Wonderful," she murmured and liked the low, throaty sound of her voice.

He stiffened. "I'm too heavy."

"No." She paused. Was he withdrawing again as he had earlier in the day? She wouldn't ask and spoil the moment. Perhaps she'd been imagining it. He'd been worried about Laev Hawthorn, and the last few days had been packed with change for Cratag, too. "No," she repeated. "I'm glad you're here, that we're together here." Finally.

"If you're glad, I'm glad," he said gruffly, then added as he began removing himself gently from her with long stretching motions. "I am damn near ecstatic. Was—was ecstatic."

She chuckled, reached out, and let her fingers trail down his thigh from hip to knee. Noticed black against the skin of his arm. "You have body art!" She was delighted.

He grunted, glanced at his biceps. "No. List of merchant Families I guarded. References and . . . identifying marks."

If he'd been killed and other parts of his body were unrecognizable. She swallowed.

"They're only good for five years. They'll go away soon."

"Oh." She yanked her mind to the present. "There's a washroom . . ." but he'd already headed there. Of course he would remember the layout of the house; he'd been through it on his walks. She found a smile. She'd given him an excellent alternative for those walks.

Stretching, she couldn't recall feeling quite as good as she did for a long time. Longer than a long time, years, eons, her whole life. The man was a fabulous lover.

Before she knew it, he was back and, to her disappointment, dressed. His face was in shadows, but he draped her robe around her. "Sorry for the tear, and I can't mend—"

She'd already repaired the rips, though she had nearly been sentimental and brain-softened-by-sex enough to let them be.

"Done, then," he said. She didn't know what he meant. Whether she was finished weaving the fabric back together with Flair, or they were done with sex . . . surely not? She refused to think so, refused to let him think so. "Done? No, we aren't."

He smiled slowly then and she returned it. Offering his hand, he said, "Let's go upstairs then, to bed." He hesitated then said deliberately, "Your bed."

"Yes."

His left hand settled heavily, intimately on her hip, he laced the fingers of his right hand with hers and pulled her close and swept her around and around. Once again her feet barely touched the floor; he was using his physical strength and natural Flair. The door opened and they danced through it.

This time his gaze was locked on hers, eyes gleaming. His body brushed hers, tantalizing her until she was glad he held on tightly, her knees were so weak.

*T*he second bout of sex—*making love—sharing themselves—sex*— more!—was better than the first. Though Cratag thought a permanent smile was on his face, his thoughts hazing toward sleep had a hint of grimness to them. He didn't figure his desire for Signet would be satisfied for a long time. Maybe the rest of his life. No. That couldn't be true. Wouldn't do to start imagining himself as part of her life, how he could fit his life to hers—and it would be him doing the compromising.

But then she snuffled in her sleep, and her hand rubbed his chest over his heart, and he let himself sink into soft sleep.

A mind screech of pure terror hit Cratag. He jerked. His sister? No! He gasped awake. Choked.

No, she was dead. He'd failed there.

But someone who was linked to him. His hand shot out. Signet was still beside him.

"*Who?*" he yelled, mind and voice.

Signet bolted straight up, stared at him.

A keening yowl, subsiding into whimpering.

Beadle!

His lack of Flair had never frustrated Cratag more. "Where are you? 'Port to me!" He couldn't get an image from the cat, nothing but dark and fear and the knowledge he was hiding from a hunter that was ripping into something else.

Fligger.

Signet jumped from the bed, heading toward her balcony. Cratag moved instinctively, blocking her from throwing the doors to the night wide. "Stop."

"Beadle," she cried, "he's on the beach. There's something out there."

"We'll get to him." He yanked on his clothes.

Signet threw up her arms, said, "Whirlwind spell," and wind-Flair spun around her. When it stopped, she was dressed, her hair arranged in a fancy braid. He was out of her bedroom door, through the sitting room, running.

He could hear nothing from Beadle over the pounding of his heart. Surely he'd have felt if the Fam had died.

Vinni met them on the landing.

"Stay inside," Cratag ordered. "Where's Hanes?" The man should have heard the commotion. Or maybe the rooms were too well insulated. Hell.

Vinni just shrugged and slapped his ass on the wide bannister, zooming down with Flair pushing him.

Cratag took the stairs three at a jump. "Call Hanes!"

"I don't need—"

"Call him!"

Hanes! We're heading to the beach. Vinni glared at Cratag, jerked a nod.

Cratag grunted. Hanes didn't know as much as he needed to teleport to the beach. Neither did Vinni, and the boy was running flat out. Both of them were behind Signet. Cratag hadn't seen her move.

A yell came from above. Hanes. Cratag didn't spare a glance. All his being was focused on Beadle's soft mewls. He was alive!

Watch Avellana! Vinni shouted.

They raced to the door nearest the beach. When Signet threw open the door, he followed her through.

She spun and stopped. "I'm 'porting down." Her face was pale and set.

"No!" He couldn't bear that they'd both be in danger.

"I know the beach in all times, all weathers. I'm going!"

He grabbed for her, but she was gone before he could put a weapon in her hand.

Swearing all the way, he put on speed, hurdled the gate to the beach steps, sprinted down.

Twinmoonslight glinted on the ocean, on the sand. A slim black shadow ran toward an outcropping of rocks.

Then Cratag saw it. A monster.

Rising from the ocean in a huge spherical shape, waving scaly tentacles. One of them held the mangled remains of . . . something . . . somethings. Another lashed out for Signet.

Cratag heard his own howl, but she'd dodged. Somehow. Flair. Safe. Lord and Lady. Lady and Lord, keep her safe.

She stumbled, two tentacles grabbed. She 'ported, a short little hop. Here. Then there. Cratag couldn't keep track of her as a shadow darting in and out of the boulders. Going to where Beadle huddled, terrified.

Then Cratag was finally there, his blazer in his hand. The one with the grip that wouldn't slip in his sweaty palm.

He ran toward her, yelling his lungs out to attract the monster's attention.

It swiveled toward him.

Seventeen

He *fired his blazer, once, twice, at the thing. Bright rays of energy* streaked through the night, striking. A bitter smell came from the sea. The monster shrieked, thrashed.

Rose and loomed, blotting out stars. A whippy black tentacle slashed near, sending sand stinging against him. He drew his sword, cut off a meter of the thing. Dark ichor spurted.

Keening.

Yelling from Signet and howling from Beadle. "Go home!" Cratag shouted, jumped away from the bloody tentacle, whirled and aimed for an eye, got it.

The monster wavered, rocked in the sea. More stench.

Cratag fired again, slicing through another tentacle.

With a horrible shriek, the grumtud disappeared under the waves, churning water. A white wake showed it zooming toward the open ocean.

Beadle ran and leapt into Cratag's arms. He felt wetness. Sea or blood?

Then warmth and softness came against his back, spicy fragrance, Signet. Her arms twined around his waist. *I'll 'port us back to the teleportation pad on three.*

His muscles stayed rigid. He couldn't relax, could only blank his mind and hope that helped.

Seconds later they were in the small panelled room. The door was open, and beyond the threshold Hanes waited, blazer out.

"No danger." Cratag's voice was guttural. He was receiving flashes of memory, of emotion from Beadle. Dark and bright. Dark sea, bright moons. Dark blood, bright teeth.

Cratag had experience in racheting down from a battle high, but Beadle was all feral animal. Attack! No, too big. Hide. Hide. Hide.

Hanes nodded at them, resheathed his blazer and turned to stride toward the sitting room.

The lights of the hallway hurt Cratag's dilated eyes. Beadle hissed, too. The whole Residence was bright.

"Lower the lights, please, to cloudy day," Signet said, her voice not quite steady. Cratag was getting nothing through their link. She had herself wrapped tight, and he felt regret. Then she hooked an arm in his and pulled him after Hanes to the sitting room.

As soon as he entered the pretty, floral-scented sitting room, he felt the true blessing of this Residence, the caring that the inhabitants had for each other and the house. A breath shuddered from him. Beadle's bristling fur lowered, his muscles eased.

Vinni was already back. He and Avellana sat, hand in hand, on a twoseat in the opposite corner. Hanes stood before them.

"All's safe here," Cratag said. "Monster on the beach. Think it was a grumtud. Chased my Fam." Beadle trembled in his arms.

To Cratag's surprise everyone looked at Vinni. The boy flushed. "I didn't make an illusion."

"No illusion," Cratag said. "Real enough. I severed a tentacle and a quarter, hit an eye, too. It headed out to sea."

Signet said, "A grumtud. We get them sometimes, usually during the day." She shivered.

Hanes nodded again. "Sort of smart, grumtuds, probably won't be back." He went to sit in a chair, still watchful. He, too, was controlling the release of battle tension.

"Oh, Beadle!" Signet crooned. "You're frightened and dirty." She reached out and he hissed at her. She pulled her hand back.

"Ssshhhh." Cratag found himself rocking the cat in his arms. "You're safe now."

Beach was scary. Terrible thing. Ate 'coons. Two, three. Almost me. Run, hide, hide, hide. FamMan! He ducked his head into the corner of Cratag's elbow, burrowing in.

"Outside can be scary," Avellana nodded.

"It's not always fun," Vinni said.

Both their gazes were understanding. Realization hit Cratag, he met Signet's eyes and saw knowledge in hers. Of all the folks in the Residence, the most innocent had been Beadle.

Once.

Beadle would never think of outside and the beach as only fun and adventure again. He'd lost a little of his joyousness. Something Cratag—and Signet—mourned and would have prolonged for him, had they known how.

Lost innocence.

Beadle had always felt safe and protected—before. Cratag had failed to protect his Fam, as he'd failed his sister.

"Perhaps we should call D'Ash," Signet said.

Only FamMan, Beadle said. He didn't look at the others, rubbed his head on Cratag's arm. His adrenaline was slowly subsiding, he was more intelligent Fam than feral animal.

Cratag's battle readiness lessened. He'd deal with the aftermath tonight, though. "Let's look at you," Cratag said.

Signet went to a side table and moved knickknacks from it.

Cratag carefully placed Beadle on his paws. The cat's white face was gray with dirt, sand clung to much of his hair, and some tufts on his sides stuck out in matted clumps.

"Some scratches, I think," Signet said. She crossed to a wall cabinet and opened it, Cratag's nose twitched at the smell of a medical no-time. Coming back with a softleaf that was gently steaming, she glanced at Beadle then handed the cloth to Cratag.

Making soothing noises that sounded odd to himself, Cratag took the softleaf and drew it over Beadle.

The cat hissed. *Don't want cleaned. Can do it Myself. Want a pillow. Want to sleep. Want to sleep lots. Inside. Near to FamMan.*

"Right," Cratag said.

There was a loud sniff. *He can't have any of My pillows*, Du said.

"I'll get one from the storage closet," Signet said, and Cratag watched as she left the room, then turned to see Hanes's knowing grin.

Cratag ignored him and continued to pet Beadle.

Vinni coughed. "Since you all insulted me by thinking I called that illusion, I will demonstrate how much control I have of my creative Flair." A huge book appeared before the windows, taking up the space from floor to ceiling. Vinni was trying to soothe them. Cratag let out a breath. Mentally he murmured to the Residence, *Draw all the curtains on this room.* Silently cloth slid over the windows, and the room seemed cheerier. He went to a wide chair and sat down with Beadle.

Pages of the book colored an antique yellow flipped, and Vinni said, "I've fashioned the book through illusion as a frame for a viz that D'Marigold Residence will play." So this wasn't a totally new idea of Vinni's, but something he had planned.

A very interesting volume, the Residence said.

Another page flipped, and the title shone in flowing script that Cratag could barely read. He was better at printing. Some three-dimensional cats at the bottom of the sheet rolled and played.

Vinni read the title, "*The History of Cats.*"

Beadle pricked up his ears, twitched his whiskers, settled further into Cratag's lap with a couple of kneadsing of his thighs. Du and Rhyz purred in approval. Avellana clapped her hands and sent Vinni an adoring look. "It's the book from the starship that tells the story of cats all the way from the ancientest days of old Earth."

"Good tales," Hanes punned, winking at Cratag, but he took a chair and sank into it, with a stoic expression. Cratag got the impression that he'd seen part of *The History of Cats* before. Maybe more than once. Cratag recalled how Laev had had a particular viz he watched over and over until Cratag thought he could still recite portions of the dialogue.

Signet walked back into the room and stopped at the sight of the huge illusion. She held a rectangular pillow the size of her torso of bright red velvet with brighter gold piping and four gold tassels. "*The History of Cats*. I've heard of this book viz." She glanced at Cratag. *It goes on for three septhours.*

His eyes widened at the news. He swallowed. *The Fams and children will fall asleep soon*, he said, hoping it was true. *Hanes is unconcerned and he wouldn't be if staying up and watching would affect Vinni adversely.*

Yes, Signet said, *tomorrow is Playday. Avellana's schedule is flexible and undemanding.*

Smiling, Signet pulled the empty table close to Cratag, set the pillow on it. "Fasten," she murmured. A good idea since the wood of the table was highly polished.

Beadle tore himself away from a story of a cat chasing mice and playing with a girl at the dawn of Earthan time to eye the large pillow. *My own pillow.*

"Of course," Signet said. "A gift from me and the Residence for staying with us."

Beadle's eyes widened, he grinned and craned his neck to sniff at it. *It smells like plant stuff. If it is Mine, it will smell like *Me.** He rose to his paws, rubbed his head under Cratag's chin, then leapt for the pillow, circling and pawing it before curling up, nose on paws, and continuing to watch the viz. Cratag missed his Fam, but liked that the cat was forgetting his experience and was content, though it hadn't occurred to him to give Beadle a gift.

As if sensing his thoughts, a bit of humor came from Signet. *Du has informed me that Fams get collars from their person as gifts. Apparently this trend was set by T'Ash.*

Cratag winced at the recollection that T'Ash's cat, a jeweler's cat, had an emerald collar.

A smile lurked on Signet's lips. She perched on the arm of Cratag's chair, put her hand on his shoulder. *I consulted Danith D'Ash, who matched us with our Fams, and she said that this new tradition has the rule that a Fam must be loving for three months, so we have some time.*

"I can order a collar now," Cratag murmured.

Beadle looked at him and grinned, and it was almost as goofy as it had been. He was bouncing back. He twitched his tail. *I liked the Fam collar of Lahsin Holly's hound.*

Cratag looked at Signet. She shook her head. She hadn't noticed it either.

Outside stuff, Beadle said helpfully. *Good smelling nuts and seeds.* He cocked his head, but his gaze drained a little of assurance. *Maybe when I go back to the beach, some shells.*

"Outside can be scary," Signet agreed. "But we love you and will always help you."

Cratag blinked . . . was it so easy for Signet to love? And how did he feel about that? He didn't know.

I can choose My own shells for My necklace . . . later, Beadle said, then the viz caught his attention again, when a black cat with a gold collar leapt across the pages.

Signet telepathically said, *I think my Du has something like that in mind, but I think amethyst would look better against his fur.*

Said so easily, without a thought for cost. When Beadle had mentioned collars, Cratag's mind had immediately gone to the state of his finances. Very healthy. He could have purchased a nice house, even a shop like his parents', but he didn't think he'd ever have that casual not-counting-cost that old noble houses did. Beadle looked good on that red pillow. Rubies or garnets would be nice on him.

Signet would wear sapphires well. He wondered if she had some. Probably. Her House was centuries old, probably had a whole load of jewels for every coloring. He could give her nothing she didn't already own or couldn't buy herself.

Vinni drifted up to Cratag. "Can I speak with you?"

Cratag didn't want to leave the coziness of the sitting room, but Signet had moved from the arm of his chair. He glanced at Hanes, who looked only half awake, the same as Avellana and her cat, sagging in the corner of the upright twoseat.

"Sure." Cratag rose, hiding his reluctance. "We can talk in my sitting room."

As soon as he moved away from his chair, Signet slipped into it with a mischievous look, and wiggled her butt. "Mmmm, cozy."

He'd thought so, but now she'd put thoughts of sex back in his head. Not that that was difficult around her.

Vinni coughed.

Cratag turned away and gestured to the door, followed Vinni down the hallway to the door of his own sitting room. Vinni didn't attempt to go in, which was wise, since Cratag had had the Residence put an alarm on the door latch.

When they entered the gray and maroon room and moved into a more masculine atmosphere, Cratag couldn't say whether he preferred it or not. Easier to talk to the boy, though. Cratag pulled the door shut until he heard it click.

The Residence had turned on lamps that bathed the room in mellow light. The maroon curtains were drawn against the night. He waved the boy toward a leather wing chair, but Vinni didn't sit. He looked up at Cratag. "You didn't know about the illusion thing."

"I still don't."

Vinni grimaced. "I played a joke on Holm HollyHeir during the feud." Vinni hunched a shoulder. "My Flair told me to interfere. It seemed the right thing to do at the time. A monster rose from the sea and chased a Fam."

Hair rose on the back of Cratag's neck . . . had Vinni used the sense of *this time* to fashion *that* illusion. But Cratag knew very little about Flair, didn't know if that would have happened. So he just said, "The Hawthorns were too preoccupied with the feud to talk about practical jokes. If T'Hawthorn or his son knew of this incident, they didn't tell me."

"Everyone else recalls. You saw how they all looked at me when they heard a sea monster had attacked Beadle on the beach. How long will that stupid mistake haunt me?" Vinni grumbled.

Cratag put his hand on Vinni's shoulder, much as he had Laev's years before. He'd forgotten how small a thirteen-year-old boy's shoulder could be, just the width of Cratag's palm. His fingers and thumb lay on the boy's chest and back. More vulnerable than he seemed with his intelligence and great Flair. "Never be surprised when an old mistake comes back to bite you on the ass. And the more people who know about the mistake, the more you'll hear about it."

Vinni was silent for a minute. "I scared Fams and FirstLevel Healer Lark and had Holm HollyHeir fighting an illusion. All the Hollys and Heathers and Hazels heard the story right away and that means gossip went the rounds. I heard from *every one* of the FirstFamilies about how bad my behavior was, how I'd used my Flair inappropriately." He rubbed his ears as if they still rung from scolds. "Mine was a stupid kid's mistake."

"Sounds like it," Cratag said.

"I was only nine, a long time ago."

Four years didn't seem that long ago to Cratag.

Vinni sighed, and Cratag lifted his hand. The boy went to a chair and sat. "Could be worse," Vinni said. "I didn't actually hurt anyone, just scared them." His jaw set. "Seemed the thing to do at the time," he repeated. He glanced at Cratag, who wasn't sure of the color of the teen's eyes, but they weren't the regular hazel. Cratag ignored the frisson along his nerves.

"My Flair didn't settle down for another year or so." Flames flickered into being in the fireplace, mesmerizing, and Vinni watched them. "Could have been worse. Only a little while later Laev wounded D'Holly, wasn't it?"

That had occurred to Cratag. "Yes, unlike your error, that isn't a teasing matter, so we don't talk about it much."

"Just one of those past events that will haunt Laev the rest of his life. Another stupid kid's error that was nearly fatal."

"Yes."

"When we're together, the other boys and I during training, we don't talk about it much, either, but we all know, even the Clovers, now. We pretty much all know stuff about each other."

"A community is like that, whether it's FirstFamily circles in Druida or a small village."

"Huh." Vinni stared at the flames and Cratag moved a chair closer to Vinni's and sat. Vinni smiled at him, a boy's smile that Cratag realized he wouldn't see anymore from Laev.

"Past events that loom large," Vinni mused. "I don't think of those often. I think mostly of the present and the future."

"Your gift," Cratag said.

"Yeah, until a past mistake comes back to bite me on the ass." He rolled the words, man-words not used much in his household of older ladies. Then his shoulders shifted again as he sighed. "Could have been worse, could have to deal with something like Laev's. More than just the FirstFamiles, most of the nobles will always remember Laev's blunder."

Cratag wondered how Laev was doing, if that mistake would haunt him during his Passages. From what Cratag understood of the dream fugues, he was certain of it, despite all the mind Healing and counseling they'd had. Again he ached to be near his "younger brother." But the boy next to him was shivering a little now and needed his care, as did the young girl in the sitting room. It was good to be needed.

"Residence, increase the heat by five degrees."

The air warmed immediately. "Thank you," Cratag and Vinni said in unison.

"My mistake was stupid, Laev's was worse, but . . . poor Antenn." Vinni frowned.

"Antenn Blackthorn?"

"Right. His biological older brother murdered some FirstFamily lords and ladies. Burned them up." Vinni shuddered. "That's how

I became T'Vine; old D'Vine died then. Antenn won't ever be allowed to forget that. Not even his fault."

"Rough," Cratag said. He'd heard stories of that event, but it had been before he'd arrived in Druida.

"Yeah. Being known for a stupid sea monster illusion is not so bad." Vinni sounded more cheerful. He glanced at Cratag and said, "Thank you for listening."

Another boy he was growing close to, forming a friendship with. Cratag nodded. "Anytime," he said and meant it.

Vinni met his eyes and nodded back.

A knock came at the door. "Enter," Cratag said.

Hanes opened the door but didn't come in. He carried a sleeping Avellana on his shoulder. "I'm putting Avellana to bed. Then, T'Vine, we should return to T'Vine Residence."

Vinni stilled, his face went expressionless.

Hanes said, "You asked if we could stay tonight because you sensed an upset coming. That's happened. Let's go back home."

Now Cratag froze himself. He'd missed whatever previous byplay there'd been between the two, and didn't like that. Something in the air stirred his own instincts.

When Vinni didn't answer, Hanes pressed, "Did you *see* anything else happening tonight?"

Vinni closed his eyes, they moved under his lids, then he lifted his lashes. "No." But he sounded uncertain.

"We're leaving." Hanes didn't catch the boy's hesitancy or ignored it. The bodyguard looked at Cratag. "We'll teleport."

"Of course," Cratag said. Maybe Vinni hadn't had a vision, but just a hunch. Cratag would have trusted one of Vinni's hunches as much as his own.

Vinni stood. Cratag thought the youngster suppressed a sigh. At being young enough that he had to mind adults against his own judgment? Vinni matched Cratag's gaze and said mentally, privately. *Please always call me "Vinni."*

Yes, Cratag replied.

"Goodnight, Cratag."

"Goodnight, Vinni, good dreams. Goodnight, Hanes."

"'Night." Hanes smiled. "D'Marigold has retired."

So much for more sex. Cratag couldn't envision himself tip-toeing across the room back to Signet's bed. She needed rest, too. They'd all been through an ordeal. She'd actually drawn the monster away from Beadle. So brave. Cratag didn't want to remember those sweaty, terror-filled moments, but didn't think they'd fade anytime soon.

"Your Fam is snoozing on his pillow with the Residence singing lullabies to him, too lazy to move," Hanes said.

Cratag smiled. He followed Vinni to the door and watched as they entered Avellana's suite to put her to bed and came back out. Hanes marched, and Vinni trudged to the teleportation room. The door closed behind them. Cratag didn't hear them leave, but after a minute there was a *distance* between him and Vinni, and himself and Hanes, that hadn't been there before.

Deep quiet descended, and the flames in the fireplace had gone out by the time Cratag turned back to the room, as if the Residence believed Cratag wasn't interested in the warmth.

Or as if it knew he'd walk the halls once more.

It was going to be one of those nights that he didn't sleep. When memories would haunt him in the dark hours.

Eighteen

*M*emories *would come.*

Cratag stood briefly under the waterfall and changed into his oldest workout clothes, soft from many cleansings.

He went down the hall, paused outside Signet's door. If she was awake and tense . . . but she wasn't. The bond between them was already strong enough for him to know she was asleep and dreaming . . . in color. He rarely dreamt in color, or recalled his dreams.

Then he checked on Beadle. The sitting room was dim but not dark, and Beadle was curled up asleep—not laying on his back with his vulnerable belly showing. Cratag sensed he slept lightly. The Residence was singing to him . . . or sending low, crystal notes of sound through the room that Cratag knew were meant to soothe and Heal.

He examined the state of the shields around the tower, all sturdy, impenetrable. The drapes closed out the darkness and spring cold. Cratag shut the glass doors to the hallway and stooped to make sure the one bottom pane that was a pet door opened and closed freely if Beadle needed to bolt.

Then he walked through the house, to ease himself—listening to the sound of the surf, appreciating the light of the stars and moons sifting through the many windows.

The Residence, of course, was too courteous to remind him it could protect itself and its inhabitants. He hesitated outside Signet's meditation room. She'd given him permission to use the room, but his brain rested better when he was on his feet and moving. Besides, he could *feel* her vibrations lingering in the room, as if the essence of her slid along and sank into his skin. It made him want her more. Not tonight. Memories and melancholy hovered.

The after-battle letdown had arrived.

So he paced the Residence for a circuit until the floor creaked under him—a signal that the house wanted him to stop his wandering—then reluctantly retired to his sitting room.

For the first time since he'd arrived, he went to the built-in bar and looked at the bottles. There was some very good scotch that had obviously belonged to the previous inhabitant and was older than Cratag was. He contemplated it; he'd never had such a quality drink. Then he shrugged. He didn't think the Residence or Signet would miss it. So he poured a shot and tasted. It went down smooth and warmed his belly.

He glanced around the room, opened the drapes. Though he wanted the fire, he also wanted the night sky. He took the chair he'd angled close to the window that looked toward the Marigolds's sacred grove. Sometimes he thought he could feel a slight emanation from the place, and if he closed his eyes and focused, it would smell rich and green and extraordinary.

Green like a farm would be. His people hadn't had a sacred grove, hadn't been farmers but shopkeepers in a small town . . . if they'd had a farm he might still be in the south.

And his sister, Estiva, might still be alive and not buried in a mass grave.

Their family would have had a house instead of four rooms over the shop. She'd have stayed for him, and he'd have taken care of her, made a place for her.

Instead she'd run off with an adventurer, a feckless man who hadn't cared for her when she'd gotten a fever and dragged after him, then died.

But Cratag had found her grave and later found the fliggering bastard and challenged him to a duel. He rubbed his shoulder and the old blazer scar. The guy had been fast and sneaky, but he'd also been in a whole lot of pain when Cratag had left him curled up from a low-level blazer shot to the balls. Would think a great deal longer before he ran off with another woman, Cratag hoped. And wouldn't be able to sire any more fliggering sons like himself.

When Cratag had held his fearful cat in his arms, he'd recalled the joy his older sister had had, the excitement in her eyes and her smile the last time he'd seen her. He was thirteen and too young and strong and needed in the shop to leave.

Estiva had just had her Second Passage and was an adult and in love. Cratag had known the man was no good, but she hadn't listened, and had gone away. She'd kept in touch with scries to him as they wandered, and he'd seen her joy fade and worry come to the back of her eyes. As the year passed before he left, too, he had seen her age. He'd hated it.

Estiva had been the best part of his childhood, had made life with their dour parents bearable. He should have been able to protect her. Why hadn't he been born first? If he'd been older . . . such was life and fate and destiny, and he didn't like it.

She'd been gone more than two decades now, and he still felt her loss.

He hadn't recognized Beadle's innocence and joy until it, too, was gone.

Things trickled through his fingers when he wanted to grab and hold on.

He dragged in a deep breath and stood and focused his gaze, all his senses on D'Marigold Sacred Grove. Wonderful. Peaceful. He stayed in the moment until his emotions were as serene.

Then he thought back to his conversation with Vinni, and his own mistakes. Could be worse. He'd made mistakes but they were long ago and beneath the notice of any noble. Now he was known as T'Hawthorn's Chief of Guards.

That was good.

For a second time that night a scream split the air. His hackles raised. Vinni's and his own hunches had come true. This night would not stay quiet.

A horrible yowl echoed through the Residence. Signet leapt from her bedsponge, fumbled on clothes.

Rhyz, Avellana's Fam, shrieked, *Passage is here*!

Signet raced to the door. Despite her hurry, it opened to show Cratag just outside. In his deep, calm voice he said, "I've learned a little about Passage, the full dream fugues are usually presaged by some short bursts of disorientation."

Signet whooshed out a sigh. "Yes, you're right. A few minutes or a septhour or so of chills and fever before the real intensity of a full-out dreamquest. And Passages are usually three long fugues."

He nodded. "You'll be the expert in this situation, like I am with security. Let me know how I can help."

Another wash of relief. She wasn't alone, and she *had* gone through these herself. They'd been nasty, but only a little dangerous.

But when they got to Avellana's room, the worst was confirmed. The child's body was convulsing in a seizure, and Signet sensed this was no precursor, but the real thing. It would be septhours before they came through this.

If they did.

Do not worry, I am here, Du said. *I will help.*

And I. Rhyz spit at Du. *She is My FamGirl.* His claws were hooked into her nightgown.

Avellana went limp, but her small chest rose and fell with hard breaths.

"Avellana!" Cratag snapped, demanding a response.

The girl said nothing, made no sign she was aware of any of them. Signet slid onto the bedsponge, gathering Avellana's sweaty body close and recalling her own Passages. "Residence, prepare to heat and cool this room as necessary . . ." Signet met Cratag's gaze. It was serious, but full of confidence in her. That buoyed her.

"I understand," said the Residence. A moment later a small, freshening breeze wafted through the room, carrying the scent of the sea mixed with other herbs that soothed.

Cratag sniffed. "Smells like old BalmHeal Residence."

"BalmHeal Residence is the authority on how a Residence can help Passage. I consulted it," D'Marigold Residence said. The curtains lightly slapped the wall in punctuation. "I transferred a goodly amount of funds."

"Fine," Signet said, settling herself back on large pillows that propped her up, moving Avellana. Signet sat around the girl, legs outside the child's, bringing the girl's torso back on hers, lining her arms along Avellana's.

Rhyz crawled into Avellana's lap, and Du stretched out along Signet's left thigh.

Beadle trotted in through the door they'd left open, stropped Cratag's ankles in greeting, and tilted his head. *I have never seen Passage. This will be interesting.* He hopped onto the bedsponge, lying along Signet's right thigh, revving his purr until his body vibrated against her leg. More support.

Once again she met Cratag's eyes. He nodded and sat on a chair higher than the bedsponge, between the door to Avellana's sitting room and the bed. Guarding them.

Avellana began to tremble.

"Rhyz?" Signet asked.

I cannot feel her, he said mournfully. *I cannot reach her. She has gone beyond me.*

Signet's body tensed, and she had to make an effort to relax. Then she nodded, leaned back against the pillows, and closed her eyes. She followed the link she and Avellana had made between them these last few days, plunging down into Avellana's mind.

Down into darkness seething with red flashes. Down too deep. Avellana was avoiding Passage, and if she didn't integrate her great psi talent with the rest of herself during these dreamstates, she would die.

Avellana! Signet called.

No response.

Signet stopped, as eerie, distorted voices and images battered against her. Feelings of helplessness overwhelmed her, a child's helplessness. Fear and dependence on others to care for you—for Avellana. Little control of her own life.

Signet couldn't go on. If she did, she might lose herself and be unable to aid Avellana. But she couldn't feel Avellana's essential spark here. The brain, memories, but not the mind or spirit. *Avellana, hear me. Come to me.*

There was a whimpering sigh.

Avellana, we must work together! Your Passage is here. This is Signet. I will help. Pray the Lady and Lord that her Flair had already been helping. This was not a normal brain pattern. Why hadn't they thought to include visits from Healers to monitor Avellana's progress, Signet's catalyst Flair? Had she missed something in her study of Avellana's medical records that would have helped?

Too late now.

Avellana, come to me. Signet tried to make her mind-voice serene yet compelling. *It is time for your Passage to free some of your Flair. To determine your psi power and the strength of it. Your Flair is very strong, Avellana, but so are you. So am I.*

I'm afraid. In the distance, Signet thought she saw a small, blurry ball of light.

We can face your fear together. And Signet's own.

Outside is Passage, that sounded like Avellana's regular voice. *It is scary and ugly. I am ugly.*

We will face your Passage together. Passage is an essential part of growing up. And you aren't ugly. You are unique.

You know my brain patterns aren't normal.

Rhyz was there, his bond with Avellana stronger than Signet's, a thick rope of gold looping down toward that little spark. The cat snorted. *Everyone knows your brain is different. You are unique.* He used Signet's words. *Come to Us, Avellana. Think how much fun We will have with your new Flair. More 'porting for sure.*

Another plaintive cry. *It is scary out there, and it hurts, too.*

Rhyz and I will be here with you. Signet had gathered her Flair, now she released the bonds on it and the puffballs streamed down to Avellana. An instant later the child giggled. *What are these?*

They are manifestations of my Flair, Signet said.

They are beautiful. They are sticking to me, like a pretty robe!

They will help protect you. Signet sincerely hoped so. Could her Flair actually change the synapses in Avellana's brain? Forge new paths so she could function more normally? That was what everyone hoped.

That was the outcome Vinni T'Vine, the prophet, *saw.*

But she couldn't think of that, since Avellana's self flew toward her Fam and Signet. She just had enough time to see that her Flair balls had positioned themselves near Avellana's Flair—which Signet also saw in balls—helping or replacing those dark and damaged, mending the tiny filaments, sending energy down them until they sparked at the end. It wasn't complete, didn't appear as if all the damage would ever be healed, but it looked like some new puffballs of Avellana's own might be sprouting.

I am ready, Avellana said, her image solidifying into a serious little girl holding Rhyz, looking solemnly at Signet. Avellana heaved a big sigh. *I suppose we all must grow up.*

Signet found herself smiling, holding out her hand and her fingers being taken by the child. *It isn't as bad as you think.*

But the next instant, as they plunged into Avellana's Passage, was terrible.

They were high, high, and a tiny girl was giggling. Holding out her arms. "Fly, fly, fly!" she screamed. Avellana at three. At a second-story window.

Avellana now shrank into Signet, whimpering again. *Scary, painful.*

Signet gritted her teeth. *We will get through this.*

I don't want to! Avellana was clinging hard to Signet, Rhyz wrapped around her neck and shoulders, also hanging on.

They didn't have a choice; the tiny girl launched herself from the sill. For a moment it felt like they actually did fly—they hung . . .

Then gravity kicked in.

They dropped.

Screaming.

Not quite as fast as they should have.

Avellana's survival instincts drawing on her incipient Flair, 'porting them in bursts along a field. Signet curved over Avellana as if she could protect her from the accident that had happened long ago. If she could have changed it, she would have.

They hit hard and shattered.

The pain was total and shocking. Hideous beyond belief.

Every bone in her body felt broken, and her head smashed open.

Darkness swirled, but was not total unconsciousness. Shrieks and screams, sounding like those distorted voices Signet had heard before. Memories. Sobbing, shaky voices, lashing anger, horrible fear.

Pain.

Wind rushing by, more teleportation—this time by experts.

Tense voices, soft hands, people surrounding her. Probing, mending her injuries. The greatest Healers of the land.

Avellana-now closing down, closing out the pain imbuing her, the terror surrounding her.

No, that shouldn't be done.

Signet braced herself. *Open up, Avellana. You must let your Flair into you, let it rush through you.*

Pain! The feeling, an animalistic groan, not even a word.

We are here, we must live through this. It damaged your Flair, but you must open up and let your Flair in.

Noooo!

Do you wish to be crippled all your life! Signet was harsh through

desperation. Hadn't she crippled herself when she let every abandonment erode her self-confidence? *Open and accept your Flair,
your pain, your fear. You survived once, and are a wonderful, beautiful person. Survive again!*

Weeping, Avellana straightened from a fetal curl and stretched,
then flung her limbs wide.

Pain, fear. They suffered through it. Eons.

Signet's puffballs vanished. Into the dark? Or into Avellana? Or
back into Signet?

A rushing filled them, spun Signet away, until she barely hooked
Avellana's fingers with her own.

Avellana cried out, a sound of surprised wonder. Inhaled deeply.
"Aahhh."

Her real voice.

Signet jolted back into her own mind and body. Separate from
the girl, but holding her close. Breath ragged and rasping as if she'd
screamed for septhours, Signet opened her eyes. Her senses spun
around her as she saw the star pattern out the window that signaled
three septhours before dawn, smelled the scent of heavy incense,
finally blinked and saw a rumpled and unshaven Cratag on his knees,
leaning over them. "It's over," Signet said, and her lips cracked.

He closed his eyes and muttered a prayer, then opened them and
kissed her forehead. Dampness. Not from his kiss, but from her
sweat. She shifted and her muscles groaned as if they'd been tense
and stiff the whole night.

Avellana lolled from Signet's arms, and Cratag caught her, lifted
her, and placed her beside Signet on the bedsponge.

Forcing herself to move, Signet rolled away, then off the low
bedsponge onto the floor, rocked inelegantly onto her hands and
knees, and looked over to Avellana.

"She's sleeping naturally," Cratag said. His hand was on the
child's forehead. "She's fine, no more shivers or sweats."

"No convulsions?"

"Those stopped as soon as you took her into your arms," Cratag
said.

Signet wiped her sleeve across her forehead, wrinkled her nose
at the rumpled bed, her own sticky clothes. Avellana's nightgown
looked just as uncomfortable. Frowning, Signet said, "Let's take her
to the large bathing pool in my MistrysSuite."

Cratag nodded and lifted the child again.

Rhyz went over to a cabinet and dragged out another nightgown
for Avellana. *I was wonderful, but need a long grooming session.*
His prance back to them was more like a stagger.

Signet took the small gown. "Thank you, Master Fam."

Nodding, Rhyz stretched front and back then curled up on the
chair Cratag had vacated.

"The bed linens need to be changed, too," Signet said. She waved
at Cratag, "You go ahead, I'll be right along." Her smile was as
tired as the rest of her, and she ached clear through to her bones.
"I can change them with a few brief spellwords." She yanked the
old ones off the big bedsponge, went to a panel in the wall, and took
out new.

"Fine," Cratag said and left, as silently as ever, but moving
slowly as if the night had cost him, too. Du and Beadle dragged after
him.

Again Signet wiped her forehead with her arm, laid out the linens, and stumbled through the couplet to make the bedsponge twice
before she got it right. "Residence, open the windows and air the
suite out, then heat it so it's fresh and warm when we return in a
half-septhour."

"It will be done." The Residence sounded subdued.

"Thank you, you were a great help with the herbs and the
atmosphere." She didn't know, but she guessed that was so.

"Avellana is finished with her first fugue?" The Residence wanted
reassurance.

"Yes, I'm sure." Signet stuffed the old linens in the cleanser.
"We'll contact the Hazels later with the good news." She shook out
her arms and legs. "I'll bathe with Avellana and be right back."

She stumbled to the bath through a mist of exhaustion. After
Cratag withdrew, Signet undressed Avellana and herself, and bathed

them both in the shallow end of the pool. It took longer than she'd anticipated. After Avellana was dried and dressed, mumbling grumpily, they returned her to her rooms and her bed.

Dressed in a heavy robe, Signet stared down at the child. She should have felt triumphant, but didn't even feel relief, she was so tired.

Avellana was safe for now.

But just how much had Signet's Flair helped?

And would it continue to do so?

Nineteen

Signet bent down to smooth Avellana's clean hair, and the door flew open and D'Hazel shot in. "My baby!"

Signet hovered protectively over the girl. "She's in a deep, natural sleep." Now that others were here she felt pride surge through her, lifted her head, and managed a slight curve of lips. "I'm happy to say that her first full Passage fugue went well."

D'Hazel brushed by Signet, picked up her daughter, and cradled her. Tears overflowed the GreatLady's eyes. Her HeartMate came and set his hand on her shoulder, staring down at his little girl. D'Hazel choked something out, but Signet didn't understand the words.

"Avellana truly experienced and survived a complete fugue?" asked T'Hazel. "We were sleeping most of the time, but were linked. Stayed away until it was over, as per the contract."

"Yes." Signet rubbed her temples.

"What . . . what of . . . later?" T'Hazel asked.

Signet wanted to promise anything, everything. "I don't know." She swallowed. "If the dreamquests continue at this strength, we may be all right." She boosted her smile, glanced at a quiet Vinni, who had slipped through the door. "I've heard that HeartMates can help, and Vinni did not link with her tonight."

"I wasn't here. Hanes and I had gone back to T'Vine Residence. I was sleeping." He snapped the words. Obviously leaving had not been his idea. "Dreaming, but sleeping. I drank my nightly tea." He straightened his shoulders. "That stops now." His gaze scanned Avellana's relaxed and serene face. His own was pale, his freckles standing out. A mixture of expressions showed in his eyes, then his fingers clenched and unclenched. "I can't help very much," he choked out. "Not even the whole of one fugue. If I do, we will bond too closely, and she will never develop on her own, be forever crippled." He turned away and marched to the window to stare out at the night-dark sky, though Signet thought he watched them reflected in the glass.

D'Hazel sniffed. "We would like to take her home, let her sleep in her own bed until she wakes, surrounded by her Residence and her Family."

A GreatLady was pleading with *her?* Signet would have to look at her contract more closely. Maybe she was completely in charge of Avellana during her Passage. Right now the edge of an ocean of fatigue lapped at the back of her mind, ready to sweep her away. Not a great time to make decisions, but D'Hazel continued to cry silently, tears dripping on Avellana.

"Go," Signet said softly.

Rhyz jumped up to T'Hazel's shoulder. The man put one hand up to steady the cat, slipped his arm around his wife's waist, and turned into her—an intimate Family grouping that caused a pang of envy in Signet. Three seconds later they had teleported away.

"T'Vine," Hanes snapped.

Vinni stiffened but faced the room again. "Avellana's Passage came when I was at home, sleeping after that tea Auntie gave me." It was said with no accusation but with complete finality.

Hanes winced, went stiff as a soldier.

"We will rearrange matters," T'Vine said, every inch a GreatLord.

Signet believed him. This ordeal was maturing him, too. She looked at Cratag, who was impassive, but she sensed he was sympathetic to Vinni, more, had been aware that the two had left when she had not.

But that was the past, and the uncertain future was upon them.

"I'm ready to return home, too." Vinni walked over and stood next to Hanes, back straight, carriage noble. Then Vinni inclined his head toward Signet and said, "Good job. Thank you." He cleared his voice. "Did you get any sense of how many fugues Avellana will have to suffer through?"

Signet hadn't, and was about to shake her head when unconscious words rose to her lips. "Twice more."

Another nod from Vinni, and he, too, was gone. Hanes swore and followed, vanishing with a swoosh. No one had bothered with the teleportation room, but all knew exactly where they were going and that the arrival space would be empty. That was a discourtesy to Signet, but she didn't care. She only wanted bed.

Cratag still stood, silent, near Avellana's bed. His jaw flexed. "I'm sorry," he said.

The weariness was streaming closer, but she caught the tone of his voice, his body ready to fight. "You were wonderful," she said.

"I did nothing."

She didn't want to spend time and energy discussing this now, but it didn't seem as if she'd have a choice. "You were here, guarding us, providing me with a . . . a presence . . . to focus on, reminding me—more, connecting me *and* Avellana—to the real world. An anchor, a rock, a boulder. Thank you." Her voice ended on a whisper. The wave of exhaustion crashed into her. Her knees gave out.

He moved fast, catching her before she hit the ground.

"You need sleep, too," he said roughly, lifting her into his arms.

"Yes, please," she said, hooking one arm around his neck and leaning into the sturdiness of him. Her other hand was over his heart, and she could feel the gentle lift of his chest as he breathed, the even beat of his heart, as well as hear it. It comforted her like nothing else had in a long time. "Yes, please," she repeated, slurring her words. "Let's go to bed and sleep."

*E*motions churned inside Cratag as if the surface of his being had trembled and cracked, letting in hopes and fears and sensations and . . . maybe . . . even a little more Flair.

The idea was stupid. He *knew* who he was, knew his place in life, knew himself. He shouldn't have all these internal ructions, should he?

But he carried a sleeping Signet to her room, her bedsponge, and laid her down on it and thought that she really was a catalyst. No matter how stable and solid you might think yourself, change was a part of life that always occurred, despite what you wanted. Shook you up like an earthquake, and you dealt with what you had left.

He stripped the bathrobe from her and stared at her long, well-shaped limbs, her slender torso and round breasts, the beautiful slope of her shoulders and her aristocratic features. His woman, for a time.

And how that stirred him up, in all ways. Making him yearn, and consider, and plot. Maybe, if he was very lucky, he'd be able to keep her as a lover for a while.

He stripped and tore himself away from her to take a quick waterfall. The huge stall in her waterfall room was made of peach-colored marble with dark gold veins that glittered, and he wondered if they were real gold. The lady had plenty of gilt . . . more coming from D'Hazel, and even more once her Flair was accepted. He figured word would be circulating by now of Avellana's successful dreamquest.

Dreamquest. Fugue. He still didn't know what that meant, though as he'd watched the pair of females he'd grown close to struggle in the trance state, cold sweat slicked his back. He let the water rush over him and cleanse it away. As he ordered the 'fall off, he did know one thing. All his life he'd developed his physical skills. Now it was time to remember his rusty long-ago grovestudy lessons and practice meditating.

He dried off with a couplet that hadn't come so easily to him the week before. Maybe doing trance work wouldn't be so hard.

If Vinni couldn't go into the trance to help Signet and Avellana, maybe he, the boulder with little Flair, could help.

Sliding under the smooth linens and tucking Signet close to his body, he let out the pent-up sigh of relief that had been trapped inside him. Sleep beckoned.

Signet smelled good. His mind automatically "reached" for hers, touched it, and knew she slept dreamlessly. Beadle was chasing a mocyn in his sleep, twitching. Du was purring, but sounded healthier. His new Family, for the moment. Beautiful. And scary.

He was beginning to suspect that if he lost either one of the ladies, there would be a big crack in his heart that would never quite mend.

*S*ignet was awakened just before dawn by the quiet. The Residence was more silent than it had been for days. The subliminal hum of different people she'd become accustomed to was gone. For an instant fear flashed through her as she recalled the deadliness of Avellana's Passage, then the image of D'Hazel's hopeful face came, and everything settled into place. Avellana and Vinni, along with their Fams, were in their respective homes. She must have plunged directly into deep sleep because she felt refreshed enough to want to stay awake.

Good morning, FamWoman, Du said. He was a champagne-colored circle on her gold sateen comforter and was purring. He didn't open his eyes.

Good morning, Du, she replied. She felt the need for . . . something.

Beadle snuffled. He was on the other corner of the bedsponge, his plump black and white self appearing much less coordinated than Du, just as curled, fur glossy and beautiful.

Signet smiled. He looked good, as did his FamMan.

"Lowest light," she whispered, and the dark became dimness. She allowed her gaze to linger on Cratag, the sheet pushed down to his waist, his broad chest with just the right amount of dark hair showing. The muscles of his arms and pectorals were well defined. A man with a gorgeous, life-sculpted body. She almost let herself slip back into bed with him, but these quiet moments were precious to her now.

Impulsively she requested cocoa with white mousse from the Residence kitchen, reached into a drawer and pulled out a simple large robe of blue silk that made her eyes look darker, and drew it over her head to envelop her. The robe was cut with large, bell-like sleeves, and a wide enough skirt to wear trous underneath, but Signet wanted nothing more on her body.

After one last look at Cratag, she hurried down the stairs and to the kitchen, slipped on a couple of clogs that she'd crafted herself, took the steaming mug of cocoa from the no-time, and left the Residence, pulling a weathershield around her. She hadn't said more than a few words to the house, but got the impression that it, too, was enjoying the quiet and was satisfied with the way the previous night had ended.

A new day.

The day following the fulfillment of the hardest and most important task of her life.

She wanted to see the last of the dawn.

The rosy glow of the sun spilling over the horizon of the ocean lit the path down to the beach. She went to a small cove that had a bench carved by the sea and generations of Marigold Flair, where she could sit and watch the colors line the sky. Pink, peach, orange, fading to the yellow, then light blue that shaded to the darker hue of the spring sky. The brightest stars still shone, their light not yet overcome by the small blue white sun.

The ocean, too, was blue and white. Wave blue with white

crests. Here the endless and varying rhythm of the surf beat at her ears, throbbed like her blood. Ever present since she was a babe.

She cherished the solitude made all the more delightful by knowing her fabulous lover yet slept in her bed, and she would return to him.

There was no sign of the desperate struggle on the sand last night, the eternal ocean had swept all tracks and gouges away like all else with its might.

Signet didn't want to think of that, so she just stood and let peace wash through her.

Before she settled into the smooth rock seat, she dropped the weathershield. She wanted to feel the sea breeze on her skin. As streaming white light shot across the ocean from the ball of the sun, she said another prayer of gratitude that this day was so different than the rest of the year. That she had a purpose, a Flair, for which people would give her respect.

No longer was she the useless D'Marigold.

In the night, Calendula Signet D'Marigold had saved a life.

The rolling surf soothed her as never before, seemed to echo her emotions in its repetitious tune that spoke of all problems being eroded by sheer determination. She lifted the mug to her lips and savored the taste of melty white mousse and rich cocoa, the contrast of light and dark flavors, of hot cocoa and cool mousse.

It was too cold to truly dance naked in sweeping ritual circles on the beach and in the surf, but she might do a little soft shuffle pattern. She chuckled. She should be dressed in narrow-legged trous and not a wide skirt, but the robe was short enough, ending above her ankles. Setting down her mug, she found a smooth, level area. Hands at her side, fingers flexed, and one and two, left shoulder lift, brush the right foot, hop . . .

A minute later when she pivoted she saw Cratag and Beadle and Du. Beadle was prancing and hopping. Du was switching his tail. She caught a surprised look on Cratag's face. She finished the spin, did a couple of more steps scuffing sand, and ended with a tiny bow.

Cratag applauded. "I've never seen dancing like that."

The style was rare. There were the great promenades and pattern dances during the social season—and the fun and fast country dances—and the waltz. A couple of antique dances like the quickstep that were obviously kept alive in the more rustic communities and the southern continent of Brittany, but these steps . . . She winked at him, smiled. "Family secret."

His expression flattened, dimming her joy. She had hurt him.

Du projected loudly, *I knew*.

Beadle said, *I can dance, too*. He tried a spin and fell over.

Signet skipped to Cratag, took his hand. Raising her eyebrows, she scanned him from short-haired head to long toes, *not* stopping at some of the most interesting places. He wore soft, loose trous and an old shirt the color of gray clouds. "I already know that you like dancing and are good at it." She swung herself by his side, bumped his thigh playfully with her hip, glanced up at him and said, "Start with your left foot, just brush it against the sand, your right foot takes all your weight."

"You would gift me with a Family secret?" He sounded astonished.

Du sniffed.

"Of course. Some knowledge shouldn't always remain a secret, but should be shared." She tilted her head and winked. "And the very secret dance I will keep to myself until . . . later." Was she actually looking that far to the future, thinking of him being permanently in her life . . . so permanently that she'd be teaching him real Family secrets?

Brief anxiety flashed through her. What if her Flair changed him so much that he wanted to do something more important with his life than stay in Druida as the chief guardsman for T'Hawthorn? She shoved the thought aside, let it roll under the next wave that broke.

"Start with your left foot,"she repeated.

He did as she said, and she walked them through a simple routine. She'd never tried to teach anyone except Du to dance before, and was pleased at how easily Cratag picked it up. Naturally, his balance was perfect. Soon she sped up the pattern and added slide steps and turns. Even his hands looked good—graceful.

His smile started slow and spread across his face until he was grinning by the end of the dance. As they ended the last spin in unison, he grabbed her under the arms and kept on swinging. Laughter spilled from both of them, and Signet's wits whirled with pure happiness.

They spun and spun. He never staggered, never let her drop. His strength was tremendous, very sexy.

Finally he stopped, and she was breathless from laughter. He slid her down his body, eyes intent. His teeth flashed again in a smile, and he said, "Let's try that dance again."

So they danced as Beadle played at the edge of the surf, keeping close to them, and Du sunned on a rock. He was the one to call a halt by rising to his four paws and stretching his back in an incredible arch. *Breakfast time.*

Cratag squeezed her hand. "I'm hungry."

Now that he mentioned it, she was ravenous. "Me, too."

She snagged her mug and they walked up the path hand in hand. Signet struggled to keep her breathing even, but Cratag wasn't out of breath. She'd have to work on her physical activity.

"I don't know when the Hazels will return with Avellana, but I have a request." His eyes met hers, and they were a deep purple. "Will you help me with some meditation exercises?"

She kept the moment light. "If you'll continue to dance with me."

"Always," he murmured.

When they reached the Residence, the house informed them that the Hazels would be returning with Avellana after lunch. Breakfast was fancy crepes, first savory with herbed eggs, cheese, and porcine, then a dessert crepe of sweet custard. A little heavy for practicing meditation, but they filled themselves anyway.

Signet drew him into the meditation room when Cratag seemed reluctant to cross the threshold.

"Your energy—"

"Pervades the Residence. I can meditate in my sitting room, in the ritual room, or the HouseHeart."

He nodded, his face serious.

Keeping her fingers linked with his, she slid one leg down to descend to the floor, and crossed them both. He did the same.

Reluctantly she put her hands on her knees, wondered how to begin, then had an idea. She peeked through her lashes to see Cratag in the proper position, his chest rising and falling with slow, deep breaths, his eyes shut. She closed her own and said, "Residence, Meditation Journey One."

Cratag's energy rose beside her as if he were curious, but before they could say anything, the Residence had deepened its already rich tones and slowed its lilt. "We will be visualizing a safe place. . . ."

The first image that flashed into Cratag's mind was the very chamber they were in—no southern continent jungle clearing, no small corner in his parents' rooms, not one spot in T'Hawthorn Residence. No. This room tinted a cool blue with a rug with a pattern that had faded into gentle pastel swatches.

This was the safest place he'd ever known.

Twenty

❦

*C*ratag cherished the feel of Signet beside him. Their knees barely touched, but he was aware of those few millimeters of skin like nothing else in his life. He was sure he was connected to her somehow mentally, maybe even emotionally—hopefully not too emotionally—definitely sexually. But now was not the time to think about sex, so he concentrated on every syllable of the Residence's words, the tone.

He became aware of a pale blueness, the yellow glow of Signet near, nudging him further . . . into emptiness.

Oddly enough, he felt a few moments of bliss, then more nothingness until the sound of the Residence's voice pulsed against his eardrums and formed into words again . . . "aware and refreshed when I count down to one. Three . . . two . . . one. Welcome."

Without volition, Cratag's lungs shuddered inward as he took a huge breath. Oxygen to the brain? Maybe. But with that breath he smelled Signet and the fragrance of old incense in the room, and, he swore, the motes of the sun themselves.

Signet turned to him, and his heart tumbled in his chest at the smile she gave him. "Excellent trance for spiritual renewal, but not so good for working with Flair. Residence, please access the ResidenceLibrary and give us such lessons next time."

"Yes, Signet," the Residence said.

Du purred. *Good dreamtime.*

Beadle snored. Cratag knew he was dreaming of rabbits again.

Signet patted his knee, and her touch went straight through him like lightning. He became achingly aroused. And in no mood to resist temptation. Grunting, he rose and picked her up, hurried from the room.

"My bedroom is closest," he said in her ear, then, "My sitting room sofa is even closer."

It was, and being with her overwhelmed the bliss of being part of the universe, the joy of learning an ancient dance. So many blessings this morning, he knew the rest of his time with her would be the best of his life.

*A*fter meditation, they filled the morning with loving . . . and with playing with their Fams in the gardens. Beadle kept close to a human at all times, and now and then Cratag saw him give a little teleporting hop. Cratag didn't know if or when Beadle would want to roam outside by himself again and decided to say nothing and let nature take its course.

All the Hazels arrived, beaming. The adults were clearly relieved and hopeful that Avellana would survive the rest of her Passage. Avellana's sister treated her with a slightly more offhand manner than before.

Avellana herself seemed both more and less adult. Her mannerisms were a little less rigid, but a new wisdom lived in her eyes.

They had a formal tea in the gardens and were joined by Vinni and Hanes. The elder Hazel girl accepted the invitation to spend the night with alacrity, wanting another tour around the Residence.

So the evening was filled with children's laughter and pet purrs again, something Cratag thought he could become accustomed to.

The three-day weekend passed with ease, though Cratag noted he wasn't the only one who often glanced at Avellana to study her for signs of incipient Passage.

They all celebrated a ritual with other nobles at GreatCircle Temple on Ioho and afterward Cratag returned to T'Hawthorn Residence and his sterile and cramped room to pack more clothes . . . and weapons. Two other reports of grumtuds had come from down the southern coast. He'd made all the Fams and Signet promise that they wouldn't go to the beach alone at any time, even though they all knew how to teleport. That hadn't helped Beadle in his fear.

By the next morning all was back to normal and on Avellana's schedule. That afternoon Laev and Vinni came to train with Cratag. They were in the middle of a muscular grappling when Cratag flipped and saw Avellana sitting in the hallway with the door open, watching. She was not in the room when they were fighting, so she was following the rules.

His instant's inattention cost him, as Laev and Vinni teamed together to keep him down. A sharp elbow landed in his gut, and he grunted then slapped the mat three times in surrender. The boys groaned and collapsed near him.

Avellana giggled, and the two youngsters jerked to sit.

"You aren't supposed to be watching," Laev said. As blood suffused his face, his body, and he began to shake, Cratag commanded, "'Port to your teleportation pad in your suite in T'Hawthorn Residence *now*. Take a waterfall, report to your FatherSire as soon as you're clean."

Instinctively following orders, Laev disappeared. Cratag sucked in a big breath. T'Hawthorn would help with the boy's upsurge of Passage. Cratag didn't know whether it was a small precursor to another Passage or the real thing, and he didn't have the luxury of helping.

He stood and turned to the other child who'd had a more horrible Passage, and might be affected by Laev's out-of-control Flair.

But Vinni was pulling her up, smiling at her with a tenderness that should have seemed odd on a boy's face. For one of the first times in his life, Cratag truly believed down in his bones a tenet of his culture—reincarnation. Surely Avellana and Vinni had been together before.

Avellana giggled again, and Cratag let out his breath. It didn't seem as if Laev's flash of Passage would impact her, sending her into her own.

As Cratag walked over to them, Vinni tensed. Cratag ignored his reaction and bowed as formally to Avellana as the punctilious Hanes would have done. "Greetyou, GreatMistrys Hazel."

"Greetyou, GentleSir Maytree," she replied, but in not quite her usual adult or imperial tone. He sensed that it wasn't just her own Passage that had changed her, but Signet's catalyst Flair was working on her. Hell, it was working on Cratag—the boulder—so it *must* be affecting the child. Enough that she would survive Passage— something Cratag discovered he wanted with all his heart, not just because she was a loveable little girl, but because of what Signet would suffer if they lost her.

Avellana looked with longing beyond him to the room, then back up at him, and clasped her hands. "After my First Passage I might get to train with others at the Green Knight Fencing and Fighting Salon." Uncertainty flashed in her eyes. "You think I could?"

He was almost staggered. She was asking *him*, as if he were an expert. Vinni was staring up at him as if he believed the same and awaited an answer. Cratag swallowed and studied her. The girl was slight, but she might be sturdier than she looked, probably was very flexible. Sparring might help her Passages. Laev seemed better for it . . . as if it evened out his moods or energies or whatever. Any physical exercise might do, but Cratag knew training.

Cratag rubbed his chin, went with his gut. "Maybe you should change into some old, loose trous and a short tunic, put a hairband or net on, and come back down. Then we'll see."

For a moment her face froze. "I always dress properly."

She always dressed like a little noble adult. So her Family would take her seriously? He and Signet took the child very seriously. How to explain that to her?

But Vinni was gesturing to himself, to Cratag, and saying, "Training is different, you use different clothes like what we are wearing." He touched her curly mane. "And you'll need to keep your hair out of your eyes."

"I don't know . . ." Avellana's voice went higher.

Maybe this wasn't a good idea. Cratag had opened his mouth to say so when Signet walked into sight behind Avellana. She stared hard at Cratag and motioned to him to keep talking, reassure the girl. Vinni shifted from foot to foot, a bad habit for anyone, keeping himself off balance. Cratag scowled. "I *am* the expert, and, Vinni, the Hollys should have broken you of that habit. Train with me and Avellana as well as them and you *will* stop shifting your weight."

Vinni bowed properly, keeping his eyes on Cratag—not one of his elegant noble bows but a good, masculine fighting bow. Cratag figured that the Hollys had taught him both.

Then Avellana shot a look at Cratag and Vinni, her mouth set. "I have some old clothes, for gardening in. Mother likes to garden, and I get to pull weeds." She touched her hair. Signet said, "Let me put it up in a coronet." With a whisk of her fingers, she did so.

Avellana smiled. "Now for clothes. I will be *right back*." She ran halfway down the hall, then stopped, looked back, again with yearning. "You *will* teach me fighting, GentleSir Maytree? So I won't look stupid when I go to the Green Knight Fencing and Fighting Salon for my lessons?"

This was probably a big mistake, but Cratag nodded. "Yes, I will teach you."

"Oooooh!" Avellana squealed as she ran back toward the stairs.

Signet let out a breath, met Cratag's gaze. He *felt* her support. "We do have some autonomy in her lessons. It's in my contract." She lifted her chin. "I approve of this decision."

"So do I," Vinni said. He folded down onto the floor into a cross-legged position and put his head on his feet. When his voice came again, it was muffled. "Anything to help her through her Passage."

Looking at the boy, Cratag added another reason to help Avellana . . . what her loss would do to this teen he was beginning to care for as much as he did Laev.

Once again, Signet echoed his thoughts. "We are *not* going to lose her."

Cratag prayed she was right.

O*ver the next week, Cratag took his affair with Signet one day at a* time. He'd adjusted to his new surroundings and his new responsibilities, and now knew D'Marigold Residence as well as T'Hawthorn Residence—except the secret way to the HouseHeart and the HouseHeart itself.

He'd been in T'Hawthorn HouseHeart two times with T'Hawthorn, but Cratag certainly didn't expect Signet to tell him her Family's most guarded mystery.

They danced together, the old-fashioned dances he'd grown up with on the southern continent and the equally antique steps she was teaching him that made up "tap."

She was as open a lover as he'd ever had, both in and out of bed, unselfconscious and sharing. She made her respect and caring for him clear, and though the link between them was there, he wasn't always able to read her emotions. Wasn't sure whether he wanted to read them. He'd learned to live in the moment as a mercenary, and be grateful for the blessings the Lord and Lady had graced him with. He was taking nothing for granted, but his imagination sometimes spiraled out of control and he thought of a long-term relationship with her. They were still very far apart class-wise, but they found other areas of extreme compatibility.

He wasn't sure, either, exactly how much her catalyst Flair was affecting him and on what levels, but his senses became sharper and his Flair expanded—not by much, and he was sure he'd never be able to teleport—but life became more comfortable as spells he'd struggled with or that had been beyond him were now mastered.

As for Avellana, she'd regained her equilibrium, but she held herself differently, and Cratag believed she viewed herself differently, too. Not a girl who had brain damage and might not survive her First Passage, but a girl who'd overcome brain damage and would survive *all* her Passages. A positive spin on a negative situation. He thought the fighting patterns he helped her master boosted her confidence. All to the good.

Vinni T'Vine was often at D'Marigold Residence.

Signet and the Residence were gracious and graceful in their handling of schedule shuffles, requests for reports from the Hazels, lessons for Avellana, and visitors on short notice.

Laev began dropping by in the afternoons after his journeyman hours to work out with Cratag during his midafternoon training time, and Vinni would often join them, so a septhour before noon was Avellana's time to train.

Occasionally Laev would stay for tea, but all were very aware that his Passage could trigger Avellana's. Laev had had his second Passage fugue after Avellana's interruption of their sparring match, and once again Cratag had experienced it. The dreamquest had been both shorter and less intense than Avellana's, and Laev was sure he'd connected with his HeartMate.

He, too, was growing into his new Flair, the new responsibilities as an adult, and the duties that T'Hawthorn was assigning him. The boy was definitely becoming a man, and developing his own opinions.

When Cratag consulted Hanes about the amount of sparring Vinni was doing—three times a week in the mornings at the Green Knight Fencing and Fighting Salon with his regular class, often before noon with Avellana, and sometimes in the midafternoon with Laev and Cratag, Hanes gravely said he'd speak with the rest of the Vine Family.

Neither Vinni nor Cratag cared for that response, and Cratag couldn't say so, but Hanes was on their side, and Cratag had heard he'd made a good argument for the training. Vinni had the standard lessons for his age by his tutor, but wasn't apprenticed to anyone. He was already considered a master of his Flair, so after his studies, his days were composed of scheduled appointments like the rest of the FirstFamilies noble lords and ladies.

Furthermore, the boy was filling out, becoming more muscular and stronger, which pleased the older ladies of his Family. So he was allowed to continue against his tutor's disapproval. Though neither Vinni nor Hanes said anything, Cratag got the feeling that changes were occurring in the Vine household. Again, this was only natural as Vinni grew, but Cratag couldn't help believing that part of it was due to Signet's effect on Vinni. He was maturing.

So many children growing up made Cratag's gut twist with pride as well as sorrow at the inevitable passing of time. Not to mention feeling his age.

*O*n the morning of Koad, the day before the weekend and Playday, Signet swept into the dining room for breakfast as if she hadn't just rolled out of Cratag's bed a scant few minutes before. She'd had to resort to a whirlwind spell to cleanse and dress, fast but not too easy on the person who invoked it. "I think that we should have an educational outing today," she said.

Cratag winced then let his expression fall back into impassivity. Avellana stopped eating her eggs, looked up, and stuck her lower lip out. "I don't want to go anywhere."

Signet just arched her brows and chose a breakfast omelette from the no-time. "That's too bad. We've been light on lessons this week." The week after Avellana's first fugue had been a week of rebalancing. "I've listened to the daily newssheets announcements, and there is an interesting case being heard by SupremeJudge Ailim Elder herself at JudgementGrove today. Very educational, don't you think so, Cratag?"

He was eyeing her as he chewed a slice of porcine. Then he swallowed and said, "I think the only trial I've been to was . . ."

He stopped. "One involving the new GreatLady Dufleur Willow." The black magic murders that he didn't want to mention in front of Avellana.

Signet's eyes widened at the reference.

Avellana fixed her gaze on Cratag. "You're talking about the black magic cult murders."

Twenty-one

*A*vellana *glanced around the breakfast room, then closed her eyes,* opened them, and let out a little sigh. "Rhyz is chasing flutterbys with Du and Beadle in the garden." With a serious look, she said, "You know he was one of the Fams who lived through that horrible cult ritual. Rhyz was Gib Ginger's Fam." Her aura pulsed, and Signet knew Avellana was sending love through her bond with Rhyz. "Vinni's Fam, Flora, was also one of the victims."

"I didn't know," Signet said at the same time as Cratag. They shared a look. She should have known, someone should have told her. No wonder Flora had had that dark, horrible memory spot . . . which was now fading until it was barely a spiderweb.

Avellana nodded solemnly. "That's why we must always be especially kind to them. And Flora is one of the first generation of housefluffs to get intelligence and Flair."

Signet grimaced. "I wish I'd known this earlier."

"You have done very well with her," Avellana said in that tone that meant she was repeating what her mother, the FirstFamily GreatLady, had said.

That relieved Signet a little. "Thank you." She glanced at Cratag, who had resumed eating. "But that trial was vized from the First-Family Council Chambers. This is JudgementGrove, available for all to watch. Have you ever been before, Avellana?"

The girl nibbled her lip. "Perhaps when I was a small child," she said. Her blue eyes widened. "I don't remember much except that the grove was beautiful and so was the judge."

"Hmm." Signet got the idea that the outing had only been a year ago.

Cratag was frowning. "We can take a picnic, right?" He sounded as if his own sense of decency was offended.

"Right." Signet smiled. "Residence?"

"Lunch is being prepared. From my understanding of the news-sheets and my connection with other Residences, and the starship wherein the SupremeJudge lives, there will be many nobles attending today's session at JudgementGrove. Also grovestudy groups."

"Oh, bigger girls and boys." Avellana smiled and went back to her food with gusto. "I want to observe grovestudy groups. Maybe..." She slanted Signet a look. "...I will not be tutored after First Passage is over. Perhaps I can go to a grovestudy group. Even Vinni didn't get to go to a grovestudy group."

Just that easily a lump came to Signet's throat. Avellana was hopeful of surviving her Passage, had no doubt. That was new and precious. The fight would be easier, now that she accepted she could, *would*, win.

"The case being heard is quite interesting," the Residence said. "It concerns the salvage rights of a merchant ship full of items from Chinju that sank off the coast one hundred and twenty years ago. The ship-master had great Flair, and the wreck and its cargo are remarkably well preserved. The Families involved are the salvager's, GrandHouse D'Kelp; the ship Captain's, GrandHouse D'Salip; and several Families who invested in the ship, including the FirstFamily of T'Reed—"

"The financier. Of course," muttered Cratag.

The Residence continued, "—and the GrandLord Alfalfa Family that insured the ship and paid out—"

"Thank you, Residence, I think that's enough," Signet said. Cratag's eyes were beginning to glaze. Avellana was frowning in concentration. "It will be interesting to hear it firsthand."

"Yes, indeed," the Residence said. "I believe a viz has been rigged." With a rich chuckle, the Residence said, "I can now be better informed."

Cratag blinked, muttered, "You're always informed on everything."

"Thank you, GentleSir Maytree," the Residence said, then added, "If you wish to find a good spot in JudgementGrove for viewing, I suggest you leave in the next quarter septhour."

"So soon?" Signet asked.

"Indeed," said the Residence. "I have been informed that the sacred circle will be opened after every case today. Do you want to teleport or go by glider?"

"Glider," Signet said.

"I will send it around," the Residence said. "It can return after you disembark, and when the day is done you can come back by teleportation or notify me if you want the glider again."

"That sounds fine."

Cratag pushed away from the table, took his dishes and silverware to the cleanser. "I'll be right down, meet you in the entryway."

He was going to get a weapon. Probably more than one.

Avellana sent a mental call to the Fams. All the cats replied they were interested in going to JudgementGrove. Rhyz wanted to touch noses with acquaintances, Beadle to explore and look at people and Fams and prey, Du expected to casually visit folk who would admire him and perhaps give him delicacies. Then Avellana rose from the table and placed her dishes in the cleanser. "I need to change." She hurried—not running—upstairs.

The girl had been dressed well, if casually. A new habit since the conversation about her training, but she was probably changing to formal clothes as befit a FirstFamily child.

A notion occurred to Signet. "Are the Hazels planning to attend?" she asked the Residence.

"One moment, I will check with D'Hazel Residence."

Signet set her dishes in the cleansing box, looked around, and said a housekeeping spell to tidy the room into pristine order.

"The Hazels do not go to JudgementGrove themselves, but members of the household will be there to report."

"Ah."

"I have been informed that T'Vine and his tutor and Hanes will go to JudgementGrove after his morning studies. He requests that they be allowed to join our party."

"Of course."

"I will provide two large hampers, with gliding spells. Vinni likes my food better than that at T'Vine Residence," the D'Marigold Residence stated. Signet wasn't sure that was true, but smiled at the pride in its voice.

She was proud of her accomplishments and her companions— lover and Fam and ward—herself. That was reflected in her clothing. She was wearing a subtly patterned golden brocade outfit—full trous cuffed at the ankles with an orange trim and her flower embroidered in rust—and a tunic with the long, rectangular pocket-sleeves that nearly brushed the ground, also trimmed in orange with rust embroidery. Her closely fitted boots were golden with rust-colored flowers outlined up her ankle and one on her toe.

Without a sound she felt an intensity in the entryway and knew that Cratag had come down the stairs. When she met him in the large room, she saw he, too, had changed into more than casual clothes—these were clothes to be seen in and noted—garments modified for a guardsman and fighter. Light brown knit trous and cream-colored raw silkeen shirt that would keep him warm without any sort of weathershield, shining black leather knee-high boots that could do damage in a fight, a jacket of brown padded silkeen showing a small embroidered hawthorn bush. On one of his hips was a holstered long-nosed utilitarian blazer. On the other was a sheathed broadsword that could only be used by a tall, strong man.

Then Avellana gave a little cough at the top of the stairs, and when their gazes went to her, she descended with the utmost propriety. Signet saw Cratag suppress a smile.

Three cats followed her down, Rhyz as dignified as his FamGirl, Du prancing, and Beadle nearly tumbling in his clumsiness.

Avellana's hair was smoothly and elaborately braided, a sign that she'd used Flair on it. Her tunic and trous were of the latest style with full legs and long sleeves like Signet's, though the wide patterned trim on the pale green appeared to be real silver.

When the girl reached the entryway, she held out a hand to each of them, and Signet was amused to see Cratag's brows go up as they both went to her instead of having her come to them. Truly, the girl knew how to behave like a GreatLady.

As soon as Cratag took her hand, he winked at Signet, grinned wickedly, and let out a piercing whistle. Avellana flinched between them, then her eyes widened as two large wicker hampers floated into the room.

"They'll follow me," Cratag said.

The Residence opened the door and the little party—the small educational outing—proceeded out to the large, waiting D'Marigold Family glider.

*D*u exited the glider near JudgementGrove first, charged with finding an appropriate place for them to sit and listen to the case. The sacred circle was open, so Beadle went zooming around with boundless joy, exploring a new, safe place. Rhyz stayed in the glider until Cratag, Signet, and Avellana exited. Signet sent the glider home.

It was a beautiful day. The sun shone brightly, and the grass was that hue of green only seen in springtime. The trees in the large grove wore pretty pastel blossoms of pink and white.

It was almost like a Family outing. Her new, temporary,

Family . . . Signet had to remind herself. Avellana would return to
her home after she'd finished her Passage fugues, and Cratag would
go back to being T'Hawthorn's chief of guards, and their Fams
would leave with them. All of them would remain friends, Signet
was finally believing that would be true, but they would not be living with her. So she should cherish this "family" outing.

She couldn't remember going to the JudgementGrove with her
parents—they'd been more inclined to have arts outings, though
she'd attended JudgementGrove with her grovestudy groups a couple of times. That had been before Ailim Elder had become the
SupremeJudge of Celta.

They arrived in time to find a good spot in the grove to see the
platform and the judge's desk well. In the time between cases, they
spread out a blanket and laid out snacks and drinks.

The ritual of closing the circle and saying the prayer interested
her, but the next case was boring, though Cratag and Avellana
listened. A business deal by GraceLords that had gone bad. Signet
would rather be in a museum or an art gallery. She began to have
doubts about the main case, but a sunken treasure ship had sounded
interesting, and the Residence was right, a case with a FirstFamily
should always be paid attention to.

After a couple of minutes, she became aware that their party
was under scrutiny by many—GreatLords and Ladies themselves
or members of their Families sent to observe. And she, Signet Marigold, was being observed.

In a discreet, supportive gesture, Cratag touched the small of her
back. *You are a GrandLady of noted skill*, he sent to her mentally.
A woman who has saved a FirstFamily's child's life.

Warmth came to Signet's cheeks, and she looked at her group
from under lowered lashes. Du was nearby and munching on a bit
of cheese, Rhyz was catnapping, Beadle was slinking through the
green grass, his plump black and white body quite evident. He kept
to the sunshine and not the shadows.

*Thank you. Let them look, I have nothing to hide, and they
might finally *see* me as I am.* She'd gone unnoticed in Druidan

society for too long. These people would recall that she'd always been invited to FirstFamily rituals and now they would know why. Then she leaned into Cratag and felt his arm come around her. She wasn't ashamed of their affair. He was a trusted and important member of T'Hawthorn's household, how could she not value that? But even if he'd been a mercenary guard, just come in from selling his sword to merchants in Brittany, she'd have been proud of him. He was a man of solid character.

Casually, she picked up a tube of water, glanced around. Most of the FirstFamiles were here, and many of the higher nobles. As others arrived, colorful clothing showed between the white bark and green leaves in a screened circle of birches that was a teleportation area.

A sharp sound resonated throughout the air, and Signet realized it was the SupremeJudge's gavel, then the bailiff cleared his throat and intoned, "There will be a half-septhour recess. All rise," and everyone in the grove did. Without looking at them, the judge went into one of the towers that framed the stage. The sacred circle was dismissed.

Signet stretched. It hadn't seemed polite to stand before, though the JudgementGrove appeared less formal than she recalled.

At that moment she heard a telepathic hail, *Greetings, all! Greetyou, Vinni.* Laev Hawthorn was loping toward them, waving a hand at Vinni, who was accompanied by Hanes and another man, striding toward them from the opposite side of the grove.

Laev, Cratag responded, *perhaps you should not—*

Signet squeezed his hand. *Come join us, Laev.* Laev's Flair was scattered, not building up toward Passage. Another new thing she could sense! Perhaps she could add that to services she could offer, Passage consultation . . . all the glances she'd gotten made her think that she'd be in demand if everything went well.

She glanced at Avellana, but the child's Flair was erratic, clumping here and there, shooting off into an aura streak, being absorbed inward.

"Greetyou, GrandLady D'Marigold," said a light male voice she didn't recognize. She refocused her vision and found herself facing a short, plump man with an ingrained smile.

"My tutor, Arcto, one of the Family, of course," Vinni said.

"My pleasure," Arcto said, bowing with the exact amount of formality that her title demanded.

"Greetyou, D'Marigold," Hanes said. He spared her a smile before he went back to scanning the crowd. His blazer was not tied down with a peacebond. Signet glanced at Cratag's holster and saw it was the one with buttons that only he could draw and fire, a better solution.

Then Laev arrived and hugged Cratag, bowed to Vinni and Signet and Avellana. As Signet said all the correct courtesies, the babel around them increased. JudgementGrove was packed. Most folk preferred to sit in the lines of trees making up the grove instead of in the middle grassy area, but that was filling up, too.

Avellana was the first to resume her seat on the blanket, which had multiplied to three blankets, one in T'Vine colors that Arcto was arranging, and another D'Marigold one that Cratag had snapped out.

A bell tolled from one of the towers, and the bailiff announced that Grove would be in session again in ten minutes.

They'd arranged themselves by the time the five-minute bell was rung, with Cratag and Hanes in positions that were the most protective. Arcto was actually the busiest—distributing the "nutritious-only" food and drink to the children, pulling softleaves from his bag and murmuring hand-wash spells for them all. He seemed devoted to both Vinni and Avellana. Then the tutor provided the group with a pithy summary of the case that even snagged Signet's attention.

Laev stretched out with a bunch of grapes near Cratag. As he watched the parties mount the few steps to the platform, Laev shook his head. "The D'Hawthorn at the time had an investment in that ship. Insured, of course, but we still took a substantial loss." He snorted. "But we've moved on, our fortune and Family is stronger than ever." He waved to the advocates and their clients on the stage. "What you see up there is pure greed, and the amount those folk are going to get from this action is going to be less than the time they've spent messing around with this, and the gilt they've paid their advocates."

"T'Reed has a Family advocate," Arcto said.

They all looked at the thin Reed men, who had features in common. "Of course he does," Hanes said.

Laev was frowning. "That might be something to consider, if any of the youngsters coming up would like to be trained in the law. . . ." He slid a glance at Cratag, "or maybe someone else who might be tired of his work."

For the first time Signet saw Cratag horrified.

Laev let out a belly laugh, tossed a grape in his mouth, and choked. With a good thump of one large hand, Cratag dislodged the grape, and it shot away into a nearby bush. Beadle pounced.

"You got an advocate in the Family, the Family starts thinking of lawsuits for this, that, and the other thing," Cratag muttered, "wasting good gilt and time."

The bell for the afternoon session of JudgementGrove tolled, and the bailiff said, "All rise."

Everyone in the grove stood, even the Fams.

"And making a spectacle of yourself and your Family in front of everyone," Arcto said disapprovingly.

"We don't have an advocate in the Family," Vinni said. There was tension between Vinni and his tutor, probably just that of a boy becoming a man and forming his own opinions. "But if one of the Family wanted to be an advocate, I'd support him or her."

Arcto opened his mouth, but the bailiff began the ritual to close the sacred circle. After the prayer, he said, "JudgementGrove is now in session, with the afternoon case being T'Reed, T'Alfalfa, T'Salip, D'Kelp, and others."

"Minor houses," Vinni said. The case title had run from highest to lowest in status.

As the first advocate started speaking with flourishing gestures— looking to Signet more like an actor than a man of law—everyone settled back down.

The case took all afternoon.

The SupremeJudge Ailim Elder seemed to watch with judicial impassivity, but to Signet's fascination, she was able to tell when the lady was using her telempathic Flair during the session. The streams of her tiny, intense flowers would circle and spiral around the person she was scrutinizing then flow into his or her head, then a brief glow of Flair would issue from the person.

T'Reed, the GreatLord himself, didn't stand before the judge— perhaps the GreatLord didn't want to be the focus of her skills. His Heir was there, and Signet believed that the man didn't notice when the judge used her Flair. Very interesting, the SupremeJudge must have a very light touch.

At that moment Ailim Elder looked directly at Signet, and she understood that she was thinking too loudly or doing something like studying the woman's Flair so strongly that it had attracted the judge's attention. Signet blushed. Judge Elder's lips curved in a hint of a smile, and she returned her attention to the long-winded advocate in front of her.

It all came down to a matter of contracts, and that had Signet paying attention again. The seamaster Captain of the ship had invested in the voyage and had died. His Heirs had taken a settlement from the Alfalfa insurers for the goods, but had not been able to prove to the Alfalfas, until now, that the man was dead. So T'Alfalfa was directed to pay out—at current high rates—the death benefit to his Family.

All the investors had had various deductible portions on their insurance policies and had suffered that amount of loss, so they would get that paid back to them—and Signet saw great relief on some people dressed several years out of fashion. The Alfalfas would be paid back what they'd paid out, and the people who had found the ship would get the rest, a very substantial amount. There was a reasonable tax to be paid to the Councils of Celta for public use.

Though the judge smiled when she spoke to those involved in the case, she made it clear that she thought the contracts had been sufficient to handle the matter and the parties involved were greedy.

She was about to raise her gavel and bang the case shut when a girl about Vinni's age ran into the grove and up the steps to the judge's platform. Cratag shifted and drew his blazer. So did Hanes. Signet was shocked. Though all eyes and wandering attention sharpened and focused on the girl, the guards in the crowd—including the bailiff, had weapons out.

The girl didn't seem to notice and panted, "Wait, wait, what about my tea set?"

Twenty-two

❦

The girl flushed and spread the material of her short and faded tunic to curtsy to the SupremeJudge. "I beg your pardon, but it took us— me—a while to, uh, document this." She threw a glance toward a small group of four girls. Everyone else looked, too.

"I am Camellia Darjeeling." Fishing a bundle of papyrus from her long sleeve, the girl continued. "My Family specializes in tea, though we are not *the* Teas." She blushed again and hurried on. "One of my forebears ordered a tea set." She licked her lips. "A very expensive tea set, from Chinju, and we were told that it was being sent to us on the ship that this case is about." She shot a look at the rest of the parties. "We didn't have insurance." With careful steps she set the sheets of papyrus before the SupremeJudge.

"SupremeJudge, this is untoward. This . . . person . . . is not a party to this action," the Alfalfa's advocate said.

"Not proper," Vinni's tutor muttered near Signet.

"GraceMistrys Darjeeling has a point and a right to be heard." The judge read the first page of the papyrus and set it aside, looked up. "I noticed that T'Alfalfa did not provide the JudgementGrove with a list of other claims it might have paid on the cargo. Do you have a list?"

"Ah . . ."

The judge shifted her gaze from the advocate to GrandLord T'Alfalfa himself. "Do you have such a list?"

"Of course." He gestured, and his advocate handed him a sheet of papyrus. He glanced at it, but Signet got the idea that he already knew everything on it. "No tea set is listed."

"Thank you for the verification," the judge said, but didn't lift her eyes as she scanned the pages on her desk. She lifted a fragile, ragged-edged scrap that looked like a letter and read it several times, then turned it over. The next pages appeared to be forms. Then she turned to a portfolio and pulled out a sheet and scanned it, then said, "A fifty-place tea set from master artist-potter Zisha is listed on the manifest."

There were several gasps from the audience. Someone muttered, "That will be worth some nice gilt."

Camellia whirled and glared. "This is my Family's heritage, we won't be selling it!"

SupremeJudge Elder coughed, and Camellia flinched, pivoted back around, and murmured, "I beg your pardon."

The judge nodded, then gestured to D'Kelp, a hearty woman with short, springy hair. She was dressed in a very short work tunic over narrow-legged work trous. She'd kept a practical, optimistic manner throughout all the arguing. The woman bowed. "Yes, SupremeJudge?"

"Have you found a tea set? Or, rather, four large boxes with the stamp of "Fragile china, max spellshield protection.""

D'Kelp hooked thumbs in her belt that was wide, tough leather instead of folded silk cloth, and said, "Can't say that I have, Supreme-Judge." She nodded at Camellia. "But we'll look for it, Grace-Mistrys, and if we find it, we'll see what shape it's in so's we all can figure out whether we can get it to you." She smiled widely. "And I'll take the price of our services out in trade. We'll negotiate that later."

Camellia swallowed and nodded.

SupremeJudge Elder swept the people in JudgementGrove with her gaze, and Signet felt the touch of her Flair. "If anyone else has documents regarding the salvage of this ship that are not insured, file them with me and the Kelps. If they were insured and you received a settlement, file those papyrus with me and the Alfalfas. If they were insured and you did *not* receive a settlement, file documents with me, the Alfalfas, and the Kelps. You may choose whether to refile a loss statement or to take the salvage."

Most of the nobles on the platform now wore scowls, D'Kelp looked philosophical.

A gavel banged, and the final blessing was said and the circle dismissed. The judge walked to her tower chambers.

"Most unusual," Vinni's tutor said. Then he seemed to realize he was frowning and smiled . . . but not happily.

"It's past our studytime," Vinni said. "You can do as you please."

"Of course." The tutor bowed and hurried away.

Hanes snorted. "I've never seen a more active gossip. He has a wide circle of friends, all like him, and they'll be hashing this over for days. Everyone will search their records and attic for anything regarding the ship. Not only nobles since this decision will hit the newssheets."

Laev said, "That's what happens when you get lawyers involved in business. Always complications. Better to take care of the negotiations yourself."

Signet began saying the spells to tidy and repack the baskets, and Hanes frowned. "Arcto should have stayed to help."

With a smile, Signet said, "It's after WorkEndBell." The case had taken so long that the first wisps of colorful evening clouds were beginning to show in the sky and shadows were long on the grass.

But Hanes was still frowning and nodded to Cratag. "Some of us take our responsibilities seriously and are never totally off duty."

For the first time Signet thought of being bound by another's will and working in a household instead of running it. It might be terrible . . . or, if you were a vital part of that household, it might be as wonderful as she'd always thought—exactly knowing your place and your duties and what was expected of you. Being so busy that no thoughts of emptiness plagued your mind . . . and certainly no loneliness infused your emotions. She smiled at Cratag.

Cratag returned her smile and helped pack up, but though he'd hidden his own emotions through the day, they'd been twinged and plucked as he saw all the circles of alliances interact around him. Making him realize for the first time that whatever his status within his household, the respect he received was because of his rank with T'Hawthorn, not because of Cratag the man. He didn't know when that had not become enough, when he'd wanted to be considered equal to Signet when he never could be.

Furthermore, all the people in the JudgementGrove had been Druidans, doing a city dance that he didn't quite understand, with shades of nuanced behavior he could not recognize and some he knew he missed. So he was irritated and watchful as he and Signet walked through the outlying trees of JudgementGrove near Laev and Vinni and Avellana. There was more than one group of grove-study youngsters milling around. The three young people in his charge—though Laev was technically an adult—were talking about the judge's great Flair of empathy.

Cratag saw it happen but didn't realize the awful significance of the whole situation until later. Laev kept glancing over at the group of five girls that included the young Darjeeling. He'd been drifting toward them, and the rest of them had followed. Cratag had seen no danger and let Laev lead the way.

Then Laev abruptly stopped.

Flair crackled in the air, enough to impinge on Cratag, pressing upon him hot and heavy and vital, like a southern summer wind.

Signet caught her breath and squeezed his shoulder. He came up next to Laev and examined the fivesome of girls. They all wore clothes shabby at the cuffs. Laev's gaze was fixed on the striking beauty with a womanly body—surely a new adult like Laev himself. She had honey golden hair waving nearly to her waist. Her tilted eyes were a deep amber, her skin was of a tanned color that made her appear a woman dusted with gold.

Another zing. "What's that?" asked Cratag. He wasn't quite sure of the feelings surrounding him. Sexual attraction. More? Dammit!

Signet glanced at him with resigned amusement.

Laev crossed to the five young women and made his most elegant bow, turned at once to the golden girl and offered his arm. The girl sent him a smile that seemed more sly than shy to Cratag, and the other four girls dropped back.

Cratag and Signet's party stood still while the others walked . . . toward the PublicCarrier plinth. Cratag was torn. He wanted to go with Laev, he had to stay with Avellana. Signet slipped her arm in his. "He's an adult now."

He pressed her arm against his side, glanced at the rest of their little group. Hanes had been keeping a watchful eye on those around them—commoners and minor nobles—most of the great folk already had teleported home.

Vinni's lips had compressed. He took a couple of strides toward Cratag and looked up at him. The boy's face was pale and set and angry. "Too late," he muttered. "I didn't *see* when this would be and wasn't paying attention, and now it is too late."

Cratag banished the sinking feeling in his gut. Maybe the boy prophet wasn't talking about Laev, but Vinni's shoulders were set, showing he wasn't open to questions.

Signet searched Vinni's face, sensing Cratag wanted answers and the young GreatLord wasn't going to talk. She was holding Avellana back, wary of the heavy Flair so dense she could actually see irregular sparks. Flair from Laev and the girls and Vinni, thick emotions from Cratag.

"Who is the lovely girl Laev is walking with?" Cratag asked, concern in his voice as they all watched Laev take the young woman's hand and lead her away from her friends.

"That's Nivea Sunflower," Avellana said.

"How do you know?" Cratag asked.

"My sister knows one of the girls in that grovestudy group and told me Nivea Sunflower had interesting coloring."

"Stunning," Signet murmured.

Cratag snorted. He'd settled into his balance as if expecting trouble, and there was a line between his brows. Vinni fell into the same stance.

As if sensing their concern, Laev lifted his head from gazing at the girl to meet Cratag's eyes. The younger man inclined his head in acknowledgment but didn't leave the girl. Signet thought she caught the whisper of Laev's thought to Cratag. *I will escort GraceMistrys Sunflower home.* Then a flash of pure joy showed on Laev's face. *I have been connecting with my HeartMate during Passage!*

Nivea Sunflower plucked at his bloused sleeve, and he bent attentively to her.

"Uh-oh," Vinni said.

Avellana might have been oblivious to Signet's and Cratag's concern, but she knew her own HeartMate's voice well. "What?"

Vinni hunched his shoulder and muttered, "Don't want to talk about it."

Avellana put on her stubborn look, but even she couldn't make Vinni talk if he didn't want to.

The crowd pressed together, and Avellana tripped. She started to fall, and everyone reached for her. Cratag caught her, lifted her, and said. "She's hot."

The girl's face had flushed red.

They shouldn't have come. What had possessed Signet to think that this would be a good thing? Now Avellana was showing signs of Passage.

"Clear the way!" Hanes shouted, using his body to push people aside. Cratag followed, cradling Avellana protectively.

To Signet's surprise, Vinni slipped his hand in hers. *This outing should have been fine. The mass of people didn't bother her, it was that upsurge of Flair. More than Laev in that group is undergoing Passage—the older Mugwort girl, too, I think. And HeartMate energy . . .* He sounded unhappy and worried.

By now the men were clearing the nearest teleportation pad of minor nobles, gesturing Signet and Vinni to come. But Signet had the huge baskets, and they didn't quite fit into the space. They all linked hands, and Signet held the bond she had with Avellana close. Anxiety flashed through her that she tried to suppress from the child. This was a real fugue, and it was already more intense than the last. "On three," she said, her lips cold. She counted down, and they teleported to the small room that barely held them.

"Give her to me." She held out her arms to Cratag.

With a brusque nod he transferred Avellana. Her skin had turned clammy and pale. Beads of sweat shone on her face.

"Residence, prepare Avellana's bedroom for Passage, now! Warm it up, release the herbs!" Signet yelled. The doors to the room whisked open. Another bang from down the hallway, Avellana's doors.

Signet ran.

*T*he Passage was hideous. Horrible, fantastic illusions burned . . . iced . . . tore through them, and Signet could only hang on to Avellana during the long, wild ride. Signet would gather her Flair, release the little puffs to be battered by ugly storms . . . tentacles, grumtud monsters . . . but the flowers bobbed and streamed toward Avellana. And Avellana's own Flair, her brain pathways, had changed and were more connected, better defined. For that Signet gave thanks.

When she wasn't praying.

Now and then she felt Vinni's unique mind touch, but it was Cratag who anchored them. Signet felt his strength at her back, enfolding her as she held the child. Solid, steady, with little Flair but a deep source of personal and grounded energy . . . that she drew on to keep Avellana from going mad with the visions, reminding the child that this was not real.

They'd fallen from the tower again.

This time, they hadn't slowed before they hit the ground and sharp spiking stones rose from the ground to impale them.

This time they died, and there was a portal of swirling stars close if they wanted to go through it, be part of that wheel, then pass on to their next lives. The glittering and fabulous light was pure fascinating temptation, but Signet kept Avellana close and filled her mind with other images. Rhyz, her FamCat, even now with them, twitching droopy whiskers. A serious Vinni surrounded by huge and pulsing Flair.

Signet heard Avellana's cry of love within herself, and they turned away from the portal and suddenly the visions were gone and they were lying on a soft and fluffy cloud in the summer blue sky, then they were rising to the top of the bowl, then beyond . . .

. . . and Avellana was asleep.

Alive and healthy and sleeping.

But before Signet opened her eyes, she knew that she, too, had changed. She'd had her own revelation when Avellana had felt her golden love for Vinni.

Signet loved Cratag.

And was he . . . could he possibly be?

Her HeartMate?

Twenty-three

Signet was too wrung out and weary to concentrate on anything but the moment. Once more her senses indicated she and Avellana had been through an ordeal. They were both damp with sweat, clothes sticking to them. Formal clothes that they'd put on to attend Judgement-Grove eons ago. Not comfortable.

Du was beside her left hip, looking skinnier than ever. She shouldn't have linked with him, though everyone had helped. Rhyz appeared bedraggled on Avellana's lap.

So she smiled weakly at Cratag—who was back in the low bed-side chair—and Vinni, who sat cross-legged on the end of the bed, frowning. The boy puffed out his breath, rose from the bedsponge. Signet knew moving her stiff muscles would make her groan.

Expression calm as usual, Cratag lifted the girl from Signet's arms. "Let's clean up."

"I'll bathe her," Signet rasped. Her hair was plastered to her head.

Gently setting Avellana back onto the bedsponge, Cratag gathered Signet in his arms. He glanced at Vinni, ordered, "Signet is exhausted. I'll take her in first. Watch Avellana, let us know if anything changes in the slightest."

Be assured I will. Even Vinni's mindspeech sounded tired.

Without another word Cratag walked to the door, and it opened for them.

Hanes, sitting in a chair brought near the door, hopped to his feet. Blood drained from his face, his hand went to his blazer. "It's over. Is Avellana . . . is she—"

"Fine," Signet said, embarrassed that an acquaintance saw her looking so disheveled. Her clothes were even binding when she tried to wiggle her fingers in a casual wave to Hanes.

Hanes stepped into the room with Vinni. "She'll be all right? Your HeartMate?"

"Yes," Vinni said.

A deep huff from Hanes. "Good. That's very good."

The atmosphere held an anxiety Signet finally noticed. *What is wrong?* she asked Cratag mentally. His muscles held a fine tension that wasn't of a physical nature, as he'd have stretched his muscles from time to time. She'd felt his hands move from her fingers of one hand to the other, from hands to wrists . . . and she was dithering from sheer tiredness. *What is wrong?*

It is near TransitionBell. Avellana's Passage was much longer this time. And, I think, harder on both of you.

Tears began to trickle down Signet's cheeks, she simply couldn't hold them back. *I had hoped that my Flair would change her enough . . . I thought it had.*

"Hush." Cratag bent and kissed her temple. "Avellana wouldn't be alive if your Flair hadn't already modified her brain patterns."

He'd said the worst of all their fears aloud!

Signet choked on a sob.

"Hush, darlin'."

They were at the door to the MistrysSuite, and it opened silently for them. Signet heard water rushing into the large pool in the bathing room. A warm mist hung in the air, along with different herbs than she'd been smelling all night . . . less astringent herbs, gentler.

Cratag carried her into the room and helped her from her clothes, his hands not lingering . . . much. Just enough to make her smile and know that she was a woman and attractive.

Signet kept to the topic. "Near TransitionBell." She thought again of the depthless space and whirling stars in the portal to death and another life. Someday. But not now.

And not for Avellana!

Cratag slid Signet into the hot pool, and she moaned aloud at the wonder of the silky water heating her skin, easing her muscles.

He waved a hand over the pool and said, "Froth, level seven."

Bubbles roiled around her, a white layer on the pool, sending up more scent of chamomile, sweet woodruff, vanilla. She moved to the underwater bench and sat up straighter so she wouldn't drown, blinked up at Cratag. "What?"

"I'll be back in with Avellana and Vinni, probably Hanes, too." Cratag grimaced. "Residence, please make sure she stays awake."

"I won't fall asleep," Signet protested.

Their culture didn't have a taboo against nudity.

"I take care of my woman."

He considered her his woman. A very good start, and looking at the broad lines of his body and sensing his aura once more, the thought teased Signet again that he might, possibly might, be her HeartMate.

Then her bathing room was full of males, and Avellana was slid, fully clothed, into the water with Signet, despite her protest that the girl's silks would be ruined. None of the men cared.

Hanes stood with his back toward her. Vinni watched to make sure Signet treated his HeartMate gently, and Cratag glowered.

"You're a GrandLady, you can remove her clothes with a word." Cratag flicked his finger. "Several words, or a couplet, or whatever."

Signet already had, and the pretty robes had sunk to the bottom of the pool, not that she could see them. She frowned at Cratag, at Vinni.

"And either Vinni or the Hazels can fix them," Cratag added.

"I can't," Vinni said mournfully, seeming glad to talk about something as inconsequential as expensive garments.

Cratag flapped his hands. "Go, now."

"I want to make sure . . . watch so . . ." Vinni trailed off.

Signet met the boy's eyes. "I'm just going to bathe her; the water is soothing her even now." Signet loosened the girl's hair from her formal braids and combed it free to float—or flop—in the water.

Vinni's lips pressed together. "I know." With one last look, he turned and left. Hanes followed with a wave at Signet, not meeting her eyes.

Cratag stopped at the threshold. "Speaking of the Hazels."

Signet paused in the middle of shampooing Avellana's hair. "What?"

"They were aware of Avellana's Passage."

Had Signet felt a connection with them? Perhaps.

"They are waiting for an official report from you."

Just what she didn't want to do, calm a frantic Family. Again. Signet allowed herself a grunt.

Cratag nodded. "See you in a bit." He glanced at the timer on the wall that the Residence had kept from being steamy. "You have twenty minutes."

He pulled the door closed behind him as he left.

*O*utside Signet's rooms, Cratag leaned a heavy shoulder against the wall, kept his breathing steady . . . as he had for hours. Prayed. Also for hours. Avellana had lived. The child was safe.

Signet was safe.

He had never been so frightened in his life as he had been lately. This job . . . this situation with this woman and child . . . was aging him. He swore he could feel hairs on his head turning gray from the stress. He was damn glad that he'd worn clothes with top-of-the-pyramid spells to handle a physical man's fear and activity sweat.

He was in too deep. He'd known that, had known it for days, but had shoved the thought aside when enjoying Signet, in and out of bed. But now his feelings were all tangled up with her, and her emotional and physical survival.

He didn't know how he'd sat by and watched Signet and little Avellana writhe and tremble, flush with heat, bead with cold sweat as their bodies turned icy. Vinni being there had made it worse. Cratag had had to hide his fear from the boy, show a strong front, *keep* a strong front even deep down, so that he didn't worry the youngster.

The sounds that the girl and woman made had shredded him. Not animalistic, pure human suffering. He'd held them both until Vinni needed a connection with them all. Vinni had limited his bond with Avellana to only a half-septhour, then he'd shut away his emotions and kept his link to them to no more than a thread. He'd sat there and watched, like Cratag. But he didn't mind holding Cratag's hand, trying to bruise Cratag's fingers.

Lord and Lady, what a night. Cratag shuddered. He didn't know how the two had survived, had sensed death was close. It still scared him down to his toenails, and awed him that Signet was able to bring the convulsing child through Passage.

He didn't have any great Flair to really experience what was going on. He'd concentrated on being exactly what she'd said she wanted, a boulder, an anchor. Lord and Lady knew what Vinni saw or sensed with his Flair, maybe even more terrible things.

Now they were all waiting to see how Avellana would be later this morning. He muttered another prayer that she would be fine, better than ever. Signet didn't seem to have any doubt, and that reassured Cratag.

He'd almost lost Signet.

No, he wouldn't think of that. She was his lover, his woman, linked to him at the moment, needing him. He liked that feeling. He thought she liked knowing he needed her, too.

Circling and cycling, his thoughts would repeat themselves if he let them. He should meditate, but after he made sure Signet was fine and supported her during her report to the Hazels, he figured that they'd crash in bed together.

Maybe the Hazels would come and take Avellana away again.

He let another tremble of his body ripple out. He didn't want to think what would have happened to Signet emotionally if she'd lost Avellana, so he thought of practicalities.

If Signet somehow survived and Avellana didn't, Signet would be ruined forever. FirstFamilies didn't forget failure. No matter how hard Signet worked, how much she sweated and bled, they'd condemn her. She'd probably have to leave Druida and all she knew. Did she realize that? She wasn't as naive as he'd originally thought, so he was sure she did. Would she consider leaving Druida worse than death? Some Nobles he'd met would, he knew. Only the city and its society mattered. Society didn't matter to Signet, though she loved the arts and sophisticated pursuits. But how could she leave D'Marigold Residence alone?

Puzzles and problems, and he was worrying about a future that might not come. Not like him, but this whole situation was unusual. He said another prayer, pushed away from the wall when he heard rustlings from the bathing room.

He opened the door and saw Signet and Avellana both dressed in thick nightrobes. Avellana was as limp as a doll in Signet's arms, with a little glow around her as if Signet had initiated a keep-warm spell on her. He took the girl from Signet and crooked his elbow. "Lean on me."

She nodded wearily and put her arm through his.

They'd only taken a few slow steps together before the door to Avellana's suite flew open and Vinni and Hanes appeared. They came close and looked at Avellana. Vinni touched her rosier, healthier-looking cheek.

Hanes put his hand on the boy's shoulder and said, "You promised not to be away another whole night this week. We must return home."

Vinni shrugged his guard's hand away, scowling. "I didn't know she was going to have another Passage fugue, did I? I can't see everything."

Tension was getting to the boy, too.

"She'll be fine, Vinni, I promise," Signet said softly.

"Tonight," he said.

"Tonight, and better tomorrow."

Vinni just stared at her, then sighed and slumped a little, believing in her optimism. He inclined his head. "Thank you, GrandLady D'Marigold." Then he bowed. Straightening to a formal posture, he turned and walked away. Hanes rolled his eyes at Cratag then followed the boy. They disappeared into the teleportation room and a moment later Cratag could *feel* that they were gone as the fizz of Vinni's anxious energy disappeared. Cratag hoped the boy didn't know more than he was telling, because Signet needed all the information she could get.

He held Avellana as Signet changed the bed linens, and they snuggled the little girl back into the safe cocoon of bed.

Signet wove toward the sitting room, and Cratag braced an arm around her, once again taking much of her weight. Her feet lifted slowly, she was shuffling, she who always was aware of her feet and had crisp steps. She went to the scrybowl and sat next to it. A spurt of anger went through him as she initiated the scry with slurred words. Why couldn't the Hazels wait until she had a decent amount of sleep?

The scry was answered immediately, the water droplets suspended over the bowl showing the Hazels standing, holding each other. Their faces showed strain.

Signet sat straight, smiled. Cratag would have thought it would be a perfunctory, professional smile, but it wasn't. It was warm and sympathetic. "I am pleased to say that Avellana has finished her second Passage fugue and is doing well."

"This dreamquest was longer than the first," T'Hazel said.

Raising her eyebrows, Signet said, "So I was told, though I didn't notice within the Passage. The Passage was rough, but Avellana is fine."

How many times and to how many people would Signet have to say those words?

"Can we come and get her?" A plea from D'Hazel as one of her hands clenched and unclenched.

"Of course," Signet said. "We are in her bedroom."

The scrybowl went blank, then there came the sound of rapid footsteps, then the Hazel parents were through the door. T'Hazel scooped up Avellana, and D'Hazel lifted Rhyz, who looked as limp as she . . . and Signet. The Hazels should just leave so Signet could have some sleep.

"We were worried," T'Hazel said.

"It was longer and should have been shorter," D'Hazel said.

Signet said, "We will deal with the last Passage quest when it comes. It may be longer or shorter." She shrugged. "Who knows?"

Cradling Rhyz in one arm, D'Hazel smoothed a hand over her daughter's clean hair. "I can feel the change in her . . . the change your Flair is bringing, mending her brain pathways."

Signet nodded, and Cratag was sure even that gesture took more energy than she had to spare.

"Perhaps you should have her checked by the FirstLevel Healers later today," he suggested.

T'Hazel nodded to him. "A good idea. We'll keep her for the day and night and return her tomorrow morning."

"Fine," Signet said. A whisper of sound.

Cratag suppressed frustrated anger at their self-absorption. Neither he nor Signet dared to be sharp with the Hazels. He put a hand on Signet's shoulder, shot a look at T'Hazel. "We'll expect you tomorrow at MidMorningBell."

With a nod, T'Hazel left, and D'Hazel followed her HeartMate.

Signet relaxed and fell over into Cratag's arms. She murmured, "I would like to spend the night in the HouseHeart . . ."

His heart thumped hard in disappointment. He wouldn't be allowed in there.

" . . . but I don't have the energy to open the door for us," she ended, closing her eyes and going limp. Cratag froze. She'd said "us" hadn't she? He couldn't believe it. A new, temporary lover wouldn't be admitted to a HouseHeart.

"Take me to bed, Cratag." She sighed out the words. "I want to sleep with you."

She was already sleeping in his arms, and he didn't want to let her go.

A whole day with Cratag with no one around but their *Fams!*

If he decided to stay with her instead of returning to T'Hawthorn Residence . . . which brought memories flooding back of the day before. Laev Hawthorn might have had his Passage last night, too, and Signet had asked Cratag to be her anchor while he was tied by blood and love to the Hawthorns. She wanted Cratag to herself for a few septhours. Was that too much to ask?

She stretched carefully, and the sheets didn't feel like her own, so she opened her eyes. He had taken her to his suite. Ah, her uncle's silkeen sheets, finer than her own. He'd been a sybarite, cherishing all his little pleasures.

But she was concerned about the man asleep next to her. The only time she could stare at him was at moments like these. His breathing was slow and deep, his Flair marching in his usual patterns, as strong as it ever was. But that wasn't the incredible thing about Cratag. His character was, the man he'd made of himself from a southern shopkeeper's son. He'd become one of the most trusted men by *the* greatest lord in Celta. Strong in every way—strong willed, strong minded, tough emotionally, and physically . . . and at this very moment she wanted his body.

Twenty-four

*T*he linens were pushed down to his hips, showing his bare chest. He'd be equally bare below. His face wasn't a noble one, features rough hewn, his scars thick and white—though she rarely noticed them—his hair was kept so short that there wasn't enough to run her fingers through.

His body was magnificent, every muscle honed and sculpted. She couldn't ask for a more beautiful lover, or a more caring one, though he hid his feelings very well. His touch had usually been tender, but she liked it best the few times when he'd lost control. And she was willing to ensure that he'd do that this morning.

She began tracing her fingers over his chest, gently flicking his tiny nipples with her fingernail. The pattern wasn't random, she'd studied him . . . his Flair, his energies, all his sensual responses.

As his most interesting muscle began to harden, she leaned over and pressed her lips to his, swept her tongue across his mouth, then rolled onto him, settling atop him, his shaft at the apex of her thighs, with the wonderful silkeen sheet between them. She rocked her hips, enjoying the slow pleasure of teasing herself and him to arousal until he was thick and hard, and strong, for her.

His eyelids cracked, and a glittering violet gaze met her own. She couldn't prevent a smug smile.

His hands clamped on her bottom, and he arched and moved so that she caught her gasp at the sweet pleasure that was close to desperate yearning. She panted now, wanting more, and tried to lift to tug away the sheet between them. He kept her easily in the exact position he wanted, the tip of him pressed against her most needy flesh. She gasped his name, and the ends of his mouth curved upward. "You started this game," he rumbled.

"Yes. Please. Inside me. Please."

"Begging prettily, I like that." Satisfaction laced his tones.

She choked on a laugh. "Anytime."

He moved fast. Yanked the sheet from between them. Rolled and speared inside of her. Desperate pleasure twisted tight inside her. Only a little bit away from ecstasy.

But he didn't move.

She had a feeling that he was going to make her lose control first, and she didn't care. "Cratag." She clamped her hands on his shoulders, tried to arch, to make him move, to take the delight just out of reach.

"Yes. My name. Say it again."

"Cratag."

"Again."

"Cratag, and third time's a charm!" she cried.

He laughed, and it was enough to push her over into shattering, a thousand pieces of her being swept away and tumbled about and then slowly melding together once more. To find that he was watching her with glinting eyes. "You are so very beautiful," he murmured. "And never so beautiful as now."

She chuckled, felt him still thick and steely in the depths of her. "I thought the same thing about you, this morning."

His brows rose in surprise. "Surely not."

"Surely so." Her hands had fallen to the bedsponge. Now she lifted them and let her fingers trace the well-defined muscles of his arms, slid her fingers to his chest, caressing a scar on the way, and put her thumbs over his nipples, rubbed.

He shuddered and penetrated her a little more, and she loved it.

"So," she said throatily. "Are you going to finish this business?"

A wariness came to his eyes.

"What?" she asked, feeling that despite everything she was going to lose this moment.

"It isn't business, is it?"

Tsking, she set her hands behind his neck and lifted to brush a kiss on his mouth. "Of course it isn't. Nothing of business in this. We have no business between us." She angled her head and kissed him again, and when she stopped her head was muzzy and she was breathless. "Only pleasure."

She kissed him once more, opened herself to all of him, her emotions and her mind to the bond between them. *Only caring*, she sent telepathically.

He put a hand under her neck, and she let her head fall back. He shook his head. "I have never had such a lover as you."

She smiled. "I can say the same."

"Look at me."

She'd closed her eyes, luxuriating in the feel of him. So she opened her lashes and stared into his eyes. They were dark now, the deep violet of evening turning to night. He flexed his lower body and the power of him moved inside her—his body, his will. She sensed a need from him that she didn't understand; then it was hidden and gone as he stroked and both of them lost clear thought and only felt.

Once again he stopped just as she was teetering on the edge of release. She sucked in a breath and narrowed her eyes at him. "Just what game *are* you playing?" She meant it to be a demand, but it was more of a gasp.

His jaw flexed, and she realized he was at the edge of orgasm too.

"I heard." He took a shuddering breath then continued. "I heard that if a man and a woman, uh, stay together, uh, sexually . . ." Red was actually tinting the broad line of his cheekbones, "they develop a deeper bond."

She blinked up at him. She hadn't ever heard that, but it was certainly an interesting idea. Not the time to ask D'Marigold ResidenceLibrary about it. "Closer than the link we already have between us?"

He cupped a hand over her left breast. "It's a physical link between us, our bodies. Our flesh will always know the touch of the other."

She liked the notion. "Are you asking me to stay in bed with you all day?" she teased.

"Yes." He bit off the word.

She twined her arms around his neck, used a bit of her renewed Flair to mold the bedsponge into a more comfortable shape beneath her, since she was going to be under Cratag for a while.

Sooner or later during this day she would make him lose control and visit a very enjoyable revenge upon him with some of her own games. So she smiled.

And she did do that sooner.

And later.

*S*he had spent the day entwined with him, exploring him. Letting him explore her with hands and mouth. He learned all her tastes, and she learned his, became expert in what drove him crazy with lust. It had been a marvelous day, and probably the worst idea he'd ever had. How was he ever going to get her out of his blood and brain and mind and heart now?

Why had he done it? He'd wanted . . . he didn't know what he'd wanted or what he'd thought. His mind had been fogged by pure desire.

They had discovered a fully stocked no-time close to the bed, full of good food as well as a couple of strange selections like six flavors of mousse. They'd experimented with them all.

There had been extremely brief toilet breaks and much longer bathing breaks and a session or two under the waterfall. He was glad he had the stamina that he did, and could only guess that her dancing had given Signet the stamina *she* had.

Finally, the Residence and their Fams had insisted on seeing them for a "civilized meal," and they had dressed for dinner. Signet looked almost as good in clothes as she did without. Her color was good, and whatever energy she had depleted in the early morning with Avellana in Passage had been renewed by the time she'd awakened him.

He bowed as he met her outside her door. She had dressed in cloth of gold with an orangish copper trim around her sleeves, tunic hem, and trous cuffs, every inch the GrandLady. He didn't think he looked so bad either. He wore one of his best tunics and trous suit, formal with a lot of fabric gathered at wrists and ankles, in the Hawthorn colors of purple and gold. Deep purple complemented his coloring more than the lighter shade that T'Hawthorn and Laev wore, and he knew he looked as good as the Hawthorn tailor could make him.

As they walked down the stairs a slight frown crossed Signet's face.

"Problem?" he asked.

She glanced at him, flushed a little.

"Ah, this morning before we conducted our great experiment—which I believe turned out to be true, by the way—I was wondering if you felt whether Laev Hawthorn also underwent Passage last night."

It hadn't occurred to him, but that was a reasonable deduction to make. "I felt nothing from him last night." Now that he thought back, that wasn't quite true. He'd felt pulses of giddy elation through his bond with Laev. Maybe that had helped keep him sane during the dark and scary septhours of the night. Couldn't have hurt.

Signet sighed, bringing him back to the moment, and they went into the kitchen.

Dinner was excellent, with an atmosphere of easy affection between them all, human and Fams. Beadle sat and grinned at Cratag, announcing that he no longer feared the night. He hopped into Cratag's lap and licked his chin. Eyes sparking, Beadle thanked Cratag for allowing him to explore outside. The link between his Fam and himself had deepened, too.

After the meal, Cratag accompanied Signet to the theater and watched a comedy and laughed a lot.

Later he made love with Signet, and then they fell asleep.

It was the most perfect day of his life.

*C*ratag *trained alone in his morning session. He'd greeted the Hazels* noncommittally when they'd arrived, but was still irritated at how they'd treated Signet. As if she was a servant of their House, at their beck and call. Yes, they were concerned parents, but they had known Avellana was through Passage and safe through their shared link. Now they were smoothing their unreasonable demands of Signet by complimenting her over tea . . . that she had provided.

Maybe he was thinking of his status in the T'Hawthorn Household, too. He checked in with the Family guards every other day. All was going smoothly, but he was beginning to feel more disconnected from the Family he'd worked with and fought for and considered himself a part of.

Maybe T'Hawthorn was feeling Cratag's dissatisfaction through their Family link, because he'd sent a gift over to D'Marigold house for Cratag. A brand-new top-of-the-pyramid fighting simulacrum. Of course T'Hawthorn hadn't called it a gift, but a new addition to his household for the guards that Cratag should check out.

The magically crafted humanoid was as large as Cratag himself, so he didn't have to pull any punches, and he was getting a better workout than any he'd had since he last took on the Hollys in the Green Knight Fencing and Fighting Salon. Even better because the simulacrum had random patterns of Flaired fighting, and Cratag was beginning to know all the Hollys' weaknesses. As they might be learning his own, so the humanoid was excellent for training.

Maybe Cratag was grouchy because he hadn't gotten a good night's sleep the night before ... as he would have expected to. He'd been plagued by disturbing dreams that he couldn't quite remember—except he'd been someplace where everyone had spoken a different language than he. The problem was, they were all people he knew and cared for—Signet, Laev, Vinni, T'Hawthorn, Hanes ... and Avellana just studied him with cool eyes.

One of his old "outsider" dreams that he hated. Another weakness.

He'd just "killed" the construct when a dark mental spear of energy hit him and he fell.

Another Passage fugue of Laev's, hopefully the last. Cratag rolled to his back on the mat. He thought D'Marigold Residence commented, but he could only choke out an unintelligible sound. They were both bonded to Signet, and she'd sensed what was happening, so she could answer the Residence. That was the last complicated thought he had. He just lay and suffered.

This *was* the worst. Like being back in bad dreams.

Oppressive darkness all around, streaking flashes of Flair he didn't understand, Laev's murky emotions. Another time when Cratag stood and watched and did little. He knew Laev battled his inner demons ... his own faults and fears and guilts, and Cratag suffered with him.

The door to the training room opened and shut, and Cratag scented his lover's floral and spice fragrance before she sat beside him, took one of his hands between her hot ones. Linked with him, and it was as if she wrapped arms around him, stood just behind him, leaning against his back. He reveled in her touch.

That was a mistake.

Through Cratag's bond with Laev, the youngster felt the surge of Cratag's tenderness for Signet. That diverted Laev from his guilt, but plunged him into another strong emotion—lust.

They all groaned together, and through a red haze of desire, Cratag felt Laev move, go to his workroom, and start feverishly sculpting a block of marble, making a HeartGift. That lasted an eternity, and once the HeartGift was created, Cratag sensed Laev's yearning, aching confusion. He wanted to touch his HeartMate as he had previously, should have been able to find her, link with her, especially now he knew who she was . . .

What? That thought of Laev's jolted Cratag back into a little detachment, into Cratag instead of Cratag-Laev.

"What's going on?" Avellana's voice was too high.

She was a distraction to Cratag. He wanted to get a better feel for Laev's emotions, his thoughts, something important was happening.

"Cratag is linked with Laev HawthornHeir as he experiences Passage," Signet said.

"Oh." There was a little silence, but Cratag felt the girl come closer, and cats' purring roared in his ears.

"Do I look like that?" Avellana sounded worried, disapproving, other stuff Cratag couldn't sort out.

"I don't know. I'm with you in Passage," Signet replied.

Du sniffed. *You look and smell much worse. Passage lasts much longer. Not pleasant.*

Cratag was aroused, and he was embarrassed and distressed that the girl might notice. He should let go of Signet's soft hand, but he couldn't make himself do so.

Rhyz yowled from a few meters away. *We are off our schedule. Time to go to the craft room. You are making a holo of Me for Me. We did not work on it at all yesterday.*

Saved by the cat.

"I'm going with Rhyz." The girl nearly ran away.

Good.

Signet said, "That's fine. Rhyz, please let me know if she needs anything."

"Yesss," hissed the cat.

Cratag sensed them leave. The purrs revved again, one furry

body pressed his side, Beadle. Another cat walked back and forth over his ankles, which he hated. Du.

The darkness and brightness and uniqueness of Laev's thoughts were receding, too, until there was a shout of triumph from him as he awoke . . . finished with his Second Passage at last.

A migraine pounded Cratag into unconsciousness.

Twenty-five

Signet bit her lip, torn between staying with Cratag and going to Avellana. Her duty to the child and a FirstFamilies contract warring with her concern for her love, her lover.

Beadle hopped onto his chest, part of which was showing through his training tunic, and curled up, smiling at Signet. *I will stay with My FamMan.*

She nodded, "Thank you." Reluctantly she released Cratag's hand. He'd been cold, then hot. She hadn't entered the link he had with Laev. She'd have been intruding on a private connection, but she'd dimly sensed the boy's fluctuating emotional storms, had been with Cratag to support him.

Slowly she rose and glanced at Cratag. His temples were beaded with sweat, his body subsiding to normal. The lust he'd felt she had felt, too, but her clothes had hidden her arousal. She was sure Avellana hadn't noticed Cratag's lower body. The girl had stared at his

gray, grimacing face. The physical evidence of Passage had frightened the child who had only awoken clean and tidy in her own bed
with her Family around her.

Signet rolled tense shoulders. Beadle would look after Cratag,
and. . . . "Residence, once I've left the room, secure it so no one can
enter."

"Yes, Signet," the Residence replied.

She hesitated, glancing at a big simulacrum that was disturb-
ingly featureless. Signet wondered who Cratag might like to best in
a fight. Who he might ever consider a personal enemy. She came up
with no one.

She had no terrible enemies herself, so she chose the worst man
she'd heard of. "Simulacrum? Can you look like the late GrandLord
Ioho T'Yew?" She wouldn't mind pounding on a likeness of that
one herself.

"Yes."

So she walked up to the construct and touched it, sending it
Flair, then watched the features form into haughty nobility with
a cruel twist. Resemblance enough, though she would never have
envisioned the lord in training clothes. "Guard Cratag until he dis-
misses you."

Its body flexed once before it took a defensive stance. She didn't
know if it was more or less disturbing now that it had a real face.
Shrugging, she left to do her duty.

But she had learned one thing through her connection with
Cratag.

He was definitely her HeartMate.

She'd think on that soon, but right now she had boots to make.

Avellana was busy creating her holos and didn't look up or greet
Signet when she entered the craft room. Signet raised her brows and
crossed to study the bright light that was ready to be bent and tinted
into shapes, but recognized nothing. She stood a couple of minutes,
but Avellana kept quiet, so Signet crossed to the door off the craft

room that led to her cobbling room. She opened the door and left it standing wide. From the corner of her eyes she saw Avellana hesitate, glance her way, then turn back to the holo.

Signet suppressed a smile, the girl loved watching her work, because it was a treat. Signet didn't often allow anyone in her private areas. She studied the cubbyholes full of rolled leathers from various animals dyed different colors. She knew what she wanted . . . some old celtaroon, the toughest leather on Celta. It still showed a hint of the natural orange stripes. The natural blue had faded to a shade of gray. The snakelike creature had been huge, so the quality of the leather wasn't as fine, but the size should make an excellent pair of boots for Cratag. Tinting celtaroon would be a challenge, especially since she usually used that leather for Marigold footwear, and the natural orange wasn't a detriment.

But she wanted to make Cratag a special gift just because she loved him, and give him a gift that would remind him of her.

She took down the celtaroon skin and eyed it, just enough for a full pair of boots without making separate shafts for the uppers and vamps for the foot area. With a little Flair, she could make each boot from one piece and harden the sole until it would be the last part to wear out.

As with all her leathers, the celtaroon skin was already prepared. Closing her eyes, she concentrated on Cratag. She'd stroked his feet and muscular calves during loveplay more than once, measuring them, setting the size and shape of him, the depth of his arch, the width of his toes, into her memory. Now she held the leather and *formed* it with her mind. The insoles would be perfect to fit his feet with extra layers of permamoss and wool. Winter-spring boots.

If he stayed—and she'd use all she had to keep him—she'd make him lightweight, breathable summer boots, and ankle dress boots, and thigh highs, and tap shoes . . .

"You're making something for Cratag," Avellana stated.

"That's right."

"You and he are lovers."

Signet froze, turned deliberately, keeping a slight smile on her face. "That is private between Cratag and me. Something I'd prefer to remain private."

The girl was looking at her with wide eyes, but nodded. "I told my mother and father, and mother said it was a concern."

"Is it?" Hot words came to Signet's tongue. She suppressed them. Her smile faded, and she gave the girl a straight look. "Both of us are very aware of your welfare. You will not be harmed in our care."

Avellana continued to nod. "I know. I would not have survived Passage without you, Signet." She came up and hugged Signet. A tight knot in her stomach eased. Avellana said, "I *feel* different inside my head. I think better. I am not as afraid of new and different things."

Signet kissed Avellana's cheeks. "Thank you, that's a wonderful compliment."

"I told my parents that. I told them that I loved you and Cratag and that you and he and Du and Beadle are my friends."

"Of course we are."

One more decided nod, and the girl stepped back. "And we all take care of our friends."

"Yes."

Avellana's eyes slid to the celtaroon boots. "I am making a holo for Cratag, and for you, because we are friends."

Signet laughed. "I'll make shoes for you. I told you so." She lifted a finger. "One pair after you return to D'Hazel Residence, because you are my friend. Other pairs if you continue to obey the rules, as we've agreed."

"But right now you are making boots for Cratag."

Signet looked Avellana in the eye. "Because he is my friend."

"All right. My father said it was all to the good that you were linked with Cratag. That he no doubt helped me during Passage, too."

"He has."

A little sigh escaped Avellana. "I didn't know. I can feel you, and Rhyz, and Vinni, and my parents, and even sometimes my sister, but that's all."

"Many people love you, Avellana. You should remember that both during the day, and in your night dreams, and during Passage."

"All right, I will. Can I stay and watch you?"

"Of course." Signet turned back to the boots and continued to work long minutes on the insoles. They must be perfect. The shafts of the boots themselves would have just enough space for Cratag to put them on and take them off comfortably, and she'd add pulls to the top. As she worked, she hummed the spells she'd learned from her father to waterproof celtaroon leather, to make them scuff and scratch resistant. After she tinted them she'd add a polish that wouldn't fade. The cut of the boots was of a timeless noble fashion that would never be dated. She'd have to consider equally timeless patterns for the ten sets of fancy decorative stitching. The Marigolds were nothing if not fashionable.

Cratag woke aching all over and couldn't recall why.

"D'Marigold Residence, GentleSir Maytree is awake," said a male voice, and Cratag sprang to his feet, saw GrandLord Ioho T'Yew, and spun a kick into the man's—ghost's?—midsection and sent the simulacrum flying back a pace.

It picked itself up and said, "Do you wish to continue training?"

Memory rushed back. Feeling stupid, Cratag said, "No." Heat came to his neck and with it the realization that his clothes and body weren't in great shape. The fight with the simulacrum had been good and sweaty. And his part of Laev's Passage had been gruesome and sweaty. He thought he might have contorted into a few shapes that strained his muscles.

"Stand down," he said, and it went to a corner, closed its eyes, and became still.

He studied it. Signet had given it the features of the late Ioho T'Yew, a wife abuser, a man women would hate and men would despise. A GrandLord who, like many FirstFamily lords or ladies, had felt a sense of entitlement at being powerful in Flair and influence and wealth. He'd led a very conservative faction of the First-Families Council.

Cratag's liege lord, T'Hawthorn, was more moderate . . . and as the former Captain of All Councils, even more powerful. Cratag didn't see Laev being that conservative, even as he matured.

Put in that perspective, the Hazels were positively liberal in their treatment of Signet and himself. Cratag shook out his limbs and did some stretches, then went to the waterfall room. Why was he so concerned about status lately? So touchy when Signet was slighted? Having "outsider" dreams again?

Because Signet had always been ignored by the FirstFamilies— allowed herself to be. Because his own life and views were changing . . . he was seeing how other Families lived, experiencing more of city life on the educational trips and nights out, instead of spending most of his time in T'Hawthorn Residence.

Because he was coming to care too much about Signet, wanted to be seen as an acceptable lover for a lady like her. He grunted and let the water rinse the dirt and sweat from him, but it didn't take his yearnings away.

As her hands worked, Signet mulled over her circumstances. The Hazels were pleased with her and implied that her future would be assured if Avellana survived her last Passage. Everyone—including Signet—had convinced themselves that since Avellana was so unique, her Passages would not follow a standard pattern either. Whatever applied to others would not pertain to Avellana.

Signet hoped it was so, but she was all too aware that her own future hung in the balance. That was secondary to the thought of the grief she'd feel if she lost Avellana, but it loomed all the same.

The Residence had reported that it was receiving inquiries about her various services and prices, and Signet would soon have to sit down and figure out exactly what she was going to do with this newly revealed Flair of hers. She could offer herself as a companion, but she didn't want to go into other people's homes, and, right now, she loved the small "Family" she had, the naturalness of it. It would be a very special person that she'd invite into her own home like she was doing with Avellana.

She set the leather in a shallow tray of deep red dye, washed her hands, and pulled out a drawer of sturdy Flair-infused threads.

No, she wouldn't be swept up and bullied into opening her Residence to another person no matter how many visions Vinni had . . . and as she set her jaw on that decision, Avellana called out that Vinni had arrived and they were going to walk down to the boathouse on the river with their Fams.

Could Signet be a "professional" friend? She didn't think so. She didn't want to put a price on her friendship, but, on the other hand, her being with someone *did* seem to change their lives. To her surprise, D'Marigold Residence had consulted with T'Ash and the NobleCouncil Clerk, and they'd contacted her previous friends and lovers, documenting such changes. She'd burned with embarrassment at the thought of all the questions they'd been asked. Whinna Furze had been lavish in her praise, as had others. Feeling belated guilt for leaving Signet? She didn't know, and that thought, too, caused her discomfort.

Maybe it was even worse . . . maybe it was as she'd always thought, that people didn't know why they liked being in her company, and once Signet's Flair worked on them and they changed, they drifted away. How many friends had she actually had? Horrifying. Depressing.

Except that Signet *knew* Avellana cared for her, as did Vinni. So did Cratag. His loving was beyond compare, tender, affectionate, passionate.

She was sure he was her HeartMate. But it was illegal to tell a person that. To do so stole complete freedom of choice from them. The usual action after discovering a HeartMate was to present them with a HeartGift . . . a gift made in the time of Passage when one's Flair was strong and wild enough to connect with them. If a person accepted a HeartGift and kept it, they could be claimed as a HeartMate.

The problem was that Signet hadn't connected strongly enough with Cratag to make a HeartGift. There were no huge tap shoes shielded and sitting in the HouseHeart safe.

And there was the matter of her pride . . . or perhaps it was the lingering hurt of abandonment within her. She wanted *him* to come to her, indicate that he wanted her permanently in his life.

But that didn't mean she couldn't make a few pairs of shoes for him anyway.

She checked their bond and found that Cratag was awake. No doubt he'd scry T'Hawthorn Residence to assure himself of Laev Hawthorn's health.

Without Vinni and his visions and Avellana, Cratag wouldn't have come into Signet's life. Would she ever have acted on their attraction when they met in rituals? She didn't think so. She fretted that he never would have either, for reasons she didn't quite understand except for their difference in status, which she didn't care much about. Nor would have her parents.

HeartMates were prized by all Families. With a HeartMate there was a better chance that the Family would be happy and prolific— or as prolific as Celtan Families usually were with one to three children. HeartMates were welcomed.

She certainly had welcomed Cratag. Her cheeks heated as she realized how long and lusty, and tender, their loving had been. She could only hope it would continue to be so. It was loving on her part, and she'd keep it as lusty and tender as she could.

She set out her first selections of threads for the stitching, then closed and spellshielded the door behind her. Through her connection with Cratag, she knew he was discussing Laev with T'Hawthorn. Laev was a concern, and she hoped Cratag would share that with her.

For a little while she indulged in pretty fantasies, that Cratag would romantically sweep her off her feet and propose marriage to her—maybe on a walk on the cliffs as they watched color come into the world at dawn; maybe when she was snuggled on his lap in the sitting room that was the most cheerful place in the house; maybe. . . .

Foolish fantasies. He'd called her his woman, but she didn't know how much that truly meant to him. He was a serious man, he'd have had serious lovers before, but he wasn't married, and Signet thought he never had been. His inner essence was that of a lone warrior. His lord's chief guard as long as that lord met the standards Cratag himself held.

Yes, a lone warrior. And did such men ever want a wife and Family?

*D*uring *her meditation times, Signet struggled with her own self-image,* self-confidence, self-*worth* over the next two weeks and the passing of the month from Willow to Ash. During her "office" time, she continued to refine the list of her services: Flair "seeing" and block-age removal through meditation sessions and "green walks," through the circles and parks of Druida. Passage consultation, though she didn't offer experiencing Passage as she was doing with Avellana. Signet didn't think that she'd be able to endure many more such ordeals.

She made appointments with T'Ash, who did Flair testing; D'Sea, the mind Healer; and GrandLord T'Heather, the premier physical Healer on Celta, to discuss her Flair and what she should be able to do and how she should do it. All of them had accessed and studied her files available from the NobleCouncil Clerk.

T'Ash had her sit in on a couple of testings and verify his results, but D'Sea and T'Heather treated her like a client, giving *her* physical, mental, and emotional tests. She both resented that and was relieved that her results showed she was well within normal parameters.

So she took small steps to becoming a businesswoman, filing a list of services and prices with the NobleCouncil Clerk based on her talks with others . . . and the staggering amount of NobleGilt—

salary for services rendered provided by the Council according to the importance of the work—that was paid to her. She'd sat and stared at the huge sum that had been transferred to her bank account. A yearly salary backdated from when she'd been seventeen.

That was a mixed blessing. A great deal of gilt, but all her previous friends and lovers were designated as "clients," since none of them had kept in touch with her.

Even with the wealth, she didn't take herself seriously. She had only one client, and the outcome still hung in the balance. No one had actually made an appointment to consult with her, and no one would until Avellana returned to the Hazels after safely weathering Passage.

Like Avellana, Signet was an unknown quantity.

She made love with Cratag nearly every night and slept with him. Neither of them hid their affair, and no one commented on it, though she thought Vinni and Avellana spoke about it. The Hazels said nothing during Signet's daily reports.

Everyone was all too aware that Signet continued to be Avellana's best chance at surviving her last Passage fugue.

Their schedules finally became second nature for Signet, and if she missed some of the flexibility of her life before, that didn't compare with having loving people under her roof.

As the days progressed without the incident of Passage for Avellana, Cratag relaxed and became slightly preoccupied. Signet didn't probe, and finally found out what was bothering him one day when they stopped for tea after a trip to a museum one afternoon and saw Laev Hawthorn and Nivea Sunflower wrapped up in each other.

Laev had stopped visiting, and that irritated Signet since she knew it hurt Cratag, but again she said nothing. Instead she scheduled more meditation lessons and time for him, both with her and by himself. He seemed better after such sessions.

*O*ne sunny afternoon Signet and Cratag were following Vinni and Avellana up the river stairs, holding hands. The Fams were still snoozing in the sun on the boathouse deck.

When the children reached the top of the stairs, their whoops sounded, and Signet knew they'd broken into a run. She chuckled, and Cratag squeezed her hand, smiled at her, and again she hoped that he might feel more than simple affection and caring for her.

"You'd think they hadn't trained at all or run along the riverbank," Cratag said.

Signet laughed again. "Their energy is incredible."

"That's why you upped the number of afternoon expeditions?"

"Three days out of five is not too many," she protested, then shrugged and sighed. "I'm not a teacher, and I don't want to be one. When she's in the city, Avellana is ever conscious of her status, so the outings balance her childish time here."

Laughing, he said, "Good rationalization."

"It worked with the Hazels." She frowned. "I got the impression that they had hoped Avellana would be through her Passage by now. Anyway, they will be sending some lessons over for Avellana that the Residence will supervise."

"Avellana will take whatever time she needs to go through Passage. We're all giving her that—you're giving her more. She seems to change a little every day."

"Like you said when we first met, we all change when we interact with others, especially on a daily basis."

"You're doing very well." In a rare gesture he lifted their linked hands to his mouth and kissed her knuckles.

Signet felt herself flush and wished it were the weekend, because Avellana would be spending it at her parents' home.

They reached the side door of D'Marigold Residence and went through. Wild shrieks echoed down the hallways. Signet felt her mouth drop open, she'd *never* heard Avellana laugh like that.

"Residence, what's going on?" Cratag asked, picking up his pace. Signet had to trot to keep up.

"The children and Flora, Vinni's housefluff, are sliding down the bannister," the Residence said indulgently.

Anxiety filled Signet. She met Cratag's glance, his mouth had turned grim.

"Didn't we forbid—" she started.

"No," Cratag said.

"No," the Residence answered, too. "They've put down a stack of training mats," it soothed.

That didn't reassure her or Cratag either. "I should have thought," he grumbled, and strode even faster.

They burst into the entry hall from a side door, and it slammed against the wall. Vinni and Avellana, with Flora on her lap, were sliding down the wide and curving polished wooden bannister. They looked over to the adults, surprised and distracted.

The children lost their balance and toppled.

They fell off the bannister.

Avellana screeched.

Vinni gasped, stopped them in midair, settled them to the ground.

Flora wasn't so lucky. In the silence her small body hitting the edge of a step made a terrible-sounding crunch of broken bones.

Twenty-six

*V*inni went white.

Avellana pulled from his hold and ran to the housefluff, scooped it up before either of the adults could tell her not to. The animal looked horribly limp in her arms. She began screaming, sobbing, shouting, "We must get to D'Ash the animal Healer, now, now, NOW!"

Signet couldn't speak, could barely swallow a hard lump in her throat. Cratag was with the children, gathering them close before she was halfway across the hall. "We will."

"We must 'port," Vinni said. "I know D'Ash's emergency tele-port pad." His voice was hoarse, his eyes miserable. Signet thought he wanted to hold his Fam himself but was afraid to take Flora from Avellana. "D'Ash's pad is empty."

Then Signet was there, linking arms with Vinni and Cratag. She took the image from Vinni's mind, connected mentally with him so that they'd all teleport together. "On three," she said and was surprised her voice didn't quaver since her insides did. "One, Cratag mine, two Vinni fine, *three*."

A loud alarm hit her ears—T'Ash Residence sounding a medical emergency. "Please go into examination room one," it said in a serene female voice that didn't calm any of them. The children were shivering with fear and shock, their faces white. Cratag was at his most impassive, but Signet saw the fast, thick pulse of his blood in his throat.

"D'Ash, *D'Ash*!" Avellana screamed.

"D'Ash is in surgery and Healing trance," the Residence said.

"We need her *now*!" Avellana stomped her foot and broke into noisy sobs.

"Five minutes max," the Residence said.

"Flora might not have five minutes," Cratag snapped. He lifted Avellana and the limp Fam and took girl and housefluff into a small room with a pretty patterned rug and a high table topped with a thick bedsponge covered in a plush dark brown cloth. Cratag set Avellana in a large cushioned chair along the wall. On shaky legs, Signet followed. So did Vinni, his brown hair sticking up in cowlicks, something she'd never noticed before. Signet stopped to lean against the table. Vinni stayed at the threshold of the room, as if wishing not to acknowledge his beloved Fam needed medical care.

To Signet's horror, Flora's fur already appeared rough; her eyes were dull. She sent her mind down the link she'd made with the housefluff and saw Flora's mind dimming, the sparks of her Flair fading, blinking slowly, as shallowly as her breath. Propelled by pity and fear, she went over to Avellana and put an arm around the girl's trembling shoulders.

Cratag crossed back to Vinni, curved a large hand on the boy's shoulder, and squeezed.

They stood in a still tableau for an eternity until the door swung open and D'Ash shot into the room, dressed in drab brown work tunic and trous that would hide stains.

"D'Ash, D'Ash," Avellana hiccupped through her tears, stroking Flora.

Flora's energy spiked a little at the woman's name then went completely dark. The housefluff's eyes glazed.

D'Ash hurried over to the Fam, curved her hands gently under the soft body, lifted. Flora's ears flopped. "I'm sorry," D'Ash said. "She's gone."

Avellana emitted a piercing shriek. Signet tightened her grip on the girl.

"No, no, *no!*"

"I'm sorry—"

"She's not gone yet! Her soul is still here. I won't let her go!" Avellana screamed. She reached out with both her hands and fisted the air.

Signet *felt* it. As if some giant grabbed her insides and pulled. Then drained her of Flair.

Her body arched then folded. She pressed her fingers to her chest. Her gasp caught in her throat, but she thought she heard howls and barks and a distant explosion of rage from a male throat—T'Ash?

She managed to move her head to see the very pregnant D'Ash crumple. Cratag caught her, but the woman was pale, and her hands had gone to her belly. Signet got the awful idea that *everyone's* Flair had been drained. Including D'Ash's unborn twins'.

Vinni fell over.

So did Signet.

Avellana huddled over Flora, panting, perspiration standing out on her forehead, then slumped.

The last thing Signet saw before darkness sucked her away, too weak to fight, was Flora's long ears twitch and her bright eyes open.

Avellana had brought Flora back from death.

*S*omething grabbed his guts. Cratag grunted a "*Fligger,*" saw D'Ash's knees give out. He gritted his teeth and moved forward sluggishly to catch her. She was the most important one to help, though he saw Signet fall, heard a thump of Vinni behind him, and Avellana slid down in her chair.

One step with darkness nibbling at the edge of his mind. Two. He knew he was in that battle zone where time slowed and stilled, but he still feared he wouldn't reach D'Ash in time, despite all his training. But he did. He caught her, let himself fall with her atop him, cushioning her. He tried to use some Flair to ease her fall, but it was gone.

He lay on the floor, breath ragged, and realized the entire Residence was too quiet, too still. "T'Ash Reshidensh?" He meant it as a demand but it came out as a slurred whisper.

The house didn't answer him, and it was a new, strong Residence. Nothing, nobody stirred. Holding D'Ash, he could tell her energy levels, the twins', were thready. Through her link he dimly sensed that her HeartMate, T'Ash, was also drained and lying in the corridor between his workrooms and here. Their first child had fainted in the nursery, along with his male nanny.

None of the dozen Fam animals in the house made a peep, mental or physical.

SCARED!

The word blasted into his mind, and he turned his head. Progress. He saw Flora crouching on Avellana's lap.

Everything inside him stilled. That Fam was dead. He'd seen her die. No question, he knew death when he saw it.

The housefluff's big brown eyes fixed on his, and she tumbled off the chair, began to crawl to him. Definitely alive and not hurt.

The Residence hadn't answered him. It, too, must be out of commission. That made him and Flora the only ones conscious, and they weren't in good shape.

Meanwhile D'Ash's pulse was beginning to skip beats. He had to move, *now*!

He didn't have to be careful of D'Ash, he was moving too slowly to bobble her as he inched from under her. The effort caused his vision to haze again, dots to swim before his eyes.

His chest rose and fell as he rocked to hands and knees. Sheer determination kept him moving. If he didn't move, he'd collapse, and people needed him, dammit.

Scared. Big hurt. Dark. Pretty lights, colors. Then here. FamBoy not awake! Scared.

"Shhh!" He lifted a shaking hand to smooth over the housefluff, once. Blinked and blinked to clear his vision looking for the scrybowl.

On counter against wall. Other side of table. Flora angled her ears, but he couldn't see the damn thing. He made it to the table, grabbed the edge of it under the permamoss sponge, hauled himself up. Continued to heft himself onto the table because the counter was within his long reach. He touched the rim of the bowl. Tipped it and water sloshed. Swore. Touched it with his finger again and rubbed a tiny amount. "T'Heather," he yelled, and it came out in regular speaking tones. "Mortal emergency. T'Ash Residence! Mortal emerg—"

The FirstLevel Healer rushed into the room from the teleportation pad outside, swearing as ripely as Cratag. Went immediately to D'Ash and thundered "Stat, Primary HealingHall," swept her into his brawny arms, and vanished.

T'Heather's daughter and Daughter'sDaughter, both FirstLevel Healers, crossed to Avellana and Vinni.

Scared, Cratag! Flora sniffled. T'Heather's Daughter'sDaughter, who had Vinni, scooped up the Fam, nodded to Cratag, and said, "Good job," and teleported away. So did the Healer who had Avellana.

Other Healers poured into the Residence. Cratag felt warm hands shift him to lie straight on the table, which was good, 'cause the blood had been flowing to his dangling head and arms. "Signet?" he whispered.

"D'Marigold is fine," came an authoritative voice.

He didn't think so but couldn't argue. He had just enough energy to keep his eyes open and watch the Healers work, finding people, summoning animal tenders for the unconscious Fams, then he, too, was teleported away to Primary HealingHall.

*T*he secret's bound to get out," Signet said as she climbed onto Cratag's lap and burrowed against him, and that was fine and wonderful.

They were on the deeply padded bench of the D'Marigold Family glider, released to go home. The vehicle smoothly pulled away from Primary HealingHall.

He'd already given a report to some of the top FirstFamily lords and ladies, including T'Heather, T'Hawthorn, D'Hazel, T'Holly, D'Grove of the older generation and T'Willow and Ruis Elder, Captain of the Starship *Nuada's Sword*, of the younger. D'Ash had begun labor and was still at the HealingHall; T'Ash was weak and with her.

Even though the great folk had tried to limit the number of their own set who knew what happened at T'Ash's, Cratag didn't think that block would hold.

"Too many people already know *something* important occurred," Signet murmured into his chest, her breath warm against him. "Healers, animal trainers, the staff at Primary HealingHall, the PerSuns called in to give energy." She pulled away from him a little, looked at him with narrowed eyes. He felt her probe. "Your energy is good, but your Flair levels haven't recovered yet. Neither have mine."

Cratag tightened his arm around his lover.

"Not that Avellana will be able to use her Flair very often," Signet said.

"Lady and Lord preserve us all." He drew her close, set his chin atop her head, then repeated what he'd only said once and in a whisper. "Avellana brought Flora back from death."

Signet's breath caught, and her fingers clutched his shirt. "And she used the energy and Flair from everyone in a strong GreatLord Residence to do so." Signet tipped back her head and met his gaze, her eyes bluer than normal. "I think we know what her extraordinary Flair is."

Signet was silent and Cratag thought about it. "You Healed her brain."

"Not me, exactly. My Flair has helped hers Heal her." Signet cleared her throat and said in a tiny voice, "Maybe that's why she is what she is."

Snorting, Cratag ran his palm down her arm. "Avellana is what she is." Something they'd said often.

Signet sighed. "If the Hazels are wise, and they are, they'll spread the word that Avellana's Flair is for holo paintings."

"Her creative Flair."

"Her only Flair," Signet corrected. "People will believe a brain-damaged child would be crippled and have only one kind of significant Flair."

"That might work."

"No one wants to make life harder for her," Signet said. "And it isn't easy to believe that someone can raise the dead. Not that Flora was very dead—"

"Dead is dead."

Again Signet looked at him, her lips curving. "Flora's soul was still . . . available . . . to be—"

"Sucked back into her body," Cratag said, making a loud slurping noise.

Signet laughed, and he eased. They'd be all right. "Avellana didn't go into her Passage. Usually an emotional event will trigger it," he said.

"Too drained herself of Flair," Signet whispered.

Cratag had to say the whole thing out loud, just once. He glanced out the glider windows to make sure no other vehicle was near and they were going fast enough that no one along the street would hear. "A seven-year-old girl drained the energy and Flair of two Great-Lords, a FirstFamily Residence, two GrandLadies, herself, three GreatLord children, and multiple Fams to return life to one small housefluff, recently deceased."

With a huffed breath, Signet shook her head. "No, I don't think she'll be called on often to return the dead to life. Who could afford it? Hmm. I bet the NobleCouncil will pay her good NobleGilt for the rest of her life, though . . . to *not* practice her craft."

"I'm not a spiritual man," Cratag said. "But bringing back a person who's died is . . . disturbing."

Signet shivered. "Yes. I suppose some people could get upset." Then her mouth firmed, and she said, "I think those lords and ladies we spoke with will quash the rumors. I'm sure there is more than one secret the FirstFamilies know that most other folk don't."

"And the starship *Nuada's Sword*, and each Family itself must have secrets. . ." Cratag stopped when he saw Signet flush. He didn't pursue it, but she said, "The tap dancing."

A laugh snorted from him, and he squeezed her. They'd passed through the D'Marigold gates, and the lovely frivolous peach-colored Residence rose ahead of them. "Tap dancing is not exactly on the same order as raising the dead."

Sniffing, Signet said, "We Marigolds are civilized, sophisticated types." Then she frowned. "The Hazels have a vested interest in not letting word get out about Avellana—"

"So does Vinni," Cratag said.

"Yes. You're right, this is not a minor matter and could possibly cause disorder." Signet's frown deepened. "What would you do if someone beloved died in your arms and you knew. . ."

Cratag thought of his sister, hesitated. Her loss was still an ache after all these years, but an old ache. Then he thought of the woman he held in his arms. "Anything," he rasped.

"And if HeartMates are in question, saving one would mean saving both. . ." Signet said and he followed her thoughts, yes, the FirstFamilies, hell, any Family might want to use a person with such Flair.

"The cost is too great," he said.

"Maybe," she said doubtfully and shivered. "Avellana must be protected."

"She will be."

"She still hasn't finished her First Passage, so the Hazels will be bringing her back to us." Signet paused. "I love her. The revelation of her talent doesn't change that."

Cratag's turn to frown. "She used this power *before* she finished First Passage, and her Flair will only get stronger?"

"Usually," Signet murmured.

"Fligger."

* * *

*T*hat night, Cratag held Signet in his arms and stared into the dark. Both tired, they'd gone to bed early. There weren't enough PerSuns—people who stored life energy and could transfer it to others without draining themselves—to handle the emergency at T'Ash's. Once D'Ash was conscious, she'd insisted all the sick Fams in the house be treated. So Cratag and Signet had accepted only enough energy to sustain life.

He let a shudder pass from head to toe.

They'd been dying. D'Ash and her unborn children, strong T'Ash, Signet. All the adults except Cratag himself. The children—little Nuin Ash, Vinni, Avellana—and the Fams might have survived. That much he'd figured when he analyzed the situation.

The completely strange, unique, and terrifying situation. He tightened his grip on Signet, and she murmured in her sleep and turned to him.

She'd almost died. Would have died if he hadn't been a big man, had less Flair to drain than others, depended more on his physical strength.

He'd been fooling himself.

He couldn't imagine life without her.

Maybe in the back of his mind, in the chambers of his heart, he'd been toying with the idea of keeping the affair going a long time, years. That wasn't unknown between a noble and a commoner.

But that was before this morning brought the sword point home to his heart.

He loved Signet.

He didn't want to live without her.

He *could* live without her. They weren't HeartBonded Heart-Mates, or even husband and wife, but without her, his life would have a hole nothing could fill.

How could he win her? A rough guard from a small town in the southern continent that wasn't on most maps and a sophisticated

Druidan city GrandLady—beautiful in manners and intelligence and sweetness, great in noble power and status and Flair.

He'd been able to pretend that a short, discreet affair wouldn't affect her in the eyes of her own level of nobility. That such an affair wouldn't affect his status as chief of T'Hawthorn's guards.

A long affair would be whispered about, and Signet herself seemed to want their relationship to be open. He'd have gone on hiding it.

But loving her meant a strong and solid, public relationship. Major changes in their lives, his life.

He didn't know if he was capable of such change.

It should have been easy: he loved the woman, he'd give up his life, move in with her. Live on her income instead of providing any of his own. Face it, any professional services he could provide her were minimal. He didn't know if he could bear taking gilt from her.

This fanciful Residence and this sophisticated Family might have had a gigolo or two in the past, but Cratag didn't consider himself gigolo material. He was like a sturdy, tough woven raw cotton tunic, gray to hide stains. Signet was the most delicate of silks . . . one of those pretty shawls that could be pulled through a gold ring.

He loved her.

He wanted her.

But he didn't know how he could have her.

Twenty-seven

$\mathcal{A}$ very subdued Avellana was escorted to D'Marigold Residence by her Family two mornings later. Signet had requested the Hazels teleport to the pad inside her office. She was tired of using her favorite sitting room for less-than-pleasant business discussions. Except for Avellana, all the Hazels were business. D'Hazel hadn't demurred, so the Hazels sat looking uncomfortable in large, softly cushioned chairs with round arms and a discreet floral pattern that matched the honey-toned panelled walls.

D'Hazel said, "Avellana's Flair is rebuilding, thank the Lady and Lord! As is everyone's." Signet felt the brush of the GreatLady's Flair, reflexively checking that no one eavesdropped on the heavily shielded office in the heavily shielded sentient Residence on the shielded estate. "The newborn T'Ash twins show excellent energy and Flair, as does all the Family."

The Ashes were known for their strength and energy.

D'Hazel continued. "They've been very understanding and reasonable."

Signet couldn't keep from looking at Cratag, who had hitched a hip on her desk. She'd rather have pulled chairs into a circle, but he had insisted she sit in a position of power. She wondered what the Hazels had paid in reparation to the Ashes.

T'Hawthorn told me it was three golden favor tokens and alliance for five generations, Cratag replied mentally, his lips twisted sardonically.

"I have considered my fee—" Signet said.

"—anything! Anything at all, Avellana must survive her First Passage." D'Hazel's hands twisted in her lap.

Avellana's sister, who sat with her in the same chair, hugged Avellana close. Avellana didn't meet Signet's eyes and seemed miserable, as if she'd suffered through a series of meetings like this dressed again in miniature adult formal clothes. "I'm sorry I hurt you," Avellana whispered. "I didn't think. I didn't control myself. I won't ever do it again." She sniffled.

Signet wanted to hold and soothe her. Later. "Apology accepted. I believe my fee is substantial enough, but I would like alliance with the Hazels for two generations."

"We're honored," said T'Hazel. His hand reached out for his wife's, and she clasped it.

"Agreed." D'Hazel stood, and so did her husband and elder daughter. D'Hazel's gaze squarely met Signet's. "Thank you."

"I love Avellana," Signet said.

"Thank you," Avellana's sister and father said in unison. They all marched to the teleportation pad, D'Hazel stepped onto it last, opened her mouth as if to give ever more instructions, then shook her head and closed her lips. With one last nod, they teleported away.

Cratag went over to reset the teleportation pad indicator, and Signet moved from behind her desk to Avellana's chair and crouched down to the girl's eye level. Avellana still didn't look up. "I'm sorry," she said in a tiny voice.

"I love you, Avellana," Signet repeated.

The girl burst into tears and launched herself into Signet's arms. Signet began to topple, but Cratag was there and steadied them both. "I love you, too, Avellana," he rumbled.

Avellana wept.

"It's a beautiful day. Let's all walk in the garden," Signet said.

"I'm wrinkling my clothes, and getting snot—"

Cratag gave her a massive softleaf, and she wiped her face. Signet said a Word and the girl's clothes smoothed.

"I'll get my new shoes dirty," Avellana said between hitching sobs. Signet had noticed that she was wearing the shoes she'd made the girl the week before.

"My crafting can stand a little dirt and twigs from garden paths," Signet said. "Come on."

With a small honking noise, Avellana blew into the softleaf again, then wiped her fingers and put the softleaf in her sleeve pocket and took Signet's and Cratag's offered hands.

Still not looking at them, she said, "I'm sorry I hurt you, Signet. I'm sorry I hurt you, Cratag." More words came out in a rush. "I'm sorry I hurt Muin. I'm sorry I hurt D'Ash and her babies—the new Jasmine Ash and Abutilon Ash. I'm sorry I hurt little Nuin Ash." She sucked in a breath and continued, "I'm sorry I hurt T'Ash and Zanth Fam and Princess Fam and Velox Fam." The hiccupping recitation took them through the Residence to the entryway.

Sharing a glance with Cratag, Signet thought that Avellana had been made to apologize personally to each of the beings listed. She even got a wisp of a memory from the girl's mind—of Nuin Ash running away from her and hiding behind his nanny—

"—and Walker Clover," Avellana named the man. "And the butler, Alf Honey. . ."

By the time she'd listed all T'Ash's staff and the animals she'd drained, they were down the front steps and into the garden. Finally she stopped and stared at her shoes, shifted.

"What have you learned about shifting your balance?" Cratag asked mildly.

Avellana sniffed. "Not to do it." She pulled at her hands as if shame washed through her, but neither Signet nor Cratag let go.

"We love you, Avellana," Signet reminded.

"I didn't control myself! I hurt *all those people and Fams*!"

Again Signet shared a glance with Cratag. "But you Healed Flora, and none of the sick Fams at T'Ash's died, did they?" Signet knew there had been no deaths.

"No."

"So the bottom line is that you saved a life and did good," Cratag said. He swept a branch of lilac away before it caught on Avellana's gold-ribbon-edged tunic.

Avellana breathed deeply, then looked up at him. "No one has said that, only that I hurt everybody."

"The cost for that life was very high," Signet said.

Nodding, Avellana said glumly, "Everyone has said the cost was too high." She sighed and wiggled her fingers again, and they let go of her hands. With a dry corner of the large softleaf she wiped her face, rubbed under her nose. "And Muin has not been allowed to visit me, nor I allowed to visit him. He is in disgrace, too."

"Sliding down bannisters can be dangerous," Signet said, keeping any scolding from her tone. It sounded as if Avellana had had enough of that.

In a prim voice, Avellana said, "We didn't break any rules you gave us."

"No, you didn't," Cratag said. "We forgot to say that one."

The little girl's shoulders slumped. "But common sense should have told us that it was dangerous," she said in the voice that revealed she'd heard that from several adults. She peeped at Signet. "But it was so fun." Another heaving sigh. "We couldn't resist."

"I know," Signet said. "Many things are hard to resist."

Avellana's lower lip trembled. "I didn't control myself." She walked stiffly along the path, carefully keeping to the stepping stones.

Signet slipped her arm around Cratag's waist, hugged him, knew he shared her concern for the girl—that Avellana would once again become too rigid. Then she caught up with the child. "You don't have to be in control of every aspect of your life, every second."

"Yes, I do." Avellana stopped. She looked at a cluster of lilacs near her nose, bent to sniff, then made an appalled noise when some of the tiny blossoms separated from the stalk and fell onto her tunic. She quickly brushed them off.

"No, you don't." Signet took one of Avellana's hands, and while the girl watched, she asked permission of the plant to take its flowers, snapped one off, shook it a little on herself, letting the florets fall on her as they might.

"You still look good," Avellana said wistfully. "Even with lilacs scattered on you. Your tunic looks good."

Signet struggled for words. "Every person must control some aspects of their life, like their Flair and their emotions that might hurt others, but we don't need to be in control all the time. Sometimes I yell and shout and stomp by myself in my rooms when I'm angry."

Avellana stared at her. "You do?"

"I hurt no one, not even myself."

Cratag grunted. "Be better off doing some fighting patterns."

"Maybe so, or dancing, or sports." Though she didn't do sports. Signet shrugged. "Everyone has Flair and talents that must be controlled. Cratag has learned to control his great strength, and not let his emotions use his strength against himself or others."

"Cratag is a hero." Avellana stared up at him again. "He saved us all. We might have all died without him. Mama is very glad he was there and is your lover, Signet."

Signet winced.

"I might have killed us all." Avellana gulped watery tears while others rolled down her cheeks.

Cratag paced forward and squatted before her, took his softleaf from her hands, found a dry corner, and wiped her eyes, then held it to her nose. "Blow."

Avellana did.

Cratag said, "You didn't know you'd endanger us all. You didn't know what your Flair was or that your fear and guilt would spiral out to all of us and drain us so you could use your Flair. You learned a valuable lesson with regard to power and Flair and . . . strength. You won't let your emotions rule your Flair and hurt others again, will you? Just like I don't let my anger or fear or guilt out during training. I've learned how to control my emotions during a fi—, when sparring. But I can be less controlled when . . . uh . . . dancing. You can't be rigid in life, Avellana. It will hurt you and might break you, and then you'll be no good to others—to Vinni."

Avellana grimaced. "I will think on that notion," she said in her adult voice.

"Good," Cratag said. He gave her back the softleaf. He stood and came over to Signet. This time he slipped his arm around *her* waist. "Life is knowing what you can control and what you can't. When control is essential and when it isn't."

"To be a complete person. . ." Signet fumbled for words and just spoke what she believed and hoped for the best. "Life isn't only about control and responsibilities and duty and common sense. It's also about enjoying yourself and fun and sometimes giving in to temptation."

The Lady and Lord knew her parents had shown her that and she was grateful. And the Lady and Lord knew she had no resistance to temptation when Cratag was involved.

"We all make mistakes and learn from them," Cratag rumbled.

When Signet met his eyes, they were cool, and she wondered what he meant. Did he think their affair was a mistake?

*T*hat *afternoon, right before his anticipated good workout with the* simulacrum, Cratag received a call from Laev.

The young man's eyes were crinkled with worry when Cratag looked into the scrybowl in the dressing room off the training room. Laev let out a sigh and smiled so deeply his dimples showed when Cratag answered—then scanned him up and down.

"I just heard you were hurt in that contretemps at T'Ash's." Laev looked a little sheepish. "And I didn't know about that until Vinni T'Vine didn't show up for our training at the Green Knight. His Family has 'housebound' him. He's not allowed out. Not even on his castle grounds, I'm told." Laev grimaced. "But you look fine."

"I am fine." Not quite, not near normal. And what sort of a word was *contretemps*?" Cratag studied Laev and saw nothing to indicate Laev knew it had been a matter of life and death. T'Hawthorn had not told Laev the real circumstances of the situation, and that gave Cratag pause. Those who knew *were* keeping the wraps on what had happened. Of course someone would eventually tell Laev— either T'Hawthorn when he gave Laev more authority over the household, or word would spread through the younger generation of noble FirstFamilies lords and ladies. After all, Vinni and Avellana were two of their own.

Cratag jerked a head at the training room behind him. "You can come for my afternoon sparring session and see for yourself." Cratag would push himself more if Laev did and that might be good. Maybe he was taking it too easy. Signet had been pampering him, and the Fams and the Residence pampering both of them with ultra-civilized treats that were supposed to make him feel better but only made him feel gawky and like a hick.

"Come join you?" Laev asked as if he'd never considered it, had never spent septhours sparring with Cratag. The young man cleared his throat, flushed a little, glanced away from the scrybowl. "Ah, not today. I have an appointment."

"Oh?" Cratag lifted his brows.

Laev's blush deepened. He leaned a little closer to the scrybowl and said in a low voice. "With Nivea Sunflower. Cratag, she's the most wonderful girl! And my HeartMate. We're courting. Today we're going on an excursion to the Great Labyrinth. I've heard that the spring flowers are all in bloom, and it's a sight to behold."

Courting agreed with Laev, the boy was glowing. "Some other time then."

"Yes. Sometime soon. I want her to meet you, and you her. Soon." He lifted a hand. "Later."

"Later," Cratag growled. The boy didn't notice, of course, he'd signed off in a blink.

Cratag realized his jaw was tight and loosened it. It was good that the boy had found his HeartMate. Wonderful.

Only to be expected of a young man who was descended from FirstFamilies on all four sides of his bloodline.

And it was only natural that a young man would prefer to spend time with his love, his HeartMate, a young woman he was interested in instead of a grumpy older-brother-friend. Cratag shouldn't feel slighted. Or envious. Yet he nearly stomped to the training room and simulacrum.

His strength and energy still weren't up to their usual levels, so he'd set the simulacrum for a lower level of power. As for his Flair, he could only manage a little mindspeak, otherwise not a twinge of psi. He wasn't accustomed to being so weak, and it angered—no, irritated—him.

He wasn't an angry man.

Not really.

Or maybe, deep inside him, where he hid it, was a kernel of anger. Maybe more than anger. There might be hurt, too. And just a twinge of despair.

All the negative emotions he'd felt for a long time . . . years maybe . . . and kept battened down and under control.

Couldn't lose control when you'd sold your sword to merchants to guard their goods on a long trek to the northern continent. Had to keep a sharp lookout for bandits who'd slit your throat as soon as spit at you.

Couldn't lose control when you were fighting for your life and the lives of other guards and your Family during the time of a stup—misguided—blood feud.

Couldn't fliggering lose control when your lord assigned you a job without a by-your-leave and you watched a young girl and boy and the woman you *loved* dying before your eyes while you were the only one who could save them 'cause you were so common as to have no damned Flair.

No, couldn't lose control *then*.

But now . . . yeah, now!

He slammed the simulacrum in the jaw, heard his own finger bones snap and an ominous rattle as the neck of the thing jerked back and fell, limp.

A scream from Signet tore through his mind, and he whirled to see her teleport to a corner of the room, rush toward him. "You're hurt! Bones are broken."

He cradled his hurt hand with the other. "Oh, yeah." Then he looked down on the equally broken simulacrum. He knew what those cost. About five years of his salary. Fliggering fligger.

Avellana, holding Rhyz close, also showed up, properly on the teleportation pad. She walked over and looked at the dead thing. "It is a simulacrum."

"Was a simulacrum." Cratag breathed through the pain.

"It was as big as you," Avellana said.

"Yeah."

A little frown formed on her brow. "We Hazels do not have one of these. Even an older model was too expensive for our use."

"My lord T'Hawthorn provided it for me," Cratag said. Signet was moving him toward the teleportation pad. "Not Primary Healing-Hall, go to AllClass HealingHall."

"I will not!"

"Yes, you will." He scraped his brain for a good reason. "Lark Holly practices there, she's the best."

"Oh."

They stepped up on the pad and even the tiny bobble jarred his hand and he clenched his jaw.

"Your hand is broken, too?" asked Avellana.

"Yes," he hissed out.

She joined them on the teleportation pad. "I have never been to AllClass HealingHall."

Signet turned on the indicator that their pad was in use, then tilted her head, mentally checking the pad of the HealingHall. "And we aren't going now," she said. "I don't know the coordinates to teleport there. We're going to Primary HealingHall."

Cratag swore under his breath.

She looked at him, concerned. "Unless you want to scry T'Hawthorn for his Healer to come here."

Cratag weighed the options. The bill from treatment at Primary HealingHall or calling T'Hawthorn's Family Healer, who would tell the whole household and rib him forevermore. "Residence, scry T'Hawthorn's and ask their Healer to come here."

"Done," the Residence said. "The Healer is on his way by glider since he does not know the Residence well enough to teleport. The siren of the T'Hawthorn Family glider has been engaged."

Great, the whole city would know what a fool Cratag'd made of himself.

Avellana stepped off the pad with an expression of disappointment. "I do like our afternoon educational outings." She walked to the simulacrum, looked at it and then at Cratag's swelling hand. His fingers felt like sausages.

"I don't think a Healer can fix this simulacrum."

"No," Cratag said through gritted teeth.

Rhyz wiggled, and Avellana let the FamCat down. He pounced on the simulacrum's hand, then hopped up on the body and walked back and forth.

"Will fixing the simulacrum and your hand be expensive?" Avellana asked.

Cratag set one foot off the teleportation pad, then the next, tears of pain stung the back of his eyes, but he answered the girl. "Very. Losing control is always expensive."

And it often hurt. But he thought this particular stupidity would hurt a whole lot less than losing Signet.

Twenty-eight

*W*hile the Healer was dealing with Cratag's broken hand in his rooms, Signet returned a scry to T'Hawthorn to discuss the incident from her sitting room. She straightened her slumped shoulders. It seemed all she was doing these days was reporting to the FirstFamilies.

T'Hawthorn answered immediately. He was a handsome man with black hair and violet eyes, the same color eyes as Cratag's. He had a hardness of expression that was actually lighter than when she'd first met him, though no one would call him an easy man. Or stupid. He sat at a desk, petting a large fluffy black cat that was even haughtier in expression than its master.

Signet got to the point that bothered Cratag the most. "The simulacrum you sent over for Cratag's use is broken."

T'Hawthorn's smile was knife thin. "Is that so? I was told that couldn't happen. It's under warranty. I'll have T'Furze provide another."

She let her breath sift out.

Waving the hand that wasn't petting his cat, T'Hawthorn said, "That isn't the most pressing concern. How is Cratag's hand?"

"Being Healed now. It gave him considerable pain. Not that he admitted it, of course."

"Of course not." T'Hawthorn's light purple eyes drilled into her. "Cratag isn't a man who gives in to pain . . . or other emotions. Usually."

Signet let the silence hang. She had a general idea of what had happened through their link. Emotions had gushed through Cratag, and he'd planned on working through them physically, ridding himself of the negativity trapped inside him—that meditation had brought to the fore, she supposed. She'd known he was capable of great emotion, but hadn't realized he'd suppressed such an amount. For how long? She studied T'Hawthorn. This man must have been responsible for a fair chunk.

She glanced at the shut door of her sitting room, double-checked her link with Cratag—sitting stoically letting the Healer work on his fingers. Then she lifted her chin and stared back at the lord and said, "Cratag was hurt that you sent him on this job without truly consulting him."

T'Hawthorn sent her a cool look that told her he wasn't used to explaining himself to anyone whose ancestry didn't go all the way back to old Earth. Signet held her ground.

His turn to let out a sigh. "I was not as diplomatic as I should have been. I was, and am, sure he understands how much I value him."

"You think so?" Signet raised her eyebrows. When T'Hawthorn's lips turned down, she said, "He might know that with his head, perhaps." She touched her chest with her fingertips. "The heart's another matter."

"I *do* value him. In every way." T'Hawthorn narrowed his eyes, and she knew then that the lord knew she and Cratag were lovers, had known for some time. "He's a part of my Family, a good man, and a good mentor to my Son'sSon, Laev. I would hate to see Cratag hurt further."

Intimating that she would hurt him more than T'Hawthorn or
Laev had ever done. Hadn't it been a scry from Laev that had
started this whole particular situation? But Signet kept her mouth
shut. She'd deal with that later, right now it was time to take the
plunge. She met T'Hawthorn's gaze. "I am Cratag's HeartMate."

The lord's eyes widened. He sat in stilled surprise for three seconds. "You're sure?"

"Yes. I know it's illegal to tell him, and I won't."

"I hadn't thought Cratag had the Fl—" T'Hawthorn stopped
before he made a rude personal comment.

"I connected briefly with him during my Passage," Signet
continued. "Though I didn't make a HeartGift, I'm sure he's my
HeartMate."

"A lot of that going around," T'Hawthorn muttered.

"Pardon?"

He didn't answer, so she went on, "I would be glad to have a full
consultation with T'Willow, the matchmaker, to prove it."

Again there was a silence as they scrutinized each other. Finally
T'Hawthorn threw up a hand in a fencer's gesture, conceding the
fight, then smiled. She'd never seen such a charming smile from him.
Saved for his Family, she thought.

He said, "Cratag is *there* after all. Destiny has a way of arranging things. I'm sorry to lose my best guard and a member of my
Family to you, but I am happy that he has a HeartMate and has
found her." The lord actually sounded a little wistful, then his smile
flashed again. "I will welcome an alliance with you, D'Marigold."
He inclined his head.

Signet's throat had tightened. This had been easier than she'd
expected. "Thank you."

The cat stretched and hopped off the desk, out of sight.
T'Hawthorn tapped his fingers together. "Now how is that other
situation affecting Cratag and you?"

Behind her the door opened, and Cratag walked in, lines in his
face showing that he'd suffered through the Healing. She looked

at his hand. His bones had knit, but his skin appeared pink and tender.

He smiled at her, not much more than a twitch of his lips, and his eyes were serious. Then he came up behind her and put an arm around her shoulders. She turned into his body.

T'Hawthorn said, "I understand that Avellana Hazel has returned to your Residence?"

"That's right," Cratag said.

"Her Flair levels are still quite low," Signet said. "I'm not sure how long it will take before they increase again to trigger her next Passage fugue."

Nodding, T'Hawthorn said, "It occurs to me that you both may need additional help." He waved a hand. "Physical or mind Healers. Ask and it will be provided."

"Thank you," Signet said. "But I think it best if we continue as we've begun—"

"—We don't want to scare Avellana with a bunch of new people," Cratag finished. "We can handle this."

"If you're sure. . ." T'Hawthorn said.

"We have the Residence, too," Cratag said. "It's a force to be reckoned with."

"They always are," T'Hawthorn murmured. He stared at them for a moment then said the formal ending blessing, "Merry meet."

"And merry part," Signet and Cratag said together.

"And merry meet again," T'Hawthorn said. The droplets over the scrybowl misted away in a violet haze, and the water cleared.

Signet let out a breath and leaned into her solid lover, who seemed to want to cradle her, reassuring them both. "That is one formidable man." She looked up at Cratag, shook her head. "I don't know how you put up with him all these years."

"You get used to him," Cratag said. He bent down and pressed a quick but passionate kiss on her lips.

Signet grabbed onto his shoulders, enjoyed the feel of him . . . the steadiness that was back in his emotions, the ease of their link.

Then she stepped away and glanced around her light and airy suite. T'Hawthorn's Residence had shown deep stone blocks and dark tapestries, dark wooden paneling, and heavy furniture. She smiled at Cratag and looked at the portrait of her parents, slight people with cheery expressions, appearing sophisticated and with little on their minds except each other and living well. "I think I like my Family and Residence better."

So do I, she heard from Cratag and didn't know whether it was a private thought or not.

*S*ignet *was worried about Cratag.*

Despite what he'd told T'Hawthorn, and the light manner he used with her and Avellana, Cratag was brooding. She'd experienced it enough herself to recognize the mood, and she wasn't used to it from him. Even Beadle's antics couldn't bring more than a brief smile to his face.

He'd accepted the events at T'Ash's Residence, Avellana's new Flair, and the new circumstances surrounding them all and moved on, like a true pragmatic guardsman. So that wasn't the problem bothering him. Signet was sure he wasn't missing his rooms at T'Hawthorn Residence or T'Hawthorn and the Family themselves, except for Laev.

Laev was the concern.

Cratag was grieving for the boy he'd lost when Laev had become a young man. Or rather, he'd have grieved less if the teen hadn't seemed to forget about him while in the throes of first love.

Laev had stopped visiting and didn't scry. That annoyed Signet.

So she decided to do something about it. She contacted T'Hawthorn Residence and asked for Laev's daily schedule. She was only a little surprised that she was given the information, but it gave her a small glow. T'Hawthorn had believed her when she'd said she was Cratag's HeartMate! More, the GreatLord had meant it when he'd said he'd accept an alliance with her.

That afternoon she set up an outing to the very upscale Enlli

Gallery where Laev would be. Getting out would fight Cratag's depression . . . didn't she know that from personal experience? Avellana needed distracting, too. Vinni's Family hadn't allowed him to leave his estate since the bannister fiasco. A punishment for both children that was especially hard since the days were now warm and lovely, perfect for expeditions. Still, Signet thought the two were in constant mental contact. The Hazels had made it clear that no one should take Avellana to T'Vine Residence. Not that Signet had ever shown up where she hadn't been invited in her entire life.

Though that could change if she thought there was good reason for such a breach of manners. She was doing all sorts of different things nowadays that she hadn't considered before.

She'd never felt so independent and free and happy. But Cratag wasn't happy, and that dimmed her own pleasure.

So she and Cratag and Avellana teleported to the main pad of the Enlli Gallery—Fams, especially cats, were not welcome there—and nearly missed Laev and Nivea Sunflower, who were waiting for them to step off the teleportation pad so they could use it. Laev had a harried expression on his face and held several bundles in the gallery's expensive wrapping.

"Why, look who's here!" Signet thought she managed a good start of surprise. Cratag narrowed his eyes. She rushed into speech. "Laev, so nice to see you." She turned with her most charming smile to the young woman, holding out a hand. "I've seen you, but we've never been introduced. I'm GrandLady Signet D'Marigold, an ally of the Hawthorns."

Both Laev and Cratag did their own minor starts of surprise at that. But they'd know she'd spoken the truth through their mingled bonds. Let that fact divert them.

Touching Signet's hand and dipping a proper curtsy in just the right degree, Nivea smiled. She sent Cratag a quick glance that seemed calculating to Signet, then stepped back as she got a good look at his facial scars. Nivea swallowed and said, "And you're Cratag, aren't you! I've been wanting to meet more of Laev's Family." The lilt in her voice was forced.

Avellana sniffed, and Signet believed she was about to comment, so thought quickly. "There's a wonderful café just down the street, The Three Goblets. Why don't I treat us to tea?" A very elegant, very exclusive, very expensive café.

Now everyone stared at her.

"You need reservations for a month for that café," Laev mumbled as if he hesitated to contradict her, with an unspoken, mental grumble that he'd tried to make reservations and had been turned down—HawthornHeir!

"I never need reservations," Signet said. That was also utterly true. Her parents had been close friends with the noble owners, who were always glad to see her. They'd also been worried about her, ready to pamper her and lift her spirits if she came by. They would be thrilled to meet Cratag and with the gossip potential.

At that moment the owner of the Enlli Gallery, GrandSir Apple, bustled up to Signet, both hands out. She gave him hers, and he squeezed them—another friend of her Family. "Dear Signet, it's been too long since you've visited." He nodded to the rest of them, then turned back to her. "I have that antique-type oil painting of my father's that you requested we clean."

Signet flushed. "I'm sorry. I completely forgot!" She let her grin break through. "I've been very busy." Unlike previously.

GrandSir Apple kissed her hands. "And I completely understand." He cocked an eyebrow at Cratag.

"Let me introduce you to a very good friend of mine, Cratag Maytree, Chief of T'Hawthorn's Guards. Have you met Great-Mistrys Avellana Hazel?"

There was a round of acknowledgments, and Signet took her hands back when she noticed Cratag glowering. GrandSir Apple was old enough to be her father, but like all the Apples, he was handsome and wore his age well.

Laev eyed her as if reevaluating her. So he hadn't given her much weight as a serious person. Her Family wasn't known for significant ambitions, but there was something to be said for being able to procure restaurant or theater seats at any time. "I'll pick up that painting next week," Signet assured Apple. "We're on our way to The Three Goblets. Could you call the Trilliums and let them know we're coming?"

A bow from Apple. "Pleased to do so, and mind you *do* pick that painting up. It was a new medium of my father's, and he would fiddle with it if he knew I had it."

"Oh, don't let him do that! I like it very much as it is. He captured the misty colors of spring at the Great Labyrinth so well." With a last smile at Apple, she turned to Nivea. "I heard that you recently visited the Great Labyrinth? A wonderful place, isn't it?" Signet gave a little sigh. "I've been derelict in the upkeep of our marigold flower beds and they are prolific, though I should check on our sundial. What part of all the noble Family offerings did you like best?"

"T'Hawthorn's hedges were in bloom. . ." Nivea rambled on about the trip as Signet got them all out of the gallery and shepherded them down the sidewalk. The street was unusually busy with a small stream of people showing off their new, gleaming Family gliders purchased this spring. She'd forgotten that annual tradition, but then her Family had never been interested in having the latest glider unless the comfort quotient had greatly increased.

When they reached The Three Goblets and were welcomed enthusiastically, everyone seemed impressed, except Cratag, so she sent him an amused smile from under her lashes along with a command of *Enjoy yourself*!

She ordered everyone's favorite beverages and consulted Nivea on her preferences.

A septhour and a half passed pleasantly entertaining Nivea— Signet had sent Avellana a look to ensure the girl joined in the proper female duty—and Cratag and Laev fell back into their easy pattern of companionship. Signet was happy to see that he was listening to Laev, feeling appreciated, and it seemed as if Laev had plenty to say.

Signet kept the occasion short enough that they were all satisfied with the company and themselves and full of good food and fancy caff—cocoa for Avellana. They rose from the table, smiling. She was congratulating herself on a successful afternoon when they left the café with a bunch of other patrons and entered the busy sidewalk. Some jostling went on.

"Watch who you're shoving," Nivea shrilled.

But she wasn't the one who toppled off the sidewalk into the street in front of an oncoming glider.

That was Avellana.

Twenty-nine

*S*ignet *watched in horror as Cratag dove for the child, putting himself* between her and the gliders. The vehicles didn't go fast. When one bumped him, it stopped and set down its stands. Cratag and Avellana flew a meter. They hit the ground, Cratag tucked around the girl, rolling. Cratag staggered to his feet, holding Avellana with one arm. His other shoulder looked dislocated. His shirt was dirty and torn, his trous in bad shape. The new celtaroon boots she'd given him didn't show a scuff.

Nivea was screaming her lungs out, and shouts erupted from others. Signet stood frozen, heart pounding, on the sidewalk.

Vinni materialized in the middle of the street, taking a chance that could have gotten him killed. He ran to Cratag and Avellana.

All the gliders on the street came to a rocking halt. GreatLord T'Holly and his HeartMate emerged from one. As Signet ran panting to Cratag, the GreatLord handed Avellana to his lady, then with quick, practiced movements, reset Cratag's shoulder.

People poured from the gliders and shops along the street, all talking and milling.

Hanes, Vinni's bodyguard, ran from the sidewalk near a teleportation area, blazer out. Then half a dozen guardsmen appeared on the teleportation pad and began organizing people. By then Signet had her arms around Cratag and Avellana, and Vinni 'ported them to Primary HealingHall.

They were met by Healers who swarmed around Cratag and Avellana, moving them all into an examination room that was becoming all too familiar.

Cratag's shirt was discarded, his tendons and muscles were Healed, as well as Avellana's bruises—and Vinni gone—before her parents burst into the room, followed by Laev. All of the newcomers were pale. The Fams trotted in and hopped onto the table where the girl sat.

The Hazels gathered Avellana into their arms, making soothing sounds. Rhyz revved his purr. Beadle meowed. Du sniffed.

Frowning, Laev scanned Cratag's bare torso for bruises, but the Healers had been thorough.

"What happened?" demanded D'Hazel.

"The injuries are Healed," one of the Healers said. "The cost is—"

"We authorize the transfer of all necessary funds," T'Hazel said.

The Healer bowed. "Done. Thank you. We anticipate more minor injuries from the glider accident. Please take this conversation to Noble Lounge One."

Only the best for FirstFamilies. In the ensuing calm, Laev summoned some clothes from T'Hawthorn Residence for Cratag, gave Cratag's boots an envious stare, glanced at Signet, then said his good-byes. Cratag changed behind a screen, then they all left the examination room, Beadle purring in Cratag's arms, the other Fams weaving between all their legs.

On their way to the lounge, they picked up an additional person, the guardsman assigned to the highest nobles. They all sat and Cratag gave the guard—and the Hazels—a complete report, including details that Signet hadn't observed, like all the noble crests on the vehicles he'd seen in the street.

Everyone's nerves seemed to settle. Avellana was less shook than anyone else, had recovered from the event faster. Signet sensed she was still linked with Vinni though he had returned home.

As soon as the guardsman was gone, D'Hazel said to Signet, "We would like to take Avellana home after this latest misadventure. How are her Flair levels?"

"I've been monitoring them," Signet said with outward calm. She had to force her mind to the question since she felt a little dizzy after all the excitement. "They are naturally increasing, but not to a point where I believe another Passage fugue will occur over the weekend." Signet's fingers were locked with Cratag's. She needed to touch him.

"I don't want to go home." Avellana scowled and crossed her arms. "I'll be home soon enough tomorrow evening for the weekend. I want to stay with Signet and Cratag. You see what good care they take of me. At home, you *smother* me. Someone's always watching."

"Someone's always watching you in my home, too," Signet said.

Avellana stuck out her chin. "Yes, but usually it's D'Marigold Residence and not a person, and he is very polite, and I hardly ever think of him watching." She turned to her parents. "Having a person always watching me at home is *rude*."

Her mother's lips compressed. "But we can't seem to trust you, can we? Not after you slide down the bannister and. . ."

"And I miss Muin!" Avellana's voice thickened, her eyes welled with tears. "I barely saw him at all today."

"You saw Vinni? Where?" asked her father.

Avellana snapped her mouth shut, obviously sensing she'd said too much.

Signet soothed, "Naturally he would have felt Avellana's danger. He teleported to the scene, as any loved one would have done. As you teleported here to Primary HealingHall."

"Vinni's Family is restricting his activities, as you well know," D'Hazel said. "We are honoring their request that you remain apart."

Looking away from her mother, Avellana sniffed.

D'Hazel sighed, glanced at her husband. He said, "We will consider speaking to Vinni's—Muin's—Family if this weekend passes well with you at home. He may be allowed to return to visiting you at D'Marigold's on Mor."

Avellana narrowed her eyes. "And the person watching me? They smirk. They *all* smirk. Or they're irritated to be watching me when they want to be assigned a more interesting duty."

"Avellana!" D'Hazel said.

"Well, it's true."

"We will consider your words," T'Hazel said. "And perhaps ask that the Residence increase its monitoring of your actions instead of a human being."

Rhyz gave a small mew. Avellana glanced down at him. "All right. I never wanted you to spy for my parents—"

The Hazels winced.

"—but I give you permission to do so until I am through my First Passage." Avellana pursed her lips then sent her parents a firm look. "I want to discuss *a lot* after my First Passage. I haven't forgotten that you said I could have the Second Child's suite."

D'Hazel protested, but her HeartMate put a hand on her shoulder and silenced her. "We agree. You're growing up, so we will discuss this after your First Passage. Right now we want you to come with us."

"Oh, very well." Avellana hopped off the twoseat and came over to Signet and Cratag, giving Signet a hug. "I'll see you on Mor."

Signet kissed the girl's cheek. "That's fine."

"And I want to continue our outings." Avellana glanced at her parents. They said nothing.

"Accidents happen," Cratag said.

"Yes." Avellana nodded in approval. "And you were a hero again." She kissed his cheek. "Thank you."

The Hazels echoed their thanks, then Rhyz jumped into Avellana's arms and they all vanished.

Signet leaned into Cratag, kissed his cheek, too, let her lips linger. "You are a hero, Cratag. Always."

His cheek heated under her lips, and she knew he flushed. "I'm no hero."

"Yes, you are. Let's go home." She scooped up Du. He was putting on weight, but was still thin and easily handled if he wanted to be. He hissed when she tucked him under her arm but didn't struggle.

Beadle hopped to Cratag's shoulder, looked down on Du, and purred loudly. *My FamMan is a big, strong *hero*.*

On Cratag's choked laugh, she teleported them home. As soon as they landed, Du hopped from her arms and raced from the room. *Perhaps so*, Du said to Beadle. *But I am faster than you and can get the best treats from the pet no-time.* There was the hint of a cat-snort. *And I live here and am alpha cat. You will go to T'Hawthorn Residence and live under Black Pierre's paw. He is snooty and mean.*

Grumbling, Beadle trotted after Du, paused at the door, and threw a look at Cratag. *My FamMan can fix anything. He is a hero.* Then the cat shut his eyes tight, twitched his whiskers, and teleported away.

Cratag rolled his shoulders, and Signet sensed it wasn't because of any remaining aches, but because of his status at T'Hawthorn Residence and how that might disappoint Beadle. By now she knew he was housed much more lowly than he deserved. If she hadn't planned on having him stay as her HeartMate and husband, she'd have pressed him to demand more from his lord.

She inhaled a shaky breath. She wasn't allowed to tell Cratag that he was her HeartMate, but she wanted to comfort him some way. A thought occurred and she glanced up at his impassive face. "I think Black Pierre is of an older generation of cats. Does he teleport?"

Cratag blinked, looked down at her. "No, I don't think he does." Kissing their linked fingers, he said. "Not that he can't, just that it might take more Flair than he wants to use."

"More Flair than Beadle uses."

"I would say so." Then Cratag smiled, and her heart simply turned over. "Beadle is a younger, more energetic cat. Loves to hunt and be outside. Black Pierre is the opposite. He likes to be inside and pampered."

"Ah." They left the room side by side, and she was pleased when they passed his suite and went to hers. Cratag opened the door of her sitting room, but they didn't stop on the way to the bedroom.

With a few Words she made their clothes fall away. "Let me *touch* all of you, make sure you're all right." Her voice was choked. "I couldn't do that at the HealingHall." She reached for him, smoothing her palms over his shoulders and chest, confirming he was whole, and safe. Keeping her hands on him, she circled him, noted that he had no new marks and let out a sigh. She stood behind him and pressed her cheek to his back, against another old scar. "Hero."

"No," he whispered.

She didn't contradict him this time, but leaned until his taut butt was against her stomach. Then she slid her hands around to find him, and his erection was large and strong. She caressed him and he sucked in a breath, let it out on a low groan, but he didn't step away from her. He let her touch his body as she wanted, always so generous that way. Patient. Though with her face against him, she could feel the slight quiver of his muscles, the unsteadiness of his breath.

She opened her mouth and licked his smooth back, and he stiffened. His arousal surged in her fingers, and she chuckled. But she wanted to see him, the ruddiness edging his cheeks, the dilation of his pupils. So she turned to rub her breasts against him, let her own moan out as her nipples hardened. She stepped away, went to stand before him, noting his hands had fisted as they often did when she wanted to play with him.

They loved fast and hard and desperately. Then they slept in each other's arms.

*W*hen *Avellana returned to Signet's Residence on the first morning of* the new workweek, they followed the usual schedule.

At MidMorningBell, a very quiet Vinni arrived, carrying a picnic basket. Signet opened the door and studied him. His face looked thinner, his body leaner, his eyes more shadowed. As if he'd fought battles that had matured him in the last few days.

He made an excellent formal bow, even with the basket. "Greetyou, GrandLady D'Marigold."

Signet opened the door wide and stepped back. "Hello, Vinni, come in."

"I was informed I could come today at midmorning break to see Avellana." He lifted the basket. "I have a healthy snack and cocoa."

The basket was large enough to hold a meal for six.

"You're always welcome here, as Vinni, my friend, or as Great-Lord Muin T'Vine."

He stared at her with his changeable eyes, but they remained green brown. A slight smile curved his lips, and he said, "Thank you, Signet." He came inside, and she shut the door.

Whatever had gone on at his household . . . and Signet could only think it had been another power struggle and Vinni had lost . . . he wasn't his usual optimistic self. Signet shut her mouth against the words she wanted to say against those who had squashed the lad. She had no parenting experience and was muddling through with Avellana, so she could not, *should* not judge others. Of course it shouldn't have been any of her business, either, but she liked Vinni, and his moods affected Avellana.

Muin's here! Avellana's mental shout could be heard by the whole household. Vinni's smile widened and reached his eyes. There was the pattering of small female feet down the corridor to the top of the stairs, just out of sight. Then a pause.

Avellana appeared at the top of the staircase and placed her fingertips lightly on the bannister. Chin lifted, she descended the steps, nearly gliding.

Signet smiled, too. Avellana was learning more from D'Marigold Residence than history and architectural lessons. Probably the whole of Signet's mother's instructions on how to charm; the previous D'Marigold had been a considerable charmer.

Vinni quivered beside Signet and set down his basket. As soon as Avellana reached the bottom of the staircase, they rushed together in a tight hug. Signet was sure that everyone on all sides of the Families closely watched the children's relationship. Vinni hadn't had a large growth spurt and was slightly below average in height, but the time would come when the six years between them would lead to some taboos—like hugging. For now Signet was glad to let them express their affection.

Cratag coughed at the top of the stairs, and Vinni pulled from Avellana and straightened to his full, not-so-tall, height. "Thank you for saving Avellana the other day. I don't know—"

"Easy does it. All is well. Just doing my job." Cratag waved a hand and came down the stairs with an athletic grace. Signet had a guilty thought about how he might look sliding down the bannister, and how they might do so together. They'd have to wait until all this was over.

Walking up to Vinni, Cratag bowed and offered his hand. "Good to see you again, Vinni."

A long sigh whooshed from the boy. He glanced around. "Good to be here. I think D'Marigold house gets more beautiful every time I see it." A wistful expression crossed his face. He lived in a sprawling castle of turrets and courtyards a few kilometers outside the city.

"Thank you," the Residence said.

Vinni made another slight bow. "You're welcome." He turned to Signet. "I would like to take Avellana on a picnic, down to the boathouse on the river, and could we . . . might we have your permission to be alone together?"

What do you think? Signet asked Cratag through their private bond.

He shrugged. *I don't see why not. I don't think either of them will consider bending even a minor rule.*

We aren't their parents, so should we be more or less permissive?

Another shrug. *The Hazels and the Vines know we've been treating them with a light hand. The two have already been punished by their own elders.*

The girl and the boy, hands linked, waited.

"All right," Signet said to Vinni. "Stay at the boathouse."

Avellana smiled at them. "Thank you."

"Thank you," Vinni echoed. He bowed deeply to Signet, then to Cratag.

This time the boy didn't pick up the basket, merely tapped the top of it and murmured an anti-grav gliding spell. Hand in hand, basket trailing, they turned and went down the south corridor that let out onto the path to the river.

In an unusually affectionate move, Cratag came up behind Signet and wrapped his arms around her. She leaned back into his strength.

"They'll be fine."

She craned her neck to look up at him. "I think so. I think despite everything, they'll find their destiny together."

He gave a little snort that she understood to mean that he still wasn't believing in the inevitability of fate, nuzzled her neck a little, and murmured, "Time for your training lesson."

Signet didn't bother to grumble, though she grimaced. Now that Laev was preoccupied with his courtship of Nivea Sunflower, and with Avellana and Vinni on a picnic, she should have anticipated that Cratag would drill her this morning. But she hadn't, and she wasn't much interested in fighting. She didn't mind brushing up on her self-defense skills that she'd learned during her last grovestudy year, but for exercise she much preferred dancing. And Cratag was an *excellent* dancer.

Since he was learning her tap dance, she supposed she could learn his fighting forms. So instead of spending time in her first floor cobbling area as usual, she went up with him to the far wing of the second floor that held his fighting rooms.

Signet had just finished the first fighting pattern, feeling almost good about it, and finally forgetting how odd the tunic and trous were when a shattering mental *Help, Cratag!* screamed through her mind.

She fell down, but Cratag continued with his pretend blow, turned a little, his head jerking up. *Vinni?*

Avellana's choking! Convulsions. Can't. Get. Her! The boy's mind dissolved into gibberish.

Thirty

Jumping to her feet, Signet grabbed Cratag's biceps with both hands, concentrated on pinpointing Vinni. She could sense him, knew the exact spot on the deck where he stood. "'Porting in one . . . and go!"

They alit on the end of the deck, Vinni was in the middle, grabbing for Avellana, who was down on the floor, turning purple, thrashing. Vinni already had a black eye and scratches on both cheeks.

Signet ran up and Avellana rolled, knocking Signet's feet from her, kicking her hard on the thigh. She scrabbled to her feet to see Cratag grab the girl.

"Hold her still!" Signet and Vinni yelled at the same time. "Turn her back to me," Signet panted.

Face grim, Cratag pinioned Avellana's hands, set a brawny arm in front of her, ignored her kicks.

Signet rushed up, got herself into position, thumped Avellana on
the back along with just the right amount of *Flair*. A gob of something went flying from the girl's mouth, out over the railing into the
river.

Cratag flipped the girl, laid her across the table, opened her
mouth, and blew into her mouth. Signet saw Avellana's chest rise
from the influx of his breath, his lifeforce, his minor Flair. He set a
hand on her chest, pressed it, lifted.

Avellana's dimming thought patterns revived, she began breathing on her own.

Vinni sank into a chair littered with bits of food, put his head in
his hands, and gave a small sob.

The girl was breathing noisily, taking great gulps of air.

"I think we should go to the Primary HealingHall," Cratag said
as he lifted Avellana.

Vinni coughed, raised his head, and scrubbed his face. Signet
reached for a softleaf, but realized she wore only the tunic, trous,
and light dance shoes of fighter training. She was momentarily
appalled at going out in public, but she stepped up to Cratag.
"Vinni, please help us teleport there. I'll have the glider pick us up
from there."

Wiping dampness from his face, Vinni grimaced. "Must we?"

"Yes," Signet said.

Avellana rubbed her head against Cratag then looked at them,
eyes wide. "Perhaps Vinni should not go with us. I don't want him
to be banished again." Her voice was little more than a croak, and
Signet sensed how it hurt her to speak.

"It was an unfortunate accident," Signet said.

"Still . . ." Avellana said.

But Vinni stood tall. "I can take responsibility for my actions."

"Did you make the food?" asked Cratag.

"No," Vinni said.

"Then you have no responsibility in this matter," Cratag said.

"I took too big a bite," Avellana said. "But I do love those iced
poppy seed cakes. Please let Vinni stay here."

"I'll soon be late in returning to the Residence," Vinni said gloomily.

"Very well. Vinni, you may return home. We'll take the glider to Primary HealingHall," Signet said. "Take care, Vinni."

"I will." He looked at his broken china, winced again.

"Take those up to D'Marigold Residence. I think it has some housekeeping spells you might use to mend them so they are as good as new."

"All right," Vinni said and looked at Avellana again. "I can come with you."

"I don't want you banished again," she said, then turned her face back into Cratag's chest, ending the conversation.

$\mathcal{A}$ *septhour later when they returned to D'Marigold Residence, Signet* was weary and Avellana was asleep in Cratag's arms. The girl's parents had shown up again, and Signet had let them deal with the Healers.

Avellana's throat was sore, and the Healers thought she'd developed a sudden and severe allergy to sweetplant that had caused the back of her throat to swell and cut off her breathing and induced convulsions.

It was touch and go for a while whether Vinni would be allowed to continue visiting Avellana, but Avellana insisted, and her parents gave in.

Cratag put Avellana into her bed and asked all three Fams and the Residence to watch over her for a few minutes, then he took Signet's hand and led her outside and to the river path. He was quiet and serious, appeared deep in thought.

The gate was shut but the security shield was off . . . as Vinni and Avellana must have left it when they went down for their picnic.

Cratag scrutinized the gate.

"What's wrong?" Signet asked.

Frowning, he moved his big shoulders. "Just have an uncomfortable feeling about this."

Ah, the reason why he wasn't saying much. He didn't talk about his feelings or any hunches or his Flair, as if he was ashamed he had so little. Apparently his meditation sessions hadn't dealt with that issue.

So Signet let him look at the gate, checked it herself with her Flair. "Seems fine to me," she said a little defensively.

His smile was brief. "In excellent condition. Nicely painted. I like the peach that matches the Residence."

"Hmm."

They descended the switchback steps. Instead of taking the short path to the boathouse, they continued to the narrow river bank. On the third to the last, Cratag slipped, windmilled, and, adrenaline giving her energy, Signet teleported them to the boathouse. She was getting very good at this.

Panting, shivering from the energy drain, she wrapped her arms around Cratag. They held each other for a moment, and he smoothed her hair, then he stepped away from her. "I have to go back and look at that step."

"Right," Signet said. The morning sun that had touched the boathouse earlier had angled until this side of the valley bottom was in deep shade, hardly touched by warmth. Signet went inside and took a coat from the closet, donned it. She had too little Flair for even a small spell. She glanced out the full-length windows at the deck, but Vinni had cleaned up well after himself, and there wasn't a crumb left. She could do with an iced cake. Or three.

Signet returned to the steps and carefully went down them, scrutinizing each one. They were all solid with no crumbling.

Cratag stood at the landing and looked at the bottom steps, something in his hand. When she joined him she saw that it was slick, green water reed. "There was some of this on the last few steps."

She sighed. "That happens sometimes when the river rises. We're close to the sea, so the river is tidal." She shook her head. "The bank is muddy. I prefer the beach, so I haven't been as careful of these steps as I should have been."

Cratag threw the weed into the river, wiped his hand on a softleaf. "The current is fast."

"In the middle, yes. We get spring runoff from as far as 241 Range."

He grunted. "Another accident." He rolled his shoulders. "I don't like how many of them have been plaguing us lately."

Signet hesitated then said, "What else could they be? They've been so . . . haphazard."

Another grunt. "Not planned enough or planned too much or something. No footprints in the mud, no sign left on the steps." He glanced at the boathouse. "Is that connected to the Residence somehow?"

"No." She wrapped her arms around herself. "The Residence knows what's going on inside its walls, of course, and if it's connected with scrystones it can monitor things like the front gate, but it can't really 'see' outside."

"Can you talk to it from here?"

"No, the close gardens are my limit."

He turned to her, held out a hand. "I'm sorry. I don't know much about Residences. Could hardly talk to T'Hawthorn's or D'Marigold's until I came here."

She shivered again. "My catalyst Flair."

He strode up the steps, put an arm around her. "Maybe. Maybe I'm just listening better." He chuckled, and it lightened his expression. "I'm getting more practice, too. D'Marigold Residence talks a lot more than T'Hawthorn's. Maybe it's that I have more status here than there, or your Residence is less busy."

"Perhaps. But the boathouse isn't connected to the Residence, and it isn't an intelligent being."

They ascended the steps slowly and had reached the boathouse path where there was a shoe scraper. Letting her go, Cratag worked diligently on the mud clinging to his boots. He said, "I didn't mean to imply that you've been careless about the steps."

Signet sighed, slid her fingers through her hair. "Perhaps I have. Riverweed on the steps, if the children had run down there—"

"—The children wouldn't have been running anywhere today. They're too conscious of the punishments they've already endured for finessing the rules. You made them promise to stay at the boathouse."

"Yes."

He came over and grasped her hands, squeezed them until she looked up at him.

"I'm not a parent," she said in a small voice.

"I'm not either." His head lifted and his gaze slid into the distance. "We do the best that we can with our children. All of us."

She knew he was thinking of Laev, of his own relationship with the young man, of T'Hawthorn's parenting of his Son'sSon, and perhaps even the character of Laev's lost father. Signet hadn't known the man well, but he'd been as rigid and arrogant as any noble she'd met. She sighed, leaned in, and wrapped her arms around Cratag. They shared a moment of quiet, the river lapping at the banks, the rush of tumbling water from a waterfall upstream. From here it was a swift current to the ocean.

After letting her breath out in another sigh, Signet smiled and looked up at Cratag, who was watching her. He lowered his head, brushed her lips, and murmured, "We need to get back."

"Yes." She tightened her arms on him, then let go and stepped aside, slipping her hand down his arm to link her fingers with his and start the climb back up the rest of the stairs. Keeping her voice as low as his had been, she said, "The last few days have been draining. For the first time I'll be glad when this is all over."

Tension from him enveloped her, and she stared up at him. "Glad when Avellana has survived her last Passage and returned to her loving Family. *You*, Cratag Maytree, may stay as long as you like. You are always welcome."

His eyes darkened, and he stopped, pulled her into his arms, kissed her until the energy between them heated with passion.

Signet! Cratag! Avellana's mental voice intruded. *The Residence is feeding me broth with meat slivers, and then I can have cocoa* *mousse and *ice cream* all made with sugar!* The girl sounded happy with the treats but there was a note of querulousness.

Are the Fams there? asked Cratag calmly, and with more ease in his telepathy than Signet had heard. One good thing she'd affected with Cratag—his Flair was more quickly accessed.

They are all staring at me, Avellana grumbled. *They don't get to eat until you come back.* She projected an image of a semicircle of cats flicking their tails. Beadle was drooling.

Cratag chuckled and picked up the pace, and they went through the gate at the top of the path into the beautiful sunny afternoon and locked the gate behind them.

*C*ratag and Signet spent the night in her bed. While he liked her suite better than his own, he was farther from his weapons, and that had become a concern. He had an itch along his nerves. He couldn't pinpoint exactly when that frisson had started, and that bothered him, as if the more he depended upon his Flair, the less sharp his other senses were. Nonsense. His Flair, his psi sense, was better than it had been.

Scrutinizing his memories, he thought that his unease had begun when Avellana had been jostled into the street. Oh, the grumtud on the beach had been a concern for a few days, but the other monsters that had been reported traveling north had been lured out to sea by fishermen.

The tickle at the back of his neck hadn't begun with the bannister incident . . . thinking about that, Cratag wondered if the draining of them all had also diminished their energy to ward off accidents . . . maybe their luck, and they were all more prone to incidents. He probably knew less about Flair than anyone in Druida.

Signet had risen and dressed, sophisticated and beautiful as always. Tougher than she appeared, than he'd ever imagined when he only knew her from glances across a room. He went to his suite and put on work clothes. A kernel of dread had lodged in his heart.

She'd spoken of the end yesterday. The end of this job—now so much more to him than a simple job. Though she'd said he could remain here, stay her lover, she hadn't said that was what she wanted.

He couldn't quite see himself living here with no income, but T'Hawthorn Residence was only a few kilometers away in Noble Country. Cratag could buy a personal glider, set a real schedule with T'Hawthorn instead of always being on call there.

He hesitated then went to the high wall safe and discreetly armed himself. Sheaths were sewn in his shirt for light, thin throwing knives near his loose cuffs. Knives in his old boots, too. He'd have to speak with Signet about including sheaths in his next set of boots . . . then he went downstairs to join the females and Fams for breakfast.

Avellana looked good, and her voice was back to normal, but he didn't think she'd eat an iced poppy seed cake soon. There was a deeper maturity in her that seemed to be more revealed as an old soul than learned. Cratag grunted. He hadn't been brought up to think in such terms, but heard them all the time in Druida, and not just from nobles. Everyone here was more concerned about the basic spiritual structure of their society than those in the south. Probably the influence of being more sophisticated and having so many Families with founders' blood. And Lord and Lady knew you could see the huge starship *Nuada's Sword* from any point in the city. Always a reminder.

Breakfast passed with minor teasing that cheered them all, and they settled into their schedule.

His mind was being numbed by some dull lesson the Hazels had sent when the Residence quietly notified him that T'Hawthorn requested his presence.

Signet, who was with Avellana and him, sent him a concerned glance. As he rose, he leaned down and firmly kissed her on the lips, waved to Avellana, then left.

The dread had returned. This could only be about Laev.

Images of Laev . . . as boy and young man . . . flashed through Cratag's mind. What did you do when you saw a young person making a mistake? For the first time, Cratag recalled his father's face when he'd left home at fifteen to find his sister. Hadn't there been sadness under his sternness? A trace of fear for his son? In his eyes, hadn't there flashed despair and the knowledge that he and his wife had driven their children away? Just before the door had slammed.

Cratag finally acknowledged that leaving his home before he was fully an adult could have turned into a major mistake if he hadn't been a big kid, had some weapons training and street savvy.

T'Hawthorn thought Laev was making a mistake courting Nivea Sunflower. Cratag sensed this, too. He and his lord hated to see Laev making a mistake.

But he hadn't been able to talk his sister out of her no-good man.

Thirty-one

The ride to T'Hawthorn's Residence was under ten minutes. Cratag disembarked from the glider in the stone courtyard, surrounded by tall walls. All glider travel now left and arrived here, a security measure he'd instituted for the Family. As he crossed the flagstones and mounted a stone staircase, he nodded to the guards stationed in the courtyard. Then he opened a tall arched wooden door and wound down some long corridors, his boot heels ringing on the stone—no pretty faded pastel rugs here, and no windows or skylights to fade them.

He felt odd. For four years this had been his home, he'd fought and killed to make his place in the Family, to rise to the chief of the guards and live here in the Residence. Now, after a few eightdays away from the place and the Family, he felt as if he was squeezing into old, too-tight armor. He wasn't the same man he'd been when he'd last sat with T'Hawthorn in the lord's ResidenceDen.

It wasn't just Signet's Flair that had acted on him, it was the job itself—taking care of Avellana, interacting with Vinni and the others. Having Signet as his lover.

His love.

He didn't know what he was going to do about that, but at least he'd acknowledge that he loved her to himself.

There was a guard standing outside T'Hawthorn's den, and that meant only one thing: Laev, HawthornHeir, was also inside. They were the last of the direct line, so when they met together, they were protected. When Cratag entered, the two bodyguards left . . . and his gut tightened. As he'd suspected, a very personal meeting.

Angry vibrations emanated from both men, making Cratag curse inwardly and wish that his Flair hadn't been newly sensitized that he could feel it.

Laev sat in one of the two tapestry chairs angled in front of T'Hawthorn's massive desk—the one with goats. That left the feminine-looking dragonfly chair for Cratag. He bowed to T'Hawthorn, who sat behind the desk, looking stern.

Cratag set his hand on Laev's shoulder, and it was shrugged away. Not good. Obviously Laev thought Cratag would side with T'Hawthorn in the touchy argument regarding Nivea Sunflower. Unfortunately, Cratag would soon learn the minute details.

"The marriage of a FirstFamily Heir is a formal business," T'Hawthorn said, gesturing to Cratag to sit while the lord stared at his Son'sSon.

Cratag's insides clenched, it was even worse than he'd feared.

T'Hawthorn continued, "There are long and delicate negotiations that must be held. The marriage of a GreatHouse Heir such as yourself means land and gilt and power are all involved."

"You just don't approve of Nivea."

Laev hit that nail on the head. Cratag didn't like what he'd seen of the young woman either. He knew that sly glance in the eyes, the teasing manner, hoping to marry "up." He'd had a couple of childhood friends with sisters like that. And if Nivea was pressuring Laev to wed her, sexually teasing him, then Cratag didn't approve of her at all.

"Whether I approve of Nivea or not is another matter. I haven't been given a chance to know her," T'Hawthorn said.

"She's shy! Intimidated by you, the former Captain of All Councils of Celta," Laev shot back.

T'Hawthorn's lips thinned, then he said, "Currently we are speaking of the alliance of Families."

"There is nothing wrong with her Family. The Sunflowers are a well-established GraceHouse with ever-increasing Flair."

T'Hawthorn steepled his fingers, a sign his patience was thinning. "I don't like that you want to marry so soon."

"She's my HeartMate!"

"Are you sure?"

"Yes! I felt it from the moment we met. That's *why* we met, because I felt the Flair and went to her." His mouth set and he sent Cratag a fleeting glance. "D'Marigold felt it, too, and others. T'Vine. I've connected with my HeartMate during my Passages. I gave Nivea my HeartGift, and she accepted it. This is right and true. We're of age. We could run—" Laev stopped on the brink of disaster.

"The last time a FirstFamily son eloped it was Tinne Holly with Genista Furze," T'Hawthorn said in frigid tones. "All know what happened then, the first divorce in FirstFamilies' history, the smearing of a noble name for generations."

"I am not a ramshackle Holly." Laev's voice was rising as he struggled with his temper. "I am a Hawthorn and a Grove and an Oak."

"You will be *T'Hawthorn*."

"I won't elope, but I don't want to drag this matter out for two years while you negotiate the best deal."

"Two years is not unusual—"

"—you don't know what it is to have a HeartMate."

Silence crystallized like ice in the room.

Cratag stood and once again put his hand on Laev's shoulder, this time gripping it with enough force that the young man couldn't displace it without an obvious struggle.

Finally T'Hawthorn said, "A HeartMate bond will not fade in two years, if you continue to love her."

"Of course I will love Nivea, she's my HeartMate."

"Laev," Cratag said quietly.

The teenager glanced at his FatherSire. "I beg your pardon." Then Laev looked up at Cratag with stormy eyes. "You don't know what it is to have a HeartMate love."

"I know what it is to love," Cratag said. "And there can be loves as strong as HeartMate love. Between a man and a woman. A father and a child."

"You don't approve of the marriage, either."

"I think, like your FatherSire, you should give it a little time."

Laev opened his mouth but said nothing when Cratag raised his hand. "Three months."

"An eternity!"

"I'm sure it feels so." He glanced at T'Hawthorn. "I believe if the HeartBond has been offered and accepted—" That happened during sex.

Laev rubbed his temples. "We aren't HeartBonded yet. She honors her parents and won't wed with me until the settlements are done."

Cratag shared a glance with T'Hawthorn. No sex before marriage was unthinkable in a society where the divorce laws were strict and the birthrate low.

"I won't wait two years," Laev insisted.

"Three months," Cratag repeated. Seeing the young man's mulish jaw, Cratag said, "I'm sure T'Hawthorn would be willing to pay for a full matchmaking consultation by T'Willow to confirm your HeartMate status."

Thumping his chest, Laev said, "I connected with her when I had my Passages, saw her and *knew*."

"I'll be glad to pay for T'Willow's time," T'Hawthorn agreed.

"He's out of town," Laev said sulkily. "Consulting at some noble estate. I don't want to wait."

"I consider marriage to be a lifetime commitment," T'Hawthorn said.

"So do I," Laev said. "I'd never bring shame on our name." He stood and straightened to his full height. "I want to marry her at next full twinmoons. *Our* TwinMoons, have you officiate. That's in a couple of eightdays. You should be able to finesse a deal with a GraceHouse Lord by then." Laev strode to the door.

"Laev," Cratag said.

The young man tensed and didn't turn around.

"If you go to a sparring room, we can work off some of this energy."

Laev's shoulders relaxed. "Good idea." He put his hand on the door latch.

"Have you restructured your space for a fighting salon?" Cratag asked.

"No."

"Ah, good, then you should look at the rooms next to yours, for your HeartMate to have her own suite. Have you shown her the rooms or talked about refurbishing them?"

Laev half-turned. "No."

Cratag shrugged. "I've learned that women like that sort of thing. Wouldn't it be a nice gift to have her suite perfect for her before she moves in?"

"Yes." Laev smiled. "Yes! I'll have to talk to her."

"After our bout? Since I'll be returning to D'Marigold's."

Laev nodded. "Sure." He left with a bounce in his step.

T'Hawthorn let out a quiet sigh. "I thank you, Cratag. I did not handle that well." The lord's jaw flexed. "The girl is an opportunist social climber."

"She is of age?"

"More's the pity, yes. They are both adults." He shook his head, a little pale. "It must be my lot in life to have my children marry where I do not wish. My daughter's first marriage with a commoner, then with my enemy's son. Now Laev with that slick girl." He stared out the window, his face bleak, recalling, as Cratag did, that day when T'Hawthorn had nearly killed Holm Holly, his daughter's HeartMate. T'Hawthorn shook his head. "If worse came to worst, I still would not disinherit him."

"Of course not. You are an honorable noble GreatLord."

T'Hawthorn grimaced. "But I think that neither GraceLord Sunflower nor his daughter are honorable nobles." He looked at Cratag. "Thank you for buying me some time, no matter how little. Perhaps the girl will be greedy enough to want to string the process of decorating the rooms out." He tapped his fingers together. "I wonder if I could convince Mitchella D'Blackthorn, the decorator, to take a trip, too." He picked up a writestick and began to make notes.

Noble politics again, over Cratag's head, but he could see machinations wheel behind T'Hawthorn's eyes. May as well leave the man to his schemes. "I'll be in the second-floor sparring room then will return to D'Marigold's."

"Yes," T'Hawthorn said. He looked up from his work and met Cratag's eyes.

Cratag tensed himself at that piercing gaze, wondering if T'Hawthorn was going to ask him personal questions. Something moved in the man's expression that Cratag couldn't quite decipher. It almost looked like sadness. But T'Hawthorn only asked, "Have you met Nivea Sunflower?"

"Briefly, and had tea with her. Didn't get a good handle on her character." Because he'd felt she was wearing a mask. Cratag hesitated. "I was there when Laev first met her . . . there *was* an energy in the air."

T'Hawthorn considered him. "You are changing if you can feel such things."

"D'Marigold's Flair."

"What did you think of the girl?"

Cratag shrugged. "Beautiful. Clever."

"Calculating? Greedy?"

"Maybe. Laev was stunned, the girl wasn't. I was with D'Marigold, Avellana Hazel, and Vinni T'Vine; my attention wasn't fully on Laev."

"I understand." T'Hawthorn tapped his writestick. "I would like your opinion of the girl—and of her and Laev together. Be sympathetic to my Son'sSon. Encourage Laev to bring her to meet you . . . spend some time with you, perhaps."

Another assignment from T'Hawthorn that Cratag didn't much like. He kept his own sigh between his teeth as he walked to the door. "I'll remind you that your daughter's marriage with Holm Holly Junior is a true HeartMate marriage and turned out very well. Your daughter is expecting a child, and I've seen how that gives you joy."

T'Hawthorn's head came up. "You're right, a blessing. But despite the clashes between us, I always respected Holm Holly Junior and knew him to be an honorable man—who has turned out to be a better man than his father. I do not like what I know of this Nivea Sunflower, and she's avoided meeting me. Nor do I like what I've heard of her father, parents." The lord shook his head. "I love Laev." A slight smile curved T'Hawthorn's lips. "And he may very well be a better man than I. So why would I dislike his HeartMate so?"

"Hard to understand," Cratag said. Another noble matter he knew little about.

With a wave, T'Hawthorn dismissed him, and Cratag was glad to go.

He and Laev had a good workout, then sat in a sauna, surrounded by nice, hot stone walls. D'Marigold's sauna was small and made of some fancy wood that didn't make him sweat as much, though it smelled better.

Cratag let Laev vent and ramble on about Nivea. Just being in the young man's presence with his preoccupation with his love made Cratag think more about Signet. He loved her. "It isn't just the sex," he said and was horrified he'd said it aloud, and Laev was turning to him with a gleam in his eyes.

Yeah, Cratag was hot. Maybe his face was red from the heat. It had certainly gone to his brains . . . or maybe not. Could he handle a man-to-man talk about love with Laev? Cratag didn't know, didn't really want to find out, but it looked like he'd raised the subject anyway.

"I'm glad to hear that," Laev said, in his best FatherSire's deliberative manner. "There is more to love than sexual passion." Then Laev's jaw clenched, and he glanced away. "Wish I was getting some sexual passion."

"It seems to me," Cratag said carefully, "that a HeartMate— HeartMates—would want to share their passion." Lady and Lord give him words. "I mean, they'd be drawn together."

"I am; we are."

"She must be very strong to deny a HeartMate passion."

"Nivea is. And she reveres her father, who thinks I'd take advantage of her. Seduce her and leave her or something. She's shy. And my GreatHouse Family intimidates her, them." Laev speared his fingers through his wet hair. "Lady and Lord knows that FatherSire can intimidate anyone."

Cratag listened to the excuses, and his spirits sank. Didn't sound like love to him . . . but wasn't *he* a little afraid of Signet's status, wary that *he'd* be thought of as a leech if he lived with her? And he didn't even care much what people cared about him. What would it be like if he was a young girl?

His mind boggled at trying to put himself in Nivea Sunflower's place, and he took a mental step back and thought of what he, a trained guardsman, had observed. Nivea not as love struck as Laev. Nivea's shy smiles matched with sharp, brown eyes weighing everything around her, like girls Cratag had known in his childhood who'd determined to marry wealthy, older men. Who, unlike Nivea, had used their bodies and sex to do so. Cratag had seen Laev's arms full of expensive gifts for her, but didn't think she'd given Laev so much as a softleaf.

Cratag cast around, trying to think of a HeartMate couple, trying to make *Laev* think of a HeartMate couple he could contrast with his own circumstances. Once again his mouth opened before he thought. "What about Vinni T'Vine and Avellana Hazel."

Laev stared at him. "What about them?"

"They're a HeartMate couple, and even as young as they are, they want to be together most of the time."

Laev frowned.

"What about affection?" Cratag went on. "Those two are very affectionate, and, ah, affection is part of true love, HeartMate love. Must be. Leastwise all the couples I've seen . . . your aunt and Holm HollyHeir, the Ashes. I'm sure you have feelings of affection for GentleLady Sunflower—"

"Of course." The stiffness was back in Laev's voice and a hint of misery in his eyes.

"—she must be very affectionate with you, too. Holding hands . . ." Cratag thought of how often his hand reached for Signet's, her fingers twined with his. "Sweet kisses on the cheek or forehead." He and Signet had shared those, too, and he couldn't believe he was talking about this. Inspiration struck. "Have you spoken to your aunt about this? I know that you've gone to her sometimes when you were troubled." Let a woman talk sense to the lad.

"No."

"Maybe you should." Feeling on a roll, Cratag said, "Have you taken Nivea to meet her? She's not intimidating. *Her* first marriage was to a commoner."

Laev stood up. "I took Nivea to meet her. Everything went fine. I'm tired of defending my love. Talking about this." Everything didn't really go fine, then. Cratag sensed Laev's aunt had cautioned him. "Waterfall, now," Laev said.

Well, Cratag had failed, not surprising. Go to the fallback position, delay, delay, delay. "Yeah, let's head for the waterfall. Are you going to spar with your lady?"

Stopping in his tracks, Laev stared at Cratag once again. "*Spar* with Nivea?"

Cratag pretended not to hear the incredulity. "Sure. If she's going to be a GreatLady, she should know self-defense." He found himself smiling. "I'm teaching Signet."

"Nivea is in her last year of grovestudy, still learning self-defense there." As if hearing his own words that revealed how young she—and he—was, Laev continued. "I don't think she likes it much."

"She wasn't apprenticed to anyone and is now a journeywoman?"

"No." Laev stepped into the tiled room and ordered the waterfall on high and hot. Water smacked the floor in a hissing wave. But the shelf ran across the length of a short wall, and Cratag joined him under there.

"Give her her own studio, her own craft room when you redecorate for her. Not only one suite but more rooms just for herself. She will be mistress here. There are some rooms I know that your mother and FatherDam made their own." Cratag finally ran out of words, though he knew he'd have to press on after he'd washed. Meanwhile Laev actually appeared thoughtful.

When they were dressing, Cratag went back to the subject. "Bring your lady to Signet's," Cratag offered. "There is no prettier Residence in Druida. Civilized. Refined. Sophisticated." All the things he wasn't.

Laev raised his brows but said nothing, for which Cratag was grateful. "Let the girl get some good decorating ideas." He looked at the gray walls surrounding them, as they had since he'd stepped into the Residence. "Lord and Lady knows, this place isn't feminine. Or, uh, have you been to the Sunflowers'?"

"It's a very nice house," Laev said.

"Becoming an intelligent Residence?" Cratag asked.

Laev looked confused. "I don't . . . I don't think so."

"Why not? The Sunflowers have been around long enough, haven't they?" Cratag might be pushing the rough, outsider manner, but Laev wasn't objecting to his questions, and that was good.

Brows lowered, Laev said. "Yes, they're an old Family." Then he grimaced. "I think they lost their Family estate a couple of generations back."

Cratag shrugged. "Too bad. Happens."

"Yeah." But Laev glanced around. "This place is sort of—"

"T'Hawthorn Residence is darker than D'Marigold Residence."

A door slammed in the distance. Obviously T'Hawthorn Residence itself.

"Come on by to Signet's."

Laev opened his mouth, and Cratag held up his hand. "At least mention the idea to your Nivea. She might like to see D'Marigold Residence. Sounded like that to me at that tea we all had together." Cratag actually didn't know; he hadn't paid that much attention to the women.

"Did she say that?" Laev said.

"Who wouldn't want to see the D'Marigold Residence?" Cratag fudged. "You said you'd always wanted to." That he did recall. He lifted his voice for T'Hawthorn Residence. "It's a very feminine Residence. A woman would like it."

Frivolous, came the low grumble of T'Hawthorn Residence. *Marigold has always been frivolous. Only good for arty types.* A window rattled.

Laev looked at Cratag and they shared a smile, and Cratag was relieved. Maybe all his babbling had not been in vain.

*S*everal *days passed, and Cratag's gut eased. They were back on* schedule, and everyone was better than before. Avellana wasn't as rigid in keeping time to the minute, Vinni had returned to casually visiting every other day. Neither of the children had asked permission to go down to the boathouse. Signet was casual, but studied Avellana now and then as if measuring the girl's Flair.

The FamCats were entertaining—Du was appropriating airs like he was the master of the house; Beadle, to Signet's and the Residence's alarm, began bringing in mice to play with, a dead bird, even the occasional skirl. He'd present his prize to whomever was closest. Vinni and Avellana praised the cat and reported to the Residence; Signet tried to coax Beadle to take his tribute outside; Cratag would salute the cat and order it to dispose of its prey outside like a warrior. The last method worked best.

Rhyz, Avellana's Fam, had relaxed, too. He was still in the girl's presence most of the time, but he wasn't always on guard.

Cratag still went armed, with knives in his shirt or jacket sleeves, and had had a session with Signet with the boots she'd made. She personally ensured that she'd set the sheaths best for his reach. His pulse had thudded hard as he looked down on her as she knelt at his feet, her golden head bent, her face intent on making the boots perfect. No one had ever taken such care of him.

No one.

How could he leave her?

But he looked around the Residence—the frivolous, arty Residence—and knew he couldn't be kept like a pet. All he knew was fighting and guarding, and neither Signet nor the Residence needed him for that.

She didn't need him for anything.

Thirty-two

Laev didn't bring Nivea to meet with them, view the Residence, talk to Signet. He gave Cratag a string of excuses that didn't sound like him.

Meanwhile, T'Hawthorn called every day, and his news was that Laev was under a lot of pressure to marry the girl.

Trying to double-check his own feelings, one evening after Avellana had gone to bed for the night, Cratag had had a short conversation with Signet in the sitting room while they'd shared the double lounge chair. "If you thought you were a HeartMate with someone, wouldn't you want to get confirmation of that from a matchmaker?"

She'd turned so quickly in his arms, he'd had to catch her knee before it damaged him. With a wide smile, she said, "Do you want to consult T'Willow about us? I think he's out of town but I can make an appointment."

"No!"

She reared back, and he realized he was making a mess of this as much as any other conversation he'd had on the topic. "He's too expensive." And unlike T'Hawthorn, Signet didn't have vast wealth to pay another GreatLord for an immediate appointment.

Signet's face set. "You don't think seeing if we're a good match is worth such expense?"

"No, I mean yes, but . . ."

Blood had drained from her face leaving it pale, her eyes shocked and hurt. "I'm sure I could do a trade with GreatLord Willow. *If* you wanted to consult."

So Cratag just went with his gut. He captured her as she tried to wiggle away and let his fear out, "It would kill me if he thought we were a bad match." He brought her close, nuzzled her neck, breathing in the scent of her. She relaxed in his arms, snuggled close. "I don't think there's any chance of that," she whispered.

"You're more optimistic than I am," he said, sliding his fingers under the tabs of her tunic at the shoulders, peeling the cloth down to see her pretty, nearly translucent breastband and her even more beautiful breasts.

But she set her hands under his chin, nudged his head up until their eyes met. "No, no, I'm not." Her lips trembled, and her pupils dilated. "You should know the worst of me."

"There is no worst of you."

"Yes there is." She drew in a large breath, "Before I met you, before I knew what my Flair was, I didn't care whether I lived or died." She swallowed, and her blue gaze slid away. "If it hadn't been for the Residence . . . I couldn't do that to the Residence. But sometimes I tempted death."

The thought of losing her curdled his gut. What would he have done in that sterile room of his at T'Hawthorn's if she'd died? He'd have felt a terrible blow. Even though he hadn't known her much then, only as a woman who'd attracted him. He might have even realized what he had lost and that would have been horrible. He gathered her close and rocked until fear dribbled away and his mind cleared, and he met her eyes again, stroked his fingers—his big, rough, scarred fingers—over her soft cheek. "An optimist," he murmured, then said it stronger. "You kept on going even when you didn't think life would get better, didn't you?"

She cough-chuckled, her eyes damp. "Yes. Before all this started I was going to the theater, where real drama belongs. A tragedy to make me feel better." A tear dribbled from her eye, and Cratag swept it away with his thumb.

"An optimist." Then he slid his hand down, over her breast, and tapped her heart. "Here you believe that everything will eventually turn out all right. Or for the best."

"Or what needs to happen will." She nodded and covered his hand with her own.

"I don't believe that. I think crap happens and will always happen despite what we do to keep it from getting in our paths and on our boots."

She smiled at that then craned around his shoulder. "Excellent boots."

He was wearing the ones she'd crafted, of course. "The best, made by the best."

Then her hands were on his head, massaging it, rubbing the shortness of his hair and causing his whole scalp to tingle and his groin to swell.

"I told you the worst of myself," she murmured.

Fligger, he hated "discussions" like this, but she was right. They had always treated each other fairly. Knowing his mouth had gone grim, he looked her in her eyes again. "I've killed men . . . and a woman or two."

She nodded. "I thought you must have." Her palms left his head to slide down his shoulders and clasp his biceps. "You're a guardsman. You had a rough life in the southern continent and made your way north." A line twisted between her eyes. "I've heard those towns bordering the Plano Strait are dangerous."

He nodded. "Very."

"But you never killed if you could help it. You never took a life lightly."

"No, I can say that's true."

She shifted until she was under him, wrapped her legs around his hips until they were sex to sex and all words left him. She was so soft and so limber and so damn female that all he wanted to do was love her.

And *her* emotions swept through him, too, through their link. Desire, passion. Love?

She said a Word, and their clothes fell away from their bodies, and he was inside her, in her heat, snug, cherished.

"I think we're a very, very good match," Signet said huskily, and Cratag damn well tried to make it true.

*S*ignet was awakened before dawn the next morning by a softly chiming ball. Blearily she stared at it. "Bright Brigid's Day!" The calendar sphere chirped. "You are expected at Meadowsweet Temple in half a septhour."

The words sank in.

Bright Brigid's Day, a craft festival for only women.

On ancient Earth, Brigid's Day had been celebrated more than a month earlier—as spring first hinted that it would be coming. Celtans had modified the dates of all the old sun and fire holidays. Unlike on Earth, here on Celta, the Solstices and Equinoxes were more important . . . as the time of turning of their own sun, their own planet, the new home of the colonists.

Today the women of Druida City celebrated the spring and creative forces in the aspect of the Goddess as Brigid. Women of every class throughout the city went to their favored temples and offered their creative work—if they chose. Some women, of course, had to sell their work to make ends meet and didn't participate, but others, such as Signet, who was a cobbler as a hobby, usually brought their work to show off.

There were Bright Brigid Day Fairs all over the city, and on this day, status was less important than like-mindedness. The Fair Signet attended was one of women who especially prized the arts.

And though most of the women were noble like herself, there were commoners who came with a sense of style that Signet could never match. She'd see actresses and artists and musicians. The greatest of them all would be the composer GreatLady Passiflora D'Holly. D'Hazel would not be there.

Signet hadn't missed a Bright Brigid's Day since she'd first gotten her monthly flow and was allowed to participate. Many of Signet's parents' friends would be waiting for her, checking on her mental state. She'd be glowing with love and a purposeful life, and they'd be pleased.

So she dressed in light silkeen trous and tunics, a pastel rainbow. The tunic had the exaggerated long square pocket sleeves that continued to be fashionable, especially for nonworking noblewomen. Frivolous, but Signet felt beautiful in the robes and smiled.

It was still dark—most liked to be in the ritual circle at a temple and say the opening blessing when the sun rose—when Signet checked in on Avellana.

The girl was neatly under the covers, her face innocent and vulnerable. The sleeping child tugged at Signet's heart. By next Bright Brigid's Day, Avellana would have been long gone from here. And everything in Signet's life would be different because the highborn girl had stayed.

When Avellana grew old enough to choose a Bright Brigid's Day group, it would not be Signet's. She would go with the highest noblewomen of the land to GreatCircle Temple.

But they would still remain friends. Signet was determined on that. She loved the girl and would make sure they kept in touch.

Signet leaned down and kissed Avellana softly on her cheek, became aware of a rumbling purr from the orange tabby cat, Rhyz. *You go away?* He didn't seem concerned, merely curious.

A fair today.

You rhyme, Rhyz said. Cats liked rhyming. Signet's lips twitched.

Take care of her, Signet said, along with a simple blessing of the day for the girl.

When she was done, Rhyz said, *I will.*

At the threshold of the bedroom to the sitting room, Signet paused, narrowed her eyes, and studied Avellana. Signet didn't think that the girl's brain pattern was completely normal, but there seemed to be stronger and straighter pathways. Signet had done that . . . helped the girl develop her own synapses. Signet's catalyst Flair had worked on the child.

Then Signet focused her own psi vision and examined Avellana's Flair. Normal levels, not bursting into bright tangles of florets pushing Avellana toward another wild Passage. Good.

Signet would have the child for a while yet.

As she left the girl's suite, the calendar sphere chimed again with the reminder, "Gather the shoes now."

Ignoring the chime, Signet went to her own bedroom and stared at Cratag. He appeared weary, the problem of Laev continued to bother him, and she didn't know how she could help except to be supportive. What she knew about boys-becoming-men was thirteen years out of date, and she hadn't been very observant then, since she'd been experiencing her own Second Passage. But she loved Cratag and yearned to help him. She also intended to keep the man.

Asking the Residence to inform him that she was at Brigid's Day Fair, she took her cloak and went to the craft room where the box of shoes was ready.

She'd always had at least one pair of shoes to offer—of the latest fashion, dyed and stitched in colorful patterns. At the beginning of the year at Samhain, Signet had started a new project that she'd hoped would stave off depression—a pair of shoes a month from the smallest women's size to the largest. She had five pairs, each of different styles. The uppers of the smallest was a patchwork of glossy leather and suede in bold jewel tones with gold stitching. The largest, a normal size she'd finished this month, were evening slippers of a delicate watered teal silk. All of the toes were less pointed, more rounded than the current style, an experiment to see if she could lead footwear fashion. Not that that mattered much anymore, but it would be amusing to watch over the next few months.

She put a glide-and-follow spell on the box and went to the teleportation pad, seeing the hint of the rising sun on the horizon. Mentally checking the temple's teleportation pad, she found it busy and waited until it was safe to travel. She'd been doing an unusual amount of teleporting lately and yet hadn't felt a total crash of energy. Perhaps it was because most of the time it was fueled by emergency adrenaline, or perhaps it was because her Flair was changing *her*, too, keeping up with the younger generation who had more energy and Flair in this area. The temple pad showed open, and she teleported away.

She smiled as she heard the happy babble of women's voices, stepped off the pad, readied it for others, and was immediately enveloped in the cheerful energy of women glad to be with other women.

"My dear Signet." Her cheek was kissed by one of her mother's friends, who then stepped back, looked her up and down, then chuckled. "I hear the rumors are true. You have a good lover."

Signet laughed. "Yes, and I intend to keep him."

The woman hummed in her throat. "I've seen him from a distance at the theater. T'Hawthorn's chief guardsman?"

"That's right."

"Ah. There's something to be said for a physical man." The woman's eyes twinkled.

Rippling notes from a flute signaled the five-minute mark before the blessing circle. Signet cocked her head. "Trif Winterberry is here?"

"Playing for us as her offering to the goddess as Brigid, and you'll never guess who else, right next to your regular table! Go." The woman stepped back, and Signet was caught in a swirl of women entering the round temple.

She hurried to the table her mother and she had had for years and was a meter from it when she saw Vinni T'Vine behind a tiny table that had a discreet sign stating "Bright Brigid Day Blessings, Free Oracle Consultations in the Lady Chapel."

Signet halted, blinked, then strode to her table and set out the shoes, small to large. Women crowded around her table.

Bright Brigid's Day Fair was a festival for women, but the aspects of the goddess weren't only hearth and creativity, but prophecy and smithing. Signet glanced at another table covered in sky blue velvet set back from the women's circle, T'Ash's, the jeweler and black-smith's, table. He'd been allowed because Brigid was his patron goddess, like Vinni would be allowed.

T'Ash had shown up at this particular Fair a couple of months after he'd been confirmed as T'Ash, lean and hungry . . . and with a table of mouth-watering jewelry for the trendsetting women. Unlike the women's crafts, which were considered offerings to the goddess and free to whomever wanted to take them, T'Ash did a brisk business. Signet's mother had speculated that he'd chosen this fair because he wasn't comfortable with the FirstFamilies noblewomen. Then her mother had laughed and said those ladies wouldn't appreciate T'Ash's jewelry as much.

T'Ash inclined his head to Signet, and she couldn't tell from his phlegmatic manner whether he was brooding about the events at his Residence or not. But at least she'd expected T'Ash and his wife, Danith D' Ash—who was missing this year.

She hadn't expected Vinni.

The previous GreatLady D'Vine might have offered her services at a Bright Brigid's Fair, but it hadn't been here.

Vinni sighed, managed a smile. "Hello, Signet. I'm glad you're here."

"I'm glad to see you, too, Vinni."

He grimaced. "All the rest of my Family are at GreatCircle Temple. I didn't want to spend a whole day with them, so I'm here." He looked over the crowd. "I like here, better."

At that moment the first ray of the sun shone through the windows, and the women quieted. Signet moved with the rest to make a circle, and to her surprise, had a couple of women insert themselves next to her to link hands. So, gossip about her Flair must be strong.

She smiled at the women, then turned to hear the blessing from D'Holly.

As soon as that was done there was a laughing rush through the room. Signet was about to wander when Vinni snagged her sleeve. "Stay a bit. T'Ash wants the littlest shoes for Danith."

Before she could reply, T'Ash was there himself, scooping up the small shoes with a long reach of his brawny arm. Then he stared at them, shook his head, and smiled at Signet, "Very interesting use of color and materials. Danith will love them."

Signet cleared her throat. "Thank you." It didn't seem as if he held the fact that she'd triggered nearly disastrous events for his Family against her. She'd sent a note of apology with bouquets of flowers on the birth of her twins to Danith D'Ash, but had not spoken to the lord. "I'm sorry for the trouble we caused."

His exhalation was almost a sigh. He shook his head. "Precocious children . . . can't entirely help themselves, as I know." With a frown, he added, "Might want to consider a good physical-spiritual training course."

"Cratag Maytree is handling that," Signet said proudly.

"Good man." T'Ash glanced at his table, which couldn't be seen. "Better go let down the spellshields and get to business." He walked away.

Signet glanced at her table and saw her offerings to the Goddess were gone and laughed.

"I could tell you who took them," Vinni said.

She shook her head. "But I'm probably too late for a beaded pursenal from D'Bergamot."

"She brought a lot," Vinni said. He hesitated a minute. "You might want to talk to Damiana, the poet," he said.

She looked at his serious face then nodded. "Very well."

Vinni was right about the pursenals. Signet was in time to pick up a shimmering silvery gray beaded one that would make a perfect evening bag. She had just the right shoes to go with it. She slipped it into her sleeve and exchanged blessings with D'Bergamot, then drifted through the round temple, greeting people and exchanging

news. She talked a little about her Flair and her changed circumstances, answered a few questions about Cratag, discussed her shoes
a lot, and diverted any probes about the Hazels and Avellana.

As she stood in line for a pastry and caff, she saw the woman to
whom Vinni had referred, the poet Damiana, looking unhappy with
strain around her eyes and mouth and trying to pretend all was well.
Signet swallowed hard. That could have been her. Had been her.
Had she appeared so miserable? She was afraid so.

But that was in the past, and if she could help, it would be in the
poet's past, too.

Thirty-three

Cratag had wakened from a restless sleep, trudged to the waterfall, and dressed before he realized that Signet was not in the Residence. With more mastery of his Flair than he'd ever had, he traced their link and realized with a small shock that she wasn't even on the estate. She hadn't said anything to him about an appointment, and he was both annoyed and worried.

He tested their link further and found her happy, sensing she was at . . . a temple and surrounded by women. There was another familiar energy signature. Vinni. Had Signet needed to talk to Vinni? About Avellana or something else? Was she having a casual conversation or an official consultation with T'Vine? Cratag tried, but couldn't sort out her emotions and was frustrated at his lack.

"Residence, where is Signet?" He didn't like how his voice came out surly.

"She is at Bright Brigid's Day Fair. One moment, incoming scry," the Residence said.

Before he could ask what Brigid's Day was, the Residence said, "Scry from Laev HawthornHeir for you, Cratag."

Going to the nearest scrybowl in Signet's sitting room, Cratag ran his finger around the rim. Laev's image formed over the water. The young man was pale, need from him sucked at Cratag's energy, and he gave it freely.

Laev relaxed, his gaze searching Cratag's expression. Cratag smiled, and Laev's lips curved slightly. Laev said, "I'd like to speak to you in a bit."

"Sure," Cratag said then glanced toward the open door of Signet's suite where Avellana and her FamCat stood.

"Time for breakfast," she announced in a loud, clear voice. She seemed disgruntled, too. That made three of them. Rhyz muttered cat grumbles. Four of them in a bad mood.

Laev's smile became more genuine. "I'll see you later?"

Cratag looked at Avellana and Rhyz. "Come at WorkBell, I'll have settled Avellana into her lessons by then."

Avellana sniffed.

Laev nodded. "Later."

So Cratag saw to Avellana's and the Fams' breakfasts—Du had strolled down from Signet's room, and Beadle shot in from the outside door. Cratag tucked into good food himself, but he didn't feel much better. Avellana sulked through breakfast, and Cratag let her, concerned about Laev. Something had changed and not for the better. He felt that bad to worse was coming.

Cratag and Avellana went to the library on the ground floor. He listened a bit to a history of the ancient Earth goddess Brigid. The Residence was making the lesson lively with viz, and snippets of plays and songs . . . even a little dance, jollying the girl from her grumpiness, but Cratag was restless. The sunlit gardens outside the full-length windows beckoned, but so did the thought of his training room.

Then he recalled that he'd be "entertaining" Laev. With a young man that age, food was necessary. Where to have this conversation? Cratag loved Signet's sitting room, and Lady and Lord knew that there had been plenty of intense discussions in it, but it didn't seem right for a man-to-man conversation with Laev.

His gut feeling told him that he should have the advantage of his own ground. Which meant the training suite at the far end of the second floor and the small room with table and chairs and a no-time. Good.

So he made sure there was tasty bread and cheeses and decent caff. Then he ran a fighting pattern against the new simulacrum armed with sword and long knife and found the pseudo human was woefully untrained in that area. He hadn't even broken a sweat when the Residence announced Laev had arrived early. Cratag had barely enough time to change into good clothes and get the food on the table.

Beadle entered with Laev, and they both headed for the food. Beadle took a cheese chunk and retreated to a corner. Laev poured himself some caff, then left the cup steaming, turned to Cratag, and stepped close for a strong hug. He gripped the boy hard and held on until Laev withdrew, turned aside. Cratag had seen the dampness in the young man's eyes. Hormones.

Laev sipped and didn't speak until Cratag had drunk.

"Good stuff." Laev looked at the liquid in his cup.

Beadle burped.

Cratag grunted. "You can always count on D'Marigold Residence to have the best food."

A fleeting smile crossed Laev's face, then faded. He drew in a deep breath and met Cratag's eyes. "I'm getting married this evening, and I want you to be there."

It was a blow. Words failed Cratag as he scrambled through a thousand to try and find ones that would stop this disaster.

The silence went on too long. Laev rose from his seat and paced the small room. "You don't approve."

"Is T'Hawthorn officiating?" Cratag thought of GreatLord T'Ash, whose month it was, "or T'Ash?"

"No, but my FatherSire is invited. The ceremony will take place in Nivea's local temple, Flax." Defiance laced Laev's voice. The temple was in a lower-middle-commoner class of town.

Beadle sniffed a Du-like sniff. *I will come.*

"Thank you," Laev said.

"What prompted this?" Cratag asked, feeling his way.

Laev threw up his hands. "GraceLord Sunflower is sending Nivea to his southern estate to supervise the crop. It's the only land they still have, their income. To get her away from me, he means. He hinted that the local landowner is interested in Nivea and would be a good match. A better match than a young man under his Father-Sire's thumb, like me. Nivea is miserable."

Scowling, Laev threw out words. "Why must others interfere?" The boy raked his hands through his hair. "Her father and his demands, my FatherSire and his. Why can't they just let it be?"

Cratag opened his mouth, but Laev cut him off with a sharp gesture. "I know, FirstFamilies dynastic marriage crap." He pounded his chest. "But we're human. I'm a man. I want my woman. What would you do if someone tried to keep Signet from you?"

Anything. Kill. Tear a city apart. The violence of his feelings surprised Cratag. He answered Laev's question. "Pretty damn anything." He filled his lungs. "But if I knew she was my HeartMate, I'd wait."

"Would you? Would *you*?"

"Yes."

Laev's laugh was ugly. He rubbed his head with both hands. "I can't wait."

Cratag didn't know what to say. "If she's your HeartMate—"

"*If!*" Laev whirled toward him. "You don't believe me, don't trust me either? But you were *there* when we met. You felt the energy."

"I felt something." Cratag pushed on. "I think you believe she is. But has she given *you* her HeartGift? And if she's accepted your gift, then she's already accepted you, so this local landowner business is smoke that's gettin' in your eyes and distracting you. You're being pressured too hard by Sunflower—"

Another awful laugh. "—and my FatherSire, and, you, too."

And by Nivea most of all. "I'm just asking you to wait a little. HeartMates are forever; she'll be there." He was spouting what he'd heard since he'd come to Druida, what most folk here believed; he could only hope it was true. "I can't see Holm HollyHeir without his Lark, T'Ash without his Danith . . ." Cratag fumbled.

"They're *married*."

"Vinni and Avellana."

"That's *different*." Laev gestured widely. "They're children. They know they will be together. You don't understand!"

"Ground yourself!" Cratag snapped.

Laev immediately stilled, settled into his balance.

"This isn't like you, Laev," Cratag said calmly. "You're a strong, intelligent bo—" He stopped too late.

"I am a man," Laev said through gritted teeth.

"A man experiencing a lotta hormones, mood swings." Cratag waved. "Upsurges of Flair." Was that right?

Laev stood tall. "I am a man who wants his woman, his Heart-Mate. And I know myself." His chest expanded as he took in a big breath, let it out. "My marriage with Nivea Sunflower will commence at EveningBell at Flax Temple. Come if you want," Laev said. "Or not."

With a too-calm inclination of his head, Laev strode to the tele-portation pad and left.

A bitter helplessness that he'd failed Laev gnawed at Cratag.

*A*s she ate her pastry at a full table and desultorily took part in a conversation about fashion, Signet watched the poet Damiana. She was a tall, angular woman with black hair and eyes and skin a darker shade of golden than Nivea Sunflower.

It took little Flair to see that the woman's Flair was blocked. When Signet noticed the silence, she found everyone looking at her. She wiped sweet-powdery fingers on a softleaf and smiled. "My apologies for being rude." Questions erupted about her psi power, and she was happy to answer them.

As musicians took the stage and others deserted the table, Signet touched the poet's hand and said, "Why don't we find a quiet place to talk."

Damiana frowned. "What do you—." Damiana coughed. "Excuse me, what do you want, GrandLady?"

With an easy smile, Signet stood and took the woman's elbow and guided her toward a door to the outer hallway ringing the temple. "You were listening when I spoke of my Flair?"

Damiana shrugged, pulled her arm away.

"I can see others' Flair. Yours is blocked."

Damiana's eyes went desperate, her mouth flattened.

Signet said, "I think I can fix that for you. Perhaps now."

The poet's breath caught. She swallowed. "Truly?"

"Yes." Signet took her arm again, and this time the woman came along. "Since it's an experiment for me, and Bright Brigid's Day Fair, there will be no charge. If you want to try."

"Yes." Damiana's fingers clamped on Signet's arm. "Of course. I'm supposed to deliver a new poem to D'Holly to set to music for the new session of the Councils, and I can't . . ."

"Ah, fear. I thought so." They were near the Lady Chapel and Signet heard murmuring voices and recalled Vinni was doing oracle appointments. Her smile widened as she realized that she, too, would be conducting a working interview. That felt good.

"The Lord's Chapel?" she asked Damiana.

"No."

"All right, there are some tiny Priest and Priestess Consultation rooms in a few meters."

"Fine."

They reached the first small room, and it was empty. The three temple priestesses were at the fair. The room was dim with heavy wine velvet curtains, richly outfitted but only big enough for two, with chairs nearly knee to knee. Perfect.

"Make yourself comfortable," Signet said. "This works best if I take your hands and we both sink into a trance."

Damiana sighed as she sat and held out her hands. Signet sensed her relief that nothing unusual would be asked of her. Signet took the poet's hands and found them dry and warm. "I'll count down."

"Yes," Damiana said in a voice already thick and slow.

Signet said a blessing, closed her eyes, and counted down, fell into a light trance, opened her psi power, and linked with Damiana.

Her Flair was dammed behind a black web. It didn't appear a difficult task to unravel the web and free the woman's natural talent. "This might be painful," Signet warned.

"Please," Damiana whispered. Signet thought she saw the web through their link.

"It could take a while—" Signet was still too unaccustomed to using her Flair to judge how long procedures might take.

"All day, all night, whatever time you need."

"Very well." Signet frowned at Damiana's construct of a black spider web. "I can remove the blockage, but it may return if it's a deeply rooted fear." Signet cleared her throat. "You should get counseling from a Priestess or Priest or a mind Healer." Signet herself should get more formal training, so she could minimize pain, recognize problems faster, be more precise.

"I promise," said Damiana.

"Let's start then, breathe with me. . ." Signet mentally *reached* for the first strand of the black web. It was slipperier than she'd anticipated.

*A*fter a couple of minutes Cratag shook himself from the brood his conversation with Laev had caused, cleansed himself, and put on his regular clothes. He glanced at his timer. The break between first and second lessons had passed. Too bad. He'd looked forward to talking a bit with Avellana, another FirstFamilies GreatHouse child, maybe tease her from her grumbles if she was still in her sulk. She'd be in the library. Time to check on her anyway.

When he opened the door to the library, she wasn't there. He frowned. "Residence, where is Avellana?"

"She and Rhyz went through the doors into the gardens during class break and did not return," the Residence said. It didn't sound worried, but a tingle snaked down Cratag's spine. "Thank you."

He could race upstairs where he might spot her more quickly, or he could run along the paths. He opted for running, throwing the doors wide and heading for the flower garden. "Avellana," he called. She was wearing spring green, he recollected. "Rhyz."

They didn't answer.

Thirty-four

Avellana and Rhyz would have heard him if they were in the gardens. Cratag's chest tightened. He turned and headed to the cliff gate. She'd been avoiding the boathouse. The gate was cracked open. Surely she wouldn't go to the beach alone against the rules? She hardly did anything against the rules, but Cratag understood overwhelming temptation, and the sea was bright and blue with whitecaps this morning. The tide was on its way out, plenty of beach. He couldn't see the beach and running down and up those steps would take precious time.

Avellana! he called mentally. No answer, though she rarely spoke to him mind-to-mind. He checked his link to her but felt nothing. Maybe he couldn't sense it because his fear was rising. He didn't have a strong enough bond with Rhyz to touch minds with the FamCat. Dammit, he wished Signet was here.

Despite his doubts that Avellana would be near the river he headed toward the boathouse.

He didn't have great psi, but his senses were hyperaware, strained to the limit, and he heard a small splash.

He raced to the boathouse path. The gate to the river was open, he shot through it, pounded down the steps, was passing the boathouse—

"Halt, or I shoot," a cool voice said.

A jumble of puzzle pieces clicked into place. No bad luck, no accidents had plagued them, but human malice. "Hanes," he said, but didn't turn left to look at the man. Hanes wasn't as important as Avellana. Cratag scanned the river. Downstream there was a spring-green-and-orange-fur-like bundle caught in the branches of a tall fallen tree jutting into the river. He took a step, and blazer fire streaked across the path close to his boot toes.

"My aim with the girl wasn't very good when I tossed her and the cat into the river," Hanes muttered. "They didn't get where the strong current would grab them." He sounded irritated. "My blazer aim is better." He shot again, grazing Cratag's knuckles. The knife dropped from his numbed left hand. He didn't dare slip his right knife into his palm, couldn't risk both hands being useless. At least it was a stunner blazer instead of a fire blazer.

"Move and there will be no way to help her," Hanes said.

Signet! he shouted along their personal bond, tested it. She vaguely acknowledged him, was deep in trance. At a fliggering fair? That he hadn't even known about.

Vinni! he yelled mentally.

Hanes snorted. "I heard that. Muin is at Bright Brigid's Day Fair." Hanes's voice hardened. "He didn't go to the FirstFamilies fair with the women of our Family. No, he went to the Women of the Arts gathering that Signet attends. She—and you—have been a bad influence on him."

"Just a boy growing up, Hanes." Cratag thought he saw Avellana wiggle. *Hang on,* he sent her, hoped she heard. But now, now he could sense his bond with her. Her mind was dim and sluggish, as if she'd been drugged. He needed to face Hanes, see which blazer the man carried. If it was the one with the range to finish Avellana off.

Slowly he turned. Yes, a blazer shot could hit her. If he didn't divert Hanes, take him out.

"A pity I'll have to kill you, too," Hanes said. "You're a good guard, for a fliggering outsider." Insult laced Hanes's tones. "Would have been my match if you were from a noble Family and had good Flair."

The sneer slid off Cratag. No time for emotions, he was ice inside and totally focused on Hanes. "I thought you loved Avellana."

"I did love Avellana. We loved her. Until we discovered she was a mutant. Can't have a mutant in the Family."

"Vinni, too?"

A rough laugh rolled from Hanes. "Outlander. Of course not Vinni. He's her HeartMate and forgives all, even things that shouldn't be forgiven, like being a mutant. Pity, the alliance with the Hazels is first class, but that might remain if they all grieve together after Avellana's tragic death." Hanes held the blazer too steadily. He was a trained guard.

Cra-tag? Avellana whispered in his mind.

Hang on. Distract, distract, distract. Until the moment was right.

"We are all mutants." Cratag knew that, though few ever talked about it. "As a people we continue to mutate as we live on Celta and our gifts grow."

Hanes's lip curled, he jerked a chin at the river. "We're not like her. *Bringing the dead back to life.* That's not right. It's against everything our society believes in."

"It's against everything you think our society believes in," Cratag said. "For myself, I cherish life, and Avellana has been given a great gift." He could sense her struggling to stay conscious. The river was cold.

"You." Hanes laughed again. "An outlander. Lord and Lady know what they teach you in the southern continent." He looked down his nose, the blazer unwaveringly pointed at Cratag. "Raw, uncivilized, ignorant. Didn't even know about Brigid's Day."

That arrow struck home. Another Druida City tradition he hadn't learned of until it was too late. Cratag didn't let his anger at himself, the tendrils of despair, show.

Hanes sent him a sharp-edged smile. "We've been keeping track of your schedule here, just awaiting an opportunity, and today is it."

"We who?"

"You don't need to know. But we can't have a *thing* like her in the Family. Too bad you came back too soon." His finger tightened on the trigger.

"So you pushed her and poisoned her food."

"I pushed her." His lips thinned in a smile. "Mingled on the busy sidewalk, pushed Avellana then ran from the direction of a teleportation pad."

"It was poison?"

Hanes shrugged. "We knew she had a sensitivity to sweetplant. The Hazels use sugar, we Vines use sweetplant. The icing on the cake was made with a high concentration of sweetplant."

"Who else?"

Hanes's finger stroked the trigger.

Time's up. Cratag glanced in Avellana's direction, smiled widely.

Hanes glanced away an instant.

Cratag leapt. He was bigger, stronger, often had fought for his life. Hanes hadn't. Advantage. But would he be in time to save Avellana?

He slammed into Hanes, took him down. The man kept his grip on the pistol. Cratag grabbed that wrist, squeezed hard, felt bones rub together, pressed a thumb on a nerve. A moan rattled from Hanes. His fingers went limp, his blazer clattered to the deck.

Hanes bucked, rolled, but Cratag was heavier, used gravity to pin him.

Shrieks pierced the air. Vinni and Signet. Here. Finally. Thuds as they landed on the boathouse deck. A splash.

"Muin, no!" Hanes yelled. He thrashed again, freed his hand. His fist slammed against Cratag's head, just missing Cratag's temple as he ducked. He gritted his teeth against the pain.

"Help!" cried Vinni.

Signet was there, swept up Hanes's blazer, pointed it at him.

"Cratag, help. Not. Powerful. Enough. To. Teleport. Avellana. And. Rhyz. And. The. Tree."

Easy choice. Cratag jumped from Hanes, ran to the boathouse, vaulted over the rail.

The frigid water took his breath. He didn't think, only swam with powerful strokes, pushing himself with his Flair, to the log, and the three caught in the branches of the dead tree. Some roots were still firmly in the ground. No, no chance of teleportation.

Behind and above him he heard Hanes mock, "You won't shoot." A whoosh as someone 'ported and the hum of a blazer.

Vinni was holding Avellana as high as he could from the water, tears running down his white face. Her tunic was snagged on one thick branch and several smaller ones. A wet and limp Rhyz was propped in another branch fork.

Cratag angled himself, kicked at the big branch, snapping it with a loud *crack*. He swam close, wrenched the branches trapping Avellana. They broke in his hands.

"She's free!" Vinni said, grabbing her. "Primm-arr–yy. H-h-healingH-hall!" His teeth chattered on the words, then they were gone.

With hands numb from the cold, Cratag lifted Rhyz and curved the cat around the back of his neck. Keeping his shoulders out of the water, he paddled around the tree to the side of the river where Signet stood on the steep bank that had crumbled. She still held Hanes's blazer, but dropped it, flung herself on the ground, and reached out her hands. "I can lift you with Flair." Tears streaked her face.

He doubted, but grasped her wrists. A second later he was on his feet on the bank and the gentle breeze felt like a blizzard wind.

She wrapped her arms around him, and they stood shivering together. Her body felt hot to him, but he'd chill her.

"He's gone. I failed," she wept into his chest,

"Not as badly as I did," he said through cold lips. All of him was cold, inside and out.

*H*e *grabbed a fast waterfall and changed his clothes and armed* himself with most of his weapons. Signet did a whirlwind spell to clean and dress herself, and Cratag was glad that he didn't have that much Flair because it looked painful. Because Signet had drained most of her Flair during the fair and this emergency, they took the glider to Primary HealingHall. Of course they stayed there for a couple of septhours while the Healers worked on them all. While Avellana and Vinni were being treated, Cratag and Signet told all three Hazels and a Druida City Guardsman the whole story. Hanes had returned briefly to T'Vine Residence, packed his things, cleaned out his bank account, and disappeared once more.

Everyone was concerned that he was still on the loose, though when Vinni was consulted regarding his bond with Hanes, he thought the man had left Druida. Hanes had tried to break the bond, but being Family and so close to Vinni, it was hard to do. He could and did hide his thoughts and might misdirect them. An unusually grim Vinni said that he would always monitor the bond.

Even more disturbing was the fact that there were others in Vinni's household who had conspired with Hanes. Vinni hoped to weed them out during another Loyalty Ceremony where all would swear solemn Vows of Honor to never harm him or his HeartMate, but Cratag wasn't sure that would do the job. Though the whole planet had recently seen the kind of curse that came when people broke Vows of Honor, people who would plot to kill a little girl didn't have much honor.

Cratag kept his mouth shut. He certainly wasn't in a position to advise anyone on anything. The adrenaline rush from the fight had faded and so had the warm glow from the Healers easing his muscle strain and bruises. Physically he felt fine.

Emotionally, he'd crashed. He had failed in his job, to keep

Avellana safe, had, in fact, been preoccupied with his own personal business instead of watching over her. Had failed the Hazels, T'Hawthorn, and, most of all, Avellana herself. Just like he'd failed his sister. He was lucky no one had died.

Avellana had sobbed out that Hanes had called her telepathically from the garden, saying he wanted to talk about Vinni, holding a sweet box. She had gone, he'd drugged her, and the whole thing had deteriorated from there.

The villain had been perfectly right about Cratag, he was an outsider and low in Flair. He didn't know all the capabilities and flaws of Residences, he hadn't known about Brigid's Day and that Signet would be gone. Still didn't know what a Bright Brigid's Day Fair was.

Next to him, Signet squeezed his Healed fingers. They were waiting for the final word on Avellana before returning to D'Marigold Residence. The best mind Healer of Celta was talking privately to the girl. The Hazels were on the other side of the lounge, and Vinni was brooding.

Both Cratag and Signet thought the Hazels would whisk Avellana home as usual, bring her back in a few days. He wondered if T'Hawthorn would recall him, if new guards would replace him. He wondered if he'd ruined his own and Signet's careers.

"Don't be so hard on yourself," Signet whispered. She was leaning against him, and he liked it. "No one could have foreseen that someone we all trusted would betray us because of Avellana's Flair." She stopped abruptly, and they both glanced at Vinni, the best prophet in generations, *the* oracle of Celta.

He caught their eyes, left the twoseat, and came over to stand before them. When he did, he flexed his knees so he was totally balanced, straightened his shoulders. Good lines.

"I supposed you figured it out."

"What?" asked Signet.

Vinni stuck his hands in his trous pockets, took them out. Hands in the pockets was not a good thing for a fighter or a man trying to explain himself. Chin firm, Vinni looked Signet straight in the eye. "I don't often get good visions about myself or Avellana. But I knew that her best chance to survive Passage was, *is* with you. That's proven true." He angled his head until his green brown eyes met Cratag's. "I also knew she would need a trained guard. I didn't know why. And you're the best. I told D'Hazel, and she checked you out, too."

The door to the examination room opened, and the mind Healer appeared. Vinni nodded at them and joined the Hazels—parents and sister—as they strode over to the Healer.

Signet touched Cratag's cheek, and he turned his head to look at her. "Your training saved her. If you hadn't been there today, Avellana would have had a 'terrible accident' and drowned."

But his ignorance had put them all in danger.

Before he could say anything, D'Hazel called out to Signet. "Avellana's having her Passage!"

*S*ignet rushed to the door, was stopped by the mind Healer, who was a FirstFamilies GrandLady, of course. A little shorter and rounder than she, the matron said, "Avellana's Flair has spiked. I believe it to be the trauma of surviving death today. Naturally she summoned all of her Flair."

"Yes," Signet said, looking beyond her to see Avellana shivering and moaning on the examination couch. A Healer and PerSun were beside the girl.

"Avellana is fine for now. I calculate that the peak of her Passage won't take place for several septhours. She is a very unique child. I'd like a moment of your time, D'Marigold."

Signet suppressed a grimace. Probably was going to tell her all the ways her bumbling had harmed Avellana, but Signet stepped aside and let the Hazels and Vinni flood the room. D'Hazel drew her daughter into her arms, T'Hazel embraced them both, Avellana's sister sat on the foot of the bedsponge and curled her fingers around her sister's ankle. Vinni stood near, still in that fighter's stance of his, but with his hands in his pockets. Like previously, he'd only link with Avellana when the worst would come. Avellana could not become dependent on him.

The boy was ensuring his HeartMate would be a strong, full individual partner in their relationship. As Signet was with Cratag. He could have died today! The thought still made her shudder, and she'd never forget the sight of Hanes—Hanes!—ready to kill him. Then he'd plunged into the cold water to save two children. She couldn't have been more proud of him.

She followed the GrandLady into a tiny office, spare of the rich appointments of the patient areas. "I was contacted by another professional in my field about a client of hers, Damiana?" The lady sat, motioned Signet to do so, too. Despite the Hazels and Vinni, and Cratag, Signet was still concerned about Avellana. She should be with the girl.

"Damiana's Flair was blocked," Signet said. "By her own fears. I helped her remove the blockage and counseled her—told her to contact a mental health professional."

"And you knew her Flair was blocked how?"

"I could see it."

"Ah, I wondered about that. I've read your records filed with the NobleCouncil. Impressive."

"Thank you." She didn't want to talk about this now, but would have to. With her Flair came new responsibilities as people took her seriously. Less independence than when folk believed she was a frivolous lady living off her Family fortune.

She thought of all the people she'd helped just by being in their lives. An odd and wonderful occurrence. "I don't want to be so passive again. I'll be signing up for study—"

"I'd like to work with you," the lady said.

Surprised but pleased, Signet said, "Thank you." Then she stood, one professional to another, even though she only had a toehold on the profession. "Excuse me, but I need to be with Avellana."

"Understood." The lady rose, too, then shook her head and sighed. "Good luck."

* * *

$\mathcal{A}$s soon as she entered the consulting room, Signet knew things weren't going well. Avellana's skin was pale and with the faint shine of sweat ready to bead. Her eyes moved rapidly under her lids. A soft crumpled blanket had been shoved aside.

"She was cold just a minute ago, now she's hot." D'Hazel was rocking her child.

The mind Healer who'd followed Signet in hurried to the couch, frowning. "This isn't good. The Passage isn't proceeding normally, as I'd anticipated."

"They never do," T'Hazel said. His arms were still around his wife. "Signet. . ."

But she was already there, tugging Avellana gently from her mother.

"I can't reach her," D'Hazel wept. "Mentally. She's beyond me." She swept a hand toward her husband, her elder daughter, Vinni. "We can't link with her emotionally."

"I can," Vinni contradicted in a rough tone. "But now is not the time. I can only link for a few minutes, when she's at her worst."

"It gets worse?" asked the mind Healer.

He threw her an annoyed look. "Yes."

Signet was concentrating on Avellana, checking her Flair puff-balls, all bunched up and milling around, misfiring sparks. Signet breathed deeply, connected with Avellana, sent the child a slight wave of energy. The girl's Flair smoothed and steadied, flowed through her brain and body.

Cratag said, "She's looking better."

A sigh of relief came from D'Hazel, then the woman ordered, "This time we'll take her home. She'll have her Passage in her own bed."

Signet pulled her mind away from Avellana's Passage to deal with the distraction, met D'Hazel's gaze. "No," she said. "We're linked, and I need to be comfortable, that means my home. Also,

Avellana's inner self associates Passage and surviving it with her rooms at D'Marigold Residence. Furthermore, D'Marigold Residence knows the herbs and scents to release at the proper time. D'Hazel Residence can't match that."

GreatLady D'Hazel's mouth worked. "You were at Bright Brigid's Fair today."

"So were you," Signet said. "I had commitments in my life when you asked me to be a companion to Avellana. The fair was one of them, and Avellana wasn't allowed to come. Hanes took advantage of that." No need to tell the woman the horrible guilt she felt. That was hers to deal with. Signet thought she knew what was really bothering D'Hazel. "I didn't get any warning from her through our link, either. I only felt Cratag's alarm."

"Me, too," said Vinni.

Avellana began moaning in rasping breaths.

"This is not good for Avellana," the mind Healer said. "It would be best if Avellana spent her Passage at D'Marigold Residence," she ended authoritatively.

Having another FirstFamily Healer confirm Signet's reasoning must have weighed with D'Hazel because she said, "Very well."

The Healer asked Signet, "Can the Hazels be part of this Passage?"

"Of course," Signet said. She didn't care. She was helping Avellana order her Flair, but the girl's psi power was rising, would soon sweep her deep into the trials of Passage.

"We'll go now," Cratag said, and an instant later he lifted Signet, who still held Avellana, and carried them both from the room. "The D'Marigold glider is waiting, and it will hold us all."

"Thank you," said T'Hazel, and that was the last "real" thing Signet was fully aware of.

Thirty-five

Signet was flying with Avellana through rough skies, full of threatening dark gray clouds. The girl wore the pretty brown shoes Signet had made her. "You finally decided to come."

"Don't let your temper get the better of you, Avellana," Signet said. "You're in Passage and will have to master it, master all your emotions to survive."

Avellana stuck out her lower lip. "You survived."

"Yes."

"And so did Muin and my mother and father and sister. Everyone I know survived Passage."

"Yes," Signet said.

"So I can, too, but this is my third, so it might be my last of First Passage."

"Yes!" Signet encouraged.

Avellana looked down. "There's D'Hazel Residence, and the tower I jumped from when I was a baby."

Signet knew that tower all too well. Knew Passage with Avellana too well, also. They'd jump from that tower again. She felt Avellana's emotions tugging at her, the wildness of the girl's burgeoning Flair. "I can't be with you the whole time," Signet screamed into the nasty wind that had arisen and was whipping their garments, screeching in their ears. "You *must* master your Flair alone."

Scowling, Avellana nodded. The wind died. Once again she pointed down at the landscape. "And that's your estate."

It was beautiful in the child's eyes, and, of course, Signet's own. Richly tinted, the greens more verdant than they were, the cliffs to the beach not as steep, the beach itself a pure white instead of sand-colored. The river was an emerald green, not muddy. The Residence itself glittered like an enameled box, white arched windows and pale peach rounded walls. Beautiful.

They zoomed and were inside the library, looking out the long, many-paned double doors to the bright flowers and green of the gardens. Where Hanes stood with a sweet box, and beckoned, smiling, his teeth bright. Merriment at doing something forbidden was in his eyes.

"I should have known," Avellana said sadly. "He always followed the rules, too."

Hanes's smile widened, and his teeth went pointy and sharp.

Passage had truly begun.

*C*ratag *held* Signet *and* Avellana *all the way to* D'Marigold Residence. Once they arrived, the Hazels erupted from the glider, and D'Hazel went to order the Residence about. Avellana's sister gently carried Rhyz, as she had from the HealingHall, and he purred. Beadle bounded out, cocked an eye at a rustling under a nearby bush, quivered, then paced Cratag as they entered the Residence to Du's vociferous mewing about being abandoned.

Everyone settled into Avellana's suite, though the circular sitting room was bright and cozy in the afternoon sun. Anticipating a long night, Cratag asked the Residence to open a couple of guest rooms.

He sat by the bedsponge holding Signet's hand and barely kept himself from scowling at the Hazels. They made him all too aware of his shortcomings. Alone with them and Vinni, with Signet battling with Avellana, he felt again like the rawest outsider from the southern continent. He didn't know how close noble Families related to each other, didn't know about city holidays, didn't know about Passage beyond what he'd learned of it in the last month and a half.

This one seemed to take forever. The afternoon passed into the evening, and they could all tell that Signet and Avellana were fighting internal battles.

He and the Residence provided food, the FamCats stayed to give comfort, and still the septhours trickled away. He kept his own small Flair steady, was there when Signet needed to draw on his energy, but he wanted this to be over, the Hazels and Vinni gone, so he could analyze and deal with his failure . . . there was a dark cloud of depression hovering in the back of his mind, and he wanted that gone, too. He wanted to pace the Residence and see for himself that all was secure. Those were things he wanted, but, as always, he worked with what he got. He was Signet's rock.

*S*ignet and *Avellana had traveled through nightmarish landscapes that* tested Avellana's emotions, opened and twisted her Flair so Signet had to straighten it, send it flowing properly. Finally they circled back to familiar features. This time Noble Country was gray and black under threatening clouds. The tower of D'Hazel's Residence speared the sky, glowing darkly. Then they were away from there, as if Avellana still couldn't face it, and back near D'Marigold's estate. The aspect here was gloomy, too, the river was black and shiny and flowed with an oily viscosity. D'Marigold Residence was a glowing peach-colored jewel. Safe.

Time moved slowly. Avellana opening the library door, going to

Hanes, giggling, and eating a fruitbar. Signet experienced it just as Avellana had, then a dark and deadly bird-shadow shape swooped down on them and Avellana grabbed her and they linked and they knew no more.

When they'd battled suffocating fear, and the darkness lifted, they were back at D'Hazel Residence's tower, and Signet braced for what would come.

*C*ratag *Maytree!" the* Residence *said sharply,* and Cratag rose from his half-doze, half-trance, wherever he'd been, the Cave of the Dark Goddess, maybe.

"Here," he said. He stood and shook out his limbs, stretched.

"It is time for you to cleanse and dress for your evening appointment," the Residence prompted.

"What evening appoint—"

Laev's wedding, the Residence whispered in his mind.

Cratag froze. Eight narrowed gazes fastened on his face. He let his expression fall into lines of impassivity as the conversation an eternity ago—this morning—filtered through his memory. Of course the Residence had heard it, and been curious enough to pay attention.

He glanced at Signet and Avellana. They weren't thrashing, and that was good and bad. Thrashing gave all the rest of them pain, but stillness always preceded a crisis. Even as he thought this, the Residence wafted soothing herbs through the room.

"Cratag?" the Residence asked.

"Not right now." The Residence would have built in time for a long waterfall, preening around, and a slow glider ride to the temple. Naturally, the temple was far across town. "Let me know when I absolutely have to leave."

"Surely you aren't going out!" D'Hazel said.

Vinni said mentally, privately, on their own personal link, *What's wrong?*

Cratag turned to him, *Laev's getting married.*

"What!" Vinni said out loud.

"You heard me," Cratag said, turned to the disapproving Hazels and said, "My apologies for my rudeness."

Vinni's face set in sorrowful lines. *I warned him this wasn't a good move, but he didn't listen. He got angry.*

"Cratag, can you stay?" asked T'Hazel.

"I'll have to think about it," Cratag answered. He met D'Hazel's angry gaze. "Important Family matter."

Her lips pressed together tightly, and when Avellana began to whimper, she shifted her attention back to her daughter, taking a damp softleaf from her husband and wiping the child's face.

Signet began to moan, and Cratag sat again, took her hand, and the tension in her quivering fingers told him this would be a bad part, maybe the worst. "Vinni," he said calmly, "You might want to help Avellana in this one."

The boy sucked in a deep breath, nodded shortly, moved to take her hand as D'Hazel reluctantly gave way.

*S*ignet and *A*vellana swayed on the top of the tower, though in reality Avellana had tried to fly from the second-story window. Signet knew she was linked too tightly to Avellana, that the girl could become dependent on her if she didn't withdraw soon, but . . . not right now.

They were falling and whimpering at the pain to come. But they didn't hit the ground, no. They plunged over their heads into an icy river, freezing water trickled into their mouths, their lungs as they tumbled in the current. They struggled toward the surface, heads broke water, coughed. The sky was gray with black clouds churning, lightning flashes blanking out all sight as they were swept away, then rammed into something hard and lost their breath, and the cold began to suck life from them.

No! Signet cried, feeling Avellana begin to sink into despair. *Remember what really happened!*

Then Vinni was there, holding Avellana close, in the Passage dream and in their link. Huge Flair swirled around them.

Rhyz, Avellana cried, looking up at a tangled mass of branches and her cat dangling limply from one as if hung.

I am here, the FamCat's calm voice came. *I am fine. D'Ash Healed me from the drug and the cold.*

And they cycled through Avellana's memories and experiences and dark emotions again.

*C*ratag, you must leave within a quarter septhour. The glider is at the front door," D'Marigold Residence said.

He was still torn. Signet and Avellana needed him—or at least he told himself that to handle the guilt and shame biting him. He *did* feel tugs of energy from Signet, but wasn't sure how much he contributed to the pair's health. Dimly he sensed what was going on—there was a falling moment and icy cold water moments, and that damned Hanes seemed a big feature. All of which he, Cratag, should have stopped. This was nothing like the times he'd been with Laev.

Who was waiting for him to show up at his wedding. A boy he'd hugged and watched accept bad turns in his life. A teen he'd trained, he'd considered a younger brother. A young man he thought was making a big mistake. Then he was on his feet and knew he had to go. He swept a glance at the people who were so much more Flaired than he, who were probably helping Signet and Avellana more. "I must leave," he said. "I'll be back as soon as I can."

"Blessings on you, and give the others my blessing," Vinni said.

"Thank you." *Laev will need his friends in the future.* Cratag scrutinized Vinni's face, wondering how much of Laev's future the boy had seen.

Yes, Vinni replied, and Cratag's heart sank.

He stopped only to get a gift that the Residence provided, then bolted from the Residence, his footsteps loud on the marble floor.

*H*is boot heels were equally loud as he marched inside the shabby stone temple where the wedding was taking place. When he entered the main circular temple he noted three things: He was late, he was very underdressed, and T'Hawthorn was not there.

At the altar in the center of the floor, hand-in-hand with Nivea, Laev glanced at him, face angry, his body stiff. Cratag stopped, acutely aware that everyone, the priestess and priest and all the Sunflowers, were quiet and staring at him. He tried to figure out where he should stand in the ceremony, but there were no cues. No Hawthorns to mingle with. Only the bride's immediate Family was there, her parents and two sisters—a big Family for nobles, maybe Laev would be lucky in that way.

The spell light in the temple wasn't strong, and Cratag figured Laev was providing the power for most of it. Cratag himself sure didn't have any Flair to add. After a moment's hesitation, Cratag circled to stand on Laev's free side. He was still about three meters from the young man. He put his gift on the floor beside him before he saw the table with others—and from the noble colors on the packages, Laev's friends had been generous. Cratag recognized a real gold envelope that T'Hawthorn used to impress. Probably papers inside, which meant a gift of property. Cratag got a bad feeling about that. Property meant that Laev might not be living in T'Hawthorn Residence with his bride. Cratag's small attempt there had failed, too.

The priest cleared his throat, and said, "We will say the beginning blessing again and the GentleSir will add his voice to the chant."

Cratag flinched, nodded.

As he recited the blessing with the others, their voices echoing in the small temple, rising upward and disappearing into the dark, Cratag realized that he was lucky in one thing. Despite the costly formal robes everyone wore—and Cratag thought Laev had paid for each one—the ritual would be a simple one, like the weddings Cratag'd attended growing up. *Not* a several-septhour ceremony usual for the marriage of a member of the FirstFamilies.

But he wished some of Laev's friends were here, the boys— young men—would have made the occasion merry instead of . . . scruffy. Had they not been invited? Family only?

He stared at Nivea, who seemed to have a glow to her skin, standing next to Laev, who stood tall and strong, breathing deeply, sending whatever anger and hurt he felt at Cratag and his Family out through his exhalations. As Cratag had taught him.

Laev looked down at Nivea with a tenderness in his eyes that Cratag prayed wasn't misplaced. She was so wrong for him. To Cratag, her outer golden beauty was cheap gilt, nothing to compare to the fine young man Laev was. A man who had suffered through his own mistakes, his own Passages, learned himself and built on that foundation to turn into an exceptional lord. A nobleman of great wealth and power and Flair. And class.

Cratag was willing to bet that Nivea had had little more Passage fugues than he himself.

There was an incredible difference between Nivea and her Family and the innate grace and honor that Laev had.

A discrepancy that must be like when Cratag and Signet were together.

Then the priestess said her blessing and the ritual began and the muscles in his gut quivered and his shoulders released tension as he knew he wouldn't tell Laev he was making a mistake. He hadn't been sure whether he'd disrupt the proceedings or not. Perhaps he should have done, but he didn't think, didn't *feel* that talking to Laev would change anything. The boy wanted the girl, *this* girl, and had convinced himself she was his HeartMate. Cratag was pretty damn sure that T'Hawthorn, and maybe others, had argued themselves puce trying to convince Laev he was doing something he'd regret. Cratag didn't need to add to the young man's burdens. And he couldn't fail at one more thing today.

Telling the truth hadn't stopped his sister from running off with the wrong man. Sometimes you had to let someone else make their own mistakes, learn their own lessons, no matter how much you ached for them.

Was that why no one had said anything to him about his affair with Signet?

The priest said his blessing. Both priest and priestess spoke of love and commitment then called for a meditation on the topic of several minutes, longer than usual. Did they, too, sense this marriage was wrong?

Meditation was easier for Cratag, now, and he sank into a slight trance, saw Laev do the same with a smile curving his lips.

Cratag felt pressure on his link with Signet that he hadn't noticed, too caught up in Laev's problems. She needed him. So he opened their bond fully and took a step off balance when her fear pushed through to him. She requested, and he gave, energy for her and Avellana. He was panting, controlling his breathing, but it had been a long day, so he stepped from the circle of light and walked quietly to the circular wall, braced his shoulders against it.

Time passed oddly, as he felt something of Avellana's Passage through Signet, tried to keep up with the wedding ritual . . . but his responses were slightly behind everyone else's. Vaguely he heard Laev's and Nivea's vows. Her voice rang with satisfaction, along with that underlying note of slyness that had rubbed Cratag wrong from the moment they'd met.

Only when he noticed a deep silence seething with angry emotions from Laev and with everyone staring at him did he understand he was supposed to respond to the question about the groom's Family's blessing.

Thirty-six

*C*ratag pushed from the wall. *He'd thought about this on the glider ride.* He said, "Huathe Laev Oak Grove Hawthorn has my blessing and the blessing of his entire Family." Speaking for T'Hawthorn, and maybe for the Oaks and the Groves as well. They would have counseled Laev against this, too. None of the FirstFamilies were stupid. But it was important that the Family blessing be said. Words were power, and T'Hawthorn would regret not being here, Cratag was sure. Cratag could be making a bad mistake of his own, but better an error of commission than omission like this morning. Action instead of inaction.

Pleased surprise lightened Laev's face, then suspicion. Had Cratag sounded so reluctant? After a long pause, he supposed he must have. Laev turned back to Nivea.

The bride's Family hastily and cheerfully affirmed that she had their blessing.

Blessings were said by the priest and priestess, and the ritual was ended.

The sound of cat claws bounding toward them broke up the little scene. Beadle appeared smiling around a dead mouse in his mouth. He leapt long and high and lit on Laev's shoulder, scrabbled a bit, and Laev had to steady him.

Blessings, blessings, blessings, the cat projected mentally. *Blessings on the mating of good Laev and the pretty lady.*

Laev laughed, stroked the cat.

Beadle stretched and placed the mouse carefully on Laev's head.

The mouse had only pretended to be dead. It jumped from Laev's head to his shoulder, then ran down his arm, across the ribbon that tied Laev and Nivea together and was stretched tightly as she'd stepped away, then hopped to Nivea's gown.

She shrieked, glared at Cratag. "Haven't you done enough to spoil my wedding?"

The mouse skittered away in the silence. Instincts stronger than courtesy, Beadle followed. Growling.

Then Nivea pressed herself fully against Laev and kissed him deeply. Cratag could see the young man's eyes mist, the haze of lust fill his body. He tightened his arms around her, slid his hands down her back to just above her ass.

Nivea broke the kiss and turned her head to Cratag with a glittering gaze. *You look at me as though I was scum. I am not the outsider, here. *You* are, with your scars and your commoner manners and lack of courtesy. Go back to your silly Calendula.* He was startled to hear Nivea speak to him, glanced at Laev, whose cheeks showed a flush of red desire.

Calendula? Cratag repeated.

Nivea laughed aloud, a rippling sound she'd probably practiced. *Signet D'Marigold. Her real name is Calendula, and you didn't even know that, did you? No, don't go back to her, she's too refined for you. Go back and live like a troll in the bowels of T'Hawthorn Residence.* Once again she kissed Laev, stood tiptoe and whispered something in his ear that made wildness come to his eyes.

"Let's go. Now. In your glider to our new home in Gael City," she murmured.

Gael City! Not T'Hawthorn Residence.

"Yes," Laev said thickly and let her lead him away without another glance at Cratag.

Not surprising. Before Beadle, Laev had been as angry with him as Nivea.

The priest and priestess—surely a married couple—said a few words to him that he didn't hear as he called Beadle back. He got the impression that they were disappointed all around. The Sunflowers gathered the gifts and left without a word to him.

There was a terrible squeak of a dying mouse. He and Beadle and the dead mouse rode back to D'Marigold Residence.

*T*hough it hurt her to do it, Signet separated herself from Avellana, narrowed the link between them to a thread. *Avellana, you must do the rest on your own. Otherwise you won't be a full person.*

No! I'm scared.

That's what you have to master. I'll be here, we'll all be here, you can feel us all, can't you?

Yes.

You have to do these last tests on your own.

Will I fall from the tower and eat poison from Hanes and drown in the river?

As much as she wanted to reassure the girl, to lie could harm her, leave her unprepared. *You may fall in the river—*

I was *thrown*.

You may experience all those things. But you survived the fall and the poison and will not *drown* in the river.

I survived poison *twice*.

Yes you did.

And I lived after the fall and the choking and the river and Rhyz lives and *Flora* lives!

Yes. Signet saw the rushing whirl of Avellana's Flair, tiny blossoms, bunched and sparking erratically. She began sorting them out.

What are you doing? What are those?

You can see them?

Yes.

They are your Flair. If you can see them, you can order them. Just relax and see if they will become steady streams.

Relax. The child laughed, and it sounded amused and adult. But she also began regulating her breathing, taking control of her Passage, and slowly, slowly, the jumbled flowers stopped their mad jumping and sparking, separated and turned into a nice flow. *I can see these because I am with you,* Avellana said. *But I will remember how to do this on my own.*

Good.

Here comes Hanes, Avellana said, and they were back in the library, seeing Hanes outside the window.

Signet felt like she was floating, observing. One more time Avellana would have to confront her deepest fears, and all alone. It hurt that D'Marigold library would now figure in her nightmares, that her worst fear now was Hanes, and that experience had happened here, when Avellana was under Signet's charge.

Then Hanes was there, smiling, his teeth sharpening into razor points, his hand turning into a beast paw and holding out a sweet box. Then behind him was another Hanes, not in Vinni's colors, huge and dark and threatening.

Hanes! He's here again. He's really here, outside the Residence!

Yes, he was. *I can feel him. Cratag's here, too. Don't worry about him here.*

Avellana grimaced. *No, only in here with me.* She turned and opened the door.

Cratag! Signet's shout nearly split his skull. He jolted from his doze . . . trance . . . something.

Cratag, Hanes is here!

That energized him. He jackknifed to sit up on the padded glider bench. Beadle protested, then hopped up to the seat, ears twitching, catching Cratag's surge of adrenaline-laden excitement. *Prey.*

"Yes." He wasn't weary now. "Open window." His window slid down. They were on the gliderdrive of the estate, the gates shutting behind them. D'Marigold Residence was in the near distance, a pretty picture. But somewhere outside lurked an evil black spider he would squash. *Prey.*

As soon as the glider pulled up to the door, Cratag jumped out, his senses stretched to catch any sound, any movement. There was a shadow darker than the brush in the small grassy area between the library and gardens, close to where the traitor would have lured Avellana out this morning. Knowing that the little girl would relive the nightmare again and again, had done so in Passage, had anger flooding Cratag.

Hanes was there.

Beadle shot straight for Hanes, hissing.

Fury filling him, Cratag loped after.

A blazer ray shot out, Cratag dodged, rolled. This wasn't a stunning weapon, but a burning one. The true "blazer."

Adrenaline pumped through him, a metallic taste coated his tongue. He ran, dived.

Hanes shot again and again. The last seared the jacket and shirt from his upper arm, burned Cratag's skin. He gritted his teeth and moved into the pain, through it. He'd fought for his life when he'd been injured before.

He kept rolling, watched as wild streaks singed the grass.

Glaring, Hanes widened his stance, held the blazer in both hands. Bruises showed on his face. No Healer would have treated him. "You ruined everything, took my life away from me. You will pay." Hanes aimed.

Beadle jumped for Hanes's face, claws extended.

Hanes yelled, whirled to strike at Beadle.

The cat kicked the pistol away and disappeared into the shadows.

Hanes spun back, but Cratag rushed him, landed a short, hard right jab to his face. Had the satisfaction of feeling Hanes's nose crunch under his knuckles.

A blow glanced off Cratag's side, missing both kidneys and ribs. That was the last he recalled of the fight. He gave in to emotion, to anger and battlesurge, and didn't calculate his moves, only grinned when his blows sang up his arms, his feet connected with too-soft flesh, and he tasted his own blood.

Then Hanes was down with Cratag's forearm across his throat.

Hanes jerked his head, spit on him. "Outsider." He thrashed his arm free, hit a strong fist against Cratag's upper arm that had pain shattering through him.

Teeth clenched, Cratag punched Hanes's. But the man jerked aside, plucked a small knife from somewhere, slid it into Cratag. He hit Hanes and the villain went limp. But Cratag had waited too long. He couldn't finish this the way a guardsman should. Couldn't make sure Hanes wouldn't wake before he did.

As darkness claimed him, he knew Hanes could escape because he'd lost control. He heard Beadle's furious yowl, *FamMan's hurt!* and blacked out.

*S*ignet *couldn't go to him. She'd been linked to Cratag during the fight,* but couldn't leave. Avellana was deep into her Passage, and Signet had been holding on to her by a thread, sending her energy, even the knowledge that Cratag was beating Hanes up. If Signet left now, she wouldn't be able to reestablish the connection with Avellana. They might lose her.

The Hazels had tensed, stared at Signet. A moan escaped.

Got the bad man, got him, got him, got him! Nice red blood he bleeds, Hanes. Biting his nasty leg. Come! Beadle yelled, broadcasting.

Vinni said, *Stay there, visualize where you are. I'll come.* The teen touched Signet on her shoulder. "I can't reach Avellana, but

I have the energy to get Cratag, 'port him to Primary HealingHall. I'll call the Druida guard."

Beadle projected a ground-view landscape of many shades of gray, dark, light, and a pungent smell of mint and blood and man. The cat howled, and Vinni was gone.

Another instant passed, and Signet knew Vinni and Cratag were off the estate, but others had arrived, took Hanes and left. A guard came to the Residence and waited in the entry hall.

Avellana shuddered, thrashed, wept, then finally opened her tear-wet lashes and said, "Mommy? Daddy?"

Signet let their connection unravel. Avellana and she would always have a bond, but she didn't need to be in constant touch with the child . . . at least not until her Second Passage, and that was a decade away. Signet rose creakily and hurried from the room, hardly hearing D'Hazel's rapid-fire orders to remove Avellana at once to D'Hazel Residence, the woman's abrupt good-bye as Signet left the suite. She lurched-trotted down the hallway to the stairs, picking up speed, hurtled out the front door and into the glider, and ordered it to Primary HealingHall, ignoring the guard. Let the Residence and the Hazels explain.

Cratag lived. Right now, that was all that mattered.

Cratag surfaced to consciousness a couple of times while the Healers were working on him. Enough to know they were FirstLevel and whatever fee he'd made for this whole mess would be owed to them, and probably more. Too late to protest, though.

These hadn't Healed him before during all the times he'd been at the Hall recently and tsked and commented on the old break in his nose and his scars.

Hanes's sneer of "outsider," which had followed Cratag like a blazer shot into the darkness, seemed branded into his being. Hear something often enough, and you start believing it. Blackness claimed him again, and the word glowed red from his chest.

When he was finally tucked into a bedsponge to rest and recover, Signet entered.

She was glowing with health, and he stared.

She flushed a little. "A PerSun gave me some energy, and you, too. I drew too much from you for Avellana's Passage."

He raised his hand, his scarred, commoner-looking hand, and saw no glow. Must have needed energy too badly, then. Fligger.

Letting out a long sigh, Signet settled herself in the comfortchair next to his bed. She closed her eyes for a moment, and Cratag could see the blue veins in her eyelids, just below the pale, fragile skin. Blue-blooded and rich and Flaired. That was Flair glowing from her, too.

All the things he wasn't.

"Calendula," he said.

She opened her eyes and smiled sweetly. "Yes?" Then she leaned over and kissed his lips softly. "You'll be better soon."

He knew what was coming. Dread crawled through his veins.

He'd failed too many times that day. He'd let personal problems distract him from his job, which was keeping Avellana safe. When he'd split his attention, he'd failed Avellana and Signet and Laev all at once. Then, instead of simply unholstering his blazer and shooting the traitor Hanes, Cratag had welcomed a fist-to-fist fight. Had failed to secure the villain, call the authorities.

He'd failed all around.

"Hanes?"

"He's in jail. Charges have been brought against him."

Someone had corrected Cratag's mistake.

"Avellana?"

Signet sighed again, this time softer and shorter. "She survived her last Passage fugue and has already moved back to the Hazels'. It will be quiet at the Residence, though I think Avellana will visit sometimes. Vinni, too, when he's finished reorganizing his household and Family. T'Vine Residence has been requesting advice from D'Marigold Residence."

About what? How to be charming? Cratag knew less about Residences now than he'd thought he had when he moved into Signet's. Calendula's. And he would never totally understand Druidans. If he'd been Hanes, he'd never have come back. Why didn't Signet use her given name?

He'd thought he'd made a place for himself, had fit in. He hadn't. He never would. He'd have to accept it.

Do what had to be done and move on.

She took his hand, held it to her heart, even when he curled his fingers into a fist.

"Come home with me, Cratag. Stay with me."

"I can't." His voice rasped from his throat.

Thirty-seven

He didn't look at her. "I can't. I have nothing to offer you that you can't get on your own. You deserve better than me."

"But I want *you*." Her voice quavered.

"Plenty of nobles will court you now."

"Now that they know what kind of Flair I have? Now that I'm an acceptable and serious woman?" Anger entered her tones, and he was glad. That would make things easier on her. "You accepted me from the start. From before . . . when all we did was lock glances at FirstFamily Rituals." She snorted. "All the time we have wasted. We belong together, come with me."

"I can't."

"Look me in the eyes and say that, Cratag. You owe me that."

He owed her so much, the change in his Flair, the change in his heart. Just knowing her. Clenching his teeth, he looked at her, and his will nearly failed when he saw the tears magnifying her blue eyes. But she was still a princess, and one who had come into her own. He gulped, forced words from his lips. "I can't come home with you. You deserve more."

She blinked away the tears, and her eyes flashed. She squeezed his fingers hard, then stood and stepped back, spine straight, chin lifted. Sophisticated noblewoman. "Yes, I do," she said with a cutting edge. "I deserve a man who knows his own worth and the worth of my love and his own." She turned on her heel in a move he'd taught her and marched from the room.

Marched. Not danced.

He wondered when she'd dance again.

He never would. Memories would be too painful.

*D*uring the next eightday, Cratag couldn't settle in his rooms in T'Hawthorn Residence. The dimness of the place depressed his spirits. Even when T'Hawthorn moved him to a huge, sunny suite comprising one entire floor in a many-windowed square tower, the light wasn't enough to make him feel good.

Beadle stayed in the tower and courtyard, outside. Otherwise the cat slunk around the place, keeping a wary eye out for T'Hawthorn's Black Pierre, who loathed him as common and ugly.

Just like his master.

To his surprise, he received a gold "favor" token from D'Hazel as well as a year's salary. He hung the token on a string and wore it when he wasn't training. He wasn't sure what it meant to him—a mixture of survival and suffering and failure.

He testified at Hanes's trial, and the man was banished from Druida, a tracking spell set into his bone marrow so he could always be found.

Seeing Signet had hurt. She'd come into her own, looked like a strong princess, not an ethereal and diffident one.

One night, after Cratag's ninth round of pacing, the Residence had snarled at him, and he'd left. He'd walked through the quiet night, under the blazing of the stars and the brightness of the waning moons, out of Noble Country and clear across town to Balm-Heal, the hidden estate that only let the desperate in.

He'd been there once before, when he'd first arrived in Druida, not knowing whether T'Hawthorn would accept him as part of the Family, give him a position and a home.

It depressed Cratag even further when he had no trouble finding the place and walking through one of the doors in the walls to the estate.

The gardens were now well cared for, the sacred grove humming with power and Flair. In the distance he could see brightly lit window squares glowing in the refurbished Residence. The Mugwort Family had settled in, made the place and themselves happy.

He wished he was.

He shucked his clothes and settled into the hot springs, hissing as the heat and herbs penetrated his muscles. He'd been training the Hawthorn guards mercilessly.

They weren't happy either. Because of him.

Neither was Signet.

Though their bond was tiny now, Cratag was compelled to check on it often.

She was busy, determined, a survivor, but she wasn't happy. Sometimes he thought he heard her weeping in the night.

He'd hurt her, and that was a failure, too. But couldn't she see that they didn't belong together?

After a soak that didn't ease his mind a bit, he climbed from the pool, dressed, and trudged back through the city. At CityCenter a silent glider pulled up next to him, the T'Hawthorn Family glider. He got in. Beadle stretched from his sleeping curl, got on Cratag's lap, and kneaded a minute, then fell back to sleep. They rode back to T'Hawthorn Residence in a silence that was only broken by the announcement that T'Hawthorn wanted to see him later at Mid-DayBell, and he was relieved of duties in the morning so he could sleep.

Cratag carried Beadle up to their tower and crawled into the luxurious linens on the nicely sized bedsponge and slept. Beadle dreamed of chasing skirls. Cratag dreamed of running and never getting anywhere.

*S*ignet *still hurt. The first afternoon and night without Cratag—without* anyone but Du in the Residence—she'd curled up into a ball and held herself and grieved and endured the pain. No other abandonment had stabbed her heart so horribly, as if she leaked blood with every breath. It was as bad as when her parents had died.

Someone from T'Hawthorn Residence had come and taken Cratag's belongings, and she didn't even rise to greet them. She had the Residence cleanse and close off the suite Cratag had used. She didn't want to see it for a while. The house even made an illusion of a smooth wall—complete with a spell light bracket—over the door, and that was fine with her. For now. She didn't quite know what the Residence felt, didn't want to add that to her own hurt.

But the next morning Du had wanted loving and adoration and special food, and the Residence had reminded her that this year she was hostessing an annual ritual, Flair for the Arts, that was coming up soon. Not to mention the requests for consultation that had begun pouring in before she'd even returned to the Residence from the HealingHall. And there was Hanes's trial.

So she'd risen from bed and put one foot in front of the other and did things in a schedule now combined of Before and After Avellana. A healthy breakfast; a walk along the cliffs—not too close to the edge; returning to the Residence to plan the party and to think about how she would craft her career, mixing the not-quite-frivolous duties of her former life with her new, more "serious" vocation.

She had life, and the Residence and Du, and a career.

And hope.

Cratag still lived, as did she. While they lived and were Heart-Mates there was hope. She could wait until Cratag worked through his stupidity and came back to her.

He'd been right, deep down she was an optimist. That got her through the following days. As the Residence pampered her and made appointments for her to work hard, as she helped others, as she meditated, Signet found strength within her that she didn't know she had.

In a moment of clarity untrammeled by emotions, she thought it odd that she, the one with the hideous fear of abandonment, had not been the one of them to walk away from love. It had been he, with an inconceivable lack of confidence, who had broken their bond.

Because once she had accepted love—HeartMate or not—life had been better, and she knew they belonged together, would be together. Just her luck he was hardheaded and didn't feel that, *know* that all the way to his bones. He felt and "knew" other things.

At night she allowed herself to be weak, wondering how long her stubborn and downright *blind-to-his-own-qualities* lover would remain away. But during the day she and the Residence worked hard, setting up her schedule, refining her services. Learning her business and her capabilities—and her limitations.

By the time the day for the annual Flair for the Arts ceremony and party had come, she was wearing less of a shell, beginning to feel lighter emotions, to *enjoy* her life. She and her household were determined this would be the best event ever.

Everyone important in the arts was coming, of all ages: the older generation with T'Apple, the artist, and his daughter D'Holly, the composer, to Avellana, who had been apprenticed to T'Apple. She had decided to become a professional holo-artist. Vinni and D'Hazel were attending for the first time as Avellana's guests. Good power and Flair for stirring creative juices and drawing abundance into the art scene.

Signet would be officiating as Lady and Priestess, and Raz Cherry, a handsome actor a few years younger than she, would be taking the part of Lord and Priest.

The day was warm and beautiful, and for the first time in a while she felt like dancing. She had a new pair of light blue shoes with sky crystals making a waxing moon crescent on the toe to dance in.

* * *

*E*xactly *as the antique clock in the hallway chimed MidDayBell,* Cratag, with Beadle on his shoulder, rapped at the door to T'Hawthorn's ResidenceDen.

At his lord's "Enter," Cratag controlled his emotions and his expression and went in, closing the door softly behind him.

T'Hawthorn sat behind his desk. "Welcome, Cratag." It was the same thing the man had said when they'd first met. Cratag couldn't find words, so he nodded. Beadle wriggled, and Cratag put him down. The FamCat began nosing about the far side of the room. T'Hawthorn's Fam, Black Pierre, growled.

T'Hawthorn ignored the cats, so Cratag did, too. His pulse had picked up rate.

"First, let me thank you for providing the Family blessing for Laev during his wedding ceremony that I was foolish enough not to attend." T'Hawthorn's jaw flexed. "I'd hoped to be smarter by this time in my life."

He tapped a large clear crystal sphere on his desk that Cratag hadn't noticed, and a viz formed of Laev's wedding near the end of the ceremony. Cratag saw himself in rumpled clothes with pale face and glassy eyes. He lurched into the ritual circle and said the Family blessing. He looked like he'd spent a month in the Cave of the Dark Goddess. No wonder Laev and Nivea and the Sunflowers had been angry with him.

"Thank you," T'Hawthorn repeated. "And thanks from D'Grove and T'Oak. They were not invited," he ended drily. He tapped the sphere, and the viz disappeared to Cratag's relief.

"Have you heard from Laev?" Cratag asked.

"Once." T'Hawthorn paused. "He doesn't look as well as I would like." The lord gazed beyond Cratag's right shoulder. "It is known that in a HeartMate marriage there is the giving and the receiving of the HeartBond during loving. The connection that joins a pair so deeply that if one dies, the other will follow within a year." A tiny shrug of T'Hawthorn's shoulders. "I don't know this from experience." Now the lord met Cratag's eyes, and Cratag saw they were shadowed by sorrow. "Laev has been wed for days—and nights. No doubt he has offered the HeartBond, or tried to." T'Hawthorn frowned. "I don't know if one can summon a HeartBond for a wife who is not a HeartMate."

There was a moment of heavy silence.

"You didn't appear at your best in the viz," T'Hawthorn said.

Cratag hooked an ankle over his knee.

"And that was *before* you fought Hanes and were blazered and ended up in Primary HealingHall. Vinni T'Vine has paid those bills, by the way. But, to continue, I doubt you were in the condition you should have been, physically and emotionally, to make life-altering decisions."

More quiet.

T'Hawthorn steepled his fingers. His face relaxed into weary sadness, and Cratag sensed with amazement that the man was sad for him, as well as grieving for Laev. "I will always welcome you here and honor you." The lord smiled crookedly. "But perhaps, like Laev, it is time for you to live on your own. Has it occurred to you that you might do some freelance guarding, for instance during the day, as you did on those outings for Avellana Hazel?"

"No one would—"

"Of course they would." Impatient arrogance was back in T'Hawthorn's voice, and Cratag finally realized the man was struggling with big emotions just like he was. For the first time Cratag spared a fleeting thought for the lord's long-dead wife. She had been a Heather, from the Healing Family. Had she been gentle and elegant, and had T'Hawthorn loved her? Had he been a different man before her loss?

Loving changed a person just as completely as any catalyst Flair.

Cratag was not the same man he'd been when he'd last lived in this Residence.

T'Hawthorn stared at Cratag with eyes the same violet as his own. Yes, he'd found Family, but still had considered himself an outlander.

The lord said, "I can spread the word that you will be taking bodyguard jobs." He hesitated. "Did D'Marigold give you any gifts?"

Cratag jiggled his foot. "Boots, three pairs of boots. The woman loves shoes."

The lord looked at the deep red celtaroon boots, and Cratag thought he saw a flash of envy. Envy! That was almost enough to make him smile.

"I heard that D'Marigold's shoes at Bright Brigid's Day Fair were snatched up in ten minutes."

And Cratag got a flicker from his lord's mind that the man had heard it from his current mistress. Cratag suppressed the shock that he'd sensed T'Hawthorn's thoughts. The lord was ultra discreet, for Cratag had never been truly aware of any of his lord's lovers or whether he had one or several or what. Maybe that would change now that Laev was not a child and living in the Residence.

"Brigid's Day Fair," Cratag echoed, nearly flinching. Beadle hopped onto his lap.

"Listen to me, Cratag, you were a hero." The lord used his most commanding voice.

"I didn't watch Avellana. I left her alone."

"In a highly aware Residence with at least two adult FamCats, one of whom was her own. Cratag, she was drawn away from you, from everyone, by someone she—and Vinni T'Vine and the Hazels—trusted. You think this couldn't have happened at D'Hazel Residence?"

Cratag got the impression that T'Hawthorn had asked the Hazels that very question, and he answered as they would have done. "No. Someone always watched Avellana at their Residence."

"And you think that's good for a child? That she doesn't know that and resent it?" Again the echo of previously said words. T'Hawthorn made a short gesture. "You think she didn't slip away? Out of sight of anyone? Wouldn't have gone to Hanes if he'd waved from their garden?"

Knowing Avellana, she would have done that.

"You saved her life. So it's not 'failure' that is truly bothering you, is it? What is it, Cratag?"

He'd never had such a personal conversation with his lord before. Cratag shrugged and answered part of the question. "I didn't—don't—know about Bright Brigid's Day. Even now." *Outsider* rang in his head.

The lord's violet eyes turned piercing, drilled into Cratag. "Are you going to make a very bad, very foolish mistake of walking away from love?"

Now Cratag felt disappointment in him rolling from T'Hawthorn, and Cratag's chest tightened.

I want to go back home, to D'Marigold Residence, Beadle said. He looked curled up and asleep, but his body quivered with interest. Hiding from Black Pierre and T'Hawthorn, but strongly connected to Cratag.

He stroked the cat, and Beadle continued, *I love you, but Signet loves you, too, and me. We belong there.*

Cratag got an image of Signet and the elegant *small* Du, a cat Beadle could intimidate with size. Black Pierre was as big as Beadle.

"Listen to your Fam," T'Hawthorn said, petting his. Black Pierre opened his eyes and sneered at both Beadle and Cratag.

Could Cratag possibly act like a GrandLord? *Be* a GrandLord? He didn't think so. Couldn't ever match Signet's style and grace, the innate power of this man before him. Not to mention the Flair that was rocketing Signet's career and had her name on many lips and in the newssheets.

Are you going to walk away from love? T'Hawthorn asked again, mentally, knowing that Cratag could hear him.

Yes, Cratag had changed, and his Flair had increased to its limits. Still tiny in comparison to T'Hawthorn's or Signet's.

But his love was huge. His love for his lord, this man who he realized was a friend; his love for Laev, so big that he ached at the thought of the young man's disillusionment, the emotional battering he'd experience; his love for the staunch and loyal and goofy Beadle.

His love for Signet was as immense as the ocean.

He might not be able to match her in Flair, but he could certainly match her in love.

He might not be a good GrandLord, consort to D'Marigold—T'Marigold—Lord and Lady help him!—but he could be an excellent partner and husband to Signet.

Raising Beadle to his shoulder and attaching him with a minor spell, Cratag answered T'Hawthorn's question. *No. I am not going to walk away from love.* He said aloud, "Though I'm not sure what I'm going to do with myself."

T'Hawthorn waved that aside. "I'll spread the word that you'll accept daily bodyguard jobs." He studied Cratag. "You could do some private fighting tutoring. Isn't there someone you've run across lately who isn't as good at fighting as they should be?"

Hanes hadn't been, that was for sure, but Cratag put the villain out of his mind. Signet. Avellana. And. . . .

"The simulacrum," he said. "The simulacrum is bad at fighting with sword and long knife."

T'Hawthorn smiled, looking like Laev. "And simulacrums' movements are modeled after real-life fighters." Nodding, the lord said, "I'll call T'Furze, let him know that. Recommend you. He'll hire you for that, for more. I know the simulacrum I purchased was a mixture of several fighters' styles."

Cratag grunted, found a smile on his own lips. "Mostly Holly. Maybe a touch of T'Ash."

"T'Ash would have done it for the amusement factor, but I'd bet you'll be a better value for T'Furze, and he counts his silver slivers. Don't sell yourself cheap, though."

"No." Not ever again.

Beadle purred. *We're going home!*

Black Pierre didn't even open his eyes. *Good riddance.*

T'Hawthorn gave a little cough, and Cratag focused on him again. "What?"

"It's the afternoon of an annual event, a ritual by the Flair for the

Arts of Druida organization. This year the rotation is at D'Marigold Residence."

Something he hadn't known. Too bad. There was plenty he'd have to learn. He might not ever learn everything about Druida and city living that natives would know, but now he *was* one of them.

So he'd be walking into a party. Better or worse?

Signet hadn't said a word, but she'd been busy, and, of course, the Residence would have had everything planned ahead of time and in order.

"Thank you." Cratag bowed, not as an underling to his lord, but as a man to his friend. "For all your good advice . . . Huathe."

Huathe T'Hawthorn smiled, and it was as tender as any he'd given Laev. "Thank you, Cratag. Visit. Often. And I'll see you again at FirstFamilies Rituals."

Cratag winced at the thought of attending those formal affairs.

Huathe laughed. "The Family glider is waiting to take you to D'Marigold's. I've already had your belongings packed and sent."

"Thanks again," Cratag said, and left with his spirits lifting. His mouth curving into a grin. He was going to a new life, finally the right life.

Beadle was out of the door before him.

Thirty-eight

*B*eadle sat on a perch in the glider that was made for Black Pierre and purred all the way from T'Hawthorn Residence to D'Marigold's estate.

The gates were wide open, welcoming. Just like Signet. The glider slid through and with every meter Cratag knew he was where he was meant to be.

Need for Signet exploded through him. He had to see her, touch her. He had to look into her eyes and say he loved her, hear her words of love in return.

A colorful flutter caught his eye, and he gazed out the window to see ribbons tied on the trees lining the gliderway, white through the spectrum to black, and dangling from each ribbon was a crystal that shot prisms of color. Ah, Signet. How could he have thought he could live without her?

The glider stopped halfway to the Residence.

Beadle made a demanding sound, and the vehicle's windows slid down. Music and laughter and voices raised in song came. Beadle hopped from the glider and streaked away. Cratag had thought the ritual would be taking place in the sacred grove, but as the song ended and a deep voice began to recite a verse—some man, some *other* man being the Lord and Priest, and Cratag didn't like that at all—Cratag realized the ritual was taking place at the cliff area where Signet liked to walk.

He exited the glider, saw another path through trees picked out with ribbons holding tiny windchimes that tinkled, and followed it to the large open area of grassy bluff.

There a couple of hundred people stood shoulder to shoulder in a circle. It appeared as if a long ceremony was winding down and the general atmosphere was of lively joy. In the middle of the circle was a stone altar he'd never seen before—and Signet.

Sharing a goblet with the too-damned-handsome actor Raz Cherry. The man had his long, elegant hands over hers, and jealousy bit vicious and deep in Cratag. How had he *ever* thought he could surrender her to any man . . . though, before, he'd have said that the sophisticated actor was the perfect match for her.

Too much alike, he assured himself as he ground his teeth. He, Cratag, her complete opposite, was perfect for her.

He stood outside the ceremonial circle and watched as the ritual ended. Outside, but this time he knew that if he'd been on time and wanted to be, he'd have been in that circle with Signet. Next year he would take part. And the next time D'Marigold officiated as Lady and Priestess of any event, T'Marigold—himself—would be there as Lord and Priest. He was looking forward to summer and private TwinMoons Rituals on the beach.

The instant the circle was dismissed, Cratag strode through to the center and the altar where Signet still stood hand-in-hand with Raz Cherry. He lifted and plucked her away from the man and held her against his chest. Looking down at her, everyone else faded away.

He sighed deeply, matching hers. Here she was, in his arms, and he never wanted to let her go. Wanted to look into her blue eyes forever. Wanted the drift of her blond hair clinging to the skin of his hands . . . and other parts of him.

"I love you," he croaked, his voice in no way matching the depth and modulation of Raz Cherry's, but Cratag was the true Lord to this Lady.

Signet's eyes filled with tears. She put her hands on his face, and he felt connected as he'd never been before—the deep blue sky overhead, the streaming sun, the woman and her land. All was his. He belonged to all.

The world and all the stars revolved around them in that moment.

Him and his love, his lover, his—

"HeartMate," she whispered, her pink lips curving. She stroked his cheeks. "You're my HeartMate."

"What!" The universe *did* spin. Or maybe it was his mind whirling. But he settled into his balance. "Can't be—"

"Of course it can," she said clearly, loudly. "Cratag Maytree is my HeartMate." Lowering her voice, she continued, "I thought I'd connected with someone during my Passages, but the touch was too brief."

"Not enough Flair," he muttered.

She tapped his temple. "Hardheaded rational man. I knew it was you earlier this month. Don't tell me you never connected with *me*, because it would be a lie."

He felt heat along his cheekbones. "I had some dreams."

"There, you see!" She beamed, looked around the circle, and Cratag became abruptly aware that he was the object of fascinated interest by a big bunch of people. "Welcome Cratag Maytree, my HeartMate, into my life and our circles!"

A cheer came, and Cratag felt himself flushing more. He locked gazes with her again. "I love you."

Signet had never been so happy in her life as she was looking up at the rough features of her HeartMate, into his wonderful violet eyes. Safe, loved, warm . . . edging to hot . . .

He jiggled her a little. "I love you."

She chuckled, knowing what he wanted, opening their bond wide, meeting him emotionally, mentally. *I love you.* She said the words aloud, too. "I love you."

His grip tightened on her. "Good."

T'Hawthorn strode into the area, between the clumps of gossiping and laughing people, straight up to them.

Cratag stiffened, then smiled. "Welcome, Huathe." He spoke the words like a host, her husband and partner and consort, greeting a friend. Signet sensed that their relationship had changed, too, become deeper, more familial.

Adjusting the sleeves of his long, formal robe, T'Hawthorn glanced at the circle inscribed in the grass, the people still lingering in the lovely weather, the bedecked altar. "I can be Lord and Priest for a wedding."

Signet's heart gave one wild thump. Wonderful! Married, here and now to her HeartMate! How could anything be more perfect. "Yes!"

Shouts came from the gathering, people began ordering the circle and themselves, choosing their places. Vinni ran to the Residence.

Huathe T'Hawthorn cocked an eyebrow at Cratag. "It is my pleasure."

D'Holly stepped forward, curtsied to Signet and Cratag. "I would be honored to take the part of Lady and Priestess." Turning to T'Hawthorn, her husband's old enemy, she offered her hands. "If you agree."

"Honored," he said.

Vinni hurried from the Residence with new candles, incense, and ribbons. Ribbons that Signet used on her shoes, but could definitely be wedding ribbons. Tucked under his arm was a pair of bright golden boots with deeper red and orange stitching. Her HeartGift, made with love and Flair and intent, though not during the time of her long-ago Passages.

As soon as he entered the new circle, people closed in behind him. Avellana took the boots from him and propped them against the altar. Vinni and she arranged the top of the sacred table, then she took Vinni's hand and they went to a spot left open for them. T'Hawthorn and D'Holly moved into the Lord's and Lady's places.

Beadle came and plopped his bottom importantly down beside Cratag. Du sat a meter and a half away, head lifted haughtily.

"All is ready," Avellana said. "You can put Signet down, Cratag."

He blinked and released her reluctantly. Kept her fingers twined in his. *I love you, Calendula Signet Marigold.*

I love you, Cratag Maytree.

And they were married right there on the cliff in the sunshine, rainbows of ribbons fluttering and wind chimes sounding in the breeze. Nothing was ever so perfect.

Except the wedding night and HeartBond.